DISTANT WORLDS

A volume in the Hyperion reprint series
CLASSICS OF SCIENCE FICTION

DISTANT WORLDS

There was a great upsurge in the popularity of science fiction in post-World War I Germany in the early years of the Weimar Republic. Of its leading writers, Friedrich Mader, characterized as "the German Jules Verne," was easily the most outstanding. Where other authors wrote stories that were scientifically sound if somewhat dull, Mader's heroes sped through wild and weird adventures that still have the power to excite and entertain. In a sense, most of his novels were inter-connected. The same trio of lively, international adventurers reappear: Professor Dr. Heinrich Schulze of Germany, Captain Munchausen of Australia, and Lord Flitmore of England, together with their wives and a company of associates. Of his many books, *Distant Worlds* is one of the most charming; it went through eleven editions and is the only Mader novel ever translated into English (1932).

In this marvelously alive work, Mader, fascinated by the geography of this earth and the universe, was not about to settle for the usual voyage to the moon or the nearby planets. His adventurers, in a space ship powered by anti-matter, zoom around to Mars, Saturn, through the asteroid belt following a comet, and out of the solar system to Alpha Centauri, landing on a planet of that system. On the return trip, they fly through the corona of the sun at temendous speed to avoid being trapped by gravitation. Mader was the most romantic of German science fiction writers, and though his stories are distinguished by careful attention to accurate and plausible scientific detail, they are most notable for their sense of fun, rollicking adventure, and by the stretch of their author's imagination which sought to encompass all the yet undiscovered universes of the galaxies.

Everything crawled and fought against everything else.

[*Page 310.*

DISTANT WORLDS

THE STORY OF A VOYAGE TO THE PLANETS

BY

FRIEDRICH MADER

TRANSLATED FROM THE GERMAN BY
MAX SHACHTMAN

ILLUSTRATED BY
ROBERT A. GRAEF

HYPERION PRESS, INC.
Westport, Connecticut

Published in 1932 by Charles Scribner's Sons, New York
Copyright 1932 by Charles Scribner's Sons
Copyright © renewed 1960 by Charles Scribner's Sons. Reprinted by permission.
Hyperion reprint edition 1976
Library of Congress Catalog Number 75-28859
ISBN 0-88355-374-0 (cloth ed.)
ISBN 0-88355-458-5 (paper ed.)
Printed in the United States of America

Library of Congress Cataloging in Publication Data

Mader, Friedrich Wilhelm, 1866-
    Distant worlds.

    (Classics of science fiction)
    Translation of Wunderwelten.
    Reprint of the ed. published by Scribner, New York.
    I. Title.
PZ3.M2643Di20   [PT2625.A24]   833'.9'12   75-28859
ISBN 0-88355-374-0
ISBN 0-88355-458-5 pbk.

CONTENTS

CHAPTER		PAGE
I.	A DARING VENTURE	1
II.	*SANNAH*, THE WORLD-SHIP	6
III.	A WONDERFUL DISCOVERY	12
IV.	THE VOYAGE INTO THE VOID	15
V.	IN COSMIC SPACE	23
VI.	PAST THE MOON	30
VII.	A SERIOUS DANGER	38
VIII.	THE GREAT ASTRONOMERS	42
IX.	MARS	49
X.	A LANDING ON MARS	52
XI.	THE TERRORS OF MARS	57
XII.	A TOUR OF EXPLORATION ON MARS	63
XIII.	THE INHABITANTS OF MARS	68
XIV.	A CATASTROPHE ON MARS	75
XV.	IN A METEORIC SHOWER	89
XVI.	THE ASTEROIDS	97
XVII.	THE PLANETOID ISLAND	100
XVIII.	THE COMET	106
XIX.	SEA SERPENTS	113
XX.	JUPITER	118
XXI.	A VISIT TO SATURN	124
XXII.	AN INVOLUNTARY POLAR VOYAGE	131
XXIII.	A NIGHT ON THE RING PLANET	138
XXIV.	A STRANGE WORLD	146
XXV.	A BATTLE FOR THE *SANNAH*	154
XXVI.	CARRIED OFF BY A COMET	164

CHAPTER		PAGE
XXVII.	THE SECRETS OF THE OUTERMOST PLANETS	171
XXVIII.	A VOYAGE INTO INFINITY	174
XXIX.	CHIMPANZEE FOLLIES	177
XXX.	LOST IN SPACE	183
XXXI.	THE GIANT CUTTLE-FISH	192
XXXII.	LEFT WITHOUT AIR	198
XXXIII.	A DISASTROUS COLLISION	201
XXXIV.	A MIRACLE	206
XXXV.	IN THE WORLD OF THE FIXED STARS	212
XXXVI.	A NEW EARTH	218
XXXVII.	THE MARVELS OF EDEN	224
XXXVIII.	CURIOUS LAWS OF NATURE	230
XXXIX.	A NEW ANIMAL WORLD	240
XL.	A NIGHT IN PARADISE	248
XLI.	SUPERIOR BEINGS	256
XLII.	IN A HOSPITABLE HOME	267
XLIII.	NEW KNOWLEDGE	274
XLIV.	HELIASTRA	282
XLV.	IN THE KINGDOM OF PEACE	286
XLVI.	A JOURNEY ON THE PLANET	291
XLVII.	MUNCHHAUSEN'S FABLES	296
XLVIII.	DEPARTURE	301
XLIX.	THE QUEER PLANET	307
L.	THE END OF A WORLD	312
LI.	THROUGH THE SUN	316
LII.	THE PLANET MERCURY	322
LIII.	BACK TO EARTH!	328
LIV.	*SANNAH*	332

ILLUSTRATIONS

EVERYTHING CRAWLED AND FOUGHT AGAINST EVERYTHING
ELSE   *Frontispiece*

FACING PAGE

"FLEE, FLEE! ELSE THE SAME FATE SHALL OVERTAKE YOU!"   72

CLOSEST TO THE *SANNAH* REMAINED THE TWO COMETS . . .
THE WORLD-SHIP WAS BEING FREED FROM HER COMPULSORY
FOLLOWING OF AMINA   210

MAJESTICALLY HE FLOATED IN THE AIR, THIS HUMAN GLOBE,
AND SLOWLY SETTLED TO THE GROUND AGAIN   232

I

A DARING VENTURE

PROFESSOR DOCTOR HENRY SCHULZE leaned back meditatively in his chair. On the writing table before him, covered with books and papers, lay a letter that occupied his thoughts.

The bell rang at the front door of his dwelling and shortly thereafter came a tremendous rapping on the door of the study.

"Come in!" called the Professor, rising from his seat.

The door opened and there appeared an elderly, yet hale and hearty-looking man of generous build.

"Captain Munchhausen!" cried Schulze and rushed towards him with delight and astonishment, both hands outstretched. "What favorable monsoon guides you from Australia to Berlin, and just at this time? I am dumbfounded! My goodness, my thoughts were just dwelling upon you in Adelaide and I was wishing you could be conjured up."

"Well, the spell worked!" laughed Munchhausen. "Here I am. And what brings me here? You know that I cannot bear sitting around inactively on civilized ground for long. Well, I thought to myself: go and take a look at what old man Schulze is doing; maybe he is planning some new bang-up enterprise; I must be there with him! And if he isn't planning any, then I'll shake him up and we'll plan one together. Eh? How do things stand, Prof?"

1

"I tell you, you come in the nick of time. Here, sit right down, old man."

Meanwhile the Professor pressed the button of an electric bell and ordered the servant who appeared to bring a flask of wine and two glasses, and then to fix up a cold snack in the dining room. "The best in the house," he urged, "the Captain is an epicure."

"Oho!" laughed the latter. "Haven't I tasted white ants, caterpillars, and water rats, when it comes to that? I take things as they come."

"But now comes something better than African hunger-fare, old friend; and I know that you prefer the better to the worse."

"Only a fool wouldn't! But now, Professor, what are you planning?"

"I really have nothing planned; but some one else: do you still remember Lord Flitmore?"

Munchhausen laughed uproariously. "Only a professor secluded from the world would think of such a question! 'Remember' is a good one. If you have gone through such adventures with a man like Flitmore, fought out such battles and enjoyed such glorious hours together as we two have, is it easy to forget him? Excuse me, Professor, but your question is . . . well, what should I call it?"

"Stupid!" supplemented Schulze, laughing in turn. "You are right, old growler. Now then! Here's a letter I received from Flitmore. He writes that he has made a hardly believable discovery."

"Hardly believable? I tell you, I believe everything he says, I believe him capable of the most wonderful things after the proofs of his inventive spirit he gave us in Africa."

"Right! But listen: he writes that his discovery wipes out the dividing spaces of the universe and makes possible, trips to the moon, to the planets, and perhaps even into the world of fixed stars. And now he is inviting me to accompany him on his first trip. What do you think of that? Can it be that he is a little cracked after all?"

"Oh, you men of science who cannot greet a new, startling discovery without doubting it! If the professors were the ones to decide these things, all the gifted inventors would land in the madhouse! I tell you I believe Flitmore can do anything. He is a genius. Send him a telegram and ask him if he will take me along. Ha, there's a trip for you! There has never been anything like it outside of the imagination of writers. I must go along!"

"That's just the point: Lord Flitmore asks me to accompany him because he knows that in recent years I have applied myself entirely to astronomy, and he has followed my writings in this field with interest and approval, as he writes. But then he asks about you and your address. He is full of admiration for the automobile you invented, the one we used to explore Australia."

"Yes, yes, the *Nora!*" said the Captain with a smile of satisfaction. "It wasn't such a bad idea. But to the moon —nope! It could never make it!"

"Well, with your technical knowledge and your inventive skill in this field, Flitmore doesn't think he can find a better engineer and captain for his World-Ship than you, and he would be overjoyed if he could get you for the venture."

"That's a bargain!" cried Munchhausen enthusiastically. "When do we leave?"

"Hold on there!" laughed Schulze. "Not so hasty, old friend! You are a rash youngster. Think it over," he continued, growing serious, "the risk is more than daring: it is a matter of life and death. Flitmore does not fail to emphasize it plainly: no man can know what dangers and what undreamed-of disasters threaten the earthly dweller who leaves his native planet and rises above the atmosphere into the void of cosmic space."

"And wasn't it also a matter of life and death in Africa and Australia and wherever else we did exploring? Did we have any idea beforehand of the dangers we were courting?"

"True! But those were earthly dangers."

The Captain shrugged his shoulders. "Listen, you grubby professor: deadly danger is deadly danger; whether it threatens on the earth or above the earth is all one and the same thing to my way of thinking, you can't lose more than your life in either place. But who else is coming along? In such an affair a lot depends upon the travelling party."

"It will not be a big party: first of all, Flitmore's wife will accompany him."

"Oh, boy! Mitzie! Hats off to her! A plucky woman if there ever was one; she proved that to us aplenty that time in Ophir."

But Schulze continued: "Then comes Flitmore's servant, John Rieger."

"Delighted, delighted! A noble, faithful soul and an amusing fellow. So he is still in Flitmore's service?"

"Indeed, and he has developed into a skilled mechanic, for Flitmore needs him as a zealous automobile driver. Finally, my young friend Hank Frieding also wants to join us. I tried in vain to dissuade him; he is all a-fire for the world voyage."

"Let me tell you, Professor, I have had a warm place in my heart for that young man since we made our voyage to the unapproachable mountains with him. That's a splendid travelling party! What has our Hank been doing since then, and where is he?"

"He has applied himself to the language sciences and is

living here in Berlin as a university lecturer. He is beginning to make a name for himself and he has made, as he confided to me, a highly important discovery in his field; but he hasn't yet disclosed anything further about it."

The servant reported that the snack was ready.

They both emptied their glasses and proceeded to the dining room.

II

SANNAH, THE WORLD–SHIP

A WEEK later, Schulze, Munchhausen, and Hank Frieding landed in Brighton and then took the train to Lord Flitmore's manor, which was located in Sussex County.

A magnificent old castle, surrounded by an extensive park and adjoined by fields, meadows, and woodlands—a little kingdom in itself—was pointed out to the arrivals as the Lord's manorial estate.

From afar they could already see towering above the tree-tops a gigantic globe that glittered in the sunlight.

"It is Flitmore's World-Ship!" cried Hank Frieding.

Schulze shook his head: "That craft must be immensely heavy," he asserted. "How Flitmore expects to rise into the air with it and even above the atmosphere, is beyond me."

But the Captain retorted: "Nor need you comprehend it, Professor! Cheer up, the genius of our English friend has undoubtedly solved the problem, otherwise he would not have invited us for the voyage."

Lord Flitmore had expected his guests at this hour and came with his youthful wife to meet them at the park gates.

He was a tall man with reddish whiskers. A serious bearing gave him a stiffish demeanor, truly English; but that was only in appearance. Although he spoke but few words, and his greetings sounded somewhat dry, you could nevertheless perceive a warm heartiness and a sincere joy.

Mitzie, his wife, a born Boer from South Africa, made no effort to conceal her feelings behind a measured dignity. She

6

came to meet her friends with a radiant smile and vigorously shook their hands.

Schulze and Munchhausen were old acquaintances of Flitmore's back in Africa; to Hank, the Englishman turned with the words: "Mr. Frieding, I have known and esteemed you too for a long time, even if I have never met you personally; for you always played a prominent and engaging rôle in the descriptions of the Australian voyage of my friends."

A veritable gala dinner was served to the arrivals; they were regaled in princely style. Then there was still a lot to tell about their experiences and work since the time they had last seen Flitmore. At ten o'clock sharp, however, every one retired for the night.

After breakfast next morning, Flitmore led his guests to the spacious meadow on which rested the enormous globe that had already aroused the amazement of our friends when they reached his manor.

"So this is your air ship?" observed the Professor as they looked up admiringly at the immense globe.

"World-Ship," corrected Flitmore. "An air ship is chained to the atmosphere, but with this craft we plan to leave the aerial region, at least the aerial envelope which surrounds our terrestrial globe; that is why we cannot properly speak any longer of an 'air ship.' The whole world, infinite space, is open to this vehicle."

"You are right," admitted Schulze: " 'World-Ship,' then."

But the Englishman continued: "What's more, I have given my globe a name of its own. The fine idea you had, Captain, when you christened your automobile *Nora,* became clear to me, and so I gave my invention the name **Sannah.**"

"In honor of your lovable sister-in-law, the courageous wife of our friend Doctor Leusohn in East Africa?" asked Schulze.

"Of course!" chimed in Mitzie. "It occurred to both of us immediately to choose the name of my far-off sister for the vehicle which is to become our home on a voyage filled with unknown dangers."

"Delighted!" cried Munchhausen. "I was especially fond of travelling with Sannah, and I am convinced that the new *Sannah* will do honor to her name, prove faithful to us, and make the voyage as pleasant as possible."

"What sort of material is your World-Ship actually made of?" asked Hank Frieding. "It glitters just like mica."

"This glistening envelope is flint-glass," explained Flitmore; "we must bear in mind that on this voyage we shall run into such degrees of heat as may not only destroy us but also our craft. Against the cold of cosmic space, which I don't believe, for that matter, to be quite so cold as is generally assumed, we are protected by electrical heating.

"But we may also whiz through world mists and cosmic dust-clouds with such speed that the *Sannah* will turn white-hot like the meteors that plunge into our atmosphere; the same thing will threaten her if we approach the sun or some other glowing world body. I therefore had the envelope of my World-Ship made up like the walls of most fire-proof safes and then covered even this envelope with incombustible flint-glass so that we may hope to be able to expose ourselves to the highest temperatures for quite a time without injury."

"But the windows?" objected Schulze.

"I do have six big windows which are made of very thick glass and permit a view from all sides. In each of these portholes is a powerful telescope, for most of the time we shan't be able to see much with the naked eye. But as soon as we are exposed to heat that may become dangerous to my windows, the pressing of a button inside the ship is enough to cover up all the windows quite snugly with a protective cover, as with an eyelid."

"I must say that your World-Ship is of vast proportions," remarked the Captain admiringly.

"They are actually small," replied the Englishman. "A Zeppelin air ship, for example, is of quite different proportions. My globe is about 146 feet in diameter; around the central point is a room some 49 feet in width, length and height, which thus has 117,649 cubic feet of space. Here we keep the provisions for the voyage in a number of pyramid-like compartments with the top down, that is, down towards the central point.

"This middle room forms the foundation for the separate rooms which spread out from it on six sides up to the envelope. Each of these rooms is 16 feet wide and about 10 feet high, so that there are always five of such rooms over each other, the one at the extremity serving as a living and observation room; ladder steps lead from one story to the other. The uppermost rooms are 49 feet long, the others become shorter as they near the central point.

"Apart from the outside apartments located directly under the arch of the globe's envelope, each of these thirty quarters offers a space of from 7000 to 7875 cubic feet, altogether about 210,000. Besides the living and sleeping rooms, I have set up workshops here: one joiner's shop, one smithy, one chemical laboratory; the remaining space serves alternately for staying in when the used-up air in the other needs renewal.

"The outside chambers under the surface are connected with each other by special passages which I call Meridian passages because, as it were, they run like internal longitude and latitude degrees inside the globe."

"It looks as though you have made use of meridians on the outside too," observed Münchhausen.

"You mean the ramps?" asked Flitmore. "These small railings, which I considered advantageous for certain purposes, also radiate, to be sure, from one point and criss-cross at opposite points, thus forming convenient longitudinal degrees.

"The six halls, which are located directly beneath the outside covering of the globe, I gave special names for practical reasons: at the top is the Zenith room, at the bottom the Antipode room, in the middle the Equator; right before us is the North Pole room corresponding to the South Pole room behind it, on the right is the East room, on the left the West room. As you see, I proceeded somewhat unscientifically with these designations, by shifting the North Pole and the South Pole on to the Equator. But all this is merely a matter of arrangement: regard the line which runs from the Zenith room past the East and Antipode rooms to the West room as the Equator and the thing is all right again."

"But with all the rooms you have named," interjected Schulze, "isn't the space in your globe quite used up?"

"Certainly not! My World-Ship has a circumference of 460 feet, a surface area of 63,585 square feet, and a content of 1,670,000 cubic feet. Subtract the space of the 30 rooms, the provisions chambers and the meridian passages, which altogether come to 350,000 cubic feet and you still have 1,320,000 cubic feet left; of these 1,050,000 are filled with steel chambers containing compressed oxygen and 270,-000 are filled with ozone; for what we need above all is air, healthy and constantly renewed air."

"You mentioned before the electrical heating," the Captain spoke up again. "I should imagine that the kitchen, the smithy, and the chemical laboratory are also to be heated by electricity, if only in order to avoid any smoke."

"Quite right," confirmed Flitmore.

"But how do you generate the electrical power?"

The Englishman laughed: "You ought to know my powerful batteries from back in Africa, Captain. But I must admit, honestly, the main thing for the electrical maintenance of my *Sannah* I owe to you. You did indeed make no secret of your wonderful invention, the remarkable accumulators which drove your *Nora*. Well, I am taking along a number of these accumulators, on the Munchhausen system, and, like you, I am producing frictional electricity by a machine, mainly driven by hand. Since the electricity produced in this manner may be stored up indefinitely in your excellent accumulators, I thus always have at hand a power source in the event that my batteries should prove inadequate."

III

A WONDERFUL DISCOVERY

AFTER these explanations Flitmore invited his guests
to inspect the inside rooms, which they did under his
guidance with the liveliest interest.

They found everything arranged with an idea to fitness
and comfort. What next struck them was that all such household furnishings as tables, chairs, bedsteads, and the like
were made of rubber, just as the walls, ceilings, and floors
proved to be laid out in thick rubber plates; but what was
made up of wood and metal: the carpenter's bench, the anvil,
the crucible, and so forth, was firmly screwed to the floor.

"I thought this precaution had to be taken," explained
Flitmore, "for we cannot know what shocks our *Sannah* may
be subjected to, should she perhaps collide with meteorites
or land roughly on some world body."

The inspection lasted a number of hours. When everything had been thoroughly examined and admired, Hank
Frieding spoke up: "Pardon me, Lord Flitmore," he said,
"you see us all convinced that no craft could be equipped
for a voyage into the universe more carefully and suitably
than your magnificent *Sannah*. But what miraculous power
is to catapult it into space? That is the puzzle I am trying
in vain to solve. Are we supposed to know anything about it
or is it a secret?"

"You are right," replied Flitmore. "I owe you an explanation. A discovery I made accidentally first gave me the
idea.

"You know the force of gravity and its laws, and you know also that science has no idea what the essence of this force of gravity actually is. The power of attraction of all world bodies is indeed an explanation of the force of gravity, but we know just as little about the power of attraction and on what it is based. Were it based upon rotation, then we should, for example, have to be drawn towards the earth's axis, whereas in actuality the attraction is towards the centre of the earth: it is a centripetal force, which is just a way of saying 'attraction towards the centre.' Quite possibly this force is connected with magnetism, and that in turn with electricity.

"Now we know that there is a positive and a negative electricity: what attracts one repels the other; thus there is a positive magnetic pole and a negative, a North pole and a South pole, and the centripetal force corresponds to a centrifugal force. In other words, besides the attraction there is also a repulsion, and the latter force I call 'centrifugal power.'

"It is clear that if our earth, in addition to its attractive force, also has a repulsive force, the former must outweigh by far with regard to its effect upon all earthly bodies; for if the repulsive force were to have an outweighing effect, all the bodies on the surface of the earth would immediately be repelled from it, they would no longer be here. That is the simple reason why this second force remains concealed from us.

"Now, however, I have discovered by an accidental combination an electrical or a magnetic current which represents this centrifugal power.

"If the current is started, the bodies through which it flows are repelled from the earth, and with all the greater force the stronger the current. If the current is broken, the attractive force of the earth again resumes its function.

"My 'centrifugal power' is, so to speak, gravitation up-side down, a magnetism which is repelled by the earth's magnetism and which has a repellent effect upon the latter.

"That is the whole secret. All the attempts I contrived had the same success; every body I charged with centrifugal power, no matter how heavy it was otherwise, rose in the air with increasing speed and vanished never to be seen again."

Our friends listened with great wonderment to these amazing arguments, and Schulze, shaking his head, said: "Well, we shall see!"

IV

THE VOYAGE INTO THE VOID

I T was a bright night; the full moon shone with undimmed lustre as the intrepid voyagers started out on their adventurous trip. Flitmore stored away in the *Sannah* still a few more cases of provisions and useful objects. The food-machine he invented and tested in Africa was also taken along in case of emergency. In large flasks and metal receptacles were preserved the chemical materials out of which, by means of the machine, he could produce tablets of a high nutritive value. This had the advantage that in small containers, occupying a very small space, food could be taken along to last for many months. Besides this, upon landing on any soil containing the ingredients needed for vegetation, he was enabled with the aid of the machine to pick out and work up these ingredients, just as the plants do which produce grain or edible fruits. But where stalks, shrubs, and trees require months, or weeks at least, the food-machine could accomplish it in a few hours. Thus this rare invention excluded famine, even if the rich stocks of provisions should give out, in the event that the voyage were prolonged beyond all expectations.

Especially important to Lord Flitmore was his photographic apparatus, with which he was able, by means of the latest process, to take pictures in their natural colors.

All were gathered in front of the entrance gate of the *Sannah*, ready to board, when Flitmore's faithful servant John came on the scene, accompanied by two powerful mon-

15

keys, whom the Englishman presented to the astounded voyagers as follows: "You see here two ministering spirits, the chimpanzees, Dick and Bobs. The first owes his name to a bad pun, for he is in fact somewhat thick-skinned and it is not so far from 'thick' to 'Dick.' The other has a striking resemblance to Lord Roberts, the Field Marshal, whom we familiarly call 'Bobs.'

"The beasts are extremely intelligent and docile, and also excellently trained: the machine for feeding the electric accumulators is operated by them quite independently. They may also be of further use to us, if fate should drive us upon a world body blessed with vegetation. Since we must expect in such a case to find there nothing but fruits completely unknown to us, the chimpanzees will protect us from tasting anything poisonous or injurious; for their instinct in such matters never deceives them."

With hearts thumping in expectation our friends entered the bottom chamber of the *Sannah*, which could more readily be called a hall than any of its other rooms. Soon it would be known whether her rise into infinite space were possible. And if this did happen—what surprises, what dangers, awaited them there?

"Charles," said Mitzie to her husband, "I want to go up to the top story and observe our approach to the moon."

"Excellent," agreed Flitmore. "Will you be kind enough to accompany my wife, Hank? In the meantime, we want to note how the earth looks while we are moving away from it. When there is nothing more to see here, we shall also come up, and that will soon be the case. For according to my calculations we shall rapidly attain the velocity of light, 186,173 miles a second."

"Is that so?" exclaimed the Professor, skeptically.

"Go up those steps, you old skeptic," said Flitmore; "as

you see, the eye-piece and reflector of the telescope are up there near the ceiling. It is a bit uncomfortable for the observer, but that's the best I could do when we have to be on the lookout below."

"Do you know which is *above* and which is *below?*" Hank called down to Flitmore. He had just left the compartment through the upper hatchway in the ceiling.

obody understood what he meant by that; but the thought that had just flashed through the mind of the young scholar and impelled him to ask this remarkable question, was only too justified, as those who had remained behind were to learn in a moment.

Hank had in the meantime closed the hatchway behind him and mounted further with Lady Flitmore from story to story until the fourteen ten-foot stairs were topped and they had reached the uppermost hall.

At the same time, Flitmore closed the entrance to the lower room airtight and looked around to see that everything was in order and that nothing had been forgotten.

The Professor was already seated upon the upper landing of the steps at the eye-piece of the telescope.

"Now, then, in the name of God and trusting to the protection of Providence!" cried Flitmore solemnly, "gentlemen, I am closing the circuit."

Here something completely unexpected occurred.

Mitzie and Hank became aware at this moment of a rumbling noise which spread throughout the whole craft.

"What does this mean?" asked the Lady.

"Everything is turning topsy-turvy," said Hank, laughing. "The men are now learning to distinguish *above* and *below* by practical experience; at any rate, they have all fallen headlong."

"How is that?" asked Mitzie in alarm: "Didn't my husband close the entrance in time? Impossible! You surely don't mean that they fell out when the *Sannah* rose?"

"No, no! With the good padding of the rooms there is no danger at all, and what we have heard is only the bumping into each other of the cases and bales in the lower provisions chambers; for no noise can pierce through to us from the rubber-covered halls."

The Lady shook her head; she did not understand it clearly, and only thought that the departure had been made with a sharp jerk which had jumbled a few things together down below. But it still did remain inexplicable that up here not even the slightest shock had been felt.

What had happened?

The men down below were themselves not clear about it when the event took place with a terrifying suddenness.

To the Professor, seated on the ceiling of the room, it suddenly seemed as if he had made a somersault and were now standing on his head; and nevertheless he had not stirred.

At the same moment, Lord Flitmore and his servant rolled up, or rather, as it now looked, down the steps, and landed on Schulze.

Simultaneously, Munchhausen crashed down like a bomb, landing fortunately at some distance, so that his body struck none of the others, or else there would have been an accident.

Thanks to his padding of fat and the gutta-percha coating of the ceiling, he escaped from his ten-foot fall without injury.

All the furniture of the rooms also crashed down and part of it landed upon the sprawled-out men, and on top of it all cavorted the frightened chimpanzees.

"Here is where all science surely comes to an end," growled Schulze, when Flitmore and John had slipped out of the luckily soft rubber chair and relieved the Professor of the burden of their own bodies.

All three stood up and Schulze noted with satisfaction that nobody was hurt.

Then he looked about.

"I'll be jiggered!" he exclaimed. "We are standing on the ceiling. It's true, the ceiling has become the floor and the floor the ceiling. Just look: the stairs are hanging upside down and the telescope is looking upwards. There! Look at that! The earth is floating above us, ah! magnificent!"

Indeed, the moon-flooded earth presented a gorgeous spectacle; it moved away at a mad speed and through the big window could already be seen, as on a map, the outlines of the British Isles rising out of the glistening white sea.

"Ho, there! You might help me get on my legs first," Munchhausen called out testily, while he endeavored vainly to slip out from beneath the large rubber table that lay heavily on his belly.

Schulze and John liberated him laughingly and then stood him up with a great deal of effort.

"I have it!" said Flitmore at that moment. "How did I fail to take that into account? Really, Hank Frieding puts us all to shame. Didn't he call out to us: 'Do you know which is *above* and which is *below*?' He was the only one who had any idea of the consequences that would result from leaving the attractive force of the earth."

"What a blockhead I am!" exclaimed Schulze, and at the moment he himself believed his assertion was correct. "It's as clear as daylight. If the earth repels us, then the direction towards the earth is no longer down, from here, but up! Flitmore, either you must completely rearrange all your rooms or else you must find out if you can make the whole *Sannah* turn about, otherwise all your stairways will stand on their head."

"That's the least of my worries," retorted Flitmore. "The stairs are ladder-like and built light, are made of aluminum and can be unhooked. We can turn them around without much difficulty; but I am worried about whether Mitzie and Hank suffered any injury, and what a state my chemical laboratory must be in! All the tubes and glasses in fragments. Too bad! Lucky thing that the electrical bulbs were fitted into the walls and not the ceiling, otherwise they would now be sticking out from the floor and be smashed by the tumbling furniture."

It was decided to inquire right away after the Lady and Hank.

The ceiling hatches had become trap-doors in the floor and the stairs, which had been put there for mounting, now had to be descended. For this they had to be unhooked and turned about, a job which took some effort but was nevertheless done.

In coming down, however, came new surprises: the ceilings and the floors of the rooms were neither entirely even nor horizontal. They showed ticklish inclines and slopes. When the first fifty feet had been surmounted, the descent stopped altogether: from here on, ceilings and floors had not simply exchanged places but had become side walls; the ceiling and floor hatches were simply doors here, and stairs were no longer needed to get to them. At the outset the new floors, which had up to now been room walls, appeared to slope downwards; farther on, however, they became increasingly acute inclined planes and at the end everything once more appeared to be in order. The next stairs could be left as they were, and instead of a descent there now began an ascent to the last five rooms.

Captain Munchhausen shook his head while he wheezily dragged his large bulk up the stairs. "Your *Sannah* is completely bewitched, Lord Flitmore!" he exclaimed. "I'll never make my way out of this affair."

"Remarkable, really remarkable," acknowledged Flitmore.

"Not at all! Quite natural," corrected the Professor with a superior air; for his diligent reflections had enabled him to solve the puzzle. "Our *Sannah* has, so to speak, become independent, a woman emancipated from the attractive force of the earth; quite modern! She now has her own centripetal force and to us her central point is henceforth always *below* and her surface everywhere *above*. She is a planet for herself, or let us say, a planetoid; she has joined the ranks of the world bodies. Sublime, eh?"

"You are right, Professor!" agreed Flitmore. "And look, in these upper rooms everything has remained in order, except that ceilings and floors incline towards the central point. A lucky thing that my chemical laboratory is located here. Not a single piece is damaged, the things have only slipped towards each other, everything towards the centre. We must see how we are going to make our way with this state of affairs and arrange ourselves as comfortably as possible. It is really annoying that I did not take these deductions into account, otherwise I should have arranged all the ceilings and floors as concentric spheres and then everything would be level under the circumstances. As it is, everything is thoroughly botched."

"Oh, it's all right, my dear Flitmore," consoled the Captain. "We shan't be greatly inconvenienced by it; just a little work until you have unscrewed the carpenter's bench from the ceiling in your joiner's shop and the anvil from the wall of the smithy, and everything will be finally restored to its proper place."

Arriving above, they found Mitzie and Hank both cheerful. Hank had meanwhile explained the occurrence to the Lady as he had quite correctly imagined it, and both were happy to learn that everything had passed without injury to the others.

"It might have been worse, you know," said Flitmore, "if our new celestial body were not so exceptionally small, so that the attractive force of its central point is extremely slight. Only the sudden disconnection from the earth's attractive power, for us and all the objects in the *Sannah*, could have such a relatively strong effect. However, the force of gravity is well-nigh eliminated in our diminutive planet."

As a matter of fact, they all felt a curious lightness of their own bodies, which moved along floatingly. So also were they able to lift the heaviest objects and move them about without effort. And this lightness, which eliminated all bodily strain, produced a wonderfully delicious sensation.

V

IN COSMIC SPACE

WITH the explanations and the chatter that now came thick and fast, the observation of the rest of the journey was being completely forgotten until Mitzie reminded them of it.

"Watch out!" said she, "we are approaching the moon at a ripping speed."

Everybody looked up.

"Sure enough," said Hank, "it already looks magnificent, but remarkably gloomy."

"Ho, there!" cried Schulze. "That's our earth you see! Dark it is, indeed; but the outlines of Europe and Africa can be quite plainly distinguished."

It was really an enchanting spectacle! The earth looked like a flat disk, about ten times as large as the apparent size of the full moon, and the moonlit continents were before them as on a desk globe: Europe, Africa, and part of Asia were to be seen at a glance, and over India and Persia the morning sun was already shining, so that the coasts stood out clearly to the amazed onlookers.

"What sort of a spook is this again!" blustered the Captain. "Why, here is where we should be looking straight out to the moon and not the earth we left on the other side! My dear Flitmore, you hired me, so to say, as captain and helmsman of the *Sannah*, but such a queer craft I really don't know how to manage. Hey, Professor! You old know-it-all, how are you going to explain this oddity?"

"Splendid!" replied Schulze, enthusiastically. "As a genuine planet, conscious of her importance in the universe, our *Sannah* is revolving around her own axis and that in about two earth-hours. Watch out, in about one hour we shall see the full moon flash up again, and as soon as we are outside the realm of the earth's shadow, night and day will change for us every hour; but we only need to proceed at the right time to another chamber under the surface of our planet in order to enjoy eternal daylight or endless night. Just as you please!"

"But aren't we already outside the realm of the earth's shadow, since we can perceive one part of the earth in sunshine?" asked Hank.

"Of course we are outside the earth's shadow," countered the Professor, "but not outside its range, which extends far beyond the lunar orbit; for the moon itself enters into the umbra of the earth during an eclipse."

"I must admit," said Flitmore, "that all this takes my breath away; my astronomical knowledge doesn't go far and I didn't take these circumstances into account."

"Indeed!" laughed Schulze. "You were also mistaken about the propulsion speed of your *Sannah*. It is certainly not the speed of light, otherwise we should long ago have passed the moon."

"Hold on," objected Lord Flitmore, "you forget that we are still going at our initial speed, which is constantly increasing; besides, I intentionally put a very weak current through our envelope so that we might observe our neighbor, the moon, at leisure."

"Do you know what is going to happen to us?" asked the Professor. "As inhabitants of a regular planet we shall be subject to the laws of gravitation; that is, our *Sannah* will revolve around the sun in an elliptical orbit, and then we shall be helpless prisoners until we come to a miserable end after our oxygen supply is exhausted."

"You are a dismal prophet, Mr. Professor," Mitzie exclaimed. "I hope your prediction will not be fulfilled."

Schulze shrugged his shoulders. "The law of gravitation stands for no exceptions; every world body is subjected to it, and since our World-Ship has become such a world body in infinite space, it must become, together with the rest of us, a victim of this law."

"If I may be permitted to ask," spoke up John Rieger, the servant, "what is this fateful force anyway, the one you call the force of gravitation?"

"That is the force," the Professor explained to his curious questioner, "which keeps all the planets, that is, all the world bodies that revolve around the sun, in their orbits. The immortal Isaac Newton was the first to establish the law of this force, which is essentially nothing but the force of gravity: all world bodies attract each other and the greater their mass the stronger their attractive force. But this diminishes with distance and is in inverse ratio to the square of the distance."

"But then, as it were, they would be falling on to each other," interjected Rieger, "the small ones presumably upon the larger, as, for example, the moon on the earth and the earth on the sun."

"Very penetratingly remarked, my son!" praised Schulze. "But the moon is not only attracted by the earth but also by the sun, and all the world bodies have a mutual attraction for one another. That is how the force of attraction causes the elliptical movement of the planets around the sun, while by this singular movement they once more overcome the force of attraction up to a certain point, so that this is precisely the force which results in keeping the universe in equilibrium."

"But what do you say, Lord Flitmore, to the fears expressed by our Professor that we shall now spin around the sun forever?" asked Hank Frieding.

"There is no danger of that," replied Flitmore. "Schulze failed to take one main circumstance into consideration. I have an altogether different view of gravitation. I believe two forces are active there, an attractive force and a reciprocal repulsive force, just as it is assumed that the molecules and atoms of a body do attract each other but yet never touch because they also repel each other. The equalization of these two mutually counteracting forces determines, in my opinion, the reciprocal distance which the heavenly bodies observe; this is also how I explain that the volatile elements of the comets, in approaching the sun, are attracted up to a certain point but from there on are repelled and thus form the tail of the comet.

"The main thing for us, however, is that the current which circulates through the *Sannah* altogether eliminates the force of attraction and allows only the centrifugal force to operate, so that no world body can force us into its orbit so long as the circuit remains closed."

"That is correct, all right," admitted Schulze. "But you see there is another thing that strikes me as puzzling: we have at all events long ago reached empty space, outside of the earth's atmosphere, whose height is estimated at some hundred miles——"

"Allow me to interrupt you here," begged Flitmore. "What do you imagine our earthly air envelope to be like in general?"

"Well," replied the Professor, "the view is held that there is no sharp dividing line between the atmosphere and space in general, but only a gradual transition through a constantly increasing rarefaction of the air."

"Quite right!" said Flitmore. "But the astronomers or astrophysicists who set up this fine theory apparently forget that the earth, in careening along through space, takes its air envelope with it. How are we to explain that, if this envelope has no fixed limits? Very simply. The air envelope of the earth is never and nowhere sharply distinguished from the space-filling element, because this element, which fills up space and is called ether, is nothing else but air."

"But then all science comes to an end!" laughed the Professor. "You will find it hard sledding with this in the scientific world."

"That's possible! But I am convinced of it. A very gradual transition of the atmosphere into surrounding space is possible only if space contains the same elements as air, of course, in an extremely diluted form. Thus the earth may, on the one hand, constantly lose some of its uppermost, thinnest air layers to space, but, on the other hand, it will constantly attract replacements from flitting space."

"Bravo!" cried Hank. "This assumption alone appears to me enough to explain how the earth, throughout thousands of years, could preserve its air envelope at the same density and in constantly renewed purity."

"That is just how," confirmed Flitmore. "And it follows further that every world body, in accord with its mass and attractive force, as well as with its speed of rotation and circulation, must have drawn an atmosphere out of space, which is condensed by its attractive force and has become densest at its surface."

"Then that means: No world body without its air envelope?" asked Schulze.

"That would certainly be the necessary conclusion of my assumption."

"Let us leave it undecided," continued the Professor,

shaking his head. "The puzzle I wanted to talk about is this: Now that we are in empty space, or, as you would have it, in extremely rarefied ethereal air, a temperature must prevail in our surroundings which comes close to absolute zero, that is, 273 degrees centigrade below zero. Now, no matter how excellent the protective shell of our *Sannah* or her heating system may be, we should still feel the effects of such a terrific cold. But I feel nothing of the kind; on the contrary, it is always comfortably warm."

"We are completely in the dark about the temperature conditions of space," replied the Englishman. "The constant diminution of the temperature is already disproved within the earth's atmosphere in which the great inversion takes place: the lowest air layer is from ten to fourteen thousand feet high and is in constant agitation and motion; above it is a calmer, dry, cold air-layer in which the temperature declines to 85 degrees below zero. At a height of 34,000 feet, however, begins the third, very equable, calm and dry layer which is again warmer, and at a height of 48,000 feet shows 52 to 57 degrees below zero. The theory of the 'radiation' of light and warmth I consider to be completely wrong; it led inevitably to entirely impossible conclusions. If you consider with what speed the earth rushes through space, so that at every moment it encounters new sun-rays previously lost in space, then it must be assumed that it could never catch any light and warmth from the sun, if the space through which it wanders were not illuminated and warmed."

"You are right, Lord Flitmore," Captain Munchhausen now joined in the conversation. "On the highest mountain peaks, which are eternally covered with ice and snow as a result of the lack of earth's heat, the sun burns more hotly than below in the dense atmosphere. Why? The thin air gives off its warmth more abundantly, and warms itself less by accumulating it; the space through which we are flying is of course far colder than the mountain air but not at all so terribly cold as might be thought, and by morning we shall learn that the sun-rays warm us up more vigorously than anywhere on earth."

"And since half of our *Sannah* will always enjoy sunlight," added Hank, "I don't think we shall ever suffer from too sharp a cold."

"I count on that too," concluded Flitmore. "I believe that so long as we are within range of sun-warmth, we shan't need any heating at all; on the contrary, the protective shell of my World-Ship will have to preserve us against unbearable heat."

"If your assumption is correct," interposed the Professor again, "how do you explain that light and warmth break through out of a vacuum tube?"

"Just because the tube has no complete vacuum," smiled Flitmore. "You forget that what I deny is the presence of an empty space, even of an air-empty space, in the domain of the knowable world."

VI

PAST THE MOON

OUR friends turned their attention once more to the moon, which sent its white light through the large ceiling window; for the *Sannah*, in the meantime, had completed a second revolution.

It now appeared to be an immense globe, closer than it could ever be seen through the strongest telescope on earth.

"We are crashing straight towards it!" cried Lady Flitmore, not without concern.

"Calm yourself, Mitzie," consoled her husband. "The centrifugal force prevents us from being dashed to pieces on its surface, it must repel us before we come up to it. If we want to, though, we can pay it a visit: all I need to do is break the circuit."

"I vote against it," declared Munchhausen. "It doesn't look at all inviting, this spot that poets yearn for."

"As if we could even breathe there," said Schulze. "Why, it has no atmosphere."

"As to that," replied the Englishman, "I still hold firmly to the view I expressed before, that every world body has its air envelope."

"Nevertheless, nobody has ever been able to observe any signs of twilight upon it with certainty," interposed the Professor.

"That proves nothing," retorted Flitmore obstinately. "In the first place, numerous astronomers claim to have noted signs of twilight on the moon, and in the second place, in pure air, as Tyndall demonstrated, there are no twilight signs at all; these are much rather due to small particles of matter in the atmosphere. For example, tropical countries, on the earth also, know what we call twilight only in a hardly perceptible degree, and surely you don't want to deny them their air. Were the air there completely free of solid matter and dust, they also, we may assume, would be unable to produce the slightest signs of twilight. That the moon shows no cloud formations only proves the lack of water on its surface. On the other hand, a star often appears in front of the lunar disk before it vanishes behind it, which can most easily be explained by the atmospheric refraction of light, even if certain scholars want to regard it as a simple hallucination."

The landscape of the moon certainly did not look too inviting, as the Captain had very rightly remarked; everything lay glassy, desolate, and dead, without a trace of vegetation or running water. But the spectacle was highly interesting and it riveted the attention of the observers.

The mountain ranges rose to enormous heights above their surroundings and everywhere could be seen the annular craters peculiar to the moon, with their precipitous ledges rising to the skies. Some eminences must have reached an absolute height of 34,000 feet.

The Professor and Lord Flitmore paid special attention to the crater Linné, whose opening was described by Lohrmann as a hollow six miles in diameter and, as such, was observed with especial clearness by Beer and Maedler, until it suddenly disappeared in 1866. In its place appeared later a much smaller crater, which both the *Sannah's* observers perceived, whereas from the earth it could often no longer be recognized as such.

They would also have liked to view the double crater,

Messier, which too has changed in a remarkable manner: under no less than 300 observations, from 1829 to 1837, both craters were round and identical; today, the single crater shows an elliptical form and the partition between the two gorges has been broken down.

It is also believed that here and there a surging sea-mist was to be seen in this crater, perhaps clouds of smoke. To our friends, the Messier was not visible, because the *mare fœcunditatis*, in which it is to be found, disappeared behind the horizon, for now the *Sannah* no longer moved towards the lunar disk in a vertical line, but skirted past it sideways.

From a number of the craters they could see bright rays emerging. Particularly did this remarkable phenomenon appear at the magnificent annular mountain-chain of the moon, the Tycho, from which many hundred separate streaks radiated to a length of 700 odd miles.

In these puzzling images, Schulze thought he recognized congealed streams of lava with a smooth, shiny surface. In favor of this is the fact that they are visible only under a full luminosity of the sun.

Flitmore, on the contrary, pointed out that the rays first began at some distance from the ramparts of the craters and then ran off uninterruptedly over plains, craters, mountains, and valleys, only to come to a sudden end at the foot of some elevation or be lost gradually along a plain. This hardly accorded with the assumption of lava streams. On the other hand, both of the explorers plainly recognized what proved to be more or less broad gaping cracks in the moon's surface.

More than once new formations were also observed on the moon, and our friends were lucky enough to see one arise before their very eyes: in the great plains of the *Mare imbrium* the ground suddenly yawned open, smoke and fire broke forth, and within a few minutes a crater was formed, out of which a stream of slime or lava poured all over the vicinity.

"Too bad that the astronomers on the earth cannot see the new volcano," Flitmore remarked regretfully. "It is too small for their instruments."

"We have observed the event and that's enough!" crowed Schulze.

"Yes," interceded Hank. "That is, if we ever reach the earth again and can bring back information about this event."

"An old dispute would be decided that way," said the Professor; "that is, if we should be believed, which is still pretty doubtful."

"What remarkable colors!" Lady Flitmore now observed, and pointed to the region of the *Oceanus procellarum.*

There really were revealed extensive spots of bright green and yellowish color.

"Can there be vegetation down there, after all that has been said?" Hank dared to suppose.

"Attention, gentlemen!" Lord Flitmore cried out. "We are now going to see a spectacle which no earthly eye has yet perceived. The moon always turns but one and the same side towards the earth, because it revolves on its axis in exactly the same time in which it revolves around the earth. Only as a result of its libration, that is, of the slight swing of its axis, we see first on one side and then on the other a small portion of the half that is turned away from us.

"Now the moment has arrived when we shall fly past the earth's satellite and get a glimpse of its enigmatical other side, and at pretty close range; for we have approached to within 6000 miles of it, while it is at a distance of 248,000 miles from the earth."

Everybody was on tiptoe for the scene that the mysterious other side of the moon held for them, although Schulze thought that it would not be very different from what they had already seen.

For observation, another chamber had to be sought out, for, as a result of the rotation of the *Sannah*, the moon was going straight down under the room occupied by the company and, besides, the *Sannah* was rushing beyond the moon's orbit.

The Englishman decided to approach closer to the moon so that all the details of the expected phenomena might be observed with the greatest plainness. He therefore shut off the centrifugal circuit and the *Sannah* hurtled towards the moon at a furious pace.

The next thing to be noticed was the enormous extent of the colored spots, which could now be plainly recognized through the telescope as green fields and arid grassy plains.

"What is that?" exclaimed Lady Flitmore in sudden fright.

Through the window fell a luminous gleam.

Lord Flitmore looked up and rushed with a bound to the circuit connection in order to put the centrifugal force in operation once more.

"What was it?" asked Hank.

"We have penetrated into the atmosphere of the moon," explained the Englishman, "and with the speed of our fall, the metal rims of the window-frames began to grow red-hot in spite of the flint-glass protection. However, the danger is eliminated; we are already rising again above the atmosphere."

"So it exists, this much-disputed moon air," said Schulze.

"There is no longer any doubt about it," replied Flitmore, "but look at that!"

The moon's surface was a bare sixty-two miles away—so high did the denser part of its atmospheric envelope rise. And now appeared landscape scenes of charming splendor.

Here too the peculiar mountain chains predominated; but they were covered with woods.

The distance prevented the naked eye from recognizing the nature of these woods, but the telescope revealed very singularly formed trees such as are not to be found on earth. Most of these growths resembled enormous clusters of grass on high trunks, so that they looked like palms; yet the trees seldom had an actual crown; most of them were horizontal branches which stretched out their bushy tips on all sides.

Megaphytons and coniferous trees of the same singular construction were to be seen elsewhere; the fronds stood at right angles from the trunks and inclined somewhat downwards, so that under the trunk no shadow could be found, apart from the meager shadow of the trunk itself and its branch-wood; only at a goodly distance was the tree surrounded by a circle of shadow spots.

In the crater hollows glistened numerous small and large lakes; waterfalls and rivulets plunged down the steep mountain walls, but larger river-courses and seas were not to be seen. The rivulets poured out into little inland lakes or disappeared in the sand of the plateau; many of them also appeared to cover up swamps of the lowlands.

Of living beings there was nought to see; Schulze expressed the surmise that at all events there ought to be animal and bird life, but most likely only in small numbers of the most modest size, so that at such a distance none of it could be espied.

Cloud formations did not appear to exist at all on this side of the moon, which was not so very astonishing in view of the absence of any substantial bodies of water. But here and there rose veils of mist which might serve to moisten the soil and to feed the sources.

"A long day and a long night is the lot of eventual inhabitants of the moon," said Schulze. "They last fourteen and three-quarters times our earth-day; all the shorter is their year, for it only lasts one day and one night, a total of twenty-nine and a half earth-days.

"From this side of the moon the earth is never seen, whereas on the other side of the moon, unlived on and uninhabitable, it stands motionless in the heavens, without ever rising or setting or changing its position. Only as a result of the libration does it rise and set for the border regions. It appears to be three and a half times as large as the moon appears to us on earth, and in twenty-nine and a half days it goes through all the phases of the moon. What a grandiose spectacle and what radiant light it has there, where nobody, in all likelihood, is able to admire it!"

Lord Flitmore decided from then onwards to accelerate the voyage into cosmic space to the highest point, and put the centrifugal current on at full power; then a repast was enjoyed which John, the artist in all things, had in the meantime prepared.

As the travellers through the universe felt the urgent need for rest, it was decided that everybody was now to retire to his own sleeping quarters and put in a few hours of sleep.

With the numerous compartments that Lord Flitmore's *Sannah* contained, everybody had a separate and very spacious sleeping chamber at his disposal.

But first the guard duty was arranged for.

It was generally recognized that a constant watch was indispensable. First, because on a voyage of such terrific speed, unknown dangers threatened at any moment; and then because especially interesting phenomena might be encountered which nobdy would like to miss seeing.

The sleeping period was fixed at eight hours, and as Mitzie insisted upon taking her turn just like the men, every "night," if that is what you want to call the period of sleep, was divided into three watches, so that out of every forty-eight hours it came to a watch of about two and three-quarter hours for each; surely no excessive watch, for after it each could sleep as long as he pleased.

The watch had to make the rounds of all the observation rooms two or three times, in order to keep an eye in all directions. Should he see danger ahead or something especially noteworthy, he was obliged to sound the electro-magnetic alarm gong which rang simultaneously in all the compartments and could be set going from any room by pressing a button.

VII

A SERIOUS DANGER

LORD FLITMORE took over the first watch.

At a terrific speed the *Sannah* hurtled into the void. By the diminution of the apparent size of the moon, Flitmore calculated that they were making about sixty-two miles per second.

"The speed will yet double in time, perhaps treble," he murmured; "but by that it will have reached its highest pace. At the present rate we should cross the Mars orbit in 9 days, at 186 miles per second in 3 days; then we should require 3 weeks to reach the orbit of Jupiter, another 25 days to reach Saturn, then 55 days to Neptune—5½ months all told. That would make 11 months till we got back to the earth, and I can count on our air provisions lasting until then, quite apart from the possibility, yes, the probability, of being able to renew them on some planet or other, which will put us in a position to spend an indefinite time in the surveying and investigation of the planets whose nature will permit us to land on their surface. Thus we could travel without any particular risk to the very limits of our solar system."

"Splendid!" called a voice.

"Oho, it is you, Professor," said the Englishman, turning about. "You are up too early; your watch doesn't begin for half an hour."

"There! I had a great sleep for two hours and I feel quite

sprightly; so I decided to keep you company during the last part of your watch; but you must be tired; stretch out for a bit if you wish, I am right on the spot."

"I don't feel a bit tired; I am used to keeping long watch."

"So we can travel as far as Neptune, if I understood you rightly. Why, that's excellent!"

"For me it signifies a disappointment rather: I wanted to explore the cosmic spaces beyond our solar system; but it now appears to be out of the question, for at a speed of only 186 miles per second we should need about 4500 years to reach the closest fixed star, Alpha Centauri, called Toliman."

"Well, do you know, Lord Flitmore, if we move around here in infinity, outside the domain of earthly natural laws, then it is not at all out of the question that we might grow to be a few thousand years old," joked the Professor.

"And be able to give up bodily nourishment and breathing in fresh air," supplemented Flitmore. "Maybe! For what a professor considers possible, must be possible. But I fear we should die of weariness if we were to travel through empty space for four and a half thousand years."

"Look at that, Lord Flitmore," said Schulze suddenly, "the sun is becoming remarkably small!"

He had cast a glance through the window and to his amazement noted that the solar disk appeared hardly twice as large as usual and had also lost in brilliancy to the same extent.

At a speed of 223,200 miles per hour this phenomenon was a puzzle; the voyage would normally have had to last four to five days of twenty-four hours for the sun to appear at such a distance.

At first Flitmore was not struck very much by the Professor's remark. "Yes," he said, "we are constantly moving farther away from our central star."

Then he also glanced up at the window.

"Holla!" he now cried out, quite bewildered. "What does this mean?"

He put his hands to his head as if he doubted whether he were awake or dreaming.

"Lord Flitmore, the *Sannah* is not making 186, but 9300 miles a second," exclaimed Schulze. "At this rate we should reach Alpha Centauri in 90 years; and more than that, if the speed of your wonderful World-Ship increases at the same rate, as may be assumed, then it may even become 90 days."

"Out of the question, completely out of the question!" Flitmore said finally. Calm and determined he went over and broke the centrifugal circuit.

"What are you doing there?" asked the Professor.

"It was high time we realized the situation," explained Flitmore. "We must already be past the Mars orbit. Had I lain down to rest and had you not recognized the meaning of the striking phenomenon, we should have been hopelessly lost. Yes, lost in endless space! It is not a question of the incredible speed of our craft, but of the tremendous rapidity with which our solar system careens through the universe. Since we had eliminated the attractive force, for ourselves, the solar system did not take us along on its voyage, but threatened to leave us behind in space."

"Permit me, Lord Flitmore! It is true that the sun is supposed to move with its satellites towards the constellation of Hercules, but only at 10 miles per second, so that this movement can hardly be mentioned in the same breath with the 186 miles per second of the *Sannah* and in no way explains our rapid separation from the sun."

"You are right, Professor; but what we have here is a movement which no earthly astronomer could recognize, but which was thought of and surmised and which has revealed itself at this moment. The whole world of fixed stars, within which the individual systems move, as does our solar system towards Hercules, in turn constitutes a great system which apparently travels there at 9300, or still more, miles per second, like a current through the infinity of space, and this is the current which threatened to lead us out of our solar system in a short time, so that we should have remained behind in the void, far from all the world bodies that might have attracted us or repelled us and thereby held out for us the prospect of landing somewhere."

"Well, I never! Then we'd have had to wait until the great world current should bring new worlds close to us."

"A good thought; but who knows how many thousands of years we might have had to wait for that? At any rate, I preferred to turn us back again to the influence of the force of attraction, for right now it seems necessary for our security that we do not leave our solar system. Now we shall presumably enter within range of the attraction of Mars and we must watch out that we don't crash down upon it with a bang. I shan't retire, therefore, so that I may be able to take the proper measures in time."

VIII

THE GREAT ASTRONOMERS

OUR friends had decided to divide their time calculations in accordance with the earth's scale in order to
avoid any confusion of ideas, and thus it was eight in the
morning, according to the clocks of the *Sannah*, when all of
them gathered around the breakfast table in the North Pole
room.

The sleeping compartments were all located in the inside
rooms, which were supplied with artificial lighting; the four
halls which were located in the equator line of the *Sannah*
always alternated with one hour of day and one hour of
night; in the South Pole room, on the contrary, unchanging
night prevailed at the time, and in the North Pole room incessant day. For this reason the latter was selected as the
common meeting place.

Schulze reported in detail on the events of the previous
night and concluded with the words: "The fact that the
earth and the moon vanished so rapidly from our horizon,
like the fact that the whole solar system threatened to escape us, is the first practical proof of the correctness of the
Copernican system."

"How so?" asked Hank Frieding in amazement. "I
thought there was nothing in the world so sure as this system and that it had long ago been proved to be correct beyond a doubt!"

"There you have your scholastic wisdom!" laughed the
Professor. "What one believes he usually proclaims, be it
out of ignorance or imagination, as indubitable truth.

"It is true that the Copernican system is extremely illuminating and best explains all the astronomical phenomena on the level of knowledge on which we stand at present; indeed, our whole physical system of conceptions rests upon the assumption of its correctness. But this correctness is just as little proved beyond a doubt as is any one of the other so-called 'scientific truths.' It is very improbable, but not at all inconceivable, that a future, more advanced, generation will turn back to the Ptolemaic world system."

"With your permission, Mr. Professor," began John Rieger, who was always striving to improve his education, "what is this anyway, the Polemical and the Copernican world system, if I may permit myself the impertinence of putting such a question?"

"Certainly you may, and I am glad to enlighten you. Claudius Ptolemæus was a renowned astronomer of the second century after Christ and lived in the city of Alexandria, in Egypt. He believed that the earth was the central point of the universe and stood immovably solid, while sun, moon, and stars moved around it, as it does indeed appear to us. This is called the Ptolemaic world system, and was generally believed in for 1500 years after Christ.

"Nicolaus Copernicus was a Polish priest who wrote a book upon which our present conceptions rest, and which appeared in 1543. Here he declared not only that the earth revolves around its axis, from which day and night arise, but also that, besides this, it moves in one year around the sun, which constitutes the stationary central point of our solar system, around which the other planets or wandering stars also revolve. This is called the Copernican world system."

"Huh," said John disdainfully, "this Ptolomaus must have been a pretty simple-minded and uneducated man, and there is nothing remarkable in what Copernicus maintained. Why, every child knows that the earth revolves around the sun!"

"Because he is told so in school, my friend. But you must bear in mind that nobody told it to Copernicus; he discovered it out of his own head."

"Just a minute, Professor," protested Lord Flitmore. "It is the ancient wisdom of the Egyptians that Copernicus warmed up again, by which I don't mean to belittle his services in any way. Back in the most ancient times there were great minds who formed strikingly correct conceptions about the earth and our solar system. They seem to have come down to them from the Egyptian priests, and to the latter perhaps from the Chaldeans. But it is the merit of these keen thinkers that they acknowledged as correct the truths which were then so unbelievable, and upon the basis of them accomplished scientific exploits.

"Think of the Cheops pyramids, which were erected 3000 years before Christ, whose dimensions are in surprisingly exact proportion to the circumference of the earth and to certain astronomical measurements of distance which have only been rediscovered lately. Their corners are in line with the four points of the compass, and in the royal burial chamber there is a mirror which looks up at all times, through a long inclined tunnel, to the polar star. Whoever was capable of making such calculations possessed abilities and scientific knowledge, a gift of observation, and a mental power which even the first great men of our modern astronomy— Copernicus, Kepler, Galileo, and Isaac Newton—did not surpass."

"You are right," acknowledged Schulze. "The ancients had tremendous minds which, without our modern auxiliaries, without telescopes and spectral analysis, achieved almost as much as our most modern scientific notables with all the advantages of the colossal work of their predecessors and the most perfect instruments.

"The Greek philosopher Bion, 500 years before Christ, taught the spherical form of the earth and contended that there must be regions on our earth on which there are six months of daylight and six months of night. Eratosthenes of Alexandria calculated the circumference of the earth with startling penetration and astounding exactness, coming to approximately the same result the Chaldeans had come to long before him.

"The geographer, Strabo, had forebodings about America, for he said that there could still be two or more unknown continents on the globe. Aristarchus made bold enough to calculate the distance and the dimensions of the moon and the sun, considering, it is true, the distance to the sun 20 times as great as that to the moon, instead of 400. Nevertheless, these were measurements which must have appeared positively enormous in those day. Posidonius furnished a truly wonderful calculation of the earth's atmosphere and of the refraction of light, and just as astounding is his calculation of the size of the sun. We have no idea what means he used to arrive at such dumbfounding results."

"Permit me," Hank interrupted the Professor, "to tell you how I imagine a sage of antiquity could have arrived at the correct conception of the distances and sizes of the world bodies.

"Let us assume that a Greek philosopher climbed the Helicon with his pupils. 'Look down,' he said to them, 'upon that field at the foot of the mountain, which seemed so extensive to us when we passed it by, and now, from above here, because of the distance, appears to be a tiny spot, a good hundred times smaller than it really is. The distance we have put behind us in climbing up from the field has brought us that much closer to the moon. And yet its disk does not look one bit larger to us than it did down below. The moon must therefore be quite immeasurably farther removed from us than that field, so that the height of the Helicon means very little in approaching it. But if it is at such a great distance then it must, in reality, be infinitely larger than it appears. The sun must be still farther off and larger, for when there is a solar eclipse the moon goes by beneath it. Also, the earth must be spherical in form; for the higher we climb the more we can survey, and that holds true for every mountain top, in Asia Minor and Africa as well as here.' "

"True enough," admitted Schulze, "such considerations might have led the ancients on to the right road. Nevertheless, we must marvel at how clear were their ideas, which were able, as a result of such observations, to rise above the conceptions of their day.

"Apollonius of Perga was such a mental giant and is said to have discovered the idea of parallaxis, that is, the method of calculating the distance of the stars. Hipparch calculated the umbra of the moon with great exactitude and deduced from it the distance from the sun to the moon.

"Pythagoras taught the movement of the earth as the reason for the apparent movement of the stars; Aristarchus recognized that the earth revolves around the sun and that the fixed stars are located at an enormous distance from us. All this, moreover, seems to have been recognized by Democritus four centuries before Christ.

"Archimedes already had the first ideas about gravitation. But all these bold advances lay fallow and forgotten for centuries until Copernicus wrote his great work, whose prophet the luckless Giordano Bruno proclaimed himself to be.

"Then came Tycho Brahe, the great observer to whom Kepler owed so much. Johann Kepler established the famous laws of planetary motion, their elliptical orbit around the sun, the law of their speed of motion in relation to their orbit, and the law of the relation of their rotation period to their mean distance from the sun.

"Galileo was the first to use the telescope, discovered the moon of Jupiter and the lunar phases of Venus; Cassini calculated the distance to the sun, from its parallaxis at the passing of Mars; Römer and Leverrier measured the speed of light; Newton established the law of gravitation; Kant and Laplace brought the universe and its laws of motion into a magnificent system and explained its origin, development, and future. Finally, Herschel discovered the planet Uranus; Piazzi, Gauss, and Olbers the planetoids; Herschel again the individual movement of the fixed stars and the existence of double stars; he was also the one who studied the nebulæ.

"Thus, when in 1838 the first fixed-star parallaxis was measured, which made it possible for us to calculate the distances of the celestial bodies outside our solar system, the great astronomical discoveries were at an end, if we disregard the wonderful revelations through spectral analysis."

"Thanks, you wisest of all professors!" said Munchhausen, laughing. "You have given us a lecture which should truly be called an outline of the history of astronomy in the last 10,000 years. But you are mistaken about one point: you have, as it were, pronounced great astronomical discoveries at an end and forgot that they are only beginning, now that we have set out to explore the universe personally."

"And now we have the best opportunity for such discoveries," said Mitzie, who had just come in. She had made the rounds through the observation rooms, as was done alternatingly every half hour so as to guard against unpleasant surprises.

"What's up?" asked Flitmore.

"We are approaching Mars at great speed," replied his wife.

Flitmore stood up. "Let us present ourselves, gentlemen," he said. "We are especially lucky in having this planet right at the spot in its orbit that we shall cross. I even deliberately selected the time of such a juncture for our voyage."

All of them followed Lord Flitmore into one of the equatorial chambers from which his wife had observed the approach to Mars.

IX

MARS

THE *Sannah*, which, since the previous night, if night may be spoken of, had had the centrifugal power circuit disconnected, was within the attraction range of the planet which, more than any other, has always excited the imagination of astronomers.

They were already so close to it that the larger formations of its surface could be plainly distinguished without using the telescope.

"Here is where all science comes to an end!" was the first thing a surprised and disappointed Schulze exclaimed. "Is this really Mars? Where are the canals, my beloved canals, which I observed so zealously and studied so ardently, the miracle, the enigma of Mars?"

Of canals, there was not in fact a trace to be seen.

Turning to the Professor, Flitmore said: "I could never get myself to believe in those remarkable canal formations and surmised that it was all optical illusion. Mars is substantially smaller than our earth, its radius is little more than half the earth's; its polar regions are immense, particularly in winter. And are the inhabitants of the tiny inhabitable zone supposed to have covered the soil with a huge network of enormous canals?"

"Why not?" asked Schulze, stubbornly. "If the irrigation of the soil required it."

"With the vast masses of ice and snow at the poles, the tremendous snowfall in the winter, and in view of the extremely rapid melting of the snow in spring most of the time, I cannot believe in the shortage of water on Mars."

"Well! Nevertheless the canals are to have regulated the flow of water, distributing it all over the soil and preventing floods."

"Very fine, assuming that they were canals of reasonable proportions and reasonable extent. But these alleged canals showed a width of from 37 to 186 miles—and pray tell me what that's for. Those are absurd dimensions for a canal! If they had at least remained that way; but here one single canal suddenly became wider, and then narrower again; if it took the notion, it would suddenly double, often within twenty-four hours, and just as swiftly the doubling would disappear again, together with the original canal in some cases; then again, an old canal would disappear and two new ones appear in its place."

"I know, I know! That was just the enigma of these remarkable canals," persisted the Professor.

"And now the enigma is solved," laughed Flitmore. "They simply don't exist, these famous canals."

"That I must certainly concede," admitted the scholar. "But the thing is only the more puzzling because of it."

Nevertheless, even without these mysterious marks the landscape was remarkable enough: the North Pole shone white with its ice and snow fields; the snowless land towards the equator looked a ruddy yellow, broken up by dark green strips; and a few small seas or large lakes struck across the continents, while broad rivers drew silvery-gray ribbons through the plains.

Almost everything appeared to be level. There were no large mountains, and smaller elevations could be recognized from the height at which the *Sannah* was only by the shadow they cast; but where the sun completely illumined the valleys, hill and dale could be distinguished.

In the meantime the World-Ship was dropping with lightning speed towards the planet and everything appeared to grow beneath their very eyes.

Flitmore hastened, however, to close the centrifugal circuit before the *Sannah* reached the air envelope of the planet, so that her outside walls should not grow red-hot from the terrific friction.

The fall was now visibly slackened until the repelling force overcame the speed of the drop and then the World-Ship began very slowly to rise.

"Shall we try a landing on Mars?" asked Flitmore.

"Hurrah!" shouted Schulze enthusiastically.

"Oh, please do!" smiled Mitzie.

"I'm for it!" said Munchhausen. "I don't feel comfortable in prison, even if it has lasted only twelve hours."

"It would be magnificent!" rejoined Hank in turn.

"And what do you say, John?" Flitmore turned to the servant.

"Sir, I have nothing to say in a matter which concerns your humble discretion; but as to my answer to this question, I should be particularly pleased to breathe free air, although, as it were, the air inside here is excellent for the respiratory organs."

"Then we land," decided Flitmore, "since it is unanimously desired. We cannot ask the chimpanzees for their opinion, and Dick and Bobs will therefore have to submit to the majority."

At the same time he broke the circuit; but as soon as the falling speed appeared to increase to a serious extent he again closed the circuit for a few seconds.

By means of this alternating opening and closing, a slow fall was made possible, which was also softened by the atmosphere of Mars as soon as it was reached.

X

A LANDING ON MARS

AS soon as the closer approach to Mars caused its attractive force to operate upon the *Sannah,* her rotating speed diminished, and as she finally sank down upon the planet her own movement ceased entirely and her centre of gravity was transferred to the central point of the Mars globe. After the full stoppage of the centrifugal force she acted like any meteor that falls upon the surface of a planet. This time Flitmore had foreseen the change and taken care that the company should not be surprised once more by a fall against the walls or the ceilings.

The shock caused by the landing was scarcely perceptible in the upper chambers, where everybody was standing at the time.

"We shall have to descend from the North or South Pole rooms," declared Flitmore. "The exit doors there, near the windows, are on a level now, that is, they are parallel to the surface of Mars and we shall be able to descend with a rope ladder."

"Let me be the first to leave the *Sannah,*" begged Hank.

"No, my friend!" replied Schulze. "I will go out first; we don't know what the atmosphere of Mars is made of. Who knows if it may not have a dangerous and perhaps fatal effect upon our lungs?"

"That's just the reason why I want to make the first test," said Hank.

"Nothing of the sort!" blustered Captain Munchhausen. "I want to go out first; my lungs are accustomed to all sorts of dust and can stand anything sooner than yours."

"You?" laughed the Professor. "You should be happy if you can gasp in normal air! Anyway, you might get stuck in the opening or ruin our rope ladder by your weight. At any rate, you're going last."

"I'll start out!" decided Flitmore. "It is my right as well as my duty, for I am the one who undertook this world cruise."

"Under no circumstances should you run such a danger, Charles," Mitzie now objected. "I beg of you to let me make the first attempt; I can come right back if I feel that there are poisonous gases there."

"If the gentlemen will be so kind as to permit me," the loyal John came forward; "all this is not right, for it is rather my humble self that should make the venture, for my possible loss would be the least serious."

But Hank Frieding put an end to this noble rivalry by the following reasonable observation: "We have the two monkeys, Dick and Bobs; let's push them forward: they run the least danger, for their instinct will protect them from leaving the craft if they suspect any unhealthy air outside."

"That's the best solution," agreed Lord Flitmore. "We should have thought of that right away! Besides, I am convinced that the air envelope of Mars differs from that of the earth only in its density."

The air-tight door of the South Pole room, to which all had proceeded, was opened; a pleasant fresh wind swept in. Dick and Bobs swung joyfully through the opening and cavorted down the ramps which were fixed to the outside shell of the *Sannah*.

"So there is no danger," said Flitmore, and, with John's

assistance, moved aside the rope ladder to be the first to risk the descent, followed by his faithful wife.

After Mitzie came Hank, and then the Professor.

Schulze called out to the Captain: "Don't venture to walk the rope ladder until all the rest of us have reached solid ground, otherwise things may go badly for us if the ropes tear or the rungs crack under your weight and your heavy bulk crashes down on us."

But Flitmore had taken Munchhausen's weight into account when the rope ladder was bought. The rope groaned and the rungs creaked in bending as the Captain walked it behind John; but they held excellently.

"Huh, how you failed to get stuck in the door opening is a miracle to me," Schulze laughed, when all had reached bottom safely.

But Flitmore explained: "As I hoped beforehand to be accompanied by our worthy Captain, I calculated all the door dimensions according to his bodily proportions."

"That was rational and fine of you, Lord Flitmore," replied Munchhausen in good-hearted humor. "Of course it would have been a joke to our wicked Professor to see me get helplessly and miserably stuck in the door frames."

In the meantime the company looked about eagerly at their new location.

The first thing to strike them was that the ground was remarkably soft; the *Sannah* had dug herself into it pretty deeply and with every step they sank into the soil.

The landscape seemed to undulate softly and the ground-swells for the most part ran parallel and straight, crossed occasionally by long mounds which ran in other directions.

Between the elevations were rather broad, even areas which seemed to be swamps and were covered with a mass of dark vegetation. The mounds were partly bare, but for the most part covered with shrubbery and woods, and in many places also with prairie grass; but nowhere could fresh green be noticed; the grass, the leaves of the vegetation, and the trees were either yellow and red or ruddy brown so that everything looked autumnal, even though at the time it was early summer in these Mars latitudes.

As evening was already falling, John was ordered to bring tents and food from the World-Ship, for all were happy at the thought of camping in the open.

Firewood was at hand in abundance; fires were lit in preparation for a warm meal and for keeping off possible wild beasts.

All of them, including Mitzie, were armed with revolvers and knives and provided with grenades.

Flitmore pointed to the far-reaching swamps. "Do you see, Professor," he said. "These seemingly endless dark streaks which run alongside each other and sometimes intersect may very easily give the impression of canals, from a great distance."

"But they do not explain the changeability of the marks observed," objected Schulze.

"Perhaps we shall find a solution for that, too," thought Hank.

"The Mars air is nevertheless quite delightful," said the Captain, breathing deeply. "I propose that we establish here an air health-resort and a summering place; we should do an excellent business."

Mitzie now asked: "How long will the night last here?"

"Not much longer than an ordinary earth night," Schulze enlightened her. "Mars revolves on its axis in 24 hours, 37 minutes, and 22½ seconds. For that, the years here are relatively long: a Mars year has 668 Mars days, which correspond to about 682 earth days. At the northern hemisphere, where we now are, spring has 191 Mars days, summer 181, autumn 149, and winter 147; at the southern hemisphere spring and summer are much shorter, namely, 149 and 147 days, but also much hotter, because at that period the planet comes closest to the sun; autumn and winter, on the contrary, with 191 and 181 days, are all the colder there, for they coincide with the aphelion of Mars."

After the repast, the night watch was divided and all turned in.

XI

THE TERRORS OF MARS

HANK had the second night-watch. He felt somewhat ill at ease on this strange world body which might conceal completely new and unknown dangers. Actual fear the young man did not have; he had too much personal courage for that, combined with bodily and mental health; but he could not put down a peculiar, oppressive feeling.

The camp was pitched on a broad mound upon which the *Sannah* had landed and which seemed to stretch out into infinity. Just as endless by daylight seemed the swamp, which filled out the one-hundred-mile-wide depression between this mound and the next one.

And this swampy lowland appeared at night to become sinisterly alive.

The young watchman could hear no distinct sounds, but he could hear a rumbling mixture of tones, as if thousands of creatures were rustling and murmuring.

So far was Hank lost in thought that something finally crept in. It seemed to be a snake, in itself no very large animal, of about an arm's thickness and approximately ten feet long; but as the gleam of the fire revealed the smooth, damp, ruddy skin, the youngster imagined it to be a ghastly monster; for it resembled an earthworm and yet its size was positively gigantic.

The head, ending in a point, showed two extremely small, pale eyes which could scarcely be recognized as such; the mouth looked like a round hole and seemed to be meant for sucking and not for biting.

The repulsive worm crawled straight up to Hank and paid no heed to the fire. Behind it emerged another and then a third—indeed, the whole slope seemed to become alive: the vermin advanced in squads, as if the swamp had sent out its army to exterminate the uninvited interlopers on Mars.

At first Hank threw a grenade at the foremost worm, which only inflicted a small wound, for it met with no resistance in the soft mass and therefore did not even explode.

The worm wriggled about, and then suddenly rushed ahead and encircled the guard's foot, crawling upon him with sinuous speed.

Seized with horror and loathing, the young man went after his knife and beat off the animal with stabs and cuts. All at once he found himself attacked on all sides. Here rose a slippery head, there a second and a third; and they coiled upon him, all these gruesome creatures, and cut heads though he might, ripping his own clothes in the ardor of his defense, the numbers were too great, and he could not rid himself of them.

A sharp pain at the back of his neck brought his hand around: he felt the cold, slimy body of one of the worms, which had fixed itself there firmly and was sucking out his blood; and already another of the hideous heads hung from his cheek.

Hank flung himself to the ground and thrashed about like mad; but he did not rid himself of them and only felt ever-new slippery mouths pulling at his limbs.

Flitmore had been awakened by the noise and stepped out of his tent. With a loud hallo he aroused his comrades and threw himself, knife in hand, upon the vermin which circled about everywhere; for not much could be done with the grenades, that he saw at once.

The Englishman succeeded in liberating his young friend;

but he himself was already entwined in the grasp of some of the worms and Hank too was soon on his back again.

Shrieking loudly, Mitzie crashed out of her tent; the repulsive swamp animals had penetrated there and one of them hung upon her right arm.

But what a sight met her eyes as she came out! She shuddered, for her foot stepped everywhere upon similar loathsome creatures, which wriggled about upon her.

Meanwhile, Schulze had also come upon the scene. The swarming, prancing creatures which covered the ground at first excited his scientific interest.

"There you have ringed worms of fabulous size!" he cried. "Lumbricides or earthworms, nothing else! Truly colossal creatures! But actually nothing amazing: there have been shellfish and snails of gigantic form, so why not limacidæ and worms? I even surmise that similar creatures populated the earth at the time of the Ammonites; traces of their existence they could not, of course, leave behind them, as they were boneless animals."

"Better help us, Professor," gasped Hank. "Then, for all I care, you may begin a scientific discussion later on about this infernal crew, in case we get out of it with our skins."

"You're right," said Schulze; "they really seem to be a pretty dangerous crew, and they are making straight for me! But hats off to you, my young friend! You are fighting like a true soldier. Bravo! That was another good blow!"

Munchhausen, who, together with John, had now emerged upon the scene, quoted:

> To the right and the left, for all to view,
> Sank the hulk of the Turk, cleft clean in two.

Hank, with a well-aimed blow, had really cut in two the body of a ringed worm, so that the quotation was very fitting.

The Professor and the servant were already in the thick of the fiercest fight; they struck about them with their knives like madmen; but the swamp must have harbored thousands of these monsters and sent them out to the very camping grounds of the unfortunate ones; the battle seemed hopeless.

What were these creatures? Molluscs whom one footstep, one knife-blow, rendered harmless! They had no paws, no talons, no bite; they were no more dangerous than leeches. But their inexhaustible numbers made them invincible and our friends saw a gruesome end before them. Far sooner would they have fought the wildest beasts of prey, lions, tigers, a herd of elephants or of buffalo.

The chimpanzees, Dick and Bobs, wrought deadly havoc among the attackers. They seemed frenzied with rage. They flung themselves upon the ground and slew and tore with four hands at once, while, at the same time, with their sharp bite they rendered dozens of lumbricides harmless.

But to what good? Ever new squads advanced!

Munchhausen, who found it hard ordinarily to move about and bend over, immediately recognized that his most effective weapon lay in his tremendous bodily weight.

He started a veritable Indian dance, jumping into the air as high as he could, and with his enormous soles squashed to a pulp everything that stirred.

It would have been a sight to split one's sides with laughter to see the fat Captain hopping around as though he were training as a ballet dancer, if the danger of the situation had not been so acute.

Perspiration rolled down Munchhausen in streams, and yet his hopping was in vain; he too felt himself encircled and wound around, and now he slipped upon the ground, which had become far too slippery, fell down and rolled around amidst the bloodthirsty vermin, not without having flattened out a whole bunch of them.

The fighters, all of whom had shed blood to some extent, were exhausted, and still the slope was alive with thick masses of crawling things. If only they could flee and take refuge inside the World-Ship! But they had their camp a good 300 feet away and between them and the *Sannah* the ground teemed with masses of the vermin, which seemed to pile upon each other in heaps.

Suddenly the air rang with shrill, hoarse cries; then the rumbling flap of wings, and huge black forms swooped down like phantoms.

In the gleam of the still flickering fire a few of these new creatures, that had descended close to it, could be discerned.

They presented no encouraging spectacle; they themselves rather appeared to be frightful monsters: they were birds which were birdlike only because of their enormous bat's wings. They reminded one more of the pterodactyl of the earth's primeval age; a clumsy head with deeply indented jaws and sharp teeth gave them a resemblance to this amazing bird. Their size exceeded the eagle's by twofold; but the most remarkable thing was that they had four feet, which were armed with enormous claws.

Sinister and dangerous as these birds appeared to be, if birds they could be called, they yet arrived as saviors at the moment of greatest need; for they cleared away the ringed worms with incredible agility and bloodthirstiness and came in such hordes that they proved the masters of even those teeming masses.

They descended especially upon the rim of the mound, and with tooth and claw seized everything that sought to crawl up to it. And now that no new reinforcements came, the numbers of the attackers at the top visibly diminished, and our friends worked away with their knives with renewed courage.

Finally, no worm was left to raise its threatening head, even if the lifeless bodies still coiled and wriggled, twitched and jerked, on the ground as though they could never be completely killed.

Schulze hastened to Munchhausen, who was still rolling about on the ground and could not rise to his feet. And now that the danger seemed to be eliminated, the Professor roared with laughter at the exhilarating spectacle; the rotund Captain was rolling around like a buoy in a stormy sea; from his head hung two worms, like lovelocks, on both sides, and around his neck a beheaded beast was coiled like a thick scarf.

Despite his merriment, the Professor nevertheless hurried to free his fat friend from his tormentors and with the aid of Hank, who had in the meantime also rushed over, helped him to his feet.

Then they all set to, plastering and bandaging their wounds which, remarkably enough, were extremely slight. All of them had lost some blood but Munchhausen had decidedly been pumped the most.

"It doesn't matter!" he said humorously. "I have plenty of it and the beasts took more fat from me than blood, I fancy. I feel positively refreshed and relieved."

"But what a dance you did, Captain!" laughed Schulze. "I tell you, an Egyptian belly-dancer is nothing in comparison."

"No trick at all!" said Munchhausen. "Where is there an Egyptian dancer with such a magnificent belly?"

XII

A TOUR OF EXPLORATION ON MARS

JOHN took over the watch while the others again lay down to rest. The night passed without further incident.

In the morning, the tents were first of all brought back to the World-Ship; nobody had much of a taste for spending another night in the open on Mars.

Breakfast was eaten close to the *Sannah*, far from the still-twitching bodies of the lumbricides slain on the battlefield the night before.

"I propose an exploring tour on Mars," began Schulze, when justice had been done to the snack.

Everybody agreed.

"John," said Flitmore, "you remain behind as guard; we don't know what may happen here. It would be best if you were to go to the top platform where you can make far-off survey on all sides. If you see anything suspicious, set the large siren going."

When Rieger had reached the top of the globe with the air-driven siren, the small company marched off; Bobs was taken along while Dick kept the guard company.

Down in the swamp nothing could be seen of the repulsive creatures it harbored; but from the movements of the surface it might plainly be perceived that the morass was teeming with agile denizens. Only at night did these light-shunning creatures seem to dare the surface.

Meanwhile, they were approaching a wood on the mound, which was made up of low trees with red foliage.

These trees aroused Schulze's lively interest in particular, for they showed quite peculiar forms. Most of them had neither branches nor twigs; the large leaves spread out in long, thick stalks directly from the trunk, which split up at the top into a bundle of such leafy stalks.

The leaves were mostly round and as large as plates, others were shaped like shamrocks, composed of three joined disks; still others showed a triangular, quadrangular, and multiangular formation, thus offering a spectacle that was completely new and unusual to the earth's inhabitants.

Some of the trees, which were richly branched, had double leaves, which snapped open and shut like oyster shells and were obviously engaged in the capture of insects.

However, there was little to be seen of insects: a few remarkable midges, transparent as glass, and legless beetles which resembled flying caterpillars and flying worms and which also moved along the ground and up the trees like them; yes, winged snails which spewed out a bluish slime, two-legged ants and spiders—these were the wonders which Schulze annexed to his collection.

Birds, too, were represented by few types; they all had the peculiarity of being four-legged, a spectacle which eyes accustomed to earthly creatures found passing strange. To this was added the fact that these birds were not feathered, but had a hairy or scaly body, which radiated, however, with wondrous, motley colors of metallic sheen. Most of the beaks revealed a mouthful of teeth and the wings consisted mainly of fan-shaped, overlapping, long and firm scales or thin horned disks.

As the wanderers stepped into a clearing there was a roar from the underbrush and the first animal they had seen on Mars stood before their eyes.

It looked just as unusual as the insect and bird specimens. Large it was not, hardly bigger than a donkey; but it had a terrible set of teeth which, like all of its flat, long head, reminded them of a crocodile. From the middle of the head an extremely sharp horn rose straight up, and, above the ears, on both sides, protruded two shorter horns, their tips bent forward. But the most unusual thing was: this dangerous-looking beast was three-legged! It had two forelegs, but only one hindleg at the end of its pear-shaped body.

Later on, more varied animal species were encountered, all small, but fully armed, and all of them three-legged, like the first one they had seen.

"Here is where all science *does* come to an end!" cried the Professor, one time after another. "Four-legged birds, three-legged mammals, and two-legged insects! I shan't be believed by a single person back there on the earth, even when I put my well-prepared evidence right down on the table of science!"

"That's how you professors are!" Munchhausen reproached him. "If you have any knowledge what the natural creations on your small earth look like, then you believe you have exhausted the whole infinite universe and you imagine that inexhaustible nature is never and nowhere capable of creating anything that does not conform to a hair with what it likes to put before your very eyes on that little grain of sand of yours which is known as the world."

Schulze lamented interminably that he could not add one of each of the animal species to the birds, insects, and plants which he had acquired. But in place of that, Lord Flitmore succeeded with several snapshots, so that the peculiar animal world might at least be preserved in the form of faithful photographic images. An especially remarkable mammal, which did not appear to be too heavy to be taken along, was bagged by Hank, at the Professor's request, with one well-aimed shot.

This beast was as large as a wild boar, with a slender, agile but firm throat, high above which was poised a roundish, queer head with a broad snout; it was three-legged, like all the other Martian mammals, and from its skull grew strong, pointed horns like the quills of a hedgehog, fifteen in all, as was established after he was downed.

"Thank you! If such a brute were to charge at you with head bent!" said Munchhausen.

"Yes, that would convert your precious body into a sieve," laughed the Professor.

"I am only curious to find out what the inhabitants of Mars look like," continued the Captain. "If the insects here are two-legged, then I presume that the people are at least six-legged; for it ought to be well-established, after all we have seen, that nature is startlingly prodigal here with the number of legs she hands out."

"I don't believe in the Mars people," said Schulze.

"Listen, Professor, what you believe is of no consequence, for you are a man of science. Did you perhaps believe in four-legged birds, three-legged wild sows, and two-legged spiders before you saw them here?"

"No! That I didn't, it is true; but——"

"No 'buts'! So if you do not believe in six-legged inhabitants on Mars, then it speaks very well for their existence, and under any circumstances, when we turn back to the earth I am thinking of relating a whole lot of very amusing things about these Mars people, even if we don't chance to see any, and I hope that you will never contradict me, for you have now seen clearly that just those things you didn't believe in really exist."

In the meantime, they had reached the end of the woods, which measured only a little over a mile in width.

At this point a hilly embankment coming from one side

connected the elevation upon which the wanderers were marching with the parallel mound strips.

This cross-running chain was especially broad and might be called a plateau; but it was not completely level throughout, and showed several rocky eminences which surely could nowhere have reached a height of much more than six to nine hundred feet.

It was decided to turn off to the right and examine more closely the nearest one of these small mountain ranges.

XIII

THE INHABITANTS OF MARS

AFTER half an hour of walking the foot of the mountain was reached, and after another half an hour the first elevation was scaled.

The prospect that unfolded before our friends convinced them right away that the legend of the Mars people could not be a mere fancy of the astronomers; for there opened up before their view a high valley filled with a great number of buildings which undoubtedly owed their origin to rational beings.

These structures also had their striking peculiarities: in the first place, they were narrow and tall, built like towers; in the second place, they all looked triangular; in the third place, they were all drawn up in the same style.

The Professor, who sought an explanation for everything and always had one right at hand, made himself heard: "The Martian inhabitants apparently build in the air like the New Yorkers, probably for the same reason: they must economize on space. As a matter of fact, the whole surface of Mars does not amount to three-tenths of the earth's surface; besides, since the terribly broad swamps seem to take up a large part of the mainland, they must economize on building space. They build their homes triangularly so as to be able effectively to stand off hurricanes and the floods which are caused by the melting of the snows; that they look so smooth and unjointed, indicates a special paste with which the builders smear the structures evenly from the outside, a plaster which is probably peculiar to Mars."

"As penetrating as ever, Professor!" laughed the Captain. "But permit me to play the skeptic this time: during all our wanderings we have encountered neither villages nor towns, not even cultivated land, nor have we spied any at a distance. So the inhabitants of Mars have no shortage of building space as yet; besides, in this sheltered valley you would hardly have a stormy hurricane; also, it is located at such a height that it is not threatened by floods. Apart from these little details, you may nevertheless be right."

"All right!" said Schulze. "You old skeptic! Let that go for a while and let's inspect the houses. The town seems to have been deserted or died out."

What the Professor called a "town" was perhaps a hundred structures of moderate size, most of them similarly shaped. They sparkled with all the colors of the rainbow, one blue, the other red, the third green; a few white as snow, others black; next to them, yellow, brown, orange-red, violet towers in all gradations of color. Because of this, in spite of their uniformity, they presented an unusually picturesque sight.

On the inside, all of them proved to be arranged quite similarly; instead of stairs, a winding path led upwards, lit by narrow side-windows. At the very top was a triangular compartment in which, upon raised mats—lay corpses.

Yes, only corpses!

"A burial place, a cemetery!" exclaimed Hank.

"At least a city of the dead," replied Schulze, "for you can't talk about graves and burials here."

The corpses were all clad in long garments of a peculiar, smooth, and very flexible material, which showed no threads or weaving. Either this material, unknown to the earth, was rolled out as thin as paper from extremely tough gum, the gum having lost its elasticity, or else it was poured out of some material known only to the Martians.

The garments also shone in the most vivid and variegated colors. The bodies were not essentially different from human bodies; but they were all very small, slender, and graceful, and in any case they revealed a peculiarity of species not to be found on the earth. This peculiarity consisted essentially of a striking skull formation: it might have been thought that each of these heads bore a hood, for fixed above the forehead sat a second, moderately arched skull-chamber thickly covered with hair.

"Two stories!" Munchhausen cried out in candid amazement. "These Martians had a two-storied brain! My, but they must have been clever!"

The rosy skin of the face and the hands, soft and delicate as it seemed, nevertheless proved to be unusually tough to the touch, like leather or the hide of an elephant.

Schulze, not out of criminal curiosity, but out of scientific interest, made an attempt to scratch the skin of a hand with his knife; but though he finally applied all his strength, he did not succeed in piercing through; the knife only left behind a deep track which soon disappeared again.

"They were equipped for the struggle for existence!" said he. "The sharp horns of the wild beasts, the claws and teeth of the birds, and the blood-sucking muzzles of the vermin could not get at them. That's all the more reason why we may expect to run into living Mars inhabitants; such a race doesn't die out!" So quickly had the Professor been cured of his doubts by appearances. But all too little was he aware of the terrors of Mars!

Flitmore photographed the interior of the dead-house, as well as a few typical mummies. After quitting the city of the dead, he also snapped it from an elevation; then our friends quit the place through a winding, down-hill valley.

At the mouth of the gorge, a low, triangular structure made of "cast-stone," for that is what Schulze called the stony material which was at once smooth and without crevices, leaned against the mountain side. He surmised that the Mars inhabitants knew how to melt a special mineral substance like lava, colored it while in a molten state, and then poured out their houses in one piece.

In favor of this was the fact that the structures in the city of the dead showed a limited number of shapes which constantly recurred in the same dimensions. The cracks in some of the damaged stones showed that the coloring penetrated the whole stone and that nowhere was there actually a joint to be found—everything consisted of one block.

In front of the newly discovered house now sat a mannikin as old as the hills, whose double skull gave the impression that he was wearing a cap of polar-bear hide; for white as snow was his thick furry hair, which fell in tufts, but no longer than is used to grow from an animal's hide.

A short beard, just as tufty, framed his face.

He regarded the arrivals with his large, intelligent eyes, obviously very much interested, but not at all with the wonderment or even the alarm which they flattered themselves would be aroused in the first Mars inhabitant to perceive their strange appearance.

As they approached him, he slowly arose. A gleaming red garment encircled his slender limbs.

And now Schulze revealed the unswerving professor: he addressed the hoary Martian in the most elegant Latin he could command; for he thought that Latin being a universal language ought to be understood by educated beings everywhere. He did not reflect that the old Romans, venturesome though they were, had nevertheless not extended the frontiers of their realm beyond the globe.

Besides, the Martian was stone deaf, as he gave them to understand by eloquently touching his ears and by the doleful smile with which he shook his head.

However, as he recognized from Schulze's moving lips that he was being addressed, he must have thought that the strange visitors were speaking the language of Mars; for he uttered some melodious words, but immediately observed from the Professor's head-shakings that he was not being understood.

He pointed at the group, which stared at him, and then raised his eyes to the skies. At the same time he lifted up his arm and pointed to a pale star.

It was the earth!

As the earth is far closer to Mars than the sun is, and the latter does not, because of its distance, shine so blindingly upon Mars as it does upon us, the earth could here be seen by daylight, standing in the heavens.

Accustomed as Lord Flitmore was to self-control, he was nevertheless upset completely by the gesture of the old man.

"Almighty God!" he exclaimed. "Can this be possible? This Martian surmises that we come here from the earth! Apparently he knows of the existence of people there, and they reckon here on receiving a visit some day from their neighboring star."

"Upon my soul! What resources these Martians must possess!" said Schulze admiringly.

"I almost believe that their eyes take the place for them of the best telescope," observed Hank. "Just look at how the man makes his eyes come far out when he looks towards the sky, and how deeply he withdraws them into their sockets when he is observing us."

"Flee, flee! Else the same fate shall overtake you!"

In fact, they were all now remarking this unusual play of the eyes, depending upon whether the Martian was turning his attention to a nearby or a remote object.

"Why don't you ask the old man where we can find others like him?" Munchhausen turned ironically to Schulze, who had come to the end of his Latin after the first vain and somewhat silly attempt to make himself understood.

Hank Frieding, however, showed that he measured up to such a task; he undertook to get the desired information.

The ingenious young man began as follows: He pointed to his own breast and stuck up the thumb of his clenched left hand; then, one after the other, he pointed to Flitmore, Mitzie, Schulze, and Munchhausen, stretching out a new finger of his left hand each time.

The Martian attentively followed these gestures, which aimed to say: "We are five."

When Hank thereupon clenched his fist again, the old man showed that he had understood and that he had a command of numeration; for with a motion of the hand he pointed to the group and then extended five fingers as if to say: "Correct, you are five."

Now Hank pointed to the Martian and again extended only his thumb. This meant: "You are only one." Then the young man looked around searchingly and inquiringly in all directions, with helpless motions of the hand, by which the inhabitant of Mars promptly guessed the question: "Where are the other inhabitants of Mars?"

Here he shook his head and a deep sadness passed over his gentle features: he extended his thumb impressively, touched his breast, then pointed his arm in a circle, always shaking his head and at the same time swinging his hand negatively, as if to say: "I am the only one here! Otherwise there is nobody to be found."

Our friends looked at him astounded; then he beckoned to them to follow him.

He led them to the edge of the mound and pointed down into the swamp.

Shuddering, they saw the tops of structures projecting out of the black slime, and the doleful gestures of the old man said: "All of them have been swallowed by the waters, all of them are rotting in the swamp or serving as grub for the swamp vermin."

Then the old man pulled himself together, pointed to his guests and then up to the earth, making them understand with violent movements of the hand: "Flee, flee! Else the same fate will overtake you!"

He made this gruesome fate still plainer by pointing down again into the swamp, then holding the palm of his hand level above the ground and raising it by jerks ever higher on his own body until it reached above his head.

"He wants to indicate that the waters may suddenly rise and go high above our heads," explained Lord Flitmore.

"Sure enough," confirmed Schulze. "The astronomers have often observed such catastrophes upon Mars. The land is suddenly swallowed up by seas and the divisions of land and water take on an entirely new form."

"In that case we shall not have very much more to discover here," said Munchhausen. "At any rate, this man knows best what he is talking about, and we shall do well not to throw his warning to the winds."

Just then the sound of the *Sannah's* siren rolled through the air.

XIV

A CATASTROPHE ON MARS

H ELLO there! That's a serious sign!" cried Flitmore.
"What can be wrong there?" Mitzie asked, worriedly.

"In any case, we ought to turn back as quickly as we can,"
urged the Captain.

Hank took the Martian by the hand and pointed out to
him the World-Ship projecting high in the distance, sig-
nifying to him that he might flee with them.

But the man only shook his head in sorrow and waved
his hand down towards the swamp. There was nothing to do
about it: all his beloved lay there and he wanted to make his
grave by their side!

Flitmore did not neglect to photograph the sole survivor
of an extinct human world; then our friends parted regretfully from the old man and hastened to reach the *Sannah*
again; for the tone of the siren had apprised them that something must be wrong there.

They came to a halt on the outskirts of the woods in order to make a hasty meal out of the provisions they had
taken along; for hunger was making powerful demands upon
them and Munchhausen had declared that he could not take
another step forward on an empty stomach after he had
been so thoroughly pumped the night before.

Bobs, the chimpanzee, plucked the golden-yellow pyram-
idal fruits from the trees along the edge of the woods and
devoured them with such obvious relish that the Captain
could not restrain himself from tasting them too. He found

them of such a delicious flavor that the others also gathered
them and took along a large stock.

In twenty minutes the woods had been crossed, for they
could no longer tarry over its remarkable things.

When John saw the homecomers coming out of the woods,
he swiftly clambered down the *Sannah* and ran to meet them.

"What is it, what's up?" Hank called out to him from
afar. "Did something happen? Did you see any danger approaching, that you gave the emergency signal?"

"Oh, gentlemen!" cried Rieger, panting towards them.
"The *Sannah*, as it were, is safe and sound, for nothing has
happened to her; but something terribly extraordinary happened which I perceived from afar, and I was afraid that if
something like it were to take place closer by, it might possibly bring us to the end of the world."

"What did you see that was so horrible?" inquired Lord
Flitmore, placidly.

"There, far off yonder, a whole mountain, so to speak, disappeared into the ground and then another one rose up out
of the depths and the water and vermin flowed down from it."

"That seems to be an earthquake, or more correctly, a
Mars quake!" said Schulze.

"Funny we didn't feel it at all," interjected Munchhausen.

"Oh, the *Sannah* was shaking more than a little," declared
the servant.

"If the undulations of the quake moved vertically against
these parallel mound lines, then there is nothing surprising
in their having been weakened so soon that they no longer
reached us," the Professor elucidated. "Earth shocks in general often show a surprisingly sharp demarcation: a valley,
a river-bed frequently brings them to a halt. It happens
that a city collapses on one side of a river, whereas the sec-

tion of the city on the other side scarcely feels the shock."

"That may be! But I vote for leaving Mars as rapidly as we can, for it seems to be as dismal and dangerous by day as it is by night."

No objection was offered to the Captain's view; but they were still a good, or rather a "bad" way off from a speedy departure.

As far as the eye could see, the whole surface of Mars suddenly seemed to have set in motion. There was a rumbling and a thunder, the ground collapsed, a reddish dust-cloud filled the air, so that for quite a while they could no longer see anything. Then a hurricane rushing towards them suddenly swept away the cloud, yet it only seemed to have been driven into the upper air levels, for a blood-livid twilight settled over the ground.

A cry of horror was involuntarily torn from all lips; only Flitmore remained calm.

They stood there as though paralyzed with fright.

Bobs, the monkey, leaped madly with frantic bounds towards the *Sannah*, which he reached and up which he climbed to his comrade, Dick.

Our friends, however, saw huge billows sweeping towards them.

At first they thought they were real water waves, that the sea had risen above its bed to swallow them up.

But they immediately saw that the land itself, with its light, soft soil, was forming these waves: mounds disappeared and new mountain chains emerged, only to sink back again and to rise once more.

The billows approached with sinister speed. As for reaching the World-Ship, which was still 600 feet away, it was out of the question.

The ground shook beneath the feet of the terror-stricken.

Now came a violent convulsion which flung them in all directions; the ground at their feet sank; they lay in the depths, but the ground rose again and they along with it. Only Munchhausen's rotund bulk forthwith rolled down the slope again; his globe-shaped body met nothing to stop it and continued its rolling motion.

Several more times the outstretched voyagers were raised and lowered helplessly by the undulations of the ground; then the convulsions became feebler and they found themselves lying in a broad hollow.

"Up with you, up!" cried Flitmore, who had picked himself up and grabbed Mitzie by the arm, dragging her up the steep slope with the strength of a giant.

It was not a minute too soon! Rushing up the hollow came a stream of slime, bringing with it a thick, tangled mass of vegetation and a teeming horde of floundering vermin.

Whoever was reached by this wave was lost; nobody would ever have been able to free his limbs from this jumble.

By the skin of his teeth, the Professor escaped the clammy flood which rolled over towards him when he had scarcely reached half-way up the slope. From head to foot he was covered with the splashed-up slime.

Hank and John, right in front of him, reached out a helping hand. The Englishman and Mitzie were already above, in momentary security.

"Where is the Captain?" cried Flitmore, his shout rising above the tumult.

"There he lies!" Hank's voice rang out.

Indeed, there he lay at the top of the ground-swell. With the last undulation he succeeded by a desperate effort in getting a firm clutch on a small mound, and he finished by being swung up without rolling down again. Otherwise the unfortunate man would surely have perished, for he would never have been able to work his way upward from the bottom of the hollow as quickly as the others, and seconds were deciding the question of life or death.

He lay there now and once more offered a picture which under less gruesome circumstances would have let loose the greatest merriment, for it was too funny for words to see how, convulsively, almost tenderly, he continued to keep his arm around the saving mound, as though he would never again let it go.

Finally, the encouragement and assistance of Hank and Flitmore brought him to his feet, John keeping him balanced from behind with powerful arms.

But now they were all confronted with a thorny problem: over on the other side, the *Sannah* jutted out from the swamp into which she had sunk. The door yawned open hard above the swamp level, upon which the rope ladder floated, covered with mire.

It was lucky that the opening had not sunk lower, else the slime would have flowed inside and there would have been no prospect of ever reaching the craft again.

Even so, to be sure, there seemed to be no possibility of reaching the entrance, however invitingly the door yawned open for them: a stretch of swamp a hundred feet wide separated the company from the *Sannah*, and that was an insurmountable obstacle.

"If only we could draw over the rope ladder!" thought Flitmore reflectively. "It is over 160 feet long and we should only need to draw it taut to be able to clamber over on it."

All of them now racked their brains to invent a means of attaining this goal.

"If the monkeys were smart enough," sighed Mitzie, after a long silence, "they could easily bring us the end of the ladder. The slimy mass is dense enough and so many roots and so much vegetation protrude from it that the light-weight chimpanzees would never sink down into it."

"Yes! If . . . if . . .!" retorted Flitmore. "But how do you expect to make them understand that? They are far from being Martians."

Nevertheless, he whistled to the monkeys, without being clear in his mind as to what good it would do if they came over.

The chimpanzees had been looking on curiously all the while; it seemed to them that something must be wrong, since they were so completely separated from their masters.

When Flitmore's well-known whistle rang out, which they were used to obeying, they clattered down the ramps to the level of the swamp. But here they halted in perplexity; the ground looked suspicious to them.

Once more Lord Flitmore whistled.

Now Bobs risked the treacherous surface. He held fast to the rope ladder with one hand and endeavored to use the jutting roots and plants as a bridge; in doing so, he dragged the rope ladder half the way over; but as he had taken hold of a middle rung and not the end, the upper part of the rope ladder was now taut and he could go no further without letting go of it.

A third whistle from Flitmore only resulted in his letting go and, now completely free, scampering across, a stunt which his agility enabled him to do.

In the meantime Dick also approached, now finding in the rope ladder a bridge as far as the centre of the swamp. Here he too let it go and finally reached the bank without incident.

"Only fifty feet!" sighed the Captain.

"Do you want to risk it?" jeered Schulze. "There's hardly any chance of your going under, you know."

"That I wouldn't," laughed Munchhausen good-naturedly, "but I'd be sure to sink in up to my middle. What good would it do you for me to float in the mire as a living buoy?"

"I must go over. I'm the lightest," said Mitzie with sudden decision.

"You?" cried her husband, a note of concern in his voice.

"Yes, I! We must get out of this danger somehow, and that's impossible unless some one takes the risk. The lightest body-weight offers the best prospect for success and therefore I am the most suitable one for the job; if I go under, then it would be surer to happen to any one else among you."

"No, no! We can never, never accept such a heroic sacrifice!" protested the Captain.

"You certainly shall! Bobs will guide me and he is already so clever and faithful that he will hold on to me if he sees me sink."

"We must fasten you with something," said Flitmore, who saw that something must be risked and that his courageous wife surely had the best chance of crossing the swamp without serious accident.

"Good," said Mitzie, "now I beg you gentlemen to look away for a minute."

Underneath her dress she wore a petticoat of strong linen. She quickly undid this superfluous garment and cut it into strips with a scissors which, as a practical housewife, she always carried with her in a handy sewing bag.

The knotted strips made a rope which was strong enough to pull her back to the bank in an emergency.

Now the young heroine took hold of Bobs' arm and pushed the chimpanzee ahead on the quagmire.

The monkey proved to be intelligent and easily guided,

and stepped forward adroitly, skilfully selecting the firmest
supports.

Mitzie, who had taken off her shoes and stockings so as to
have a better grip, could not cling like the chimpanzee to the
shifting roots and branches, so she clung all the more firmly
to the arm of her protector while the men on the bank held
tight to the rope which had been tied around her under the
armpits.

It was, after all, a rare spectacle to see the gentle Lady
crossing on the arm of the monkey; yet the attention of
those standing on the bank was drawn solely to her footsteps. Often they trembled when they saw her foot sink in;
but the Lady was so nimble that each time it happened she
had already set the other foot upon some firmer point and
quickly shifted her weight there before the first foot had had
time to sink in deeper.

A long, protracted crossing would have spelled her
destruction; by this agile hopping forward, which Bobs
scarcely accomplished more skilfully, she succeeded in making use even of very dubious props during her flight, turning them merely into fleeting springboards for the next step.

"By all the elves and fairies!" the Captain could not contain himself from crying out in admiration. "Lord Flitmore, I believe your wife could skip across the sea, with such
skill; before a foot can sink in, it is already elsewhere."

"You marvel at it, don't you, my portly Hugo," gibed
Schulze. "I should like to see you in the Lady's place, how
lightfootedly you would stamp through the mire. That you
can hop around like a ballet girl you proved to us last night,
you gentle worm-crusher."

Now they all breathed freely; Mitzie had reached the rope
ladder and drew out of the slime the end which had sunk
into the swamp; but the halt necessitated by it on the uncertain ground was to become disastrous for her.

She stood upon a thin tangle of interwoven tendrils and roots, which forthwith began to sink as she bent and carefully drew the rope ladder out of the swamp; a difficult task, for plants and—oh, horrors!—fat worms also hung from the rungs.

The men on the bank pulled promptly at the rope when they saw Mitzie sinking; but she shouted back to them with an energetic "Stop! Stop!"

It would have been a bad business for the poor young woman to be dragged by a rope through this mire with all its refuse, and she would surely have reached the other side in a sorely mutilated and torn condition. Yet she did not think of this, she was concerned solely with not jeopardizing, so close to the goal, the success of her dangerous venture.

The men on the bank looked at her in anguish, ready to haul in the rope the minute Mitzie was in imminent danger of her life. She was already imbedded in the slime to her waist when she finally pulled up enough of the rope ladder to reach to the bank.

But what was this? She undid the rope which was to give her the last hold.

"Mitzie, what are you doing? What are you thinking of?" cried Flitmore in unmistakable terror.

"The smartest thing!" the Lady shouted back.

She quickly tied the end of the rope to the lowest of the liberated rungs and then shouted over to them: "Now then, quickly! Haul away!"

With feverish haste the men pulled the rope through their hands until the rope ladder grew taut; it now reached right over to the bank.

Mitzie had meanwhile sunk in the slime to her neck, but kept herself up by her arms which held firmly to a rung.

As the men now gripped hold of the ladder and pulled at

it with all their strength, the sacrificial heroine was once more lifted out until she was now imbedded in the quagmire only to her breast.

Drawing the rope ladder taut had been a hard piece of work!

The end of the ladder was now tied as firmly as possible to a strong shrub. Despite this precaution, Munchhausen still had to hold it down with all his weight and the Professor had to hold himself in readiness to grab at it in an emergency; only then did Lord Flitmore and his servant, together with Hank, climb the uncertain bridge across the swamp, for it was necessary to liberate Mitzie from her terrible position.

Terrible indeed it was: she was hardly able to hold on; her wearied arms were painfully stretched and the clinging fingers felt like letting go at any moment. It was lucky that she did not hang free in the air, else her strength would surely have given way before aid arrived. The sticky muck she was stuck in diminished to a certain extent the bodily weight that hung from her arms and threatened to tear them from their sockets.

But she felt that in spite of the greatest effort of her will and muscle power, all her energy was leaving her: a thousand arms seemed to be pulling her into the swamp, more and more alluring became the temptation to let go and suffer no longer the terrible torture which dulled all fear of death, so that to sink down, to choke, to fall asleep, appeared to her as the only solution.

With all this, she did not utter a sound; but the blood hammered in her temples, everything around her became black, her fingers opened up: it was the end!

This was her last dark but far from terrifying thought; and then she lost consciousness.

But at the very moment that she let go the rung, in dwindling consciousness, Flitmore had reached her and grasped her wrists with a hold of iron.

"I'm holding her," he gasped; "now let's see how we can bring her up."

This was no simple or easy task!

Hank, who was an extremely agile gymnast, hooked his feet into the rope ladder, and dropped head downward, hanging from his knee-joints.

Then with both hands he took hold of the Lady and with an unspeakable effort lifted her out of the slime.

"I have her!" he finally groaned. "You may let go, Lord Flitmore."

Flitmore released the wrists which he had held through two rungs; for he could not, of course, pull his wife through the intervening space.

He quickly wound his legs around rungs and rope and indicated to John to do likewise.

They now reached down the upper part of their bodies and took Mitzie's limp form under the arms. It was none too soon, for in his difficult position Hank could not have held it another minute.

Flitmore and Rieger now drew the unconscious body on to the rope ladder, where they first laid it down so as to draw fresh strength.

In the meantime Hank had also swung himself up again.

The Lady could now be brought all the way to the *Sannah,* although not without difficulty, where Flitmore's efforts soon succeeded in bringing her back to consciousness.

Now Schulze and Munchhausen had to undertake the trip.

The Captain moved ahead and the Professor followed.

The former found it difficult, for his round girth made crawling along the narrow ladder well-nigh impossible.

It was a precious picture to see this great bulk advancing slowly and clumsily upon the swaying foot-bridge.

Reaching the middle, the Captain declared in a loud but highly pitiable voice: "It's all off! I'm at the end of my strength. Here I stay if I have to stay here over night and roll off into the swamp."

"Cut out those bad jokes, Captain," exhorted Schulze from behind. "I'm pushing you with all my strength."

"Ugh, what good does it do? It's as if a flea tried to push an elephant! I tell you, I'm checkmated."

"You delight me, most charming fellow! And what is to become of me? Am I supposed to leap over you? I am not in the slightest versed in mountaineering and I should at least require an alpine stick before I'd dare to venture on this dangerous scramble."

"Ha! You heartless scoundrel! Am I built out of square granite? Am I a rough boulder that you want to drill the iron tip of a mountain stick into my sides? Get that idea out of your head or I'll roll down with you into destruction, like an avalanche!"

"Naw! A rough boulder you are not," laughed the Professor gaily. "You are rough only on the inside, old growler; on the outside you are but too smooth and rounded off, that's just the disastrous part of it; a plunge downward would be a sure thing if I were to venture the scramble. Therefore, onwards!"

"Not another step!"

"But I can't stay here over night."

"Then turn back."

"What! Do you think I'm going to turn back when we're so near to the welcome harbor, and wrestle through the night with bloodthirsty vermin? Forward, forward! Twilight is falling."

Flitmore had meanwhile sent John, who now reached the Captain and fastened a rope around him.

Thus, pulled and pushed, he finally landed in the *Sannah*, to the great relief of the Professor, who was now also safe and sound.

All efforts to tear the rope ladder loose from the shrub and draw it back into the World-Ship proved vain.

"Let us leave it behind," declared Flitmore, "I have plenty of others."

"No!" protested Hank. "The bridge that saved us from death and for which Lady Flitmore risked her life, on which she so courageously bore the ghastliest torments, should not be left behind; I'll loosen it!"

Flitmore shook his head: "And what about you? You won't find it easy to turn back on the loosened ladder."

"Leave it to me, everything will be all right!" said the young man, lighting a cigar.

Hank readily clambered back.

He cut off a piece of the linen rope, tied it to the piece of rope which held the ladder to the shrub, and lit it with his cigar. Then he quickly scrambled back and actually reached the *Sannah* before the rope had caught fire from the slow fuse and burned through.

As soon as this happened, the rope ladder proved easy to pull in.

Once more they were all side by side in the World-Ship. Bobs had made for it as soon as Mitzie let him go to pull the rope ladder out of the quagmire. Dick had been the first to shoot over the bridge as soon as it was set up.

Night had meanwhile fallen; both of Mars' moons shone in the sky.

Flitmore shut the door and let the centrifugal current stream through the World-Ship.

The *Sannah* rose with increasing speed and, as our friends saw, just at the right time; for beneath them the moonlit land suddenly broke out into motion again. It must have been convulsed by an especially violent shock, for from afar there suddenly came an enormous dark wave: the sea roared forward and swallowed up the trembling land as far as the eye could reach, and with it undoubtedly also the last inhabitant of Mars.

XV

IN A METEORIC SHOWER

"TOO bad we are moving away from Mars so quickly," said Schulze regretfully. "It would have been highly interesting and instructive to observe at close range in daylight the changes which the earthquake produced on the surface of the planet."

"We are in no hurry," replied Flitmore, "now that we are safe and sound, and it is an easy matter for us to spend the night in the atmosphere of Mars. I take over the first night watch and will break the circuit every ten minutes so that we may sink again; Mr. Frieding will do the same in the second watch and you, Professor, take over the morning watch and carry out the same manœuvre; only you and Hank must look out that you do not break the circuit for too long, so that we may not have a rough and perhaps dangerous landing."

Both promised to take every precaution, which they lived up to, so that at the break of dawn the *Sannah* was only a mile or so above the surface of Mars.

It was an amazing picture that now presented itself to our friends: the sea bottom had risen and the former mainland, which had sunk, was covered by the sea, at least for the most part.

But now it appeared that similar catastrophes had been visited upon Mars before this, for the new mainland rising out of the sea bottom was studded with towns and villages built of many-colored stones, which gleamed out from under the slime that had settled down in their streets and all around them.

"Now I first understand how the whole population of Mars has been wiped out, gradually, bit by bit," said Schulze. "Another one or two such enormous devastations and even the animal life on the planet will be extinguished, down to the sea creatures and the most hideous swamp vermin. At the most, only the birds may escape extermination."

The orbit of Mars was now finally left behind and Flitmore proposed to travel towards Jupiter, the giant among the planets, and then to pay a visit to Saturn before starting back on the homeward journey to the earth.

With this proposal everybody was in agreement.

They now set about adapting the various rooms to the changed centre of gravity of the *Sannah*, for her rotation had begun again and it was necessary to remove from the walls or ceilings all the furniture and fittings in the rooms, which were arranged on the basis of a different centre of gravity, and to screw them down to the floor.

Shortly thereafter the *Sannah* landed in a swarm of meteors.

For the purpose of prolonging the voyage, Flitmore had disconnected the flying circuit, when the uproar broke loose. In the beginning, it was only isolated and very small meteorites which hit the casing of the World-Ship, but soon they clattered down upon it like a regular hailstorm. No damage was being done to the strong casing, for the meteors were scarcely larger than hailstones; but in order to step out of the path of any danger, Lord Flitmore again let the current stream swiftly through the *Sannah* and instantly the influence of the centrifugal power made itself felt, for the meteors gave the World-Ship a wide berth as a result of the repelling effect it exercised upon all bodies subject to the force of gravitation.

Flitmore invited the travelling company to proceed to one of the chambers located on the night side. "I think that on the shadow side we shall enjoy a magnificent spectacle of sparkling shooting-stars and meteors," he opined.

"You forget," objected Schulze, "that the meteorites only sparkle when they enter into the atmosphere, as a result of friction with it."

The Englishman laughed. "I forget nothing; if we see sparkling meteors, then that's fresh proof of my supposition that all space is filled with attenuated air."

"But then wouldn't the earth have to glow also?" asked Hank.

"It is protected by its atmospheric envelope, which shields it from friction with the elements of space."

Be that as he would have it, it was a fact in any case that they got to see whole swarms of sparkling meteors, large and small. It was a delightful display of fireworks.

"You were indeed right, Lord Flitmore," Schulze now conceded. "But it remains a puzzle to me why, if their friction with the thin world atmosphere is obviously enough to ignite the meteors, the earthly falling stars should begin to sparkle only when they enter into the earth's atmosphere."

"The thing is very simple: just because before that they are not subjected to any friction at all, or else to slight friction. You see, I explain the procedure thus: the meteoric showers have indeed their own movement, but the world atmosphere probably divides this movement in its path, possibly, also, every meteor, regardless of how small it is, has its own air envelope which it draws to itself out of the atmosphere of space; in this way friction is eliminated or limited.

"But if the earth lands in such a meteoric shower, the

attractive force of the earth makes the meteors hurtle down at a terrific speed; upon entering into the denser earth's atmosphere they are suddenly deprived of their air envelope, the resistance of the air divests them of it to a certain degree and then the friction arises which is translated into a sudden blaze.

"If we now see sparkling meteors here, the case is certainly a different one, in so far as no denser atmosphere causes the blaze-up but rather the exceptionally accelerated fall. These meteors must have landed within the sphere of attraction of a planet, perhaps of Jupiter, and are now hurtling towards it through space at such a terrific speed that the resistance of the relatively calm world atmosphere divests them of their air envelope, in the event we assume such. At any rate, their friction with the world atmosphere becomes strong enough to make them white-hot."

John Rieger listened mouth agape to these imposing arguments of his master, which inspired him with all the greater awe since he did not understand any of them in the least.

But thirsty for knowledge as he always was, he turned to Professor Schulze, who knew better how to adapt himself to his understanding.

"Humbly asking your gracious permission, Mr. Professor," he began. "You say so many highly instructive things about the motors or shooting stars; but if you would once be so kind as to explain to me exactly what these sparkling motors really are, I should be awfully obliged to you."

"With pleasure, my friend," replied the Professor, readily. "As you have quite correctly observed, meteors and shooting stars are essentially the same thing. They are larger or smaller bodies to be found in world space. Now when the earth comes close up to them, they are drawn towards it and they hurtle with greater or lesser speed towards the air envelope of the earth. The swifter they hurtle downwards the hotter they become, but all the more, also, do they lose in falling power, so that farther down they do not fall any quicker than those which fell more slowly at the outset.

"The heating may reach several thousand degrees; that is why they begin to gleam and to melt at the surface, whereas on the inside they remain pretty cold. When they reach the earth, they are not particularly hot, which may be because their fall becomes slower the further down they go.

"Most of them, however, do not even reach the earth because they have already become so hot high up that they dissolve into gas: then they are shooting stars. If they do reach the earth they are meteors. That's what they are also called if they appear especially big and bright. If they exceed the brightest stars in brilliancy they are called bolides; if they spread a wholly extraordinary brilliancy, often as bright as day, they are called fire-balls; but these appear only very seldom and always separately, whereas shooting stars and meteors occur in whole swarms.

"Naturally you want to know now where these things actually come from. Many assert that meteorites, that is, small meteors, come from the moon. But it is certain that shooting stars and meteoric showers come from the comets. In the first place, their paths are entirely similar to those of the comets; in the second place, it has already been observed that comets that come too close to the sun or to Jupiter dissolve themselves into meteoric swarms.

"The famous Biela comet is an especially instructive example of this. In 1846 it came too close to Jupiter and because of that burst into two pieces which returned at the right time in 1852 but were nowhere to be found in 1858, when they were to have appeared again. Since then they have not been seen; but when the earth crossed their orbit in 1872 and 1885, it landed in a meteoric swarm which delighted the eye as a magnificent hail of shooting stars. These were the remains of the proud comet. This meteoric swarm was called the Leonides because it seemed to come from the constellation of the Lion; in the end this meteoric shower also disappeared."

"That makes it clear to me," said John with satisfaction, "that the motors come from the comets; for the comets are indeed called 'lily-stars,' because they have, as it were, a golden mane."

The Professor said laughingly: "Bravo, my lad! But you still don't know what elements these meteors are actually made up of. They contain all sorts of them: silicate, magnesium, iron, nickel, copper, hydrogen, oxygen, also carbon, and undoubtedly organic elements, that is, traces of plants or living beings which inform us that other worlds also have these, as we have just seen with our own eyes on Mars; sometimes they even find diamonds inside of a meteoric stone. Most of the time they are larger or smaller pigs of iron."

Now the Professor was moved to impart some especially interesting information to John concerning the meteorites: "You see," he said, "there sometimes fall from the skies some pretty substantial pigs of iron; often a whole hailstorm of meteors comes down. It is reported that in the year 823 such a hail of meteors in Saxony crushed people and cattle and brought about the destruction by fire of thirty-five villages. The famous doctor and chemist Avicenna gives an exact description of falling meteorites which came down around 1010 in Egypt, Persia, and elsewhere. On October 1, 1304, fiery stones fell near Friedeburg like hail and caused great damage. On November 7, 1492, a 260-pound meteor fell near Ensisheim, and a part of it hangs to this day in the local church. On September 4, 1511, a terrific rain of stones fell near Crema, which darkened the sun. About 1200 meteors fell down, among them some weighing 260 and 120 pounds; they crushed birds, cattle, and fish; also one monk.

"And similar events occurred by the dozens in Germany, France, Spain, and Italy, killing off many people. A great number of these meteoric falls were described in detail, often by reliable scholars and professors. In fact, scientific commissions investigated the aerolites or aerial stones, yet in spite of this, science refused to believe in them; yes, the French Academy of Science solemnly declared it to be absurd to assert that stones could fall from the sky. To be sure, they were fundamentally refuted by a vast rain of stones which followed immediately in France; but from this you see how tenacious is the skepticism of many people who consider themselves the luminaries of the world."

John Rieger could not quite follow all this; but he had still one more question on his chest regarding the meteors, which he now introduced as his masters were silent: "You have named so many occurrences of stone rains, Mr. Professor, but all of them from the old days. Does it mean that such things cannot happen nowadays in our enlightened epoch?"

"There you have one of the skeptics!" cried Schulze, laughingly. "So you too are not yet convinced, my son Brutus, that the fall of meteors upon the earth is a fact? Listen: even nowadays they frequently take place. For example, near Mugello, close to Florence, a hail of meteorites in a glowing condition descended on February 3, 1910, and covered the streets, fields, and vineyards, destroying numerous plants. After this rain of fire, the veil of smoke suddenly parted and revealed a comet of radiant splendor."

"And that really and truly happened?"

"Really and truly; it was in all the papers and is so well authenticated that an educated man must believe it."

"Well, then, naturally I believe it too," said Rieger, self-consciously.

XVI

THE ASTEROIDS

ON the following day, a day being calculated at twenty-four hours, the *Sannah* came into the midst of the planetoids.

"The discovery of these planetoids or small planets, which are also called asteroids," instructed Professor Schulze, "has once more shown that the natural laws set up by science can never serve as something certain and fixed for all time. Up to now it was actually believed that the planets moved around the sun almost on the same level, and this was considered one of the great natural laws. Then these diminutive planets were discovered by the hundred, whose eccentric orbits demonstrate the weakness of the alleged law."

"But wasn't only *one* planet supposed to exist between Mars and Jupiter?" interjected Mitzie. "How is it that they were found by the hundred?"

"That's another one of those riddles," explained the Professor. "At the outset, they were inclined to believe that it was only a matter of one large planet which had been smashed into little bits by an explosion or a collision with a comet. They are exceptionally small and you could, for example, ride around the whole of Atalanta in two hours with an express train. In addition, their feeble light makes it enormously difficult to observe them from the earth and you cannot determine their mass and extent with any certainty."

"All the more valuable are our observations at close

range," said Flitmore. "Look, Professor, we're coming past
one of these dwarfs again."

"Ah!" cried Schulze, "this is interesting: not a trace of
globosity! It's a Rocky Mountains whizzing through space.
It ought to be about 186 miles long, 30 miles wide, and at
most 2 miles high, apart from its points and peaks."

"Take good note, these planetoids have no rotation, they
do not revolve around their axes, nor do they have any light
of their own, since their small size caused them to cool off
and freeze quickly," added Flitmore.

"In such formless lumps," laughed Munchhausen, "there
aren't any axes anyhow."

A lengthier observation of the remarkable heavenly body
actually showed that no rotation was to be noticed. If it did
take place, then it must have proceeded exceptionally slowly.

Hank remarked further: "All that we see here shows such
an irregular form one might conclude from it that, in spite
of the latest views on the subject, we nevertheless have before
us fragments of a planet."

Not without a malicious triumph, the Professor then made
a discovery which caused him to cry out: "And yet, my wise
Hank, you are mistaken: just look at that! Here is a planetoid of spherical form which is spinning quite gaily around
its axis; and it is giving forth light, even if it is somewhat
dull."

Flitmore regarded the unusual world body. It was hardly
to be called spherical, for it seemed so flattened out that it
looked more like a Swiss cheese, at least like one curved at
the top and bottom. The rotation was unmistakable; for
mountain peaks could be recognized at the rim which visibly
changed their position within a quarter of an hour. From
this could be calculated a rotation period of five hours. That
the planet had its own light was indubitable.

Lord Flitmore shook his head. "If I had found this asteroid in glow, then my view would surely be refuted, providing that it had not formed a short time ago or been suddenly heated up by a collision. It is far from unlikely that now and then the power of attraction affects such a rotating body, that a larger fragment coming close to it plunges down upon it and unites with it, in which case it would temporarily acquire a luminous glow from the violence of the impact. I rather surmise, however, that this light is phosphorescent or comes from luminous elements, radium and the like. I think the matter is worth our being convinced by an inspection and landing on the object of the dispute."

"Lord Flitmore," warned the Professor, "you will run the risk of making the *Sannah* glow and burning us all up."

"Should it become too hot for us," laughed Flitmore, "we shall simply make a quick getaway."

Since a timely flight made possible an escape from any danger, all of them resolved to undertake the landing, and the master of the World-Ship shut off the centrifugal current.

XVII

THE PLANETOID ISLAND

AS the *Sannah* landed on the planetoid, Flitmore proceeded with Schulze to the nethermost room, the floor of which rested on the surface of the world body. Here he waited to learn if any noticeable heating of the walls was taking place, before risking the descent.

The Professor continued to put his hand to the floor; for he believed that a tremendous rise in the temperature must follow; but he could perceive nothing of the kind and even the applied thermometer rose, within half an hour, only one degree.

"Either the protective shell of the *Sannah* is of a wholly remarkable excellence," said Schulze in astonishment, "or you prove to be right, Lord Flitmore. But the planetoid is far from frozen into ice; whatever it may be, it is radiating warmth, for the temperature is rising, even if you can hardly notice it."

"I think we can risk going out into the open," opined the Englishman. "The only question left is what the atmosphere is like."

They now mounted to the North Pole room where the others awaited them. The lid was cautiously opened and Dick pushed to the slit. The monkey did not shrink back; on the contrary, he shoved his head towards the opening, a sign that no poisonous gases were streaming in.

Lord Flitmore now opened the door wide, and Dick and

Bobs leaped joyously into the open, to scramble immediately down the ramps.

Flitmore stepped under the doors and looked out. The side of the planetoid on which the *Sannah* lay fast was turned away from the sun, that is, night had fallen on it at the time; only, it was not at all dark down below.

Large black expanses were indeed visible, but they floated like islands in a luminous sea. It was not as bright as day, it is true, but there was a wonderful, enchanting, soft shimmer in every color gradation: here everything glistened green, there it glowed in red, elsewhere in blue and violet; in some places a milk-white light broke out, which sent its wispy rays high into the air, just like an electrical searchlight.

Here and there, multi-colored mist clouds floated over the ground. A gentle air current sometimes drove them onward, and according to the coloring of the rays which rose from the ground over which they hovered, their colors also changed with fascinating effects.

A fragrant, lukewarm breeze fanned Flitmore, and when he saw that the chimpanzees had reached bottom and were tumbling about on the luminous ground without a sign of discomfort, but much rather with exceeding pleasure, he attached the rope ladder and let it drop out.

Then he took the lead in stepping out on it.

A loud "Ah!" of rapture sounded from Mitzie's lips as she stepped out of the door after him, nor did the others who followed restrain their surprised outcries of admiration.

"Everything is in Bengal lights to celebrate our arrival!" cried Munchhausen, as he carefully, but with eager zeal, clambered down the swaying rope ladder, which creaked and groaned under his weight.

Soon they were all gathered below. It looked like a meadow they had stepped on to, and the grass gleamed with a green shimmer; but even the ground itself, wherever it was visible under the grass, shone phosphorescently with a white and yellow glow; everything seemed illuminated!

Flitmore was the first to break the silence.

"Let's give a name to this wonder-world which we have discovered and which affords us a new insight into the Creator's omnipotence! Mitzie, I want to name this beautifully and exquisitely shimmering star after you."

"No, my dear!" protested Mitzie resolutely. "I neither feel worthy of lending my name to such an extraordinary splendor, nor is the homely sound of it well suited to designate this exquisite, radiating world; it needs a sonorous name."

"Then you shall have the right, in any case, to select the name," said her husband, and added courteously: "in case the gentlemen have no objection."

"Well, then!" Mitzie made herself heard: "I bear in my heart the picture of a proud and charming princess, a heroine to whom all of us, except Mr. Frieding, who is not fortunate enough to know her, owe infinitely much, a noble soul whom we admire, a golden heart we learned to love. I can see her sparkling eye flashing through my mind and the sound of her name is ringing in my ears."

"Tipekitanga!" cried Munchhausen, enthusiastically. "Bravo, bravo! Our Tipekitanga truly deserves such an honor!"

The Professor and Lord Flitmore were also agreed on Mitzie's proposal, and the former remarked: "It's a happy thought to bestow upon our planetoid the name of a dwarf princess; for these world bodies are dwarfs among the planets and the one we have stepped down upon appears to me by its luminous jewels to be a princess among the asteroids."

After this question had been settled to the satisfaction of

all, a journey of discovery was undertaken upon the newly christened planet.

"Let's wander westward," proposed Flitmore. "I assume that the view of this light world is most alluring at night and we are moving away from the sun in this direction."

This proposal, too, met with no objection and thus our friends moved through the luminous fields, going into new raptures with every step.

The green meadow adjoined a flowery field: each of the red, yellow, and blue flowers radiated its own peculiar light; they thought they could see the lustrous juice of the stalk rising up and coursing through the fine veins of the petals.

The white light streamed from the ground in places that were bare of vegetation and which seemed to consist of gleaming chalk or limestone.

Then came bushes and shrubbery with delicate violet foliage, trees between whose subdued leaves beamed orange-red and golden yellow, as well as purple and silvery gray fruits, which lit up the surroundings like Venetian lanterns.

Wondrous above all were the silver-gleaming brooks, which wound through the fields, and the flashes of white light from the foam of the waterfalls which plunged down from rocky declivities. These massive rocks which towered out of the flatlands, and in some places lay like huge cubes on the plain itself, were the dark spots which had struck our friends at the very outset. On their part, they enhanced the beauty of the whole, and the fascinating impression of the multi-colored light would surely have suffered had not the shadows effectively broken it and heightened it.

As in a world of romance, were pools and lakes whose waters glistened in various colors, from the lightest blue to the darkest violet, from the softest rose to the most sombre purple. Above them hovered the billowing, light-pierced mist clouds which, driven by the night breezes, swept over field and meadow in fluttering strips.

The mountains, which could be climbed over in places, always proved to be of moderate height and offered no special difficulties. The stones were dark as a rule; yet, even here were interspersed layers of glittering minerals and they enjoyed an especially marvellous spectacle as they wandered over boulders of scintillating stone of all colors; it was as if they were walking over diamonds, rubies, sapphires, and other fine stones which flashed in their own light and at every step rolled against each other with a melodious tinkle and wondrous flashes and glitter. Flitmore diligently took colored photographs, which later came out wonderfully and constituted a glorious and lasting remembrance of the many-colored splendor of Tipekitanga. Schulze gathered stones which, it later turned out, continued to preserve their illuminating power.

After five hours of wandering, interrupted only by a half-hour's halt for breakfast, our friends saw the sun rising behind them.

As Flitmore had correctly assumed, its brightness extinguished the main attraction of the wonder-planet.

The lustrous colors even now did indeed reveal a splendor with which nothing on earth could compare, and the separate light of the ground, the water, and the plants could be plainly distinguished. But the magnificent spectacle which it offered in the dark of the night was no longer to be seen.

Up to now the wanderers had proceeded as in a fairy dream, revelling in the never foreseen bliss of what they saw. Now the long-familiar light of the morning star brought an awakening, yet it could not wipe out the impressions which had been imperishably stamped upon them.

But what was this? Before them, out of the luminous green fields, rose the *Sannah!*

They required no more than an hour to stand once more on the spot from which they had started the glorious round-trip.

In five hours Tipekitanga had completed the revolution upon its axis, the wanderers had required little more than six hours to circle the whole planetoid around its equator: truly a dwarf princess among the planets!

XVIII

THE COMET

FOR a few hours more our friends continued to stroll in the daylight upon blissful Tipekitanga. Now they also tasted of the luminous fruits, after the example of the monkeys, who eagerly consumed large quantities of them, had assured them that they were courting no danger.

These fruits not only proved to be refreshing and juicy, of a delicious and very variegated flavor, but they must have contained a singular, strengthening, and invigorating power: after tasting them they felt in extremely high spirits, a joy of life never known before filled their minds and new strength seemed to pulse through their veins.

Even Munchhausen boasted: "I feel myself as fresh and light as if all my weight had vanished and I might rise into the air like an ethereal being."

All of them had to laugh when they regarded the bulk of the Captain and heard him compare himself to an ethereal being.

"Well, you might look like a balloon, anyway," said Schulze. "Don't restrain your feelings, for we should appreciate the rare spectacle of you rising into the air."

However, they were still far from seeing the stout man rise. Large stores of the excellent fruits were gathered for the *Sannah*, even though nobody knew how long they would keep.

The short hours had in the meantime slipped by and the fields and meadows once more shone in all their beauty.

But in the skies rose a radiant comet which nobody had previously noted.

"It is showing us the road for our further voyage!" said Flitmore.

All of them re-entered the World-Ship, the current was switched on, and the many-colored brilliancy below them flowed together into one mellow shimmer. Gradually Tipe-kitanga again became the quiet radiating star it was when they first saw it; it sped along its path before their eyes into the dusky distances.

All the more splendidly shone the new comet, to which all attention was now directed.

John Rieger, in his unquenchable thirst for enlightenment, turned once more to the Professor. "There is much I do know, but I should like to know *everything*." And thus he began to speak in the manner peculiar to him:

"Honorable Mr. Professor, unless it should seem of little import to you, I should like to ask whether you feel inclined to give me a scientific lecture, in the way you know so excellently, on certain points of the astronomic science about which I am, so to speak, still relatively ignorant."

"If I can serve you in any way, my dear boy, then I am always ready," replied Schulze. "Let's hear what it is you would like to have explained."

"Just that, the comets, just what is the nature of such a star, where it comes from, and just why it should have a tail."

"Well, my dear friend, those are in part catchy questions: a wholly definite knowledge about them really does not exist and the authorities are far from agreeing; yet I should be glad to tell you how the whole thing stands according to the present state of science.

"Where the comets come from is relatively the simplest thing to answer: some of them are part of our solar system and recur regularly, about 6000 of them, of which even the smallest are visible to the naked eye. They run an elliptical course; but whereas the ellipsis which the planets describe around the sun is almost a circle, the path of the comets is like a parabola: it runs almost straight until the end, that is, up to the point where the comet turns about in order to return to its point of departure. The circling time of these comets is sometimes very short, they may return every three to six years; it may also be very long, like the Donatic comet, or the great comet of 1881, where it ran as long as 3000 years.

"But there are also comets which come from immeasurable or even infinite distances, like heralds from the world of fixed stars. In approaching the sun, their paths twist very sharply as a result of the solar attraction, turn around the sun, and then disappear, never to be seen again in our solar system.

"However, it is just that attractive force of the sun or even of a planet, particularly of gigantic Jupiter, which may exercise such a disturbing influence upon the path of such a comet that from parabolic or hyperbolic, it becomes elliptical. Then our solar system has, so to say, snared the cosmic vagabond and he must thenceforth always recur in a regular cycle.

"But also the other way around: the elliptical path of a comet may be transformed into a parabolic or hyperbolic path, and then it is lost to us. Thus, for example, the Lexell comet, discovered by Messier in 1770, got into a bad scrimmage with Jupiter, after coming too close to it. The period of recurrence of Lexell was calculated at five and a half years; it also appeared that this comet was first captured for our solar system by Jupiter in 1667.

"In 1779, the cosmic vagabond once more approached Jupiter and even went through its moons. The rightly an-

gered planet cast the invader out of its orbit for a second
time, so that it now has a period of recurrence lasting twenty-
seven years.

"Early in 1886, the Lexell comet made a new attempt to
approach Jupiter, and for a full eight months it kept within
close range of that planet. Because of this its path was once
more altered and it acquired a cyclic period of seven years.
Thus it became visible again in 1889. It may be calculated
in advance that this cheeky fellow won't leave Jupiter alone
until he finally loses all patience and throws the comet out
of our solar system for repeated house-breaking."

"Yes, but what about their tails?" again asked the inquisitive John.

"Just so! At the outset the comets have no tail and are
very feeble in light, although they undoubtedly radiate their
own light. It is only when they approach our sun that they
light up more brightly and send to the sun one or more,
often oscillating, radiations, which bend back with a strong
diffusion and envelop the core of the comet with a radiant
cloud mass which is called 'coma,' that is, something like a
'mane.'

"Many comets develop several more or less twisted tails.
Thus the comet of 1744 let out six fan-shaped tails; it was
so bright that it could be seen with the naked eye at midday in the vicinity of the sun."

John was not yet satisfied and asked further: "But how is
it, since the comets are without a tail by nature, that such
a one grows out of them when they reach the sun?"

"That's done by the power of attraction of the sun, my
lad. Certainly, it is now sufficiently understood why the
radiations which at first strive towards the sun, are bent
backwards and thus form the tail turned away from the sun,
the twisting of which depends upon the relation of the re-

pelling power to the speed of the comet's orbit. Many assume that the sunlight exercises this repelling effect, others think it to be an electrical manifestation.

"As for the elements which make up the comet, they seem to be of extremely slight density; at least the tail must be a very thinly distributed dust or vapor cloud, for the stars gleam through it without being darkened and without a break of light."

"In spite of that, it's entirely possible," said Flitmore, "that under favorable circumstances the air of the earth might be poisoned by comet gases, so that all life would be destroyed in an instant. What preserves us from this fate is, in my opinion, the fact that the centrifugal power of the earth enables it to repel these elements."

"But how is it," Mitzie now asked, "when a heavenly body, let us say the earth, collides with the nucleus or the head of a comet?"

"That's a question by itself," responded the Professor. "In general, it is the comet that gets the worst of it. We see how the approach of the sun dissolves a part of its nucleus into volatile elements which, in the comet of 1843 for example, formed a tail of 198,000,000 miles. If the comets draw the tail back again, then they suffer an enormous loss of matter and thus become increasingly lighter in mass until they finally dissolve entirely.

"On the other hand, it cannot be denied that the collision with the nucleus of a comet might hold serious dangers. Many a comet moves with such tremendous speed that an impact of its firm mass, if it were of any considerable size, would make the struck planet white-hot."

"But I think," objected Hank, "that of late even the nucleus of the comets is considered to be a nebulous, gaseous mass without solidity."

"In face of the facts, that's a wholly untenable view," protested Schulze. "Just think, the meteors which fall to the earth are sometimes blocks of iron of tremendous weight. And these fragments do not even appear to come from the nucleus but from the tail of the comets.

"At all events, it is believed that in 1872 and 1885 the earth collided with both heads of the Biela comet, since the tail at that time was moving in quite a different direction from the descending meteoric shower. Should this be correct, it is nevertheless to be taken into consideration that what we had there was a comet demolished by Jupiter and already in the process of dissolution.

"But that it is at all possible for a comet to go past so close to Jupiter or even to whiz through the glowing corona of the sun, as also happens, without being completely dissolved into smoke, shows that it must have extremely firm elements capable of resistance."

"I can contribute another proof of it," confirmed Flitmore. "Years ago I visited the so-called Devil's Canyon in Arizona. It's an oval crater ring which rises 130 to 160 feet above the surrounding heights; its diameter is some 4000 feet from east to west and some 3700 from south to north. The inside gorge declines steeply for 600 feet, the basin thus being about 500 feet deeper than the plain around it; it must have been still deeper before, but ruins and boulders have rolled down into it for centuries, for the structure of the rock is very loose.

"Drilling revealed that under the mass of ruins the rock is completely broken up and reduced to cellulose pumice stone. The pulverized sandstone is mixed with finely distributed nickel and at a depth of 800 feet below the present valley bottom, solid masses of iron were encountered which proved to be meteoric iron.

"Right around the crater were found whole masses of meteoric iron stones, whose weight ran from 1 gram up to 920 pounds, and which, aside from the predominant nickel-iron, contained combinations of phosphorus, sulphur, carbon, and even diamonds.

"In scientific circles, therefore, the conviction was reached that long ago the solid fragment of a comet plunged down upon the earth from the west-northwest at an angle of 70 degrees. The block probably had a diameter of about 500 feet. It drove a hole 1100 feet deep into the earth, during which the developed heat of about 2000 degrees Centigrade melted the sandstone into pumice stone. The wreckage of rock that spattered up formed the crater wall around the basin."

"There we have it!" Schulze said. "Rocks of sizable diameter may just as easily be contained in such a comet head, or even still larger masses. The impact would not only destroy, under certain conditions, all life upon the struck part of the earth, but the rotation of our planet might undergo a change which would make the periods of day and night other than what they are; and, in addition, the earth's axis might shift in such a manner that the seas would fall towards the equator and swallow up the mainland."

"Let's hope this remains a supposition," Munchhausen now made himself heard. "In any case, however, we ought to pay attention, so that our dear *Sannah* may not come much closer to that comet up there; for it seems to be pretty well established that the nucleus of a comet is not always so small as many assume."

"We are protected against a collision by our centrifugal power," Flitmore assured him. He did not dream at the time that precisely the opposite was to be the case.

XIX

SEA SERPENTS

THE conversation about the comets had been carried on during luncheon; that is why Munchhausen took so little part in it. For while he was engaged in the tremendous yet so pleasant task of soothing his appetite, he let the others argue about anything they pleased—it made little difference to him.

John felt himself so enlightened by what had been explained to him about the comets that at the end he exclaimed enthusiastically: "Astronomy is indeed the most praiseworthy science, so to say, for it deserves the highest praise for its understanding of the most obscure and difficult matters as well as for the special interest and importance of the facts it reveals."

"Dear friend," rejoined the Captain, washing down his last bite with a gulp of wine, "astronomy is lacking in only one letter to deserve the praise you give it. But since it is without this letter, it takes but second place."

"And what is this letter to be, if you will be kind enough to allow me this question, most honorable Captain?" asked John, wonderingly.

"The letter G," Munchhausen replied with conviction. "Higher than astronomy and all other sciences, stands gastronomy."

"Gasteronomy?" repeated John, pricking up his ears. "Excuse me, please, if I am unfortunate enough not to know that there is such a science, I who flattered myself into thinking I knew all the sciences, which is the reason why I should appreciate it very much if you were to teach me this science also."

"That's not taught, it's enjoyed, my son; it is a science to which you must be born; it deals with eats and drinks, and teaches what tastes good and is beneficial, as well as what is to be done in order to prepare tasty foods and drinks. Its manual is the cook-book, which has but little value without a born genius for it. Moreover, in order to be an efficient gastronomist, it is enough to esteem and enjoy these pleasures, even if one does not understand the art of cookery. Look, without astronomy and all the other sciences, man can live and be happy, but not without food and drink; yes, without these most essential of all necessities, he would be in no position to devote himself to any other science; that's why gastronomy is the foundation and soul of all the sciences."

"That sounds pretty good," thought Rieger, reflectively. "I too am in little mood for science on an empty stomach."

"There!" triumphed Munchhausen. "The most important question is not how swiftly a world body moves, how far away it is from us and what elements compose it, but whether there is something good to eat on it, and astronomy can't reveal that to us."

"It seems to me more important," laughed Mitzie, "to know what creatures live on a planet to which we plan to pay a visit; for I shouldn't like to meet again with such repulsive vermin as we found on Mars."

"Trifles!" growled the Captain. "Give me a good meal and I don't give a fig for all the lumbricides and other monsters."

"Oh, indeed!" jeered Schulze. "We didn't see much of your 'fig' on Mars when you were rolling around on the ground."

"Nonsense! Any one who has fought and conquered sea

serpents, as I have, couldn't be afraid of such harmless vermin."

"Sea serpents? Really, those mythical sea serpents?" asked Hank, eagerly.

"Positively! A monster 130 feet long and as thick around as a forest fir."

"Please tell us about this wonderful adventure, if I may permit myself the impertinence," begged John.

"Yes, that was a tough affair," began the Captain with a smile of satisfaction. "Well, we were sailing off the coast of Cape Horn when the second mate, Petersen by name, came towards me and said: 'Captain, the back of a whale is rising out of the water.'

"I looked over. 'No,' says I, 'those are dolphins,' for I saw five backs in a row above the mirror of the sea. 'There was only one at first,' Petersen assured me, 'but now it seems to me too that they're dolphins.'

"The creatures moved along, yet we saw neither head nor tail come up, and suddenly I exclaimed: 'Man alive, those aren't dolphins either; that's the back curve of only one monster, of the sea serpent!'

"What a shouting and running and screaming there was! The sea serpent, however, seeing that it was recognized, stopped its hide-and-seek and raised its revolting head above the water. It rose like a huge mast and soon its head hovered above the ship. The otherwise fearless sailors scurried away from it like cowards and crawled into their holes. I alone remained at my post and the horrible reptile craned its neck towards me, its enormous jaws agape."

"Naturally! Such a fat tid-bit must have been welcome to him!" laughed Schulze.

"Please!" protested the Captain. "At that time I still had a youthful slimness and great agility, as you shall soon

see. It chose me as its victim only because I was the only one
left on deck.

"I didn't feel any too good, I'll admit, as those murderous
jaws yawned upon me. Up in the air the thick neck curved
into an arch, while the head of the serpent sank down towards me.

"I sprang aside; the head pursued me. In despair, I darted
across the body of the monster as it lay along the rail. The
sea serpent turned its head around its body, still behind me.

"Then, at the moment of the greatest danger, a saving
thought came to me. The upper body of the reptile now
formed a ring above the deck and with the boldness of
despair I leaped through this gruesome ring with both feet.
A circus acrobat could have done no better.

"What I hoped for took place. In the thoughtlessness of
its fury, the serpent this time also pursued me with its head,
which promptly slipped through the ring formed by its own
body. This made a regular knot.

"Then I ran the length of the deck for all I was worth.
The hideous creature sought to follow; but now the knot
tightened around the neck of the sea serpent. Too late it noticed this disastrous fact; it could no longer draw out its
thick head; its furious movements only drew the knot tighter,
until it was finally choked, strangled by the knot of its own
body.

"Limply hung the repulsive head, with its eyes popping,
and with a dull thud the upper body of the huge reptile collapsed upon the deck, while its tail continued for a time to
churn the sea convulsively.

"I called up the shivering sailors and said to them: 'There,
pull aboard the whole beast, we want to turn it over to the
Oceanographic Museum on the Falkland Islands. As you
see, I have captured the serpent and in spite of its terrific

resistance I tied a knot in its neck until it choked to a miserable death.'

"I tell you, the sailors, who did not dream of such a simple and natural remedy, now acquired a positively superstitious respect for me, relied on me, and followed me blindly. I have my timely leap and the thoughtlessness of the sea serpent to thank for it."

"Hooray for him!" cried Schulze mockingly, and all of them joined in and drank to this great hero and dragon-slayer whose miraculous presence of mind, as Lord Flitmore slyly observed, would preserve the whole company of voyagers against whatever danger might come along.

XX

JUPITER

THE *Sannah* was approaching the largest of all planets, Jupiter, and Flitmore hastened the approach by a temporary break in the centrifugal current.

"Be careful!" warned Munchhausen. "I have great respect for the highest of all the Olympic Gods and greatly fear he may play us a trick, like the late Biela comet, if we approach him too impertinently. Imagine our predicament if his tremendous influence should part our *Sannah* in two, perhaps just at the moment when we are enjoying a carefree slumber in our respective compartments. Then our fine company would be separated and we might never see each other again."

"Do not worry," laughed Flitmore. "I'll see to it that we don't give Jupiter any cause for such gruesome measures. We only want to observe him at close range."

"Aren't we going to land on it as we did on Mars and on enchanting Tipekitanga?" asked Lady Flitmore eagerly.

"That depends entirely on how conditions on the planet look to us."

"Has it any atmosphere at all?" inquired Hank.

"Presumably a very dense one," Schulze informed him, "for it shows a very strong albedo."

"The earth's astronomers, as a matter of fact, are doubtful if their telescopes really show them the surface of Jupiter," spoke up Flitmore. "They count on the possibility that what they see are only products of condensation, that is, signs of density of its air envelope. In any case, no map can

118

be drawn of it as there can be of Mars. For what is perceptible is extremely changeable. Only two dark streaks remain
constantly visible."

But John had already heard the Professor speak of an
"albedo," a word entirely new to him, especially as it was
supposed to show the presence of a dense air envelope. He
could not let it pass, he had to instruct himself on this point,
too, and therefore he asked: "Mr. Professor, to make matters short, permit me to ask you a straight question, which
seems to me necessary for my full education. Now, you have
just said that Jupiter has a strong torpedo, I know the word
from warships, but I don't understand how it can have anything to do with atmospheric conditions. It must be an entirely different sort of torpedo."

"Yes, my son," laughed the Professor. "It is quite a different sort of torpedo and it's spelled 'albedo.' Albedo is the
mean relation of the light masses radiated to and from a
body."

"So that's it!" replied John, hesitantly; it was obviously
very unclear to him. He had a very weak albedo, for the
light that Schulze's wisdom radiated towards him was only
very incompletely radiated back from his features.

"I'll explain it to you in greater detail," said the practical Englishman. "You see, when the sun shines upon a
black object, this sucks up or, as scholars say, absorbs
much of the light. The black element throws back little of
the light that beams upon it; consequently, it has a weak
albedo. But should the same sun rays fall upon a mirror, it
throws it back almost unweakened, it flashes so brightly that
you can't look into it; consequently, it has a very strong
albedo.

"Now it is known how much sunlight strikes Jupiter or
any other planet and how bright it would have to appear

were it to radiate back the full light unweakened. So that the less its brightness is in relation to this radiated light, the less is its albedo, and vice versa.

"The earth has an air envelope which is so thin that it lets through much light and throws back little of it; for it is the dull ground that must throw back again the light which strikes it, but only part of it—most of it is swallowed up. That is why the earth has a weak albedo. Were it covered with a sheet of snow its albedo would be far stronger, since snow radiates back light profusely.

"A very dense, vaporous, and cloudy air envelope likewise throws back a strong light. If, therefore, a planet has a strong albedo, that is, appears very bright in relation to its radiancy from the sun, it is assumed that it has an especially dense atmosphere; this is the case above all with Venus. Mars has pretty much the same albedo as the earth, and Mercury is the only planet which reveals a slighter albedo, that is, seems to have a thinner air.

"To be sure, it should not be forgotten that a reflecting surface, a snow-covering or some special light that the planet might radiate, could produce a strong albedo just as well as a dense atmosphere; complete certainty is thus lacking even in these conclusions."

"Look here, Lord Flitmore," spluttered Schulze, rising crossly, "you took me along as the astronomer of the expedition; but if you yourself are so thoroughly acquainted with astronomy, then I don't see what good I'm doing here!"

"Calm yourself," laughed Flitmore: "I have indeed equipped myself with some astronomical knowledge, for I intended to voyage through the star world; but I am far from being as well versed in the whole field as you are. Besides, it doesn't hurt in such a voyage if several or all of the participants have some idea of the science. I say, Munchhausen, decide for us as an expert in a quite similar case. Ought a ship's captain to know nothing about steering a ship?"

"What a question!" exclaimed the Captain. "You couldn't trust him with the command of a ship; he's got to understand it thoroughly and be able in an emergency to take the wheel himself."

"Then isn't a helmsman superfluous if the captain can take over his work?"

"Nonsense; it is even necessary to have a first and second helmsman."

"There you have it, Professor," laughed the Englishman: "we have a wholly similar case here."

They soon drew closer to the great planet, the cubic content of which is 1270 times greater than the earth's and 5 times as far away from the sun, namely, 480,000,000 miles.

In nine hours and fifty-five and a half minutes, this colossus revolves around itself; its days are therefore not so long as those of the earth; but for that, its orbital journey around the sun takes almost twelve earth-years, namely, eleven years, three hundred and fourteen days, twenty hours, and two minutes.

As they approached, they felt even in the protected rooms of the *Sannah* that Jupiter emitted a great warmth, which caused Flitmore to exercise caution towards its force of attraction and to alternate with a rise and fall of the World-Ship.

In the meantime the planet could be closely studied.

At first they saw luminous clouds which were being driven by a raging hurricane, more swiftly than Jupiter itself was revolving on its axis.

Where the torn clouds permitted a look through, was revealed a stormy sea of flame through which were drawn a few dark streaks of frozen rock.

"That corresponds," said Schulze, "to the calculations of the density of the planet, from which was to be concluded that Jupiter would be in a fluid state. In the same way, its bright radiation means a light of its own and the indistinct, partly transparent borders indicate a changing vapor envelope."

"So we can't even think of a landing here, my dear," said Flitmore, turning to his wife.

"Well, then, on to Saturn!" she asserted.

"It won't look any better there, my Lady," objected the Professor. "The ringed planet has the least density of them all, only one eighth that of the earth and three fourths the density of water."

"Come now," Munchhausen called out merrily, "is it more fluid than water? Then it must be made of stiff grog! Let's go!"

The moons of Jupiter were still being studied with interest when, in the course of time, they made themselves visible: the moon on the inside, closest to Jupiter, was surrounded by a thick layer of clouds; still they could see from the luminous parts that shimmered through and the dark spots that showed themselves in it that it was already in the grip of congelation and on its flaming surface floated cindery islands. It is somewhat larger than the earth's moon.

The second satellite, shimmering with a bluish white, almost exactly as large as our moon, likewise showed fiery liquid and frozen spaces.

The third, the largest and brightest, was in an even ruddy glow, which flickered yellowishly. It was extremely flat at the poles and turned about very rapidly.

The fourth moon of Jupiter, which sometimes appeared weakest in light and at other times exceeded the others, was surrounded by a luminous, sharply defined envelope of steam.

"These moons," remarked Schulze, "afford the short Jupiter nights an extremely dubious illumination, for the three innermost moons are darkened by umbra, and in every other respect could not compete with our earthly moon."

Besides these four commonly known moons, our friends also saw the four smaller, recently discovered, moons of Jupiter, as well as three others, until now never seen by men.

XXI

A VISIT TO SATURN

AS the heat became gradually unbearable, the centrifugal power had to be switched on, full current, so that the *Sannah* might speed out of the realm of this inhospitable planet as quickly as possible.

When this was attained, Flitmore slowed down the flight again. He wanted to get a closer look at Saturn, too, and as this planet was pretty remote in its course, it was necessary this time to put a little distance between the solar system and the *Sannah* until Saturn had approached far enough for them to be within the realm of its attractive power.

This might take a couple of days if the switching on and off of the current were effectively alternated; and this was necessary, for with a steadily switched-on current the solar system would fall behind the *Sannah* in a short time, she would not only fly beyond the path of Saturn but also beyond the path of Neptune and would then have no means of returning to the solar system, having passed beyond the sphere of attraction of the sun and its planets.

On the other hand, were the centrifugal power to be shut off for good, the World-Ship would be subjected to the force of attraction of the sun or a planet, perhaps it would even revolve around the sun like a planet, in accordance with the law of gravitation.

This waiting time was utilized for all sorts of work in the various shops; photographic negatives were developed and musical entertainments organized; they gathered frequently in pleasant conversation or read books from the abundant library which the far-sighted Lord Flitmore had taken along. Above all, however, Schulze had to deliver astronomical lectures, for Mitzie, Munchhausen, and Hank Frieding felt the need of supplementing their knowledge in the field that was of greatest importance in this cosmic voyage, not to speak of John Rieger, who listened most devoutly to the lectures and made constant use of the right already granted him to interrupt the speaker with questions on every occasion.

During this time, Munchhausen's birthday was celebrated with great pomp, and kitchen and cellar produced the best that could be conjured up by the culinary art of Lady Flitmore and John. But the banquet was crowned by the incomparable fruits of Tipekitanga, which appeared to have preserved their freshness completely. They had lost neither their luminosity nor their nourishment and flavor.

Finally Saturn was sighted and the *Sannah* was surrendered to its force of attraction.

Schulze made use of the occasion for a brief repetition of what he had already said in his lectures on the ring-encircled planet.

"As already said," he declared, "Saturn is not even as dense as water. It undoubtedly has an atmosphere and is the second largest planet, 780 times as large as the earth by mass. Its period of rotation takes only ten and a fourth hours, consequently, it has less than five hours of day and five of night, both being equal; such is always the case at the equator. All the longer does its year last, namely, twenty-nine years, one hundred and sixty-six days, five hours, and six and a half minutes, by earthly calculations."

"Magnificent!" exclaimed Munchhausen. "Here's where

we descend; just think, when you get to be a hundred years old here, it is equal to two thousand, nine hundred and some odd earth-years. That beats Methuselah!"

"Only we're going to have some difficulty in descending," asserted the Professor. "You might land in a fine brew, perhaps a stiff grog, as you supposed; you would be very nicely preserved in it."

"Positively wonderful!" the Captain replied.

"Well, we shall soon see what the ground conditions are like," continued Schulze. "If this undense mass should be as liquid-fiery as Jupiter, then you'll just have to abandon any idea of landing."

"Absolutely!" agreed Munchhausen. "Yet I hope that old Saturn is not holding such a disappointment in store for me."

"As I said, we shall soon see about that," repeated the Professor. "The most interesting thing about Saturn, in any case, is its rings; also, it has no less than ten moons; however, since we are right in a position where we can see for ourselves, I shall not dwell any further upon it, for if things are not the way I think them to be, I should only be held up to ridicule."

The *Sannah* had moved beyond the path of Saturn as the planet approached her, and thus she sank at first towards its night side.

Flitmore had expected that the rings of Saturn would be composed of vaporous masses, although he did not consider it impossible that they might be made up of solid matter or, as is also hazarded, of a dense cloud of very tiny satellites.

He aimed at reaching the innermost of the three rings of Saturn, which is relatively dark and reveals vague outlines; and reach it he did.

In spite of its breadth, this ring is the narrowest of the

three; it is not quite so broad as the bright outside ring and less than half as broad as the middle ring.

The *Sannah* found a firm base and rested upon it.

It was just the time for retiring, and all of them turned in to sleep except those who were keeping watch.

In the morning, as they were all gathered for breakfast, Captain Munchhausen spoke up as follows: "Professor, you have contended that a night on Saturn lasts five hours, on the average. Then why doesn't the day show up? Or have we perhaps overslept the short day?"

"Not that," rejoined Schulze; "but we are located on the ring, where conditions are fundamentally different. Here day and night each last half a Saturn year, which is about fourteen and two-thirds earth-years. During this somewhat prolonged night, the ring is dependent upon the feeble light of the ten moons of Saturn and of Saturn itself which, in accordance with its rotation, illuminate it periodically."

"Hold on there!" shouted the Captain. "And are we going to sit by here and wait until it becomes day?"

"Certainly," said Flitmore. "But calm yourself, Captain. Saturn is now at the point in its path where the sun will rise in two hours on the plane of the rings we are in, after almost fifteen years of night."

This proved to be right; two hours later it was day; it is true that the sun scarcely shone with the brightness known on the earth, for Saturn is nine times farther removed from the sun than is the earth.

Now they risked a descent upon the ring. It proved to be made of very light, porous elements and revealed numerous holes and gaps which went through and through.

Quite enchanting and truly magnificent was the outlook upon the enormous globe of Saturn, on which could be seen huge mountain ranges.

The ring, too, was far from level, and showed numerous elevations, some of them pretty considerable mountains; but their wanderings were rudely interrupted by a gap which ran across the full breadth of the ring. The view that the whole ring consisted only of meteoric blocks was now, it is true, visibly refuted, however definitely its advocates declared it to be the only possible view.

Later on, our friends observed that all three rings were separated, by numerous more or less broad splits, into separate pieces which did not touch, but that these parts came closer together under the expansive influence of the sun's heat.

"Splendid! Magnificent! Wonderful!" exclaimed Schulze repeatedly. "How much better we can observe things from here than can all the earthbound astronomers with their best instruments. When I just think of how long it took before it was even known that Saturn is encircled by a ring!"

Since a split in the opposite direction soon made any further advance impossible, and the investigation of the rings seemed to offer little more of interest, it was decided to proceed instantly to the planet itself.

Soon the *Sannah* sank below the lower air layer which surrounded the rings, and after a short but terrifically swift plunge entered the atmosphere of Saturn.

Here Flitmore promptly slackened the falling speed and the World-Ship sank lazily to the ground.

"My Lord," John asked his master in the meanwhile, "why do we never go down into the lower room when we want to undertake a descent? We could thereby get a bird's-eye view of everything, the closer we came to it; here up above, however, we see nothing but the ring which is moving away from us."

You see that towards his master John adopted no such

choice language as when he spoke to the learned Professor;
not because of any lack of respect, but because he knew from
years of experience that Flitmore would not stand for many
phrases.

Flitmore gave his loyal servant the following information: "You see, John, to prevent the descent of the *Sannah*
from becoming a disastrous plunge, I must alternately switch
the centrifugal power on and off. But by that, the centre of
gravity is changed every time in the lower and side chambers: if I switch on the centrifugal power, we are drawn towards the centre of our craft; if I switch it off then Saturn
draws us to itself. You will remember what results this
had when we left the earth. It would be exactly the same
here: in the lower chamber we should be thrown alternately
from the ceiling to the floor and vice versa; in the Pole rooms,
we should be hurled back and forth from the wall turned towards Saturn, to the floor. Up here, however, the centre of
the *Sannah* lies at our feet exactly like the centre of the
planet, and my object is not to change the centre of gravity in any way. That's the reason why, during our descent
upon Mars and Tipekitanga, we had to abandon any observation of the terrain we were approaching, although it's too
bad.

"You do know that I took this circumstance into consideration while building the ship and was myself surprised by
the topsy-turvy effect of the centrifugal power; otherwise I
should have taken the precaution of arranging mirrors on
the outside which would enable us to see what lies below, from
this Zenith chamber."

A soft thud showed that the surface of Saturn had been
reached. The *Sannah* came to rest.

That this surface was neither red-hot nor fluid, they had

been able to ascertain from the ring, otherwise the plan to land would of course have been out of the question.

Eager to see what new wonders would be revealed to them here, our friends left the craft from the North Pole room after the hatchway had been opened and the rope ladder let down.

XXII

AN INVOLUNTARY POLAR VOYAGE

IT was night when the company landed on Saturn; but since all of them were eager to get into the open, the tents were set up, this time in the immediate vicinity of the *Sannah* so that a prompt retreat might be made should some dangerous occurrence menace them; the frightful night on Mars was but all too fresh in their minds.

Heaps of wood and faggots were abundantly supplied by the *Sannah;* Lord Flitmore had provided for all emergencies. There was no need of searching for firewood in the darkness.

A fire was started and after the meal had been eaten they all turned in to sleep, except for Hank, who took over the first watch.

After two hours, he was relieved by John, and two hours later Munchhausen took his place.

The Captain took a childish delight in seeing the first sunrise on Saturn and in being the first to see this new world under his very feet, by daylight.

But, remarkably enough, it would not become day! When his two hours of service ran out, it was just as dark as before. He reckoned that the night had now lasted more than eight hours; since the period of rotation of Saturn took ten and a half hours, it should really have approached nighttime again.

It had been agreed that right after break of day Munchhausen was to wake them all, but day did not break and he waited yet another hour; he would have been so happy to be the only one to see the sun light up the land.

Finally he aroused the Professor.

"Look here," he said to the sleepy-headed one, "the deuce take all astronomical science and yours in particular. There is no such thing as your short Saturn nights. D'you know how long this night has lasted already? Nine full hours!"

Schulze had roused himself and looked at his watch.

"True enough," he growled, "you're right!" Then he looked helplessly into the sky, as if he might discover the sun somewhere, despite the darkness that prevailed below.

"Here's where all science comes to an end!" he burst out.

"Right you are, all science comes to an end and makes itself ridiculous in the face of the facts," rumbled Munchhausen. "Do you know for sure that night doesn't last fifteen years on Saturn as it does on its rings?"

"Nonsense!" exclaimed the scholar, although he himself did not know just where he was at. "That holds for the polar zones but not for these broad ones."

In the meanwhile the others had arisen and wondered why day had not yet come.

Schulze was thoughtful while breakfast was being taken; he turned over in his mind again his knowledge of Saturn.

Suddenly he cried: "I have it! We have a solar eclipse here, caused by the rings of the planet."

"Well! then it will pass over right away," said Munchhausen, breathing freely again; for the puzzling darkness had really made him anxious. "It is true," he added, "there'll be no sunshine today; night will soon fall; but in six or seven hours we shall see daylight again."

"That's what you think!" contradicted Schulze. "Nothing of the kind. This Saturnian darkness lasts several earth-years. I assume that we are now somewhere below twenty-three and one-half degrees latitude and therefore have to reckon with a solar eclipse of ten years."

"Great news!" blustered the Captain. "So we are to wait around here until the ring shadow has been kind enough to move away or the sun smiles mockingly at us for an instant in order to disappear again? Or are we supposed to explore this queer celestial body with torches?"

"No," laughed Flitmore. "We simply rise again and land upon a more favorable latitude."

"Saturn certainly seems to be an inhospitable planet," said Mitzie. "In many regions there are almost fifteen years of night, and then ten years of solar eclipse, which makes twenty-five years of darkness and only five years of daylight!"

"That's certainly the case, as far as this zone is concerned," confirmed Schulze. "But take heart, there are well-lit regions and we are not going to remain here very long."

The continuation of the journey was promptly undertaken.

"Unfortunately," observed Lord Flitmore, when they had once more gathered in the Zenith chamber, "the *Sannah* is not built as a dirigible airship. I now see what an unfortunate mistake that was. Equipped with a few motors, it could find its way through the atmosphere, whereas now we must leave our landings to chance. As soon as I switch on the centrifugal power, our World-Ship no longer takes part either in the rotation or the circulation of Saturn. The former is of no account, for by rotating upon its axis the planet only turns another side to us, and it makes no difference whether we descend upon the one or the other.

"But by circulating along its path around the sun, Saturn whizzes by underneath us as soon as we have freed ourselves from its attractive force by the centrifugal current; we haven't the means of calculating this movement exactly, and consequently we cannot determine our landing place as we should like to."

This proved to be fateful indeed; for when Flitmore decided to descend after a while, the *Sannah* was at the North Pole region of Saturn.

When the hatchway was opened, such an ice-cold air streamed in that they all provided themselves with the warmest furs before stepping out into the open.

A magnificent view dazzled them as they descended the rope ladder; as far as the eye could reach was a wilderness of ice and snow, broken by fantastically jagged and wildly cloven icebergs which glistened under the rays of the sun with all the colors refracted by light on crystal.

In the distance, towered a great mountain which reminded them of the glacial ranges of the Alps; in short, it was a splendid landscape which awakened a feeling of devoutness in every heart.

However, there was no point to a prolonged stay here; the icy wastes of Saturn did not tempt our friends to an exploration so long as they still hoped to find more interesting fields for their discoveries. Still, the enchanting polar landscape yielded its greatest beauties to a few photographic plates.

Suddenly Mitzie cried out in astonishment as she regarded the sky: "What has happened to the ring? It seems to have vanished; I can't discover a trace of it from one horizon to the other!"

All of them raised their eyes, and Munchhausen declared: "There's a fine trap for you! Here we are at last, landed on an entirely different planet, in fact on a glaciated Saturn moon. That's what happens when you sail into the blue and cannot even look out to see where you are moving and what is situated beneath you! Or perhaps the Saturn belt is bewitched and can make itself invisible by means of the famous radio-electrical rays of Manfred von Rothenfels? Ahoy, Prof, let's have some light from your scientific arc-lamp, unless this enigmatic disappearance has made you think as usual that all science has come to an end!"

"Why not?" replied Schulze coolly. "Science doesn't come to an end here at all, quite the contrary! Every budding astronomer knows that the rings of Saturn are not to be seen from the greater part of the polar zone, for the simple reason that they are below the horizon. Farther south we should see just the outside ring, and it is only by crossing the polar circle that the inside rings would gradually emerge: so everything is in order and nothing else was to be expected."

Another remarkable fact now struck Hank as he sought to lift a loose ice-block. The substantial fragment proved to be unbelievably light in relation to its bulk. Since this could not come from any lesser power of attraction of the planet, nor was due to any looser structure of the ice than is the case with ice on the earth, it had to be assumed that the ice on Saturn, as such, and consequently also the water, weighed less and was less dense than the ice on the earth.

After they had convinced themselves of the unusual lightness of the block, and ascertained the same thing with other pieces of ice, they turned back to the comfort of their craft.

"We ought not in future to land so planlessly," declared the Englishman. "We must think up some means by which to free ourselves from a position which makes us the football of chance. Here, Professor! Set your great mind to work and make it possible for us to choose a landing place at our own discretion."

Before Schulze had really set his mind to work, Hank Frieding advanced the following proposal: "Let's spread a net directly beneath the window of our Antipode room. An observer can lie in it; if the centrifugal power be shut off, then he lies flat on his stomach over the window; if the current be started he falls back softly into the net. In any case, he can keep on observing the surface of Saturn and let us know in the Zenith room, by electric bells, whether we are rising, falling, or should finally land. Three agreed-upon signals would be enough. In addition, since there is a telephone in every room besides the electric-bell system, he can also make reports by telephone, should there be anything special to announce."

"Excellent!" praised Schulze. "I want to take the observation post."

"Nothing doing!" countered Munchhausen. "I've been hankering for a long time to be the first to see what Saturn looks like at close range. The solar eclipse cheated me out of my hope; now at least I want to achieve my aim as the observer at the masthead, which an old seaman like me is best fitted for."

The Professor smilingly shook his head. "Your specific weight, noble Hugo, makes the matter too risky; the strongest nets would tear like cobwebs were you to lie in them."

"Oh," said Flitmore, "I have on board a hammock which is woven out of such strong bast cords that the few hundredweight of our Captain couldn't tear them apart; also, it is so large that it offers him plenty of room, so let's grant him the satisfaction."

The Professor would indeed have liked to make the first discoveries, but he did not want to dispute them with his old friend, and thus was Munchhausen, equipped with a fieldglass, let down into the "masthead," as he called it, as soon as the net had been fixed firmly in place.

Then the centrifugal power was switched on and the Captain, lying on his back, swung in the hammock directly beneath the window, which moved away from the icy ground upon which it had till then rested.

Thus he looked up into the icy fields, which seemed to swing above him and looked truly threatening with their mountains and crags. It was a singular, sinister sight to see these sparkling masses hang over you as if they were about to hurtle down and pulverize everything. However, Munchhausen knew well enough that all this only appeared that way because the *Sannah* now had her centre of gravity in her own centre. Saturn would hold its surface, all right!

XXIII

A NIGHT ON THE RING PLANET

MUNCHHAUSEN was zealously at his post, the electrical contact always in his hand. If he gave a short bell-signal, Flitmore switched off the power above, and the Captain landed on the window-pane with his fat belly, which fortunately was so huge that it could have withstood even more violent shocks.

In such cases it seemed to Munchhausen as if the world had turned around with lightning speed: the planet which he had looked up to till then, because he swung below it, now suddenly appeared to be below him and he had to look down upon it from the *Sannah* swaying above him.

When Munchhausen gave two bell-signals, which meant the switching on of the current, he plumped right back into the hammock and suddenly saw the window and Saturn above him again.

This recurrent and very sudden change, which created confusion every time it took place and made it impossible to get one's bearings, might have caused an ignorant person to doubt all reality and his own senses.

Just imagine what a feeling it must be to have the ceiling at which you are looking, suddenly, in one second, become a floor on which you lie and then, just as suddenly, again become the ceiling above you. And that is how it changed every few minutes.

"Lucky that I am lying at this post, instead of the Professor or some other inexperienced landlubber," thought

Munchhausen. "They would get seasick with a vengeance; the movement suits an old sea-dog like me to perfection."

And out of sheer gaiety over the affair, he gave the signals much more often than was necessary.

But he soon made an unpleasant discovery: the *Sannah* always remained turned to the North Pole of the planet and it was impossible for her to reach the more southern regions of Saturn. Along its whole length, the planet was marching past the World-Ship and as soon as the centrifugal power was switched on, it moved away on its path, whereas the shutting off of the current only brought about a plunge towards the Pole.

"We ought to be at the South Pole," growled the Captain; "then the celestial body would sail by under us and we should be able to descend as soon as the equatorial belt came under us. But now it has left us for good and won't come back; so I don't see what we can do."

He reported this observation to Flitmore by telephone.

A consultation was held above and the result of it communicated to him.

Schulze explained through the telephone: "Since we are in the favorable position of being on the inside of the Saturn orbit, that is, between it and the sun, we shall now keep the current working uninterruptedly. The *Sannah* will thus bisect the arc described by the planet in the coming hours and approach a point in its path which it must reach immediately thereafter. Then you must keep a sharp lookout as to when the planet is approaching us again, so that we may submit in time to its attractive force and then, by a proper opening and closing of the current, allow ourselves to be drawn down until we are able to land on its equatorial regions. Come up here for dinner now; you can then sleep quietly for five hours, for we shall require some seven hours to bisect the vertex of the ellipse by the shortest possible arc."

Six hours later Munchhausen was stretched out again and now saw how Saturn was indeed rushing by from the other side; by bisecting the vertical arc of its elliptical path, the *Sannah* had caught up with it.

It was now necessary to switch off the centrifugal power so as not to be flung back again by the repelling force of the nearing planet.

Then began again the alternating closing and opening of the current in accordance with the bell signals of the Captain, and thereby also the merry ball-game the *Sannah* played with his rotund body, flinging him back and forth between window and hammock, as the centre of gravity of the World-Ship was shifted to her centre within or to Saturn's centre without.

On the one hand, this alternating manœuvre prevented a premature crash to the surface of the planet; on the other hand, a too great removal from it: after the rings had been passed, they remained within the atmosphere of Saturn.

When the South Polar zone had been passed over, from the Zenith room the rings looked like narrow circles. As they approached the equator, there was soon little more than the rim of the innermost ring to be seen, beneath which the *Sannah* was sailing by.

In the meantime the gaze of the Captain was riveted on the prospect before him: seas and high mountains, rivers and lakes, softly curved hill-ranges, green fields, meadows and sinuous streams; then again craggy cliffs and yawning canyons as black as night.

When the *Sannah* reached the equatorial zone, Munchhausen gave the landing signal with three long-drawn-out bells.

It was an alluring mound-dotted plain onto which the

World-Ship descended; but night fell again as the company dropped the rope ladder and stepped onto firm ground.

Of the ten moons of Saturn, whose period of circuit grows with their distance from the central body and amounts only to twenty-two and one-half hours for the innermost one and no less than seventy-nine days for the outermost one, the four inside ones stood simultaneously in the sky. Yet their feeble light was not enough to conjure up the brilliancy of a full-moon's night on earth. The narrow rim of the ring was dark; the inside rim was never brightened by the sun anyway, and the illumined surface of the ring showed itself only in the daytime, but never at night.

Mitzie took the first watch this time, and Munchhausen insisted on the second, towards the end of which the break of day would take place, for no solar eclipse prevailed here.

This time they were going to content themselves with three hours of sleep, so that they should not miss the short day.

Lady Flitmore, who was to get but one more hour after her two-hour watch and was anxious above all not to oversleep the Saturn dawn, decided not to lie down at all, but to keep the Captain company in his vigil; with this in mind she had snatched some sleep before the descent and felt fresh enough to stay awake for ten, and if necessary, for twenty hours without growing tired.

All was quiet; only Lady Flitmore, a loyal guardswoman, sat close to the flickering fire, adding a log from time to time.

A slight elevation of the ground served as her seat. The ground here was composed of bleak stone, which felt remarkably warm, so that Mitzie found no need of spreading a cover over her seat; the rock did not even feel hard. She thought it must be some sort of pumice stone, and she was confirmed in this by the striking lightness of some of the stones lying about her. A chunk as large as a big pumpkin, which she sought to lift, felt as light to her touch as a rubber ball.

It occurred to her then how remarkably light also had been the ice at the pole, and she thought to herself that these unusual phenomena must be based upon some natural law peculiar to Saturn.

Then her gaze roved about. The bleak space was not greatly extended; it was hemmed in by a thicket as tall as a man, which seemed to be formed of reeds or reedy grass, above which towering trees of sinister blackness lowered from a distance.

She raised her head to the sky: so clearly did the familiar constellations greet her that she suddenly felt herself back upon her native earth and the whole world-voyage seemed only a dream. And was it not really so singular as to be possible only in dreams?

But in the midst of these old, familiar constellations, a dark, narrow arc divided the whole celestial vault into two unequal parts. It was the rim of the ring, which showed her beyond a doubt that she was on a strange planet. She was told so also by the four moons which wandered, uneven in size and differing in brilliance, about the sky, and one of them had just been darkened by the shadow of its central star.

There too radiated the comet which she had first seen from Tipekitanga, in an almost dazzlingly golden brightness.

And look! On the horizon below rose a fifth moon! Yes, it was indeed a strange world! Despite the constellations, which did not seem one whit different than when viewed from the earth, she was nevertheless far removed from the earth! What had her husband said? 769,860,000 miles, more than eight times the distance of the earth from the sun!

She shuddered as she recalled this enormous figure, and yet what did it mean compared to the distance of the fixed stars high above? Practically nothing! They seemed to be neither closer nor farther.

She was frightened out of these thoughts by a shadow that darkened the gleam of the fire.

A bird fluttered about with scarcely audible wing-beat. It circled the flames, approached and retreated, flew up and swooped down again.

"An eagle," thought the Lady, measuring with her eye the enormous spread of its wings.

But the wings were noteworthy indeed. They were not feathered, nor yet the wings of a bat, these thin, mottled sails with the broad, sharply outlined rim.

Mitzie shook her head. "If it weren't for its enormous size, I might take this bird to be a moth, a nocturnal butterfly," she murmured half aloud.

The first was now joined by a second and then a third. Noiselessly they encircled the fire, whose blaze, fanned by the wind of their wing-beats, bent low only to flicker up more brightly.

One of these sinister birds now flew by close to the young woman. It had a singularly thick head with an elephantine beak like a fire-hose, and two round pop-eyes as large as walnuts between which twitched two plumes, like huge feelers. The body was cylindrical and very hairy; the hairs stood up as stiff as a hedgehog's, but most remarkable were the six thin legs which this unusual creature had attached to its body.

Gripped with horror of these monsters, she snatched a burning faggot out of the fire to protect herself against them.

She was instantly confronted with the need of defending

herself from attack, for one of the birds flew straight at her.

With the burning end of the stick, Mitzie struck out at the repulsive head with all her strength. It seemed to have no skull but to be made of a soft mass, for the blow did not smash the weapon and produced no sound other than a dull thwack. But the bird sank stupefied to the ground and when Mitzie struck at its head again it was instantly squashed into a pulpy mass.

Just then Munchhausen appeared on the scene. It was not yet actually time for his relief watch, but in expectation of the discoveries he hoped to be the first to make, he had enjoyed but a restless sleep and had awakened before his time.

"What hideous monster is this you have laid low, you Amazon?" he asked, astounded at the quivering body on the ground. "Sure enough, here comes another one of them. Ha! there's one that aimed at me. No, my friend, I wasn't meant for you!" And with one blow of his rifle-butt he crushed the hideous invader to the ground.

The third bird had in the meanwhile disappeared.

"A sort of butterfly wing," he said, "two antennæ, a snout, six horn-armored legs, and not a bone in its body—all pulp! Lady Flitmore, these are night-butterflies. You're laughing at me, but you are quite wrong. I myself don't believe what I am saying, but that is what they are and nothing else. Moths, that's what these creatures are, monster night-moths! You look truly frightened, and I shouldn't feel any too comfortable if these two-horned birds were to swoop down on me. But I don't believe that these night-creatures are capable of inflicting damage on any one of us. Just look, they are made of butter; a slight pressure suffices to squash their bodies to a pulp."

This was manifestly the case, and Mitzie was inclined to

be ashamed of her fright; but the unknown always arouses a certain terror and the Captain himself had not been able to fight off a feeling of horror at this huge butterfly.

"You see," he explained, "it's only human. What has never been seen always frightens one at first. But you had better get some rest after this horror, my watch is beginning."

"I have no idea of turning in now," laughed Mitzie. "I am keeping you company; I am curious to see my first dawn on this planet."

"All the pleasanter for me," Munchhausen asserted, "but we might as well sit down." And with that he plopped down upon his plump cushion.

XXIV

A STRANGE WORLD

DAY began to dawn. Rosy clouds swayed above the horizon and immediately afterward the distant mountain peaks lit up, rimmed by the golden flood of the first sunfire.

Munchhausen and Mitzie gazed about them.

What an unusual landscape! Hill and valley, slope and plain, waterfall and stream—these made no particularly strange impression upon them, although a small waterfall, which tumbled over a low rock close behind them, already offered a riddle.

The water splashed up high and thick flakes of foam floated in the air. The spectacle might have been understood had the water hurtled down from a height of three or four hundred feet and not, as they could see, from a height of ten or twelve feet at the most.

"Wow!" exclaimed Munchhausen, dumbfounded. "This pygmy of a waterfall behaves as if it wanted to enter into unfair competition with Niagara, or the Victoria Falls in Zambesi."

But far more striking was the plant world: what had looked at night like reeds as tall as a man, turned out, in the daylight, to be grass. Here rose green tufts seven feet high, over which swayed huge blades; the grass was broader than a hand's breadth, the blades thicker than a thumb, and the timber forest behind it seemed composed of herblike growths with enormous, tender stems and leaves, the smallest of which far exceeded the size of banana leaves. Flowers shot up amidst them, spreading out like parasols or hanging down like church bells.

But nowhere could you see a growth that resembled a tree; the tallest giants of the forest, which might have reached some 200 feet, were knotty reeds several yards in circumference, crowned with fronds and spikes, or horse-willow and fern with gigantic pinnula.

Yet how lovely and overwhelmingly magnificent were these tangles of grass and these forests of herbs with the floral splendor of their colorful brilliancy!

"We must arouse the sleepers!" urged the Lady, after shaking off her first astonished admiration.

"I'd far rather make an exploring trip first on my own hook," grumbled Munchhausen, "but, in the first place, that would be a spiteful betrayal of my comrades, and secondly, what is more decisive, without a substantial breakfast under my belt I am physically incapable of a world-renowned exploring expedition."

They awakened the whole company, who soon appeared in front of their tents, rubbing their eyes, and then gazed in astonishment at the crushed giant-butterfly, and praised Mitzie's courage.

"Hurrah!" cried Schulze as he looked about him. "Here we have something entirely new again, entirely super-earthly, these rolling plains, these fabulous forests! We must take a walk through them before we do anything else."

"Nothing doing!" resisted the Captain. "Everything in proper order! First a good breakfast, then I am ready for anything!"

"You are right," agreed Flitmore. "It is better that we satisfy our bodily needs first; then we can make uninterrupted use of the day, which is quite short enough. And the first need will be a refreshing wash; there is a lovely stream-let close by us."

It was agreed upon, and all hurried to the nearby stream in order to make a thorough wash-up.

"My, how remarkably soft this water is, almost like oil," Mitzie was the first to remark.

"True enough, it seems to be much more fluid than earthly water," confirmed Hank. "It flows through the fingers like mist and is as fine to the touch as gossamer."

John ran the few feet to the camping ground, seized a thin piece of wood, with which he came leaping back, to throw into the water with a plop.

The water spurted a good ten feet high, in a finely divided spray, like a fountain. All of them stared speechlessly at this new wonder. But Rieger cried: "That's no water at all!" and he pointed to the wood, which had sunk to the bottom of the stream like a piece of lead, and stayed there.

"Well, this is where all science does finally come to an end!" cried Schulze. "This is fresh, clear water, but of a lightness that would enable it to float upon our heavy, earthly fluids, like oil or alcohol; it seems to be correspondingly volatile and to evaporate very quickly; I feel that from the strong prickling when it dries on the skin. Lady Flitmore, on Saturn your biggest wash would dry in half the time it takes on our inefficient earth!"

To Munchhausen's relief, they now turned to the preparation of breakfast.

It was amazing how quickly the water reached its boiling point. The Professor tested its heat with a thermometer. "I thought so!" he exclaimed, "only 128 degrees! The water of Saturn comes to a boil at that low temperature."

He now proceeded to an examination of the soil, and removed the rock with a pick which John brought him from the *Sannah*. The fragments of rock hacked out of the ground reminded them of bones: they were full of hollow spaces, porous, divided into cells, with thin but very tough partitions. The medium-sized chambers were filled with air or gases, while throughout the larger cohesive chunks of rock ran watery veins.

An attempt showed that most of the stones floated on the water of the stream, although the water itself was pretty light.

As they went on, they found heavier bits of rock which sank down into the water, but nevertheless appeared to be amazingly light.

"Now the riddle of the slight density of this planet is solved," said Flitmore. "The density, or what amounts to the same thing, the specific weight of Saturn is only one eighth that of the earth's, three fourths that of water's, namely, of earthly water's.

"It was therefore supposed that it must be in a glowing fluid state, from which, it is true, such an extremely slight density would not be quite comprehensible. That's why even our Captain presented the supposition that the matter of the Saturn mass might be hot grog."

"Too bad it isn't," laughed Munchhausen.

"Well, you shan't be lacking grog much longer," Flitmore consoled him. "Now we have discovered here a firm, substantial ground, by no means as soft and elastic as the much denser ground of Mars and yet of such lightness that it explains everything. The water has a correspondingly lighter weight than on earth, and even the plant world seems to be of light material, which defies tempests not by its stiff bulk but by its elastic flexibility and the toughness of the fibres."

"The animal world is certainly also adapted to these conditions," said Schulze. "Let's be on our way! I am burning with anxiety to undertake a voyage of discovery."

As our friends entered the grass forest, and behind it the timber forest of the giant herbs, they found the Professor's supposition fully confirmed: they were nowhere confronted by a vertebrate animal which might have revealed a firm bony structure; only insects and mollusks were to be seen.

But what frightful monsters they were!

Although they differed essentially in details of structure and form from all earthly species, they nevertheless revealed a startling similarity in general with the latter, and they were accordingly designated.

At the very beginning, Munchhausen declared that these monsters could not be embraced under any other general name than that of "dragons"; for that is what they looked like, with their unnatural size and horrifying appearance.

Here were snail dragons and caterpillar dragons and such as bore a resemblance to beetle larvæ by the feet at the front of their bodies; really thick, plump, and yet agile creatures of the size of weasels, cats, and sheep. This comparison, however, could serve for the last two only; for they were two and three times as long as a weasel.

Far more gruesome reptiles were the wood-lice and centipedes; they crawled and turned about as large as crocodiles and when they swayed aloft with half their bodies, their ghastly heads and quivering legs swung so menacingly above the heads of the wanderers that they had to defend themselves against the monsters with well-aimed shots.

Ant and bug dragons, horrible spiders taller than a man, were even more dangerous; but the true giants of the animal world on Saturn were the armored beetles, which stamped about like hippopotami, elephants, and rhinoceroses and nipped at the strange invaders with their jaws.

They had to be constantly on guard; for these beasts clambered around on the mighty shrubs which often bent even beneath their slight weight; but they did not escape Lord Flitmore's skilful snapshots.

A sort of stag-beetle suddenly caught the Captain unawares about his middle, with its terrible jaws. Flitmore was so zealous with his photography that he snapped even this remarkable picture before coming to the rescue. Hank Frieding had in the meantime killed the monster with a few shots; but the jaws of the dead beast had to be chopped away before Munchhausen could again breathe freely and regain his humor.

"Of course, this slobberer had to hunt up the juiciest bit right away," he jested, while the beads of sweat still stood out on his brow.

They had to guard especially against the locusts and grasshoppers, which hopped about like kangaroos.

A sort of earwig also made itself very unpleasant.

In the air droned midges, horse-flies, and gadflies with transparent wings, ranging in size from sparrows to doves. Still larger were the wasps and bees, the winged ants, and steely-blue dragon-flies. The giants of the bird world, however, if one may speak of them as birds, were the butterflies, which had the most delightful colors.

But now a flat-bodied monster crawled forward, with long arms at the end of which two enormous claws stuck out; simultaneously it swung its tail, bent high above its back, towards Lady Flitmore. At the end of this tail was a sharp prong which was very thick beneath the point, obviously containing a poison-gland.

"A scorpion dragon!" shouted Munchhausen, and aimed his rifle.

Yet it would have been too late had not Mitzie herself,

with remarkable coolness, sent a shot directly into the puffy poison-gland so that it burst, oozing out a yellowish fluid until the prong fell limply.

Only, the scorpion gripped the arm of the young woman with one of its claws.

Now John came to the rescue: he was armed with an axe in order to clear a path where necessary. With a well-directed blow, he parted the claw from the body of the giant scorpion, which thereupon abandoned all further attack.

With great effort, Lord Flitmore then succeeded in breaking off the convulsively closed claw and freeing the arm of his wife from the vice. But the courageous Lady carried off a painful bruise as a reminder of the encounter.

Most of the forest giants had soft, flexible, tender, yet tough and elastic stems of an unusual size; they were simply gigantic herbs.

But next to them were shrubs, bushes, and copses, also with reedy branches or with stems which were filled with an extremely light pulp, and finally, gigantic ferns and horse-willows. Real wood, however, was nowhere to be found; in its loose, light structure, everything corresponded to the slight density of the planet.

Appropriate to these were the tasty, juicy giant fruits, almost entirely berry fruits, some with stones, like sloe and juniper berries, others like raspberries, blackberries, or even gooseberries; many hung in juicy clusters or like huge bananas and beans; finally, there were shrubs like the hazelnut, with hard-shelled nuts as large as cocoanuts.

Of course, all these splendors were given names according to the earthly growths which they most nearly resembled. In reality, they differed essentially from all the berries of the earth not only in size, but also in form and flavor, though not in their disadvantages. By unanimous judgment, the first prize for spiciness and quality was given to a sort of cactus fig without thorns.

The two chimpanzees made themselves at home and clambered up wherever a fruit tempted them. They had been trained by Flitmore to throw down their booty at command, and it now stood them all in good stead; for most of the fruits hung so high that they were not to be reached from the ground and, for heavy persons, the climbing of the swaying, flexible and for the most part very broad stems and reeds, presented especial difficulties.

In the fights with the various creatures of the forest, the apes also joined in, strangling several locust and caterpillar dragons, and tearing to bits or biting to death several giant spiders and centipedes. From combat with the armored beetles, however, they carried off all sorts of wounds, but were saved each time by their master's bullets or John's axe.

XXV

A BATTLE FOR THE *SANNAH*

THE enjoyment of the aromatic berries, which were not, however, a match for the luminous fruits of Tipekitanga, was marred by the many repulsive and even dangerous creatures which populated the strange forest.

But there was still another thing that compelled our friends to hasten their departure.

This was a furious hurricane, which broke loose quite suddenly and under the violence of which the herb-trees and shrubs bent to the ground and thus made further progress well-nigh impossible, indeed, even threatened the wanderers with the danger of being smashed and crushed beneath them.

Some of the beasts fled into the holes in the ground, which were to be found on all hands, and must have been the result of the activity of these giant insects themselves. Others rushed to the tree-tops, to which they clung as the storm roared by and whipped up everything like the waves of a sea.

The return was difficult and not without danger, and although they had not penetrated deeply into the forest, it took a long time before they put it behind them; for the greatest caution and many roundabout ways had to be taken to avoid the plants, which bent over so far that they literally touched the ground.

Fiercely though the storm raged, only a few of the shrubs were broken, so elastically did this Cyclopean plant-world adapt itself to conditions.

At last the edge of the bush forest was reached and, breathing freely again, our friends entered the small clearing on which the *Sannah* rose before their eyes.

They thought to seek shelter within their craft from the hurricane, which now sent down a fine, drizzling rain that soaked all their clothing. This drizzling rain, so thinly was it distributed, filled the air with an impenetrable mist, so that even before sunset it became fairly dark, and the entrance to the North Pole room half way up the *Sannah*, that is, about seventy feet high, could no longer be seen.

The chimpanzee Bobs, as the nimblest and at the same time the most impertinent and inconsiderate of the whole company, was the first to clamber up the rope ladder and had already disappeared into the mist before the others reached the spot.

Suddenly a frenzied screaming was heard from the invisible heights.

"Hello! There's something wrong up above," cried Flitmore. "And it was an irresponsible piece of lightmindedness on my part to leave the *Sannah* behind us, in the solitude of a strange planet, without human protection."

Just then a large, but apparently not particularly heavy, body rolled down the rope ladder.

"Aha! It looks as though one of those repulsive Saturn-beetles had made itself obnoxious up there," said the Captain. "Well, Bobs has made its improper behavior clear to it and torn its head off until it hangs to its hideous body by only a hair."

"Don't call this creature repulsive and hideous," the Professor called out. "It is highly interesting." With a scientific eye, he examined the dor-beetle which lay at his feet; for a dor-beetle it was, this beast comparable in size to a young calf.

In the meantime the screaming of the ape did not cease, and they soon saw Bobs, with a pitiful look and bleeding arms, swinging his way down the rope ladder in hasty flight.

"Oho! There you have it, Professor!" cried Munchhausen. "It looks as though a few more of your highly interesting beasts had made a nest for themselves up there in the *Sannah*. I propose that you go right up, since you have such a tender feeling towards these creatures. You can make your studies there without disturbance; for we shall follow you only when you have come to an end and have added the invaders to your beetle collection."

Schulze made a long face. No! He did not trust himself to go up, although he could see nothing but mist when he raised his eyes. But since Bobs had taken to flight, there must be something wrong.

"Let's set up the tents again, the storm is subsiding," said Flitmore, drily. The hurricane had torn down all the tents.

"Does that mean we are to leave the *Sannah* to her fate for a while?" asked Hank.

"There is nothing to be gained in letting ourselves in for some unknown danger, in this mist, with night falling, and taking up a battle with rabid monsters," replied Flitmore, shrugging his shoulders.

"But neither tent-walls nor ceilings are a protection against this drizzling downpour," the Captain reminded them. "We are already drenched to the skin and under such conditions Lady Flitmore may catch a dangerous cold."

"How do you know that there are disease germs, especially cold-germs, on Saturn?" interrupted Schulze.

"Bah! You can catch cold anywhere," asserted Munchhausen, "and it's a dry bed that protects you from it, not a learned germ theory. As for myself, an old sea-growler, I can stand dampness and cold air. I am only concerned about you and particularly about the gentle Lady."

" 'Gentle Lady!' " laughed Mitzie. "Did you know me in Africa for a wax doll to think I have to be rolled up in cotton?"

"Not that, but at that time you were a Boer girl and now you are mistress of an English castle."

"But no softer than I was then; England took none of my Boer blood from me."

"I can vouch for my wife," confirmed Flitmore. "Have no worries about her."

"Only," said Munchhausen, whose soaking bed did not look very inviting despite his sailor's boasts, "only, now that the Professor has mentioned the question of germs, who knows but that Saturn may have much more dangerous germs than those on the earth? Perhaps even very huge ones!"

"Calm yourself," said Hank suddenly, "I will risk the venture and hope to exterminate the monsters that are up there."

"Don't be foolhardy, young man," warned Lord Flitmore. "There is no point to it. Let us wait till morning, when we can examine the situation. Maybe by that time the beetles will have withdrawn voluntarily, if only to seek food; for they will find nothing in the North Pole room and they surely will not be able to open the doors leading from it."

"Yes, let it be, my young friend," Schulze also joined in. "Bobs would never have fled if the odds had not been very great."

"I have my plan, which involves no risk for me," insisted Hank. "Foolhardiness is not of my nature; if I find that there is danger, I shall turn back."

"Come, come!" threatened Munchhausen. "You showed us in Australia more than once that you hold back from no deadly dangers; I haven't so much confidence in your caution."

"Just let me try," Hank cried down from the rope ladder, up which he climbed as nimbly as a cat, so as to cut off all further argument.

Behind him came the chimpanzee Dick. He had become especially attached to the young man, who always took a kindly and solicitous interest in the ape.

But John too clambered up, calling after Hank: "I permit my humble self to follow right behind you, for three of us ought to be in a better position to calculate our moves than if you and Dick were alone to inoculate a battle." "Inoculate" was intended to mean "inaugurate," a term which John seemed to prefer to the homely English word "begin."

Hank reached the black, yawning entrance to the North Pole room. It was now fully night and nothing could be discerned within the room, although a creeping to and fro, a squeaking and a chirping could be heard which announced that a great number of uninvited guests had made themselves at home within, and that it would not be wise to venture close to them in the dark of the night.

Nor did that enter his mind at first; rather he now gripped one of the ramps which went around the whole circumference of the World-Ship like meridians and crossed her zeniths.

The climbing of the ramps on the smooth, curved surface of the globe was not without danger. The darkness alone, which excluded any feeling of dizziness, favored the venture and Hank was an agile acrobat. John Rieger too found no insurmountable difficulty in the climb, and Dick the ape certainly not—it was a joke to him.

At last all three reached the top where, at a height of 150 feet above the ground of Saturn, they stood at the highest point of the *Sannah*, that is, above her Zenith chamber.

Groping about him, Hank found at his feet the electrical button which made possible the opening of the window from without, and so they descended into the dark room by the ladder steps, closing the window behind them.

Then Hank turned on the electric light and said to John: "First of all, let's each take along one of the rubber stools, which ought to be excellent shields against the claws and jaws of the fiends."

"But then, shooting may become necessitous down below," urged the servant. "At least in so far as I am concerned, I am lacking in the indispensable ability of shooting with my one effective arm."

"We'll shoot only in an extreme emergency, my friend. It is no small matter to shoot with long-range fire-arms in a closed room; even though the bullets might not bound back from the thick, rubberized walls, we might nevertheless damage and destroy things that were best avoided."

"But there are, so to say, revolvers in the arsenal, which is located here."

"Excellent! We can more easily risk shooting with those. Let's each stick one in his belt; but load them first! And now, our main weapon must be a hunting-knife; that we take in our right hand."

"With your kindest permission, unless you have something essential against it, I should prefer rather to stick the knife in my belt too, and take in my hand this Thomas-hack, the Indian axe, since there are in this closet all sorts of excellent armaments from all countries, and I can get around better with an axe-blow than with a knife-stab."

"Just as you wish, John, take the tomahawk; and we will use the revolver only in an emergency; will you be able to fire it with one hand?"

"I will flatter myself by replying affirmatively, for if that were not the case, I would surely look like a fine clodhopper."

"Now, then! Now for the passage to the North Pole room! I go first, Dick follows me, and you close the door after turning off the light; in the meantime I'll light up the passage. When we come into the North Pole room, I will first put on the light; that will blind and startle the monsters so that they won't attack us right away."

Before Hank opened the door which led into the North Pole room from the passage, he extinguished the light in the latter so that all was in darkness when he entered the room. He did it cautiously, covering himself with the rubber chair, for hard by the door stood a beast that first had to be pushed aside. It needed all his strength, for the six-footer offered tremendous resistance.

Now the young hero swiftly turned on all the lights, one right after the other, so that a blinding brightness broke out in the room.

He speedily surveyed the situation. A dozen armored beetles, the size of half-grown calves, had made themselves at home in the room; but besides them, there were also four enormous wood-lice, whose agility and nimbleness gave Hank more to worry about than the beetles with their chops and claws.

Dick gave the signal for the assault: he leaped forward pluckily and landed on the back of a wood-louse, which twisted and turned under his strangling grip, his ripping nails, and biting teeth without being able to escape; the chimpanzee speedily settled its fate.

The beetles were at first blinded, as Hank had correctly assumed, and did not stir. As though warding off some menace they reared their front legs and opened their chops.

"At them, now!" ordered the young man and let go at

the nearest foe, driving the hunting-knife through its throat.

John in the meantime swung his tomahawk, or his "Thomashack," as he called it; he had thrown away the obstructing shield and now split the soft head of a wood-louse, while Dick, who seemed to prefer battle with the wood-lice to an attack upon the plate-protected beetles, promptly began to tear the third to bits.

It seemed to be a pretty easy struggle, for eight of the monsters had already been incapacitated and a ninth had fled through the window, without the heroes having suffered more than a few bruises. In addition, three wood-lice lay dead and the fourth was no more to be seen.

"Only three more enemies!" shouted Hank, jubilantly. "The victory is ours!"

Only, he had exulted too soon; it was the last of these enemies that made the job a hard one; their eyes had grown used to the light and they were now on guard.

With one of them, Dick was engaged in a desperate struggle. The beast had fallen on its back, but with the powerful claws of its six quivering legs it held the ape fast, pinched and tormented him till he howled, and snapped at him with its jaws. In vain did the chimpanzee seek to free himself; could he have done it he would have thought only of retreat, as had Bobs before him. He bit away in a frenzy and broke two of the monster's legs with his forearms, but he was held fast in the vice behind him.

The second beetle had passed over to an attack upon Hank, who in the certainty of his victory had lost all prudence—it had been so easy up to then.

As ill-luck would have it, the jaws of the beetle found his throat; they could not bite it through but they squeezed it so tight that the poor fellow might have been strangled. "Help, John, help!" was all his choking voice could cry;

then he dropped the hunting-knife, with which he had struck his adversary a feeble blow.

But John was in no position to help; he too was menaced, even though not mortally. Held by the right arm, he could no longer utilize his murderous axe and he groped with his left arm for the revolver in his belt.

At this moment of their greatest need, Flitmore appeared in the window, followed by Schulze. Their worry over Hank and John had left them no rest. In the upward climb, it had gone badly with Lord Flitmore, for he collided with the falling beetles, which almost threw him off his balance.

One look now showed him that the main work had been done, but that Hank was in great danger. He hastened to behead the aggressor and to tear the jaws of the cut-off head from the throat of his young friend. Immediately thereupon he sought to revive the now unconscious fighter.

John had meanwhile succeeded in blowing the light of life out of his enemy with a few revolver shots and then freeing his arm with some effort.

The Professor had now come to the aid of the ape, who rapidly left the dismal spot, even though the danger had passed.

And yet it was not entirely past: a shriek of horror rang out all at once from Schulze's lips.

The fourth of the wood-lice, which had apparently disappeared, had only crept up the wall and suddenly plunged from the ceiling upon the Professor; not with evil intent— it had simply lost its footing.

But what difference did that make? The luckless Professor felt himself surrounded by a fat, ringed body, gripped by countless, swarming feet. He thought that his last hour had struck.

But John and Flitmore both reached him at the same time

and they destroyed the last of the hideous creatures, its dismembered body twisting to the ground with all its closely set feet twitching.

Hank had now come to his senses again and felt his throat; he had the feeling that a terrific jaw was still squeezing it in its grip. But there was nothing of the sort, only the pain was there to make him imagine things. Soon he breathed more easily and was able to rise gradually to his feet.

Now Mitzie appeared at the window with drawn blade; but fortunately she found nothing to do with her weapon. Behind her came Munchhausen, puffing and sweating, so hastily had he climbed up in order to bring whatever aid he could to his friends.

"Well, well, I sure came too late," he gasped. "Too bad, too bad that nobody's in deadly danger, it would have been a pleasure and an honor for me to save him."

"It's alright enough to joke now," said Lord Flitmore, "but our heroic friend, Hank Frieding, was literally up to his neck in danger, and was saved by the skin of his teeth."

The Captain turned to the rescued fighter with admiration: "It's true! You are blue in the face and your throat shows traces of strangulation. We've got to cook you up a grog right away!"

The corpses of the beasts were now thrown out and the horrible traces of the struggle removed, as far as possible; then John hauled in the tents and the apes now also risked a return to the *Sannah* and helped transport what was needed.

The fighters, however, washed up and put on new clothes, whereupon the evening repast was served in the Zenith chamber, far from the battlefield.

XXVI

CARRIED OFF BY A COMET

"LET us look up some other region of the great planet," Flitmore proposed the following day.

"That is a good idea," said Schulze approvingly. "I will admit that the animal world here in the tropics is loathsome and unpleasant, however interesting it may be. Quite possible that other latitudes will reveal new wonders and less horrors."

An abundance of fruits, and especially nuts, were then gathered and brought into the *Sannah*, for nobody knew whether the next landing place would be equally fruitful.

Then a few empty kegs were filled with water from the stream which had proved to be such an excellent and welcome drink. With block and tackle, they were hoisted up.

This precaution too was taken, because they could not foresee what the drinking-water conditions might be in other spots.

"Let's hope that we may also discover a Saturn man, that is, rational beings like ourselves," declared Mitzie. "I cannot imagine that such a tremendously big celestial body, possessing all the conditions necessary for human existence, should not be inhabited by man!"

"Such men, to be adapted to the density of the planet, as are the animal and plant world," jested Munchhausen, "would have to be extremely lightfooted, and we should run the risk of being deported as 'burdensome aliens.'"

"A risk you at least would run, friend Hugo the Stout," said Schulze. "The 'burdensome alien' is undoubtedly yourself, and the Saturnites might easily regard you as a heavy menace to their light planet."

"Ouch!" cried Munchhausen. "Only a born Berliner could turn out such a pun."

"Seriously speaking," resumed the Professor, "I don't believe in Saturnites, for up to now we have not discovered a trace of the work of man, and furthermore the long winter and the solar eclipses are not particularly conducive to the existence of humans."

"I incline to Lady Flitmore's view," countered Hank. "Humans could adapt themselves even to these conditions; perhaps the long winters are not especially rigorous. And as for human traces, the world of Saturn is so enormously large in comparison with the earth that it simply doesn't mean anything if some regions prove to be uninhabited. Perhaps they haven't even been explored yet by the Saturnites."

"Of course, you're at liberty to have your own point of view on the matter," rejoined Schulze. "But what do you base it on? A baseless supposition hangs in the air."

"Oh, I base it on exactly the same thing as does our Lady. For we are all agreed on one point, that this wonder-world, with its plants and living beings, could have been produced only by the will of a personal and rational Creator."

"Of course! There's no argument about that," Schulze flared up. "We can safely leave it to half-educated and weak-minded people to believe that impersonal forces conjured up personalities and that the reasoned ordainment of the world is the accidental product of unreasonableness."

"Right!" continued Hank. "A personal, reasonable Creator would create nothing without purpose and intention. Mars, for example, was inhabited by beings similar to man; it seems to have fulfilled its purpose before having died out, if only to offer erected quarters at a later time, under more favorable conditions, to a new race. Saturn, which is almost 3000 times the size of Mars, and seems to offer rational beings far better conditions for living, can hardly be conceived as having been created as a paradise for giant insects."

"Bravo! that's what I thought," cried Mitzie approvingly.

"Permit me to say that both sides are right," Lord Flitmore intervened in the dispute: "North America was sparsely populated for thousands of years and showed vast tracts of unpopulated land which nevertheless had excellent living conditions to offer man; today it has a very dense population and that is just what it was intended for. We may assume the same intention for Canada, which has begun to be populated only in recent times. The same thing holds true for South America, where the most magnificent areas are still entirely or almost entirely uninhabited."

"From that we may learn," interjected Mitzie, "that the settlement of habitable countries is realized only in the course of time."

"Quite true, my dear! Consequently, when you justly assert that Saturn is habitable for human beings and is therefore intended for such, still you are far from any right to conclude that it has already fulfilled what it was intended for, namely, that such beings already live on it. It may be a world which is reserved for later occupation. Perhaps its rings may soon fall to pieces entirely and plunge down upon its surface so that the eclipse will come to an end at last. Perhaps its rotation period may also be accelerated thereby; then nothing should prevent it from being populated from the earth, after the means have been found of reaching it within a few days."

"There is nothing can be said against that," thought Schulze. "But, my dear Flitmore, since we are now ready to hunt up some other region of Saturn, I beg you to assign the observation post to me this time. I will endeavor to choose the most promising landing-place."

"Hold on there, Prof!" warned Munchhausen, "you won't be able to stand it. I tell you, you'll be jounced between the ceiling and the hammock until your bones are a pulp, since you are not provided with such an upholstered body as I have. You are a landlubber, and, believe me, you'll be miserably sea-sick."

"Landlubber, indeed! Do you think I can't stand a rocking movement? Perhaps I travelled to America, Africa, Asia, and Australia by land!"

"All right, try it; but you'll remember what I told you!"

So the Professor proceeded to the hammock at the Antipode room, gave the signal for the start, and promptly flew out of the net and landed on the window on his face. With every signal he gave, he bounced back and forth between the hammock and the ceiling, but he bore up manfully under this ball-game which the *Sannah* was playing with his body, and found the ever-changing sights highly interesting.

But what was this? Saturn suddenly disappeared below him with lightning speed and was nowhere more to be seen!

Schulze rubbed his eyes, he strained his eyesight to the utmost: was it only the sudden fall of night that had robbed him of a view of the planet? But the *Sannah* was rising right on the day side, between the sun and the path of Saturn; so long as the centrifugal power was switched on, the planet would have to keep its sunlit side turned to the World-Ship, because it rotated beneath it while the *Sannah* took no part in its revolution.

With a constantly closed circuit, it should have taken a few hours at least before night fell.

So it couldn't be that, and yet nothing could be seen far

and wide except dark cosmic space. The sun shone on the *Sannah* from the other side; in the Antipode room reigned the deepest night.

So startled was the Professor by this completely unexpected and inexplicable occurrence, that for a long time he strained his eyes and brain without either seeing anything or finding a solution for the riddle.

Finally it occurred to him that the most sensible thing would be to have the current broken so that, as a result of the force of attraction, the *Sannah* might again approach the missing star.

He gave the corresponding signal a number of times; quite in vain! He remained lying in the net and the centre of gravity of the *Sannah* remained unaltered in its own centre.

Something was out of order, perhaps Flitmore had not succeeded in shutting off the centrifugal power.

"What's wrong down below?" Flitmore's voice inquired through the telephone.

"I might ask what's wrong up there?" returned Schulze. "Saturn has disappeared, gone completely! Why don't you break the current?"

"It is broken! I shut it off at your very first signal."

"Then your switching apparatus is not working!"

"It is! It is quite in order. Something else must be wrong; come along up here."

Shaking his head, the Professor rose from the hammock and proceeded, first descending and then ascending from the middle, to the Zenith room.

Here the voyagers had enjoyed a very singular spectacle from the very start of the departure: in spite of the blinding sunshine, a comet stood radiant in the morning sky and presented an enchanting sight.

Flitmore had proposed to give the comet a name.

"The astronomers on the earth have undoubtedly already given it a name," he said, "but we don't know it and we have first rights to give it a private name for our own use."

They all agreed to call it "Amina," in honor of the loyal Somali Negro girl with whom they had gone through so many adventures in Africa.

Remarkably enough, the comet seemed to come steadily closer and the sun to recede ever further. A few luminous bodies, like planetoids, whizzed past the *Sannah.*

In the meantime, Schulze again gave a signal; Flitmore cut off the centrifugal current. Immediately thereafter the same signal was repeated.

"The Professor must have forgotten the meaning of the signals," laughed Munchhausen.

Right there is when the telephone conversation was held, after which the Professor came to join them.

When he entered, his surprising observations were being ardently discussed, without, however, an explanation being found for them.

"Let's have luncheon," proposed Munchhausen. "A good meal sharpens the mind."

Before, and all during the repast, the Professor observed the remarkable comet. Then Hank proceeded to the Antipode room and reported by telephone that there wasn't a trace of Saturn to be seen and that everything was covered with darkness.

"I have it," cried Schulze. "We are stuck in the middle of the comet's tail and are being borne along with it, and at a speed that passes all human understanding."

"Holla!" cried Flitmore. "You may be right! Let's hasten to switch the centrifugal power on again, so that we don't plunge right into the nucleus of Amina."

And he instantly closed the circuit.

But the result was completely inexplicable. The *Sannah* seemed to come appreciably nearer the head of the comet; then it remained apparently motionless in one spot.

This they were able to infer from the fact that a few pieces of meteor, which were now quite close to them, continued to maintain the same distance.

"This apparent standstill," explained the Professor, "only proves that, together with those meteorites which form a part of the comet's tail, we are being carried along in the tail of Amina."

Lord Flitmore made a few more attempts by switching the current on and off, but the only result was a slight change in the position of the *Sannah;* the comet seemed to hold it as if by an invisible thread.

In spite of the most exacting investigations, nothing could be discovered to show that the centrifugal power apparatus was in any way out of working order.

Nobody had any advice to give, nobody found an explanation.

At last, Flitmore let the current stay on at full force, as the surest way of averting a collision, and perhaps, after overcoming the puzzling resistance, of getting loose from the comet.

"The *Sannah* is being carried off by the comet, no doubt of that," he said. "Let us yield to our fate until somebody hits upon an explanation or until some equally unexpected circumstance liberates us from this painful situation."

The *Sannah* completed her rotation, and night fell in the Zenith room.

After the watches were divided, they turned in to rest, with mingled feelings.

XXVII

THE SECRETS OF THE OUTERMOST PLANETS

THE next day the comet Amina, with the *Sannah* right behind it, crossed the path of the planet Uranus, which was discovered by Herschel on March 13, 1871.

"Uranus is about twice as far from the sun as Saturn," explained Schulze, "namely, about 1,769,850,000 miles. It is 90 times as large as our earth and is only feebly illuminated and warmed by the sun, since it receives 400 times less sunlight than the earth, which is nevertheless still equal to the light from 1500 full moons. It seems to be symmetrical and dusky, and is probably molten and consequently somewhat luminous. Its density is virtually that of water and its specific gravity is about one-tenth that of our earthly planet.

"It has four extremely small, dim moons. The sun appears 360 times smaller to it than from the earth, and rises for it in the west and sets in the east.

"Its equator seems to stand almost vertical to the level of its orbit, so that the Poles lie in this level and every point on this heavenly body has the same climate; but notice, this climate also undergoes the most extraordinary changes at every point; for the longest day lasts two and a third earth-years at five degrees latitude, and forty-nine earth-years at ninety degrees!"

The *Sannah* came fairly close to Uranus, but in vain did Flitmore hope to be torn away from Amina by the force of attraction of the planet while the centrifugal power was shut off: the comet's tail continued unswervingly to carry the World-Ship along with it.

Yet Schulze was at least enabled to make a few new discoveries: he found a moon of Uranus, the Oberon which Herschel discovered in 1787, circled by a ring similar to that of Saturn, something wholly new in the field of astronomy. Further, he discovered two additional, but very small, dark moons, one of which circled between Oberon and Titania and the other between Ariel and Umbriel, the two innermost moons which Lassell discovered in 1846.

Another twenty hours later, the comet was already cutting through the orbit of Neptune.

"Neptune," explained the tireless Professor, "is remoter from the sun than Saturn and Uranus put together, namely, 2,775,870,000 miles.

"Neptune seems to have but one moon, has one and a half times the density of water, and is surrounded by a cloudy atmosphere. It receives a thousand times less sunlight than the earth, but for that, its moon, which moves backward, is larger and brighter than the Uranus moon; it circles Neptune in five days, twenty-one hours, and four minutes. The planet itself is supposed to be in a molten state."

The *Sannah* did not come as close to Neptune as it had to Uranus; however, three additional small moons could be discerned, of which two pursued a normal course: a new violation of the preconceived law.

"With Neptune our solar system comes to an end and even at a distance 10,000 times as great, there is nothing any more but empty cosmic space, traversed only by comets and meteorites."

This was Schulze's final assertion; but he was mistaken: one and a half times farther removed from the sun than Neptune was a tenth planet-orbit, and the world-travellers sighted a dark planet, which might have been smaller than the earth.

True to the custom of designating the planets of the solar system by the names of Roman gods, the new star was called "Vulcan" by Flitmore, "because of its limping course," as he termed it.

Unfortunately, the planet could not be examined more closely, because of its remoteness and the great speed at which the comet's tail carried the *Sannah* along.

XXVIII

A VOYAGE INTO INFINITY

THE *Sannah* spun around in endless darkness; the sun still hovered in the sky as a small star, its planets no longer visible to the naked eye.

The comet alone spread light and brightened the side of the World-Ship turned toward it. After leaving the solar system it had drawn its tail closer and closer to itself, and with it the *Sannah*, which now revolved at a slight distance from it like a satellite and received from its nucleus not only light but also a moderate warmth.

"The further a comet moves from the sun, the slower becomes its speed," began Schulze one day. "That is a rule which I found confirmed by Amina also, at the outset. In the meantime, however, the speed of our comet has become so swift again that it passes all comprehension and exceeds even the speed of light."

"Just think, the nails of our hands and feet grow but one thousand-millionth part of a twenty-fifth of an inch per second, whereas in the same period a snail could traverse fifteen-thousandths of a twenty-fifth of an inch. And we know that a man, in relation to the growth of his nails, progresses much more rapidly than our comet in relation to the speed of an ordinary pedestrian," observed Flitmore, laughingly.

"What is speed, anyway?" asked Munchhausen. "Everything is only relative; the flea surpasses the snail in agility, just as a sparrow surpasses Captain Hugo von Munchhausen."

"Right you are!" agreed the Professor, laughing. "The one surpasses the other; that's how it is in the winged world also: the vulture travels 50 feet a second, the quail 55, the carrier pigeon 87, the eagle 100, the fly 172, the sparrow 216, and the tern as much as 290 feet. Electricity runs through the cable wires with a speed of 2484 miles a second, the voltaic current does three times as well, and in an overhead telegraph wire electricity reaches the speed of 22,356 miles a second. Light speeds through water at 13,972 miles per second, through air at 62,100, and through space at 186,300 miles a second. And yet it requires about 4½ years from the closest fixed star to the earth.

"However, I estimate that our comet is reaching about 50 times the speed of light, so that within 5 weeks it will carry us into the fixed star world! As against this, what significance has the so-called runaway star with its 186 miles a second?"

"If only our air holds out," said Mitzie, thoughtfully.

"If what the Professor calculates is true, that we should reach the fixed star world within five or, let's say even ten weeks, then our stores of oxygen ought to suffice, unless some special circumstances intervene," Flitmore assured her. "If we can then only get loose from the comet and land on a habitable star with wholesome air!"

"Hurray! We're off to the fixed stars!" cried Hank, enthusiastically. "I would never have dreamed it."

"Yes, we are travelling in God's wonder-world," observed Flitmore, thoughtfully. "Well, then! Did not the Creator send us His herald out of infinity to take us in tow? Let us trust in Him to preserve us on a voyage that no living being has yet made or even thought to be conceivable."

Now John spoke up, after having listened attentively: "So all you gentlemen think, so to speak, that it is educated to believe in the Bible? I always thought that under modern conditions it was more educated not to believe in a God, as we hear so often; but down real deep I often felt that something would be lacking, the main thing; and then I noticed that my masters were pious, and yet educated and reasonable."

"Yes, my lad, that's how the matter stands: if you don't believe in a God, most people will say to you that you are very reasonable and highly educated; for the half-educated are, as has often been said, always the great majority. Whereas if you hold firm to your belief in the Creator, this majority will jeer at you, but the really intelligent will consider you reasonable and educated, and so you will be."

"Then I would much rather believe, just as you do!" declared the good man.

Meanwhile the *Sannah* was whizzing farther through space and no end was in sight.

XXIX

CHIMPANZEE FOLLIES

TO make possible the electrical heating and lighting, as well as the development of centrifugal power, the electric accumulator had to be freshly charged twice a day.

This was taken care of so punctually and with so much zeal by the apes that Lord Flitmore was able to let the work be carried out without supervision. The apes enjoyed it immensely.

Flitmore had certainly arranged the electrical power plant with ingenuity: he had set up two large cylindrical cages, like those usually made on a smaller scale for captured squirrels. When the squirrels leap along the bars, the cage revolves around its axle and the small animals are tireless in the activity by which they set the cage in rapid rotation.

In exactly the same way, the chimpanzees apparently took the greatest pleasure in running around their cages, without dreaming that they were thereby performing a great service; for the ingenious device utilized the rapid rotation of the cages for the production of electrical energy, which was stored up in the accumulator.

One day, amazing sounds rang out from the music chamber, ghastly discords indeed, as when a young child bangs around on a piano, and yet the malefactor was developing such a fingering skill that one might have thought it was a trained piano player, who had been brought to such orgies by an extravagant humor or a sudden madness.

Our friends were gathered in the Zenith room, save for the servant who was making his rounds; they were absorbed in books or steeped in thought. But when this infernal row commenced, they all looked up.

"Can John be practising on the piano?" asked Mitzie. "He plays beautifully on the flute, but the pianoforte is strange to him; yet how he can undertake such a thing without any knowledge, when the discords must be tearing away at his own musical ears, is a puzzle to me."

"You are mistaken, my dear," said Flitmore. "John is never so impertinent as to touch the instrument; you know that he has never yet taken any unmannerly liberties; he is too modest for that, almost too timid."

"Then it's a ghost," said Munchhausen, hollowly, "for it is exactly midnight in the music chamber."

"Listen! There sounds the trumpet in the midst of it! It is a duet," observed Hank.

"Incomprehensible!" murmured Flitmore.

"Come! Let's look into it," said Schulze, curious to solve the riddle.

"Ugh! Wouldn't you like first to make a few keen guesses calculated to explain this miracle scientifically, most estimable Professor?" Munchhausen begged ironically.

"So that you can have the laugh on me and my science afterward, you old scoffer? Nothing doing! I myself put appearances above all attempts at theoretical explanation."

"Well, let's get along!" called the Captain, and started out with all the others behind him.

A veritable infernal noise now rang from the music hall.

"Some one's playing with at least six hands!" laughed Hank.

"And the trumpet! What terrible sounds!" cried the Lady, and held her hands over her ears.

An electrical globe burned in the music chamber, by the light of which they saw Bobs leaping away from the piano, while Dick had just succeeded in tearing apart completely the abused trumpet.

Bobs had this time become weary of his cage and the artful fellow had succeeded in opening the door by groping through the bars until he found the latch and drew it back.

Finding himself at liberty, he also opened Dick's prison and, disposed to all sorts of misdeeds, proceeded with his companion to the music chamber far below. The opening of the connecting doors had long ago ceased to be a mystery to the clever apes.

Here the two conspirators hatched the dark plan of arranging a musical entertainment by themselves for once, instead of always keeping Professor Schulze company as inactive listeners.

Bobs opened the piano without difficulty; nor did he fail to put some notes on the stand, notes for the 'cello, it is true, which didn't bother him at all, for he had put them there upside down anyway.

Then he flounced down upon the piano stool and began belaboring the keys with an agility that did honor to the natural speed peculiar to the ape.

Dick, in the meantime, cautiously opened the instrument cases; this he had imitated from Flitmore. He regarded the various musical instruments and then grabbed the trumpet, whose metallic sheen caught his eye.

Oh, he knew quite well how the thing was held in the mouth and that the nether part had to be pushed in and out as quickly as possible, and he succeeded, with violent snorts, in conjuring up a few horrible sounds, biting through the mouthpiece in the act.

But when the whole company now appeared in the chamber, the apes felt something coming which was highly unpleasant for them; so they took speedy leave and fled to the adjacent chemical laboratory, where they climbed all over the shelves, without failing to throw down a few flasks of corrosive fluid.

Munchhausen followed right on their heels and shook a threatening stick at Bobs, who bared his teeth and grinned mockingly, as if to say: "Come on, Fatty! You are threatening in vain; with a bulk like yours, you'd do well not to climb up after me."

This obvious mockery could not but enrage the Captain.

"Wait, you scoffer!" he cried, and seized the pedestal of a distiller, which he flung up with such skill that the three iron feet dug painfully into the unprotected hide of the chimpanzee. Wounds there were none, but how it did hurt!

Bobs let out a loud screech; he found it inconsiderate and presumptuous of a man who was not even his master and played neither piano nor trumpet. He thirsted for revenge.

A large flask stood next to him. He might have thrown it down upon his assailant; but not even in righteous anger did Bobs act so clumsily. He tore out the glass stopper, held the big flask and poured its contents down upon the man below, who had just bent to pick up a new missile.

"Help, help! The beast is murdering me! Bobs is covering me with vitriol; he is burning up my naked skull!" cried the Captain.

Frightened, Hank came running to him; he believed he would find the Captain already eaten away, perhaps robbed of his eyesight, for there were in fact a number of flasks with sulphuric acid on the stands.

But one look at Munchhausen's dripping skull promptly reassured him; his nose, trained in chemical fumes, told him instantly that it was merely spirits of wine, which would of course make one's head feel hot, particularly since its rapid evaporation produced a sensation of cold which, when terror and imagination were added to it, might be thought to be a frightful burn.

"Calm yourself, Captain," Hank called out to the terrified seaman, "fortunately it is only spirits of wine."

"Deuce take your spirits of wine! It's vitriol or some other acid, which is taking off all my precious hair and maybe eating away my whole scalp."

"I assure you that nothing of the sort is happening; but you are dripping like a water-rat! Here's a towel. Dry yourself and then you can wash your head and change your clothes."

That surely had to be done. Munchhausen went off like a drenched poodle and Schulze laughingly called after him with the consolation: "Bobs had good intentions, spirits of wine is good for the scalp and makes for a rich growth of hair."

"You can laugh all you want now," said Hank to the Professor, when Munchhausen had left the room. "But I tell you, a cold chill ran through me when I heard the poor fellow groaning like that. Just look, there are sulphuric acid, hydrochloric acid, carbolic acid, and a lot of other dangerous fluids. I must always close the laboratory in the future and take along the key; the apes might have caused a terrible calamity."

"They may yet," thought Schulze, and looked up at the two chimpanzees, who were crouching up there among the flasks.

But Flitmore now called the two malefactors and they promptly came down, quite meek and docile, accustomed to heeding the word of their master.

Punishment had to be inflicted—the educational principles of Lord Flitmore demanded it. So the obviously penitent sinners were put into solitary confinement for twelve hours. They were well acquainted with the dark, narrow closet, and knew that it was a well-deserved punishment; for they leaped into it voluntarily with humbled mien, bent down, and without resistance allowed themselves to be shut up.

As soon as they had gathered in the living-room, Munchhausen too appeared in dry clothing. He continued to insist that the fluid which burned so sharply had been vitriol. "Fortunately, my skin proved to be acid-resistant," he added, "and even my clothes suffered no damage; a very remarkable material, I tell you!"

XXX

LOST IN SPACE

FOR days and weeks the *Sannah* tore along with the comet, and this voyage through the apparent void began to have an increasingly oppressive and anguishing effect upon the feelings of all.

Where were they? Whither were they rushing? In infinity! Into the never-ending!

Nobody concealed from himself the terrible danger in which they all were, the dreadful fate that threatened them.

For the time being they were still able to maintain a wholesome amount of air in the rooms, by means of the abundant stores of compressed oxygen and ozone. But no one could tell how long this voyage might last or whether it would ever come to an end.

Indeed, according to human foresight, it seemed highly improbable that a heavenly body offering human beings the essential necessities could be reached within an appreciable time. And then, who knew if such even existed in the fixed-star world to which they were rushing?

Only the belief that they stood under a Higher Protection, and that a God who knew also the ways of the infinite was their guide, sustained them when they thought of themselves as prisoners in the rooms of their craft.

Who could tell whether this might not become a life imprisonment, which would not last long, it is true, for within a few weeks, unless relief intervened, their lives would be extinguished!

Then they would watch each other die, without being able to render any aid, and in the end all would be still and dead. A tiny globe laden with human corpses would then careen through the universe, and in the end, probably plunge upon some distant sun and with all it contained be dissolved in an instant into glowing gases!

Only John remained inwardly calm and content, for he did not foresee the possibilities so clearly and thought that his master knew well enough whither they were travelling and where they would land.

Meanwhile, Flitmore spared the oxygen stores as much as possible, so as to postpone the final catastrophe as long as might be. All of them began to feel the consequences: it was a bad air, weak in oxygen, which pressed upon their lungs; nor were their moods very healthy ones.

Truly! that is how the unfortunates must have felt who were shut up in a submarine, prevented by an accident from emerging to the surface of the sea, and watching each other slowly choke to death!

The time was passed with all sorts of work, with entertainments, with concerts, and the reading of good books; but their thoughts always wandered off, gripped by the disquieting question: What is to become of us?

Again and again Schulze studied the starry sky and made calculations, a work which, even though it offered but little consolation, at least engaged his thoughts.

"We are travelling towards the constellation of the Centaurs," he said one day after concluding some observations and calculations, "directly towards the star Alpha Centauri, which, so far as is now known, is closest to the earthly solar system. The approach can already be noted with the naked eye: Alpha Centauri may be recognized plainly as a double star; several constellations are already seen to be essentially different from that which they appeared to be when viewed from the earth, and some of the stars are visibly gaining in size and brilliance."

"It is of the greatest interest to us to find out at least the direction of our voyage," asserted Flitmore. "But have you also taken the aberration into consideration?"

"I have thought of that, but in this case there can be no aberration, for the *Sannah* is moving straight towards the star Alpha or Toliman."

"What may this be, if you will permit me to ask, this 'apparition'?" asked John.

"Since the earth moves through world space with enormous speed," explained the Professor, "the position of the observer constantly changes with the earth. If you therefore train a telescope on a star, then the light-ray which meets the extreme end of the telescope, the objective, requires some time before it reaches the other end, the ocular.

"This time is very short, it is true, but the earth has moved on in that instant, and the direction of the telescope has been shifted. Consequently, in order to be able to see the star at all through the telescope and to continue observing it, the telescope must be given another direction than that followed by the rays of the star: the ocular must be set back in the direction of the earth's movement as much as the earth moves in the time required by the light to pass from the objective to the ocular end. Because of this, an apparent shifting of the star takes place, that is, it is not seen in exactly the spot in the sky where it is actually situated, or rather was situated, when the light left it which now strikes our eyes.

"But when the observer moves straight towards the star, there can be no aberration; it is at its greatest when you move towards its rays in a vertical line."

"So we are now travelling towards such a star?" John asked again. "Shall we soon be there?"

Schulze laughed, shrugging his shoulders. "What do you mean, 'soon'? Do you know how far from the earth these fixed stars are? Alpha Centauri is closest to it, and yet its distance is calculated at four and a half light-years, three and a half at the least."

"What is that, if you'll permit me, this 'light-year'?"

"It is the distance that light traverses in a year, namely, the trifle of 5,876,000,000,000 miles."

"And you call that a trifle? Really, you must be joking."

"Yes, yes, my lad; for such figures are so enormous that unless your humor is called to your assistance when you speak about them, your senses begin to whirl. Or do you want to have some sort of an idea of what it means: Toliman is from 18,630,000,000,000 to 24,840,000,000,000 miles distant from the earth."

John shook his head helplessly. "And that, so to say, is supposed to be our closest fixed star?"

"It is! There may be some that are nearer the solar system, but up to now they have not been discovered, that is, no smaller distance has been established by measurements. Alpha Centauri is 9000 times farther removed from the earth than Neptune, that is, 277,000 times as far off as the sun. An express train would require 1,250,000 years to reach it."

Rieger's eyes went wide. "A million years?" he stammered. "And we are going there?"

"And why not? Only we are going a few million times faster than an express train. For Amina, our comet, is a swifter vehicle, as you see. And if I spoke before of trifles, then it was not merely a jest; for Sirius, the bright dog-star, is from 8 to 9 light-years from the earth, 1300 times as bright, and 40,000 to 50,000 times as large as our sun; the

Polar star is 40 light-years away; Canopus, the brightest star in the southern sky, shines from 10,000 to 15,000 times as brightly as the sun and is one and a half million times as large. That is the very least; it may even be a hundred, a thousand, a million times larger; it's beyond our calculations. Deneb in Cygnus may be just as large or larger than Canopus, and that also holds for Rigel, the brightest star in the constellation of Orion, at its lower right-hand corner.

"This magnificent star of pure white light may be 500 light-years from the earth, that is, 30,000,000 times as far off as the sun, the brilliance of which it exceeds by 20,000 times. If we were to designate the distance from the earth to the sun by one twenty-fifth of an inch on a sheet of paper, we should need a strip 18 miles long to designate the distance to Rigel, on the same scale. Do you now grasp what a trifle the distance to Toliman is?"

"Certainly, considered from a relative point of view, so to say."

"But now, there are among the fixed stars huge suns, beside which these unimaginable colossi are only solar dust; namely, there are some 52,000,000 fixed stars up to the seventeenth magnitude; up to the twenty-seventh magnitude there may be a billion, that is, a thousand million. But the parallaxis of only about 60 of these stars is known to us."

John, who eagerly snapped up every word unknown to him, and twisted it around in his unique manner, asked inquiringly: "And what is to be understood by the name 'Polaraxis'?"

"Well, now, how shall I make that clear to you? Do you see this point here in the middle of the ceiling? Well, I train a telescope upon it from one end of this room, and you train one from the other. These telescopes are inclined to each other at an angle whose point is the object observed. Well, the angle formed by the lines which go from the object through both our telescopes, in relation to the distance of these from each other, is the parallaxis of the object. We can therefore just as well say that its parallaxis is its angle of inclination formed by both our telescopes, trained upon one object, in relation to the distance from each other.

"Now, if we know the distance from one end of the room to the other, and the angle which our telescopes form with the even floor, then we can calculate the height of the triangle, formed by the object in the ceiling, by the two points at which the light travelling through our telescopes from the observed object, hits the floor. We can consequently calculate how far the object in question is removed from the floor.

"Now you can see, my friend, that if, instead of the object in the ceiling, we consider through our telescopes a star which is thousands of millions of miles away, then the incline of our telescopes towards each other is so infinitely small that it seems to be virtually nil. We can therefore find no parallaxis for the star.

"But the further removed we are from each other, the more will our telescopes incline toward each other if we train them upon the same object. It may therefore be hoped that the parallaxis of a star can be found if it be observed at the same second from two distantly removed points on the earth, the distance between which is known, and if both observers measure the angle which the direction of their telescopes forms with the plane. Or this can be done just as well by a single observer regarding the star from the same spot at different times in the night, when the rotation of the earth has shifted his standpoint some thousand miles or so.

"But such distances, in many cases, proved to be too small, no measurable inclination of the observation directions towards each other could be ascertained; consequently, the fixed stars showed no notable parallaxis.

"So a far larger base-line was chosen for the triangle; the stars were observed at intervals of half a year. At the time of the first observation, the observer found himself at one end of the earth's orbit; at the second, at the other end. This meant a distance of 186,000,000 miles between the two points of observation.

"Great was the bewilderment when it was found that even here there was no measurable parallaxis for the fixed stars! Only by means of extremely refined instruments did Struve, in 1836, and Bessel, in 1839, succeed in measuring the first fixed-star parallaxis. In this manner, they found for star sixty-one in Cygnus a distance of nine and a half light-years. Bessel had the excellent heliometer, put together by Fraunhofer, to thank for his success. This is the same Fraunhofer to whom we owe, more than any one else, the progress made in spectral analysis."

John promptly snapped up this word also and said humbly: "If it isn't too much for you, Mr. Professor, to enlighten my humble self on this obscure point as well, I should appreciate it especially to learn what I have longed to know for some time, what this business of Speck-Stral-Anna-Lissis really amounts to."

"And know it you shall," laughed Schulze. "Look, if a ray is sent through a polished glass, it breaks up into colored bands and streaks. This is called a spectrum. The narrower the light ray, the plainer is its spectrum, and you may observe among the colored bands more or less broad dark lines, the so-called 'Fraunhofer Lines,' named after their discoverer. Furthermore, bright and colored lines also divide the spectrum, and Kirchhoff and Bunsen showed that from these streaks, lines, and bands, may be determined the elements which are to be found in the source of the light as glowing gases; they may even be identified as regards mass and composition.

"In this manner, we ascertain the elements contained in the sun and the stars; the spectroscope tells us.

"But it has told us much more. When a light-source moves rapidly, the spectral lines shift towards the violet end of the color spectrum if the light source is drawing nearer, and towards the red end if it is moving away. From this it is possible to estimate the speed of the movement of the fixed stars even."

"But I thought that the fixed stars did not move," objected John.

"That's what was believed formerly; but now it is known that they have their own movement. This may also be observed through the telescope, if it be trained perpendicularly towards the visual line. There are stars which have already moved a full-moon's breadth in the sky in 200 years, which in reality means millions of miles, in view of their great remoteness. Thus Arcturus races along at 400 miles a second, which is a thousand times faster than the fastest shot; Alpha Centauri too has a rapid motion of its own."

"But what does it look like on Alpha Saurus, towards which we are flying?" John now asked.

"Toliman is the third brightest star in the firmament; but it can be seen only from the southern hemisphere. It is equal to our own sun in brilliance, size, and heat."

"Then we shall burn up!" cried John, horrified.

"Certainly, if we come too close to it," Flitmore now intervened in the discussion; "only we hope that this will not be the case. At several million miles distance, the Professor can hardly ascertain our direction exactly. So it is still possible that we may land on a dark star."

"How is that? So there are dark stars too, so to speak?" cried John, surprised again.

"Certainly," confirmed Flitmore. "Our earth is such a

star, so are the planets, in so far as they no longer radiate any light of their own. The sun lights them up very brightly, often more brightly than the most radiant fixed star; but that comes only from the fact that they are relatively close to the earth and appear to it in the brilliancy of the sunshine that brightens them.

"From the distance at which we now are, we no longer see a single one of the planets of our solar system; just as little do they see from the earth the dark celestial bodies of the fixed-star world which no longer possess any light of their own."

"Yes, but supposing this to be the case, how do we know that they exist?"

Flitmore wanted to reply, but Munchhausen interrupted him: "If you don't mind my saying so, Lord Flitmore, the luncheon is steaming on the table and the Lady might feel hurt if we let her artistic work grow cold before doing it the necessary honors."

"*You* would certainly feel very much hurt by it!" rejoined Flitmore, laughing, "but you are right, there is a time for everything. Well, John, have patience; after the meal I will explain to you how we know that there are dark stars, even though they cannot be seen."

XXXI

THE GIANT CUTTLE–FISH

THIS time, however, John's inquisitiveness was not so punctually satisfied as he might have expected from his master's reputation for reliability.

But this was due to an extraordinary circumstance, an unforeseen event which might easily have been disastrous for the *Sannah* and her occupants.

Towards the end of the repast, a violent rattling was suddenly heard, broken by thunderous blows which shook the World-Ship from one end to the other. It was obviously a hail of meteorites which was descending upon the *Sannah*.

Fortunately, the first stones to strike the outer shell were small ones, and by pressing the corresponding electric button, Flitmore was able to close the protective metal plates or eyelids over all the windows, so that any shattering or damage might be prevented.

But such substantial chunks soon rebounded upon the surface of the craft that the worst was to be feared and even Munchhausen interrupted his gastronomical activity.

When the banging and thundering ceased, Flitmore, together with John, Hank, and the Professor, made the rounds of the *Sannah* to determine whether the ceilings had been damaged or broken through at any point. To their great relief and satisfaction, they found that the excellent metal shell had held up under the furious hailstorm and revealed no damage. On the outside, it must have sustained bumps, abrasions, and cuts, which could not be examined at the moment, for on the outside yawned empty space. The main fact remained, however, that the casing had not been pierced and the precious air could therefore not escape.

As the men returned from their rounds, Munchhausen had completed his repast, which he had continued to consume after overcoming his first fears.

"Your coolness is enviable," said Schulze, shaking his head; "while we, impelled by concern for our lives, look to see whether the *Sannah* has sustained some disastrous injury, you just go on eating calmly as if nothing had happened and nothing was to be feared."

"I suppose you consider that awful light-heartedness and greediness," retorted the Captain. "In reality, however, it is rational philosophy and thoughtfulness. For, tell me yourself: if four of you go off to look into some damage or other, why should I roll along like the fifth wheel of a wagon? And finally, either the *Sannah* has sustained a dangerous injury or it hasn't. If it was undamaged, then the interruption of my repast would have been unnecessary, to say the least; however, if a dangerous leak had been found, then there'd be absolutely nothing to do about it. On the contrary, on an empty stomach you are much more helpless and weak in the face of danger than with the feeling of repletion, which enables you to reflect calmly."

"Is that so! In any case, with that well-filled paunch of yours you might have been able, under certain circumstances, to block up a large hole, until we could caulk it over to prevent the air from leaking away," jeered Schulze.

"Don't mock," warned the Captain, with dignity, "I shall always be ready for such a sacrifice and, as a matter of fact, I once saved a large ship from sure sinking, in that very way."

"Oho! Tell us about it!" cried Flitmore, seating himself in a chair.

"With pleasure!" declared Munchhausen, readily. "It was not so long ago; my increasing bulk was already making it hard for me to serve as ship's captain, when my stately ship one day ran into an undersea reef which was not marked on any sea-chart. We sprang a leak of such size that despite all the pumps the hold was filling up at a breath-taking speed. We seemed destined to sink, for a coast on which we might have landed was nowhere in sight. The rocky point which had proved so disastrous to us must have been a part of some submarine island.

"I went below with the ship's carpenter and two sailors to see if there was any way of stopping the leak; but all was already under water. I worked my way along a narrow beam, above the gurgling water, towards the ship's hull, when suddenly I thought I saw a serpentine creature splashing around below me. Soon three or four such serpents about twenty feet in length rose to the surface. No doubt about it! A giant kraken, also called polyp or cuttle-fish, was inserting its horrible tentacles into the ship through the leak; its body, soft and elastic though it was, could not enter because of its colossal size.

"Suddenly a giant tentacle jerked up at me, and as I sought in terror to escape it, I lost my balance and plunged into the water.

"Immediately, the sea-monster clasped me with all its tentacles and sought to pull me out towards it. Fortunately, it was now I who was too big. My belly was pressed against the hole so that it stuffed it up completely, while I could still keep my head above water.

"My companions promptly jumped in to help me: they wanted to cut through the tentacles of the polyp with their knives and thus liberate me from the stifling embrace. But I immediately recognized that we had here been shown the only way to save the ship and I didn't hesitate a moment about offering up my life, if need be, in order to save craft and crew.

"So I shouted to the sailors to sheathe their knives, and to tie strong ropes around each arm of the kraken instead. They really didn't know what this was for, yet, accustomed as they were to follow me blindly, they carried out the difficult and not undangerous work.

" 'Now draw the lines taut,' I called, when they had finished, 'and tie them to a cross-beam, so that the tentacles are stretched out!' With the aid of a few more members of the crew who had come in, this was done and the cuttle-fish had to release me as its arms were drawn away and held by force.

"Half dead, they fished me out of the water, and I lost consciousness while they were carrying me up on deck, a feat which required no less than six men.

"But the polyp was held fast, and its colossal, soft body was pulled so tight into the leak by the tightly drawn cable that the hole was completely blocked up and not another drop of water could come through.

"By the time I came to, the water had already been pumped out sufficiently to enable the carpenter to get to the damaged spot and caulk it up, during which time, as the work progressed, the arms of the kraken were cut off one after the other, until the monster was finally released without a single one of them, after the last crevice had been nailed up behind him. Now the ship was saved, thanks primarily to my bulk; for, had I been as slim as you, gentlemen, the revolting monster would easily have pulled me through the hole, I should have died a miserable death, and my ship, crew and all, would surely have sunk to the bottom."

"A health to your blessed circumference!" cried Schulze, filling his glass and raising it aloft.

"And to your noble spirit of sacrifice," added Flitmore, clinking glasses with the smirking Captain and joining in the general hilarity.

"That was, so to speak, an adventure that might be called magnificent," said John, "but if I may permit myself, Milord, to remind you, you promised to explain to me how one can know that, besides the luminous solar system, there are also dark stars in existence, in spite of the fact that they cannot be seen."

Flitmore willingly gave the information, beginning by saying: "In the first place, it may be assumed; for the fixed stars are nothing but luminous, glowing suns, mostly much larger than our earthly sun. Now if several dark planets circle around our sun, then why not also around the millions of other suns in world space?

"Then, we distinguish three classes of fixed stars, according to their brilliance. The first class embraces the white-light stars, which are still at their highest incandescence, that is, they are the most recent. Among these are Regulus in the Lion, Sirius in Canis Major, Vega in Lyra. The blue stars also belong here.

"The second class embraces the yellow stars, similar to our sun, which are inferior in temperature and brightness. In the third class are counted the red-glowing and orange stars.

"Between these classes and within them, however, there are all possible intermediary and transitional stages, and many astronomers even distinguish a fourth class of blood-red stars of little brightness, and a fifth, which embraces only a few stars which yield a spectrum of hydrogen.

"The first class includes most of the fixed stars, the second about half of the first, the third approximately an eighth part. From this they conclude that a star remains twice as long in the first state as in the second, and four times as long in the second as in the third.

"I might tell you further that the fixed stars which, when seen from the earth, appear the brightest to us, are called stars of the 'first magnitude,' the next in brightness 'second magnitude,' and so forth. But this is not to say that the stars of first magnitude are in reality the largest and brightest. Millions of stars far greater and stronger in light shine down upon us more feebly just because they are at a much greater distance from the earth.

"But now to come back to the dark worlds: we see that the fixed stars are in the most varied stages of glow, many of them already having been extinguished, and thus what is easier than to assume also that millions of long-ago extinguished celestial bodies are moving about in space, unable to reveal to us the feeble light they receive from their suns?

"Some astronomers assume that the universe contains thousands of millions of suns and hundreds of thousands of millions of dark worlds, of enormous size at that. They do not believe that the space of three to four and a half light-years which separates our solar system from the world of fixed stars is a solitude empty of worlds, but that a few million dark bodies may be situated there, such large ones that our solar system may revolve around them. For there is nothing to prove that luminous and non-luminous cosmic bodies cannot also revolve around an extinguished dark star, provided it be large enough.

"From all this," Flitmore now concluded, "you see that dark bodies, as well as inhabitable ones, must exist a-plenty. God grant that we shall find such a one in due time and be able to make a happy landing upon it."

XXXII

LEFT WITHOUT AIR!

THE weird journey of the *Sannah* with the comet had already lasted five months, and Toliman was still so far off that it could not be said when they would reach it. Lord Flitmore's food machine was now being put into action more frequently, so that the dwindling stores of foodstuffs might be preserved as long as possible. It produced a very nourishing, strengthening, and agreeable food, which, however, could not long take the place of foods grown by nature.

"Unfortunately your supposition about Amina's speed is proving to be wrong," Flitmore said one day to Schulze.

"Quite so," replied the Professor, "I overestimated it considerably. When you have no sure data for a calculation, it is easy to go wrong tenfold, and a hundredfold when such amazing figures are involved."

"A poor consolation," sighed the Englishman, "but what is even more disturbing is that I also figured too optimistically when I thought my oxygen stores would last for eleven months: we haven't been under way half that time and they are all empty but for one small chamber; as for ozone, that is altogether gone."

"How much longer will the air last us?" asked Munchhausen.

Lord Flitmore shrugged his shoulders. "With the greatest economy, and I mean the *very* greatest, three weeks; then we are done for."

"Let's economize!" said the Captain, drily.

"That we shall; but we are due for bad times and who knows whether all our economizing will do any good!"

From now on the meagre remains of oxygen were so scrupulously rationed that the air in the *Sannah* was all but worthless.

The consequences were soon to be seen: only the most imperative activity was engaged in, for the unfortunates felt themselves overwhelmed by dullness and sleepiness. They lay around, sniffing for air, and surrendered to the leaden stupor that held them in its grip; for they consumed less of the precious air while asleep.

The more they hungered for air, the less appetite they had for food or drink. Pallid and haggard as ghosts, they dragged themselves through the rooms, seeking better air; but everywhere it was used up and poisoned.

No longer from day to day, but from hour to hour, their torments increased, and those on watch had a hard time fighting off sleep, so as to be able in turn to arouse their choking comrades, who otherwise would never have risen again!

"Invent something that will produce artificial oxygen or make the exhausted air fresh again!" the Captain panted. "I'm at the end of my rope, Lord Flitmore!"

Flitmore smiled feebly and sadly and looked at Mitzie, who lay back in her chair with closed eyes, gasping convulsively. "If only I could! If God does not help us, we are lost. But help must come *soon*. I have estimated that at the rate we are using it up now, the oxygen will last us another four days. We can't go on like this; we absolutely must have better air, there is no time to lose. We must put an end to this economy. I am resolved upon distributing in the next twenty-four hours all that is left of our stores. Then we shall at least live again, one last time. What comes after that is in the hands of the Almighty!"

With these words, Flitmore slipped away to open the ventilator which was to let the condensed oxygen course through the only room that was still occupied.

The Lady raised herself as in a dream and left the room with lagging footsteps.

Hank, who felt uneasy, followed her. He found her in a room where the two chimpanzees lay choking on the floor: much as they hated to do it, they had had to remove the apes so that they would not also contribute towards breathing away the last bit of air from their human companions in misery.

"What are you thinking of?" Hank asked the Lady.

She looked at him wearily: "What do I matter? The main thing is to preserve the life of the men until God sends them relief. I will not rob them of their last chance."

"Do you want to choke to death here?" cried Hank, in horror.

"Here or there, it's all the same," said the Lady, smiling.

"But in another hour you will be done for here; there you can hold out another twenty-four, and in comparatively good air, for Lord Flitmore intends to change the air thoroughly."

"Then go, perhaps your life will be prolonged by it until help comes, and it will not fail to come, I am sure of that."

"No, dear Lady! We cannot permit such a sacrifice. And there is no sense in it."

"Who knows?"

"Then I shall remain here also; then——"

He got no further. A terrific blow shook the *Sannah*, a crash and creaking rang through the metal casing like rolling thunder. Every room trembled. Then silence reigned.

XXXIII

A DISASTROUS COLLISION

"GOD have mercy on us! What was that?" screamed Lady Flitmore.

"I hope the others have met with no misfortune!" cried Hank.

And as fast as their feeble strength would permit, they hastened back to the Zenith chamber.

"What has happened?" Munchhausen called to them.

"That's what we want to know," returned Hank.

"Where is my husband?" inquired Mitzie, worriedly.

"Here he comes," said Schulze, breathing freely again.

Lord Flitmore entered. His face was deathly pale.

"Thank the Lord! You are safe!" cried the Lady, forgetting all else.

"Let us prepare to meet our end," rejoined Flitmore, hollowly. "We are beyond hope, and the next few hours bring death along with them."

"No more oxygen?" asked the Captain.

"A huge meteor has scraped the *Sannah* and smashed its casing, and of course it had to be just where our last oxygen chamber was located. It has vanished into empty space. Just as I was about to open the ventilator, the crash came. I had some idea what had happened and looked through the side window into space, which was lit up by the light of the comet that streamed through the broken ceiling."

A profound dejection overwhelmed them all. Only John moved away silently. He himself did not really know why; yet the thought occurred to him of looking at the damage and making a tour of the World-Ship so as to ascertain whether everything else was in order.

In order! Yes, if only they could get air! It was a fatiguing trip through the rooms void of oxygen, and often enough the servant felt his strength fail him. Nevertheless he dragged himself along heroically.

In the North Pole room, he found the two dying chimpanzees lying on the floor. They moved him to pity.

He raised the faithful beasts, who clung to him convulsively.

"You shouldn't be forced to suffer so long," said he. "We will all three of us step out where there is no air at all. Then we can die right away!"

Immediately, he proceeded to the hole in order to plunge with the apes into empty space, for he thought they would plunge downward; the force of attraction of the centre of gravity of the *Sannah,* which would hold them to the surface of the casing, was beyond his comprehension.

It was not any thought of suicide that drove John to this apparently desperate step; he could no longer form any clear notion; his blood hammered dully in his temples, his lungs wheezed and rattled, and his nostrils sniffed in vain for air. A dark cloud dimmed his mind. No; the same thought that had impelled Mitzie to sacrifice herself now dawned in the back of John's mind as he climbed up to the hole: he wanted to leave all that remained of fresh air to be breathed by his masters. And added to this was his pity for Dick and Bobs, for whom he sought a speedy end.

Meanwhile, the others in the Zenith room looked forward to a slow and terrible death. In any case it could not be long before a charitable unconsciousness would overtake them and spare them the anguish of further torment.

Lord Flitmore was composed and submissive to God's will.

Hank and Mitzie proved to be just as calm; what irked them was only that they could not sacrifice themselves for the others—it would no longer have been of any use.

The Captain was the most uneasy: he chafed in the stifling atmosphere and yearned for a fresh sea-breeze. He continued to mumble something or other under his breath, which did not sound as if he had made his peace with the iniquitous world. Yet he was no coward and no skeptic.

Silently he admired Professor Schulze, who seemed to have forgotten everything for the moment and, hard though he fought against the lack of air, was still completely absorbed in his scientific zeal during this last quarter of an hour of life.

The collision had aroused his inquisitiveness and he sought intensively the reasons for it.

"It is clear," he said finally in a weak voice. "A new comet is the cause of the disaster; this new comet sailed through the tail of Amina and a solid sector of its own tail struck our *Sannah*.

"Also, we are farther removed from the head of our comet than up to now; a violent struggle over our humble selves seems to have broken out between the two comets. The new comet wants to tear us along with it and Amina does not want to surrender us! It would be really interesting to live and find out which of the two wins. If the *Sannah* gets loose from the comet Amina, the other comet will probably carry her back to our earthly solar system."

"Truly interesting," said the Captain, mockingly. "Only it's too bad we shan't live to see the end of this struggle and that the return to our solar system won't matter much to us. For what does it matter to us where our huge coffin lands? Yes, if you could announce to us that a star of hope was shining somewhere close by, where we might land in half an hour, then I'll admit that your observations would serve some reasonable purpose."

In choppy sentences, often broken by the vain gulping for more air, Munchhausen had spat out his words. But Schulze replied somewhat dejectedly: "The latter prospect doesn't look so good, it is true; Alpha Centauri has come comparatively close to us, in fact, you can already distinguish the luminous satellites of its solar system. But we should still need at least a few days to reach any of these, even if we were not being held up right now by two comets wrangling over us."

"So there is no hope!" muttered Munchhausen; and now again silence fell in the room. Only a moaning and rattling could still be heard.

Flitmore bent over his wife. She had lost consciousness and it would be better for her not to return to it. It would be pointless and gruesome to bring her back.

Hank looked about him with dimming eyes; he missed John. "Rieger is gone!" he breathed.

Nobody said a word in reply.

Schulze continued to stare up at the window.

Suddenly it darkened; a shadow fell upon it and all at once the Professor was aroused to new life by the great astonishment he felt.

"Here is where all science *does* come to an end!" he cried. "There stands John Rieger, our faithful servitor! Right in airless space! Yes, he still lives, he moves, he seems to be wide-awake! That's the sheerest impossibility!"

In the meantime, John had knelt upon the thick pane, waving for help and banging on it with all his strength.

"He is in despair! Naturally, he can't stand it another second without air. But how did he get there and why?" continued Schulze, shaking his head. "Shall I let him in?"

"Of course!" said Flitmore.

"I don't care!" agreed the Captain. "Even though our last breath of air will escape when we open the window."

"There's Bobs too! Why, he's dancing around as usual and turning somersaults!" cried Hank in astonishment, while the Professor hastened to open the window to let in John, whom he imagined to be in the throes of death.

But before Schulze had opened it, Rieger remembered that the doors could be opened from the outside.

He was obviously in a tremendous hurry and could not wait until those on the inside admitted him; he pressed on the button and the thick metal plate turned slowly on its hinges.

Now the air would vanish completely into empty space, but what difference did it make, in the long run? It was poisoned, anyway, and a speedy end would be more welcome than a long-drawn-out battle with death.

But just then a miracle occurred!

XXXIV

A MIRACLE

SCHULZE, who stood quite close to the opening, felt a fresh breeze float in.

Although all and every science evidently came to an end here, he spoke not a word, but opened mouth and nostrils to breathe in the precious, revivifying air.

"There! Are you choking on that horrible air below?" John shouted down, sticking his head through the window. "All of you come right out here!"

"Why, can you sniff in airless space?" the Captain called up from below. He was indignant; for it seemed to him that the servant was playing a most unpleasant joke on him. Perhaps he had lost his senses, poor John! Or was he already a corpse, a spirit, which needs no air? In any case, he, Munchhausen, still needed air to live, he realized this only too keenly!

But John called down: "The most magnificent atmospheric conditions, so to speak, prevail here on the outside! Really, dear Mr. Captain, a precious atmosphere, and the most remarkable thing is that you don't fall off the *Sannah:* I came up from the North Pole window to this point. I was on top all the time, and then when I thought that I should have to climb down the ramps with the greatest caution, because down below things are like that, it proved here to be altogether different and we never went down, but always up. The monkeys are turning capers all around the whole *Sannah*, until you'd think that they were sure to fall, to plunge off into empty space; but they remain constantly in the completest uprightness of their physical position."

The last part of this spluttering speech was delivered to Professor Schulze, who had meanwhile climbed out and only breathed, breathed, breathed.

At last he spoke up: "That you can run all around the globe of the *Sannah* without falling into space, is quite correct, and of course we are always on the top of its surface. But that there should be such excellent air in empty cosmic space—why, it's impossible and absurd; here *is* where all science simply comes to an end!"

But now he turned back and called down into the room: "Why are you staying down below there and fighting for air? Come on up; there is an air out here which actually brings you back to vigor and health! Of course, it is an impossible circumstance and the sheerest absurdity to believe it, but I assure you that it is nevertheless a fact!"

In the meantime, a fresh breath of air had made its way below and swept to the nostrils of Flitmore, Hank, and Munchhausen.

The Captain tottered to his feet and moved his bulky mass with difficulty, enjoying every gulp of the precious atmosphere.

As he rose through the window with head and shoulders, he remained breathless for a moment and propped himself upon the frames with his arms. And now he breathed and puffed like a steam-engine.

"Ho, there!" urged Schulze. "Come out here altogether!"

Munchhausen shook his head: "Don't urge me to superhuman efforts. I want to get my second breath here. Ah, magnificent, delicious!"

"But, man alive! If you stuff up the whole window with your belly, those below will never get out alive! Haven't you any regard for your fellow-man?"

"Right you are!" stammered the Captain, ashamed of

himself. "I just didn't think of it from the sheer joy of the air I was gulping." And he crawled out completely.

Now came Lord Flitmore and Hank, lifting Mitzie into the open.

The Lady was still unconscious, but when she was stretched out in the air rich with oxygen and ozone she soon came to, and in a short time felt herself once more strong enough to rise.

A walk was now taken around the World-Ship, a delightful walk! All the windows they passed were promptly opened so as to let the exhausted air escape and the fresh atmosphere stream in.

"And to think that we were within a hair's-breadth of being stifled to death while the air of life was all around us!" said Munchhausen. "We should have died simply because we did not realize that there was actually no need for it. If John had not stepped out into the open by accident, or rather by divine ordinance, our ignorance would have cost us our lives."

"But it is beyond me how we could have reached a corner of cosmic space filled with air," opined the Professor. "No one could have been expected to think of such a thing."

"Yes!" rejoined Flitmore, in afterthought. "I should have thought of it, and been certain of it. Here you have another example, Professor, of how we humans, who consider ourselves so intelligent, are struck with blindness, and often incapable of drawing the most obvious rational conclusions from what we have already ascertained."

"How is that?"

"Well, I did argue it out with you that, according to my view, the ether which fills cosmic space can be nothing but attenuated air and that every planet or rather every revolving body condenses the air around itself by its power of attraction and must thus surround itself with an air envelope.

"What conclusion was therefore more obvious than that this must be the case with our *Sannah*, also? Why should it not also surround itself with an atmosphere which it drew to itself out of world space?"

"There you are!" cried Schulze, striking his temples. "What an old ass I am! And that's the kind of a man they call a *professor!* The thing is as clear as daylight! We did not notice anything during our landings, because we did not leave the *Sannah* until after she was already in the atmosphere of a world body. But if, in the meantime, we had only once opened a hatch the least bit, then fresh air would have streamed in to us!"

"Of course!" said the Englishman again, "we didn't risk it, we didn't even think of it, because we were always under the delusion that there was no air on the outside to be breathed, but rather death and destruction, and that only the air-tight closing of the hatches to prevent the escape of the inside air could save us from choking to death."

"I could not, of course, have thought of it," said Munch-hausen, "but that Lord Flitmore and, above all, you, the wisest of all professors, should not have thought it out, is a disgrace to all humanity. What? Here you had us shut up, as in a mine-pit or a submarine, until we were almost suffo-cated, instead of saying: Well, boys! Let's open the gates, take a walk outside, and breathe some fresh air. Henry Schulze, you are always talking of science coming to an end, as if you had ever known even its commencement!"

"If I may permit myself to have understood correctly," John now intervened in the discussion, "it seemed to me from your respective remarks as if this air must have been there all along."

"Certainly," said Flitmore, "since our departure from the

earth our *Sannah* has had a legitimate atmosphere which was being constantly enlarged and renewed out of space-ether."

"Ah," called out Lady Flitmore. "Then we could long ago have taken some of these wonderful walks in the open. Too bad we didn't know about it; but now we shan't fail to take advantage of it."

Truly fascinating was the walk in the open. Not only because of the fresh air, which, it is understandable, was the most important thing to them all at the outset, but also because of the changing views that could be enjoyed.

The surface of the globe offered enough room for a promenade; the circumference of more than 450 feet permitted them to circle the whole *Sannah* in any direction within two minutes.

In this way, the whole starry sky could be admired.

Closest to the *Sannah* remained the two comets; yet it seemed as if both of them were moving away in opposite directions; by this the World-Ship was being freed from her compulsory following of Amina, apparently because the new comet also had drawn the *Sannah* to it without, however, being able to take her along entirely, since the force of attraction of Amina was still enough to hold the World-Ship back.

Most of the constellations in the northern and southern skies appeared not very much different from what they had looked like when seen from the earth; the remoteness of these stars was so great that the three and a half light-years closer or farther that they had come, were as nothing.

But those constellations to which they had come appreciably closer (in reality, only to some of their stars) appeared somewhat changed or else markedly shifted.

They were now in the realm of the fixed stars, and yet

Closest to the *Sannah* remained the two comets . . . the World-Ship was being freed from her compulsory following of Amina.

really only in the vicinity of a strange solar system from which the fixed-star world looked to be just as far away as it had when seen from the earth.

Schulze expressed this observation as follows: "We are quite close to the solar system of Alpha Centauri and yet far removed, somewhere in the constellation of the Centaur, as it looks from the earth; for the other stars of this constellation are mostly at sky-distances from us—and, from here, seem to belong to a remote fixed-star world.

"Regarded from the earth, we are here among the fixed stars; but regarded from here, the fixed stars are just as remote from us as the earth, whereas, on the contrary, the earthly sun seems to us to be a part of the fixed-star sky."

"A case quite similar to ours," related Munchhausen, "was that of a ship's crew in the Atlantic Ocean. Their drinking water had been exhausted for days and all of them were torn with thirst. At the moment of their most urgent need, they met a steamer from which they earnestly begged the aid of sweet water. 'Draw it up!' was the answer, 'you are floating in it.' As a matter of fact, the suffering crew had long before reached the mouth of the Amazon River, which is so broad that they saw no land and were on the verge of dying of thirst, only because they believed that they were still surrounded by salt water."

XXXV

IN THE WORLD OF THE FIXED STARS

THE fresh air stimulated the appetite mightily, and Munchhausen was the first one to notice it.

"How would it be," he said, "if we left off wandering in the air for the day and proceeded to imbibe something more solid? I feel as if I hadn't eaten a thing for a week."

"Our meals have certainly been pretty scanty of late," laughed Lord Flitmore; "the lack of life-sustaining air wasn't conducive to arousing a real hunger."

"Not even with me," confirmed the Captain.

"Which is saying a good deal!" gibed Schulze.

"Come, John!" Lady Flitmore proposed. "Let's hurry to the kitchen to prepare a feast as soon as possible; we ought to celebrate all our birthdays today."

"Bravo!" exclaimed Munchhausen; "bravo, Milady, that's an ingenious idea. The fact is we *have* all been born to a new life today."

Mitzie went below with John, and the others followed.

While the first two proceeded to the kitchen, the others remained in the Zenith room.

"I believe," Flitmore said here, "I have now also found an explanation of why the comet Amina carried us off. You know, gentlemen, that according to my view all bodies are invested with an attractive and with a centrifugal power, and attract and repel each other accordingly, until they arrive at a distance where attraction and repulsion are equalized and eliminate each other.

"Now it appears to me that the centrifugal power predominates in comet-matter. That is how it happens that the masses of this matter which are dissolved by the approach to the sun, are repelled from it with such momentum that they form a tail of many million miles."

"That would also explain," added Schulze, "why a comet, whose centrifugal power is rendered inoperative, to a certain extent, by the speed of its course, can be shattered and dissolved when it comes very close to Jupiter and whizzes through the corona of the sun, but never plunges down upon those bodies."

"That's right too!" nodded Flitmore. "But centrifugal power attracts to itself centrifugal power; only thus is it comprehensible that a comet can carry along such an enormous tail and later pull it into itself, whereas the celestial bodies which cross this tail, carry off none of it."

"But the meteoric showers and falls of aerolites?" objected Hank. "The fact of the matter is that parts of a comet or its tail *are* drawn down by the earth."

"Of course!" admitted Flitmore. "What must be borne in mind is that while the centrifugal power is dominant in the comets, there are individual parts which are nevertheless magnetic positives. That would explain the loose tail-formation, since parts of it could be found which would be mutually repellent to a certain degree. At all events, it would be clear why the comet was bound to attract our *Sannah*, loaded with centrifugal power, and carry her off with it."

"I understand," said the Professor. "And partly the terrific speed of the voyage, partly the existence of attractive elements in the tail, prevented us from getting loose by switching off the current."

"That's how it looks to me, at any rate," said the Englishman. "Then the other comet tore us free from the realm of attraction of Amina without, however, being able to grip us. The mutually antagonistic forces finally brought our *Sannah* beyond the sphere of attraction of either comet. And now I shall disconnect the centrifugal current so that we may be pulled by the solar system of Alpha Centauri and, if we discover some favorable planet, land upon it."

Since this was generally considered best, Flitmore instantly shut off the centrifugal power.

The feast that was now brought up set them all a-tingle, and there developed a comfortable and merry mood which was doubly refreshing after the sufferings and mortal dread through which they had passed.

Then they turned in for a delicious sleep such as they had not enjoyed for a long time.

As our friends assembled in the Zenith room the next morning for breakfast, bright sunshine streamed through the window, a sight which was greeted with the greatest astonishment and jubilation; for since they had left the earthly solar system, the pale light of the comets and the gleam of the electric globes had been the only light to illuminate the *Sannah*.

Immediately upon finishing the meal, they all hastened into the open to enjoy the new spectacle.

The surface of the *Sannah* radiated in the brightest sunshine. Its flint-like casing, however, prevented overheating. It was like the sudden appearance of warm, sunny springtime after a long and frosty winter!

"So there are two suns, so to say!" cried a most astonished John. "Which, if I may say so without being fundamentally wrong, ought not to be the case."

All of them looked up at the blinding morning stars which certainly appeared to shine like twins, right next to each other in the sky.

Remarkable as this seemed to be, they could nevertheless not keep gazing at them for long; eyes could not endure such brilliancy.

"That's right," said Schulze. "Toliman is a double star." And he promptly launched into a lecture on double stars which was quite in place.

"The existence of such double stars," said he, "has been known only for some decades. The telescope of the astronomer had indeed, long before that, revealed that where the naked eye appears to see a single star, there may really be two or even several of them, and the cloudy glimmerings of the Milky Way dissolve under the telescope into dense masses of countless stars, so that Herschel at first assumed that under sufficiently strong instruments all star-clouds would prove to be such accumulations. Yet it is only because of their position in perspective and their infinite remoteness, that these stars appear to be so close to each other, that they dissolve into a connected image before the naked eye. In reality, they are separated from each other by vast distances and are not at all what are called double stars.

"The real double stars are two suns of a solar system, one of which encircles the other. Bessel was the first one to announce in 1847 that Sirius in Canis Major, as well as Prokyon in Canis Minor, had dusky companions.

"Twenty years later, the companion of Sirius, which Bessel had divined by mere calculation, was discovered by Alvon Clark. It looked half as big as Sirius, that is, 12 to 15 times as big as our sun, but 10,000 times weaker in light. Its distance from Sirius is equal to that of Uranus from our sun.

"From the very peculiar movements of Sirius, Bessel calculated the period of circling of its companion at 50 years; more recently it was also fixed at 50.38 years.

"The double stars encircle each other mostly in very long

ellipses, which holds only for the optical manifestation and not for the actual orbit. The period of encirclement of the double stars, in those cases where it could be determined by the visible change in their position, amounts to a minimum of 5.7 years. Double stars with a shorter period of encirclement are too close to each other for even the best telescopes to enable us to see them apart.

"But here is where the spectroscope brought us new revelations; in the spectra of certain stars, period double lines were seen which revealed with certainty that two bodies were sending light to us, of which one was moving towards us and the other away. From the shifting of these lines, the period of encirclement could be estimated by mile-seconds, even without knowing the distance from each other of the heavenly bodies in question.

"All spectroscopically discovered double stars have very short periods of encirclement, lasting from one day to three years.

"Thus the Polar star was recognized as a double star with a four-day period and only 1.86 miles a second in speed, its companion must consequently have been extremely close to it.

"Thousands of such double stars have been discovered and it can be said confidently that they seem to be the rule, and a solar system like that of the earth, with its single sun, the exception.

"But there are not only double stars, but also manifold systems, like the cloud-spots which reveal from one to four central nuclei. Systems up to ninefold have been discovered and if these numerous systems appear with comparative rarity, they may nevertheless be very numerous, for the smaller suns, luminous though they are, can no longer be visible to us at such a distance.

"A threefold star, Gamma in Andromeda, is a scintillating

jewel ranking with the most magnificent of them all. Even small telescopes show us all its beauty; its main star shines with a golden-yellow light like a topaz; its neighboring star, which is a double star, radiates a wondrously blue brilliancy, like a flashing sapphire.

"As for the double suns which we see before our very eyes, the two stars seem to be quite close to each other from here; in reality they are twenty-five times as far apart as our earth is from its sun, that is, virtually as far as our farthest planet, Neptune, is from the earth.

"Whereas Neptune moves around the sun in 165 years, the mock sun of our Toliman needs 81 years to circle its central star, which is about twice as large as the earth's sun."

"And now," said Flitmore, "may this dual-sun system of the fixed-star world reveal its divine wonders to us!"

XXXVI

A NEW EARTH

THE *Sannah* hurtled towards Toliman. The closer it came to the two suns the larger they appeared and the farther the distance between them.

But on the way towards them, there was a white-lit star that Schulze recognized through the telescope as a dark planet, which shone in the light of its two central suns and showed the phases of the moon. The Professor calculated its circumference as twice that of the earth and its period of rotation at fifty hours.

"Let that be our next objective," declared Flitmore. "After this tremendous voyage, we are all in need of a resting-place and if we find that this promising planet offers us the necessary means of life, we ought to make it our next stop-off; then we shall be secure for the time being."

"Yes, and maybe break our necks when we contrive to find our way back to our poor earth!" supplemented Munchhausen. "I am beginning to get a little homesick for our distant planet; but God alone knows whether we shall ever see it again! I confess that I should be sorry indeed if it were to remain beyond our reach forever."

"It would be too bad," admitted Schulze, "if only because we should then be unable to enrich the knowledge of astonished humanity with the report of our magnificent discoveries. It might be centuries before anybody would think up Lord Flitmore's invention again and establish contact between the earth and the planets of its solar system. On the other hand, I am not at all in a hurry with the homeward journey; for I have an idea that the most wonderful discoveries are still ahead."

"Do you believe that the planet we are approaching might be inhabited?" asked Mitzie, who would have been happier than any one else to meet human beings again, and who kept thinking with horror of Saturn, and no less of Mars, where only monsters and repulsive creatures populated an otherwise desolate world.

"Everything is possible," the Professor rejoined, emphatically. "The great geometrician Lambert said that since the microscope reveals that everything on earth is inhabited, then everything in the universe which is at all habitable, must be so also."

"Yes, whatever is habitable!" interjected Hank. "We saw that on Mars and on Saturn, although rational beings seem to have died out on the former and not yet to have come into existence on the latter. But we will have to assume that an infinite variety of conditions must prevail on the countless planets: on one of them, life may be made impossible by an unbearable heat, on the other, by inhuman cold; one may have too abrupt a climatic variation, another, an unfavorable atmosphere; and so on and so forth."

"To be sure! We admit all that," opined Schulze. "But all that does not exclude life, nor the emergence of rational beings. Just think of how on the earth already there are living things capable of enduring unharmed the most terrific degrees of heat or cold. Formerly, the opinion prevailed that the presence of life in the great sea depths was impossible because of the tremendous hydrostatic pressure. Today, it is known that a very manifold life exists at the bottom of the sea and that the deep-sea creatures are remarkably adapted to the conditions under which their life is lived. This is why Lambert declares that living creatures on the various celestial bodies will be formed in accordance with the prevailing conditions, and there is simply nothing to be said against that."

"At any rate, Lambert has unfolded a daring dream," said Flitmore. "I certainly don't want to say anything against it, for even the wildest dreams may prove to be realities. He seems to have had in mind that after death, people are provided with bodies which permit them a new life on other planets, and that they then migrate to the place most suitable for them. For example, he thought that comets were the most suitable spot for astronomers and that centuries there would be as brief as hours are to us."

"I can't say that he's wrong," answered the Professor: "Is it not owing to a comet that we are able to penetrate into the fixed-star world? What an inspiring thought for a stargazer, to travel with a comet through the impenetrable depths of the universe on a never-ending voyage and be able to make ever new discoveries, to see close at hand what he hardly dared dream of on earth!

"Klein shows himself more sober when he says that in all probability it is only a small proportion of planets that are populated by rational beings; but since the number of planets runs into hundreds of millions, it would probably be a pretty considerable number. Moreover, he says further: 'Many of them may be populated by beings who far excel us in intellect. Here we may give our phantasy free rein and be convinced that science has no proofs either for or against the correctness of our visions.' "

"And in that connection it should be kept in mind," Flitmore intervened, "that Klein takes into account only such heavenly bodies as would supply human beings like ourselves with the necessary means of life."

"Those are the only kind that concern us for the moment," said Schulze. "In any case, we cannot at the present time pay a visit to any planet which does not permit us to live and breathe on it; and though it be populated by creatures ever so wonderfully adapted, it is out of the question for us to make their acquaintance so long as we ourselves are lacking the necessary adaptation."

"At the most, we might observe them from the *Sannah*," Hank declared.

"Not a bad idea," was the Professor's approving reply. "At all events, many great astronomers believed in the habitability of the planets even of the earth's solar system."

The next day, they had come so close to the new planet that the mountains could be recognized by the shadow-spots and the peaks at its rim, rising in places to very great heights. Sparkling areas of great size told of seas, and towards evening they saw the coloring of the land, mirrored lakes, and rivers gleaming like silver.

Flitmore found it necessary, by means of a partial switching on of the centrifugal current, to slow down the approach, which was taking place at a growing speed; for he had switched off the current so that the force of attraction of the new planet might operate upon the *Sannah*.

He took but little rest, while Hank let the World-Ship fall and rise in turn. Then Flitmore relieved the young man and himself took the final measures to insure a smooth and safe landing.

When Flitmore thought that the *Sannah* had already sunk deeply enough into the atmosphere of the planet, he turned on the current and went outside. Had the current been switched off, it would have been dangerous to go outside, for then it would no longer be the central point of the *Sannah* but that of the planet which would operate as the centre of gravity, and a fall from the World-Ship would ensue.

As Lord Flitmore stepped out, the *Sannah*, under the influence of the centrifugal power, still rose at a moderate speed.

It was a delightful breeze that fanned him. It seemed to Flitmore that it had something alluring and invigorating, unlike any air that his lungs had ever before breathed. An indescribable joyousness filled him as he inhaled this balsamic ether which seemed permeated with a strange, wondrously pleasant perfume.

There was no doubt that this was no longer the ordinary air-envelope of the *Sannah*, it was an entirely new and unknown atmosphere which could, however, be inhaled without fear.

After Flitmore had ascertained this, he hurried back, however much he would have liked to linger without. The landing now had to be accomplished with speed and caution; then this delightful ether could be enjoyed to the full.

Flitmore awakened Schulze.

"I should like you, Mr. Professor," he said, "to turn the current on and off according to the bell-signals I give you. I plan to go to the observation net of the Antipode room, from which I can survey the landscape below. Then I can see to it that we land on a suitable spot."

When Flitmore had taken up his post, he saw that the World-Ship was hovering over a mountain-peak, whose tip was now so close that the surrounding landscape could no longer be seen beyond it. Only in the far-off distance could he discern hill-bedecked plains and vast seas, without being able to recognize smaller details.

He reflected whether it might not be better to rise again until the rotation of the planet should bring level land under the *Sannah*; yet, was it not of small import where they landed? And beneath him smiled such a heavenly, enchanting lake, encircled by fairy-like shores of luminous beauty, that he thought there could hardly be a lovelier spot than the one which the Creator had brought beneath his eyes.

So he gave the signal to turn on the current only to the extent needed to soften the fall, and a few minutes later the *Sannah* sank down smoothly upon a flowery meadow on the shores of the lake.

The window of the Antipode room touched the ground; Flitmore could see no more, a barely perceptible tremor indicated the smoothly accomplished landing: the World-Ship had settled firmly and rested securely upon the strange planet.

Flitmore now ran upstairs and found the whole company aroused and full of eagerness to see what would be revealed to them.

XXXVII

THE MARVELS OF EDEN

"AH! Glorious! Superb! Wonderful!" exclamations of enchantment rang from every one's lips as the air, fresh and yet filled with an almost dizzying perfume, flowed through the opened hatchway.

The whole company hurried out to climb down the rope ladder; and the landscape that smiled up exercised such a charm over them that they really did not know whether it was a dream or a reality.

In addition, they were all overcome by the rare feeling that the descent required a wholly unusual exertion; it would really have resembled a mountain climb, difficult and wearisome, were it not that the rich ether they breathed had filled them with such virility and overbrimming desire to try their new strength, that every effort brought them a sort of ecstasy and put every thought of exhaustion out of their minds.

Munchhausen, the last to descend, felt these strange, inspiring feelings most plainly, as was comprehensible from his immoderate bulk.

"I am floating!" he exclaimed in rapture. "I feel lighter than a feather! In the heyday of my youth I never felt so fresh. I am more than rejuvenated, I am reborn. I feel so light that I can scarcely walk; I feel as if I could fly!"

They had to laugh when they looked up at his great figure and heard him talking of lightness and flight. Schulze called up to him: "Indeed! A mountain like you, Captain, taking flight is a positively priceless thought! Excuse my uncourteous merriment, but I can't help it. No! If Lady Flitmore were to float away, it would be highly regrettable and painful to us, but still not astonishing in view of the lightness we all seem to feel here. But we aren't getting any gray hairs yet from the danger of your floating."

"Now, there!" growled the Captain in comic indignation as he stepped down on the ground. "You still remain unreasonable, unintelligent, and skeptical, you old Professor! Just wait and see if you don't live to view the miracle of Captain Hugo von Munchhausen floating out of your sight like a gay sylph, to your shame and dismay, and no matter how much you would like to hold him back."

The Captain as a gay sylph! This idea was too delicious not to arouse a general roar of laughter.

Munchhausen joined in with the others, but nevertheless raised another protest. "You don't think I could fly, just because of my rotund figure? You see how little logic people have! For what is rounder and fuller than a balloon? Does that prevent it from rising and floating about, eh?"

"Yes, Captain," replied Hank. "But you aren't inflated with hydrogen gas!"

"This hulk of mine can't be holding much besides air at the moment," asserted the rogue. "At least, I feel myself pretty empty and starved, even though it is a shame to admit it in view of this celestial landscape. At any rate, I shall be able to esteem all its charms to the utmost only when I have put a substantial breakfast under my belt. Hey, John! You haven't forgotten to bring along the food?"

"No, honorable Mr. Captain," John hastened to assure him. "How could I permit myself to be guilty of such a neglect of duty? I have already lit the semaphore."

He pointed to the pot-bellied samovar, the Russian tea kettle.

" 'Semaphore' is not so bad!" laughed Schulze. "You certainly are an extremely handy chap, John! A semaphore is a telegraphic signal device, and a samovar is not quite that."

"Ah, Mr. Professor," Rieger apologized, "I can't remember these Chinese terms so well, for the Chinese language was not taught in my school and therefore you can understand why I now say 'semaphore' or 'samopher,' which do sound pretty much alike."

The educated servant knew that tea comes from China and therefore he believed that the strange name of the teakettle must be Chinese.

"He isn't so far from being right with his 'semaphore,' " said Flitmore, in defense of John. "The rising steam from the boiling kettle is truly a telegraphic signal which announces from afar a delicious beverage."

Soon they were all seated with steaming teacups and spicy cakes, although, aside from the Captain, they scarcely felt any physical needs out of sheer fascination at the marvels surrounding them.

Here was the meadow on whose soft carpet they had pitched camp.

"A soft carpet" was no mere phrase here: the finely feathered grasses with their transparent green were, in fact, as soft as down.

And the flowers of this exquisite meadow! They shone in every color; but what gave them an especial charm was that unequalled delicacy, which put to shame even the spring blossoms of earth.

So transparent were these blossoms that the background could be plainly seen glimmering through them as through the finest colored glass. But as the light fell upon them, it was thrown back in the most delicate shades, so that a color-ful cone of radiance seemed to spread out from them.

This curious, yet so remarkably fascinating, transpar-ency seemed to invest the whole plant-world of the blissful planet with its singularity. There were bushes with splen-did large flowers like hanging bells, swaying like plates and saucers, like small balloons or soap-bubbles stretching up-wards in round, oval, cylindrical, or composite forms; in the background rose forests of fruit-laden trees, some with slim, others with gnarled trunks, their graceful limbs swinging low with leaves in all imaginable patterns; and all things blinked and glittered where they threw back the light, and appeared thoroughly transparent where the beams of light shot through.

These transparent forms were often like crystals and prisms, and broke up the light into all the colors of the rain-bow. From the color of the object, together with the color of the rays shining through it, came the most wondrous tints and the most delicate combinations, so that even the deepest shadow gladdened the eye with the myriad richness of its colors.

And then the lake, smiling up at the sky! A blue of a tint not to be seen on earth, an aura of sapphire. Hard by the shore, it was so transparent that each of the many-colored grains of sand at the bottom could be discerned. But where the color-beams, which crossed and fused in the air, were re-flected in its waters, you would find areas of the most varie-gated shading till the eye was bewildered and knew not which was loveliest, only to be riveted again by the golden sheen, the silver shimmer, the rosy aura here and there, unable to turn itself away from the fairy-like beauty of the scene.

But turn itself away it must: the islands and islets, the marvellous curve of the shore, the coves and headlands, the banks on the other side, the hill-ledges, and the imposing declivities with their jagged combs and unusual forms—all these commanded its attention and drew forth ever new exclamations of wonderment.

Every moment somebody in the company believed he had discovered something new which surpassed everything seen before. They called each other's attention to many things, and eye and heart gloried in an uninterrupted holiday of rapturous enjoyment.

"Eden, Eden!" exclaimed Flitmore, won away from his customary reserved calm. "What other name could we find to give this paradise? And if the whole planet were otherwise a cheerless, terrifying wasteland, this one spot would justify us in giving it the name of the region that held the garden of paradise."

"Right you are," said the Professor in turn. "Eden it shall be!"

Hours passed before the round of sight-seeing and admiration was interrupted by Hank's proposal to undertake an excursion upon the planet, since they had all had sufficient rest.

All were agreed, for a youthful enterprising eagerness, as well as inquisitiveness, inspired even the older men. Only the Captain raised objection, drawing forth his watch.

"We have been sitting here a good four hours," said he. "The time indeed passed swiftly, for we have enough to look at and enjoy. But it did leave traces on my stomach. It's a far cry from breakfast and I vote for a luncheon."

"An incorrigible eater!" roared the Professor. But Flitmore said: "Our friend is right, let us first satisfy the inner man, so that we may then extend our voyage of discovery that much further. It would be too bad if a feeling of hunger compelled us to interrupt it or even to turn back."

So the luncheon was prepared and served amid constant merriment and in a very sprightly mood, a mood that might very justly have been attributed to the wonderful air and the magnificent landscape.

XXXVIII

CURIOUS LAWS OF NATURE

JOHN was the first to appease his appetite, while the Captain was still chewing away.

"I should find it very interesting," began Flitmore's servant, "to ascertain whether the wood of our earth sinks in water here, as appeared to be the case on Saturn."

With that, he threw a stick of wood far out into the stream which seemed to form the outlet of the lake, for they were located at its extreme end.

Their eyes followed the stick. But the greatest astonishment was reflected in their faces, and Schulze sprang to his feet with the cry: "But *here* is where all science *does* come to an end!"

The wood had not sunk, but it floated back upon the stream, straight into the lake; that is, it was floating upstream!

"Is such an optical illusion possible?" asked Hank. "The stream does appear to have a slope, and yet it proves to be an affluent to the lake and not an outlet; the ground then must rise there and not descend, as it appears to do."

The Professor had stepped right to the edge of the stream.

"It is no optical illusion," he said, shaking his head. "We have a riddle before us here: the stream undoubtedly has a slope, and a pretty sharp one from its mouth, but its waters actually flow into the lake; in other words, it is flowing uphill. This is simply contrary to all the laws of nature, but it is a fact just the same!"

The others came closer and convinced themselves that

what the Professor said was so: they saw how the bottom sloped appreciably at the mouth of the stream and they could plainly see the flowing of the waters which ran in the opposite direction. Further attempts with leaves and branches, which were thrown into the stream, only confirmed this.

"That's enough to bereave you of your senses!" cried the Professor, who could not calm himself. "How are you going to explain a thing like that?"

"Let us abandon explanations for the moment," declared Flitmore. "Let us rather accustom ourselves right away to the idea that the natural laws of our earth-world do not hold equally for all worlds."

Munchhausen alone had remained seated; he could not leave the rest of his meal in the lurch just because a little water was flowing upstream, which didn't constitute any particular danger and therefore left him fairly cold.

Schulze, in his perplexed excitement over the hair-raising wonder, for which he thought everybody should be forgetting everything else, grew dreadfully indignant at Munchhausen's unfathomable indifference.

He therefore shouted somewhat peevishly at the Captain: "How can you remain seated there so calmly, eating away as if it were the most natural thing in the world? If you stuff yourself with such gobs, you'll end up by not being able to take a step."

"Oh," rejoined Munchhausen placidly and rose to his feet; "not walk any more, is that what you mean? I can hop, dance, and jump, if you want me to. The food hasn't made me a bit heavier, which can easily be understood in view of my moderation; on the contrary, I feel myself lighter than before, now that I again have something under my belt. Just look at this!"

And in order to show how light he felt, the stout old fellow took a leap into the air, which was pretty risky for a man of his bulk.

Schulze looked on, frozen with terror, Flitmore watched with serious mien, but Hank, Mitzie, and John broke out into convulsive laughter. Such a spectacle outdid anything comical they had ever seen.

Munchhausen had leaped a good ten feet high! Majestically he floated in the air, this human globe, and slowly settled to the ground again.

Then Flitmore, without changing a muscle in his face, permitted himself a witticism: "You have become the merest soap-bubble, Captain," he said, "if only you don't burst on us!"

But Munchhausen came to earth again speechless; he looked about on all sides, rubbed his eyes and was obviously of the opinion that he was in a dream.

"I have it!" cried Hank. "Haven't you read Jules Verne's book, *Hector Servadoc*, Mr. Professor? A very similar phenomenon is described there, which is to be explained simply by the slighter power of attraction. Obviously the planet Eden has a very slight power of attraction, which considerably diminishes the force of gravity, almost eliminating it. This might also explain the enigmatic conduct of the stream, at least to an extent."

"My young friend," said Schulze, "you yourself will not persist in this explanation if you reflect a little; be the force of attraction and gravity ever so slight, water will nevertheless not run uphill. Besides, the force of attraction of our planet cannot be so slight: to judge by its mass, it should be greater than the earth's, although I will admit that we know very little, if anything, about what the force of gravity really is, and can consequently build nothing upon the cor-

Majestically he floated in the air, this human globe, and slowly settled to the ground again.

rectness of such deductions in spite of many seeming proofs. But I would sooner believe that all of us, because of our long stay in the *Sannah,* are so heavily laden with centrifugal power that our weight is thereby almost eliminated."

The Professor did not, of course, believe in such a possibility himself, and it did not make the conduct of the stream one whit more comprehensible. But as a man of science, he had to contribute some sort of an explanation and if, in such a case, no weighty explanation is at hand, then even the feeblest one must suffice, so as to soothe the scientific conscience which, whenever possible, allows nothing to remain unexplained.

Just then Dick and Bobs appeared, returning from a voyage of discovery which they had been making in the vicinity on their own account, having a splendid time with the magnificent fruits of Eden's forests.

But look there! The chimpanzees were flying through the air, for they leaped from sixteen to twenty feet high and must have been putting a good eighty feet behind them with every jump.

"Holla! there's something jolly for you!" cried Hank merrily. "If we are all laden with the same centrifugal power as the chimpanzees and the Captain, then we ought to be able to do a remarkable Indian dance!" And immediately he took a leap which brought him some twelve feet high in the air above the heads of the others.

It was uncommonly funny to look at him, startling and incredible though the whole thing seemed; but it was a great temptation to each to find out for himself whether he were endowed with the same ability to fly. So John and Schulze also made the attempt, and even Lady Flitmore could not resist it and, gathering up her skirts, leaped into the air.

"Oh, how wonderful!" she cried.

As a matter of fact, there could hardly be a more delightful feeling than this easy, effortless rising into the balsamic air and then the soft downward float. All physical weight seemed to vanish and you felt as if you were a free, disembodied spirit.

The Englishman alone stood still and watched, with visible satisfaction, the successful attempts at flying made by his comrades and his wife; in the meantime, he arranged his photographic apparatus and took one snapshot after another.

Munchhausen also participated zealously in this merry skipping, after having convinced himself that it was no dream, but that like all the others he actually possessed a new and fascinating talent. The voyagers found his antics especially amusing, and often they remained standing in order to enjoy the comical picture of the flying barrel, while the generous Captain never took in bad part their hearty, but never jeering or malicious laughter.

When all of them paused for a while, Munchhausen cried: "Ho there, my estimable Flitmore! Are you the only one who considers it beneath his dignity to participate in such a splendid ballet? That won't do! Come off your high horse and get up into the air of this paradise! For a good quarter of an hour we have been offering for your entertainment and merriment a spectacle such as was never seen before and you keep on snapping your fingers. Now we'd like to feast our eyes on your jumps."

"Yes, darling!" said Mitzie. "Try it just once. I tell you, there cannot be a more wonderful feeling."

With all his dignity, Flitmore was neither a pedant nor a prig, and he was far from refusing to enter into any gay performance. He did not have to be asked twice, but executed a series of such remarkable leaps as earned him the approval of the onlookers.

"But now," Munchhausen uttered the warning, "after these exercises, which are so beneficial to the digestion, we really ought to start out on the exploring trip we had planned."

Remembering the fateful occurrences on *Saturn*, John took the precaution of closing the door of the Pole room, through which they had left the *Sannah*. They did not consider it necessary to leave a guard behind; nobody was to be excluded from the journey which all surmised would be so interesting.

When the stream was crossed, an enchanting prospect unrolled before the eyes of the travellers.

To the right, the mountains continued in a long chain of barren rock, overgrown summits and slopes, gradually subsiding in the distance to low hill-ranges which melted into the horizon.

From this side, the stream moved up in a smooth incline.

Straight ahead, the mountain chain declined in steep slopes which did, however, permit descent, if made with caution.

To the left, the rocky walls fell perpendicularly, for the most part, to bottomless depths.

Schulze estimated the heights on which they stood at from twenty to twenty-three thousand feet above sea-level.

"I doubt," he said, "whether we can reach the lowlands in three marching days."

"We are in no hurry," rejoined Flitmore.

"Of course not, if our provisions last," admitted the Professor.

"We certainly have taken along enough for four days," said Lord Flitmore, "yet I have no doubt that the forests which lie here and there along our route will offer us an abundance of edible food."

"That may certainly be assumed and we shall soon be in a position to find out whether or not it is so," Schulze acknowledged. "On the other hand, I fear that we shall be submitted there to a pretty unbearable heat, for the temperature at this height is strangely mild."

"We shall see about that, also," retorted Mitzie; "right now, such considerations should not prevent us from undertaking the descent."

Meanwhile the travellers let their gaze roam over the distances; but first, a phenomenon, comparatively nearby, aroused Hank's attention and admiration.

"Above the declivities yonder," he said and pointed to the left, "a mighty waterfall is plunging down; and I thought that Eden's waters flowed uphill!"

"True enough!" cried Schulze. "The waters are roaring and raging, foaming and shooting to the bottom just as on the earth! Here is where all science *does* come to an end!"

Munchhausen laughed heartily: "There we have it again!" he said. "Hardly an hour ago the Professor was distracted because a stream was flowing *uphill*, and now it is already incomprehensible to him how one can flow *downhill!*"

"Yes," said Schulze in an aggrieved voice, "it does challenge reason: if the laws of nature are to be reversed here, then at least they ought to be so in all cases. But one time this way and another time another way, that's simply inadmissible scientifically."

"Well now! Then here is where your science goes to pieces completely," laughed the Captain.

In the distance they could discern hills and valleys, rivers and lakes. Among other things, a very large lake with several islands.

At the left, the sea-coast was not very distant; in part with precipitous shores, in part with gently sloping ones, it extended to the horizon, through bays and fjords, headlands and promontories, outlined in wondrous beauty.

There were also several islands rising out of the sea, some of them very large, and many with massive hills of astonishing height, which stood up threateningly like dark giants.

Snowpeaks were nowhere to be seen.

The mountain ranges and hills of the flatlands seemed to be well wooded or covered with soft green mats. Through the spyglass they could distinguish woodlands and meadowlands, and sometimes broad prairies. Huge stretches looked as if they might be cultivated land; but this could not be ascertained with any certainty from so great a distance.

No traces of human habitation were to be found; but there were remarkable rock formations in the valleys and on the plains, as well as on some of the heights: boulders, towers, peaks and cliffs, which rose singly but were usually so close to each other that they gave the impression of villages and towns.

Oriented thus far, our friends began the descent in a straight line, for at the right the mountain-chain extended beyond their vision, while at the left it stood perpendicular.

Here it was possible to descend in a straight line; but caution had to be exercised, for there was no lack of abrupt declivities.

As they began the downward climb, they again observed the feeling they had experienced in the morning, when they left the *Sannah* by rope-ladder. It seemed to them as if every step meant a special effort, as if some invisible obstacle had to be overcome, yes, as if it was not really downhill they were going, but uphill; yet their efforts did not tire them out. Rather they produced a peculiar satisfaction, as if here exertion did the rested body as much good as, elsewhere, rest did the exhausted body.

"Captain, be on your guard!" Schulze suddenly cried out in concern. "Your foolhardiness will yet cause your fall, your belly is getting the better of you!"

"Bah!" Munchhausen called back from his position at the edge of a rocky wall, which hung over a depth of some hundred and sixty feet. "I don't feel a touch of dizziness, although usually I have not been immune to it, especially since I have taken on weight and age. Dizziness is really something an old sea-dog ought to be ashamed of, and I am happy at being free of it here. Besides, my belly will never get the better of me, it is as light as a balloon, as you ought to know by now."

Just then the incautious man made an awkward movement, which was fatal in such a spot; in fact, he slipped and plunged into space.

A shriek of terror rang from all lips, only Lord Flitmore remained quiet; but the deadly pallor which covered his face revealed that he was no less horror-stricken than the others.

The plunge into space was the first thought to grip the minds of the terrified onlookers; in reality, there was no plunge, but Munchhausen, who had grown dreadfully pale when he lost his footing, floated softly downward and in about twenty seconds landed at the foot of the rock, without even stubbing his toe.

Flitmore was the first to find tongue. "How hard it is for us to get rid of our deeply rooted old notions!" he said. "Didn't we find out only a short while ago how lightly the air here bears our bodies, how swiftly we rise and how gradual is the coming-down? And yet we were unable to draw the proper conclusions from this."

"Yes, but this is something quite different," asserted his wife. "To jump up from level ground doesn't look dangerous, but falling from a height is another thing."

"And yet there is no real difference, for we jumped so high that under earthly conditions the fall back to the ground would have been disastrous," countered Flitmore.

"Yes, we are a lot of simpletons," Schulze confirmed him. "Here we are, tormenting ourselves with a difficult descent which, while it isn't wearying, is extremely annoying, when we ought to have known how easy it would be here to float down. Well now, let's be on our way!"

The Professor was to learn that Lady Flitmore was not entirely wrong in her observation; for as he left the less abrupt ledge and touched the rim of the steep rock-wall, he did not dare to make the leap into space. The new knowledge could not so quickly overcome the fear of such a risk.

Here Flitmore came forward and without a moment's hesitation took the decisive step. And look! he floated down as gently as the Captain had before him.

Of course! It was bound to be thus!

Mitzie followed her husband, as she would have done even had the matter been more hazardous.

Schulze was now ashamed of his weakness and he hopped out even before Hank and John, together with Dick and Bobs, had taken the chance.

They were soon all gathered around Munchhausen, shaking his hand in congratulation, as if it had been a deliberate audacity which caused him to set them the worthy example.

XXXIX

A NEW ANIMAL WORLD

THE descent now proceeded very swiftly, accomplished by leaps into the air and glides from steep terraces, almost like those of birds in flight.

They were pretty far down when the first halt was made, not in order to rest, for nobody felt a trace of fatigue, but because the Captain declared that it was again high time for a little snack.

Besides this, Schulze also requested a halt, for the first forest had been reached and he desired to get a closer glimpse of its plant and animal life. The beautiful bird-songs and other sounds that emerged from the forest made it clear that living things existed there, whereas the blissful valley on the heights, despite its marvelous beauty, had appeared not to contain any living creatures; at least, none had been seen.

The tree trunks which the Professor first examined upon entering the forest, showed a firm and tough structure; but whether the material of which they were composed could be called wood, was very doubtful, for it was transparent like resin or amber, or rather about as transparent as these; otherwise it was as fibrous as wood and even revealed layers like rings, although the bark consisted merely of a thin, tough skin which was quite translucent.

The coloring of these trunks ran from a golden yellow to a dark brown, from crystal-clear to silvery white.

The leaves for the most part were green in the most variegated shadings, also yellow or ruddy and not essentially different from those of the trees of earth; only they were also transparent and of very graceful forms, worked out in the most intricate patterns.

There was no lack of shadows, despite the translucency of the foliage and the trunks. The density of the tree-tops weakened the light at many points, in such a way that only a feeble shimmer of color played upon the ground, like a deep but multi-colored shadow in comparison to the lighter spots.

There were also pine trees and they were of a peculiar charm since their fine needles, which looked like glass, showed all the colors of the rainbow. You could see red, yellow, rose-colored, orange-red, violet, golden, silvery, sky-blue and dark blue firs and pines, if these earthly names may be applied to the similar species on Eden.

No tree was without edible fruits; these too were transparent and thoroughly relishable, as the chimpanzees proved by devouring them, seeds and all.

The fruits were of the most varied sizes and colors; from the size of huge pumpkins to that of a plum, all the intermediate stages were represented. In the large fruits, the seed looked like a cocoanut. For the most part, these pits were floury and very nourishing; they were a perfect substitute for biscuits and bread and had a strong and pleasant flavor.

The fruits were delicious and satisfied both thirst and hunger. Some of them were as sweet as sugar, others were not sweet at all, but all were aromatic and remarkably pleasant to the taste. The pine trees bore edible cones which were fairly dry and reminded them of chocolate such as had never been tasted on earth.

Finally, our friends discovered that even the branches and leaves of the trees and shrubs were edible. This too they learned from the zeal with which Dick and Bobs gnawed away at them.

Munchhausen was particularly enthusiastic over the discovery of one, or rather of several kinds of fruit, which he immediately called "grog fruits" and was thenceforward able to discern with a remarkable botanical penetration. They were actually berries, but giant berries like oranges, which grew on low shrubs. Both the stems and leaves of these shrubs were warm, almost hot, to the touch; the berries contained a really hot, fragrant juice with a distinct aroma, very strong in scent and taste, as if it were actually grog or punch. But it did not intoxicate; rather it had an unusually invigorating and fortifying effect.

The Captain distinguished between the grog-fruits that were strong and those that were not so strong, and he favored the former by far.

To be sure, our friends did not find out these enjoyments all at once, the number and variety of the fruits was too great. But it was only a comparatively brief time before they had tasted everything and could now make whatever choice was to their liking. They no longer thought of touching any other foods than those which could be had in Eden's woods and forests, and which, it appeared, nothing could excel in any respect.

Of poisonous plants or any other kind of harmful growths, there were apparently none to be found on this blessed planet.

Right at the entrance to the forest they also made their acquaintance with its insect and bird life.

The former revealed nothing repulsive or horrible. There were harmless beetles and reptiles, moths and butterflies, distinguished for their lovely forms as well as their beautiful colors and, what was particularly notable, they exhibited a transparency similar to that of the plants and blossoms. They glittered, shimmered and iridesced, sparkled, glistened and vibrated like luminous jewels.

The birds were unfeathered and had only a parti-colored coat of down which was, however, vividly tinted and wondrously lovely; their wings too were unfeathered and their structure might best be compared to that of a butterfly, except that the wings also were covered with down and, when at rest, were not outstretched but folded to the body, which had the same curvature.

Where human beings could almost fly, these birds must surely be able to rise to great heights with these simple instruments of flight.

All in all, the bird and insect life of Eden was indeed singular; but it did not seem so utterly diffcrent from that of the earth, and above all, it had nothing repulsive, sinister or dangerous about it, but rather such attractive features as to gladden eye and heart.

Especially inspiriting was the uncommonly lovely singing of the birds, which out-rivalled anything that the nightingale or any other feathered songster on earth could do. What melodies rang out here, inspiring and engaging their souls! Each bird was his own composer, trilling his individual concert, master of the whole scale, but never in discord with any of the others. It seemed as if one stood forth alone while the others accompanied it in a harmonious undertone.

Our friends had listened for some time to these fascinating warblings, munching the while their delicious fruits and admiring the living jewels which crawled and hopped about the translucent moss or whirred from flower to flower, when suddenly Mitzie uttered a low shriek.

They all turned to her, for till then every one had occupied himself with his own observations.

But what was this they now saw!

A large quadruped, more like a huge lion than anything else, had padded softly upon the scene and without further ado laid his mighty mane upon her lap!

And Lady Flitmore? She was stroking it!

The first horror which the appearance of the great beast naturally aroused had elicited the faint outcry from her lips; she had first noticed the lion, as our friends later termed him because of the similarity, when he appeared before her, and before she could leap to her feet or think twice about the matter, the animal had already stretched out on the ground and nestled his head in her lap.

When he now gazed up at her with large, intelligent, soft, harmless eyes, she was pervaded with such calmness and so great a liking for the fine, proud and apparently kindly creature, that she began involuntarily to stroke and fondle the majestic head.

Flitmore, as cool as he always was in the most dangerous moments, rose quite slowly so as not to frighten the beast, whose reputedly wild nature might conceivably break out.

He took the precaution of drawing his revolver, and moved softly towards his wife; the lion raised his head.

"Let him alone!" Mitzie begged her husband.

"I won't touch him if he is not dangerous," Lord Flitmore assured her.

And he thereupon put his left hand on the lion's head.

The animal only gazed at him.

The Englishman now gripped him under the jaws, always prepared to shoot a bullet into his head as soon as he showed wicked intent.

But the animal proved to be understanding and tractable. A slight pressure sufficed to raise him and a gentle shove from the side caused him to turn about quite docilely and disappear again into the forest.

"Oh," said Mitzie, "what a relief!"

"I can well believe it," remarked Schulze. "I should think that you would feel relieved at getting rid of this dangerous beast so easily; we were all trembling and quaking for you."

"No," said Mitzie, "you misunderstand me, Professor; this gentle creature inspired a little terror in me, but only for a moment, before I saw the harmlessness in his eyes. No, it was not that! I meant that I was relieved to find that the beasts on this planet do not seem to be so different from those on the earth. You know, on Mars and on Saturn the world seemed so dismal, and that was still in our own solar system. I had already reconciled myself, without being at all happy about it, to having the remote world of fixed stars turn out to be even more unusual and ghastly."

"It's lucky," thought Munchhausen, "so far as we can conclude from what we have seen, that the animal world of Eden isn't very vicious, bloodthirsty or dangerous."

"Let us not lose our caution," warned Flitmore. "This time we came off well; but nobody can guarantee that we won't encounter something more serious."

"I'm no longer afraid of the lions of Eden," the Lady declared confidently. "That would be base ingratitude and contemptible distrust."

In wandering farther through the forest they met with many more representatives of the mammal kingdom; yet all seemed like harmless enough creatures, marked by a striking beauty and gentleness. But this was not due merely to the color and splendor of the hide and the grace and elegance of the limbs, but particularly to their features, which immediately attracted attention by their intelligent expression and uncommonly friendly look. There were animals which reminded them of the stag, the deer, the zebra, the antelope, the giraffe, the horse, of hounds, cats and wild boars, or other earthly species. Not one of them seemed to know what fear was.

Suddenly John stood frozen in his tracks.

Before him swayed a large serpent with a remarkable, glittering body. He had stepped upon it and now expected the bite of the reptile at any moment. It twisted and turned, baring its sharp teeth.

Dazed with terror, he did not even think of stepping back so as to free the snake from his weight and perhaps escape its revenge.

The luminously streaked body now entwined itself around his legs and down again; but the serpent did not bite, it only moaned.

A cry from Flitmore finally brought John to his senses. He sprang aside, and the reptile, freed from the weight of his heavy foot, glided noiselessly and slowly away.

"Really, even the most poisonous creature seems to have lost its terrors here," exclaimed Schulze. "You should run into such a serpent on the earth, John! You'd never come out of it unharmed."

The company now walked out into the glittering savanna; but they halted in astonishment, fear and, at the same time, fascination.

What monstrous animals were these, grazing before their eyes! Mammoth-like elephants, the unicorns of fabulous memory, buffalos and giraffes, camels, huge bears, spotted and streaked tiger-cats, panthers and leopards, lions and wolves, sheep and goats—all meandered about amongst each other and peacefully chewed the translucent grasses or reached up for fruits from the high shrubs and trees at the edge of the forest.

What a multifarious herd this was, scattered over the vast plain!

These creatures showed such a striking similarity to the
designated earthly species that our friends were not in the
least perplexed about giving them the corresponding names;
on the other hand, they did reveal a number of distinctly different features, particularly in that they seemed to represent
a higher, nobler stage, or as Mitzie expressed it: it was the
animal life of the earth, in part with its extinct species, in an
idealized, perfected form.

"Shall we risk marching through them?" asked Munchhausen.

"Forward!" commanded Lord Flitmore. "We are threatened with no danger from these beasts."

But Hank remarked: "This planet increasingly justifies
the name we gave it at first sight. Is it not a paradise beyond
the dreams of the wildest imagination?"

XL

A NIGHT IN PARADISE

LIKE a fairy dream were the wanderings of our friends through this flower-laden garden of Eden.

They soon lost the slightest fear of touching even the large and carnivorous-looking animals, stroking them, to which they responded understandingly and with a certain gentleness, be it that they softly licked the friendly hand or that they bent head or trunk in recognition of these strange friends. Even the nimblest, the most muscular and massive of these creatures restrained themselves so carefully in their movements, that you could see in this a conscious care not to inflict injury.

Had any one of these mammoths wanted to give vent to some temperamental show of spirit with his trunk, as he might towards his comrades or kin, then even Munchhausen's solid bulk would have been hurled to the ground in a twinkling.

But all these animals knew how to behave themselves.

The second sun was beginning to set—the first had disappeared beyond the horizon an hour ago—when it occurred to our friends to pitch camp.

The fruits of the forest had so lastingly appeased hunger and thirst that even the Captain had not once emphasized the need of a meal during the whole long journey, which had been accomplished mostly in leaps. And he was one of the most zealous jumpers, getting the greatest fun out of sailing over the high, broad backs of the largest colossi.

Even during camp-pitching he showed himself still unwearied of engaging in this exhilarating sport; for right around the camping ground wandered a few huge mammoths.

John and Hank set up the tent, while the others watched the circus performance Munchhausen was giving, more for his own amusement than for the entertainment of his companions.

Loud *Bravos!* and stormy applause rewarded his most successful leaps.

The star number of the performance, however, was a trick which he did towards the end, and quite unintentionally, for it was not called for in his program!

He had taken a position behind an enormous bull elephant and jumped up in order to leap over the full length of the colossus.

But at that very moment, the idea entered the mind of the mammoth to take a leap into the air himself, and thus it happened that in the midst of his joy-ride Munchhausen landed on the back of the sailing animal.

For one second he rode through the air like a genuine circus rider; but his feet had no firm hold, he swayed, and would have fallen down head first had he not had the presence of mind to spread his short legs so that he sat like a horseman athwart his unusual steed.

It was a grand picture! Lord Flitmore did not fail to perpetuate it on a photographic plate.

"One colossus upon another!" Schulze cried merrily.

John and Hank left off work in order to enjoy the incomparable spectacle.

Gazing about him proudly, as if he had bridled a dragon and deliberately mounted it for a joy-ride, the Captain remained seated upon the mighty pachyderm like a globe, his short legs stretched out straight, unable to grip the broad back of the monster with them.

Friend mammoth now landed, and with an agility nobody would have believed him capable of, Munchhausen leaped to his feet and with an elegant curve swung himself down to the ground again. Merriment and laughter and lengthy applause greeted him after this masterpiece, so that the mammoth looked about in surprise and shook its head; it must have thought: "There's something wrong with those people's upper stories!"

Mitzie now assisted John and Hank to gather fruits for the evening meal, and there was no lack of them in the vicinity. The various grog-fruits were to take the place of the usual warm tea.

Twilight fell when they sat down for their snack.

"Well," said Munchhausen, "you thought we would need three days to reach the plain, honorable Professor! We have not only reached it, but we have already crossed a goodly part of it on the first day's march."

"Nothing wonderful in that!" declared Schulze. "I was thinking of an earthly pace, afoot, step by step: but after you, my inventive old sea-dog, showed us the ingenious art of travelling by leaping and floating, we might be farther yet than we are now if we had not stopped so often along the way. Another thing to take into account is the length of the day which, I might say here and now, has lasted a full twenty-seven hours from the rising of the first sun to the setting of the second!"

"Isn't it remarkable that we don't even feel tired?" asked Mitzie. "And after such a long and eventful day! I, at least, don't feel the slightest need of rest or sleep."

"That's how we all seem to feel," said Flitmore. "I believe that we have already adapted ourselves to the conditions of the planet; perhaps the delightful air and the refreshing, invigorating strength of the fruits helped us along. We should be far more vigorous here than on the earth, since the day is twice as long here as there."

"No need for it," interjected the Captain. "Why such colossal energy, when there is nothing here to make you exert yourself or tire yourself out?"

"I am worried by only one thing," said Hank. "How are we going to pass the long night, which lasts from sunset to sunrise, if we don't feel a bit tired?"

"We shall lie down to sleep only when we feel the need of it," proposed Mitzie.

"Agreed!" the Professor assented. "We will talk and study the marvels of Eden's night until we feel that it's time to go to bed."

"Honorable Mr. Professor," John asked. "What season of the year ought we to be having here? From the blossoms, it looks like spring, but otherwise like summer; but on the other hand, if I may permit myself such an uncourteous remark, it is not so hot on the plains here as you had supposed when we were still up there."

"To tell the truth, I can't tell yet just what season it is," responded Schulze. "I suppose we are at the beginning of spring, in any event, we have virtually equal day and night."

"The Professor will excuse me, but I permit myself once more to ask if I understood rightly that the day is now four hours longer than the night."

"Certainly, my lad; but only because we have two suns here which are opposed to each other at the present time, that is, are farthest removed from each other on their orbit, so that more than half of the planet is constantly illumined and the second sun shines almost two hours after the first one has set. When the suns are in conjunction, that is, closest to each other, when one may temporarily cover up the other, then they rise and set for us simultaneously; maybe it gets much hotter then. But we have no way as yet of knowing anything about the course of Eden's seasons, we don't even know the length of the year, which may last only six earth-months or, perhaps, a thousand. But one thing seems certain to me—there are no big variations in temperature; for if there is practically no difference to be noticed between sea-level and twenty thousand feet up, if so splendid a plant life flourishes there at such a height, then winter's cold and summer's heat cannot be excessive, otherwise we should have seen traces of glaciers up above, while down below here there would have been no such manifold animal life in a region which is closer to the poles than to the equator."

In the meanwhile dawn had broken.

"Ah!" cried Mitzie, suddenly, "Nature is taking care of our evening's conversation!"

"Splendid!" smirked the Captain.

"Highly interesting!" cried the Professor. "Really, not half bad!"

And after Hank too had joined in with his "Magnificent!" John felt himself obliged to express his approval by crying out "Truly important!"

Imposing it certainly was, this display of fireworks revealed at the stroke of dawn. Fire-flies and phosphorescent beetles, large and small, rose into the air; you could see sparks, stars, and flames, some of them twinkling and disappearing, others glittering constantly.

What was new and especially majestic, however, was the play of colors about these living meteors and starry showers; yellow, red, blue, or green light streamed from them according to their species.

On the ground too it was lively and bright; here the

sparks and lanterns of glow-worms and luminous snails and caterpillars drew past each other, like glistening jewels, topazes, rubies, emeralds, amethysts, and sapphires.

"Oh, gentlemen, a northern light!" John suddenly cried out and pointed, not to the north, but to the east.

"That's a moon," the Professor corrected him. "Truly a worthy moon for a night in paradise!"

The moon, which rose above the mountains, had an indescribably beautiful and hazy rose-color. Only the most delicately tinted wild-rose bud or the blooming hue with which an airy cloud above the sea of the Italian Riviera is tinged at sunset, might be compared with it.

Soon the lunar disc, about twice as large as the satellite of our earth, floated free in the dark sky among the twinkling stars. And now it shed its enrapturing rose-light over the whole landscape.

All at once a new life seemed to awaken. Birds whirred through the air and gave voice to wonderfully soft music, crickets chirped in melodious tones; small animals, like hares, weasels, and hedgehogs, the last-named with multicolored, transparent quills, bounced around gaily, playing and scuffling, skipping and dancing, and turning remarkable somersaults.

In short, there was plenty to see, to hear, and to admire, had not the charm of the magical, Bengal moonlight alone been enough to keep them all awake. Who could have slept through such an entrancing, yes, truly paradisal night?

And new flowers too opened up their calyxes, unusually tender delicately formed patterns, shining whitely with golden-yellow filaments, and rose-tinted by the moonlight; bright-blue and red bindweed, silvery nasturtium and other blossoms unfolded to the rosy moon and exhaled a perfume which seemed to excel in sweetness all the aromas of the daytime.

The rosy moon shone for eight hours; but hardly had it set when a somewhat smaller moon of a light blue color rose on the opposite horizon.

Its mild light had an unusually soothing effect. Everywhere, quiet settled down; the animal world began to slumber and the calyxes of the night-flowers closed up.

But new blossoms sprang up again, large umbels, motley poppy-heads, and an intoxicating perfume mingled with the drowsy light.

Our friends also fell into silence and at last they felt the need of sleep.

Schulze led the general retirement to the tents, with the following words: "Even the nights in this paradise do not seem to be meant entirely for sleep. At any rate, the time during which the rosy moon is shining does not seem designed for sleeping, but rather for waking life. But the blue light induces sleepiness. Well, we have enjoyed ourselves for four long hours and there are still ten hours till sunrise; let us utilize the time for a night's rest."

"Let me take over the first watch," implored Hank, "I don't feel sleepy yet."

"Good! After three hours, wake me up, so that I can stand the middle watch," said Flitmore.

"And I ask for the morning watch," declared the Professor, "if only for the purpose of astronomical observations which may be of value to us."

Thus it was agreed upon and all retired save Hank Frieding.

After an hour and a half on guard, the youthful sentinel discovered that the planet Eden had not merely two moons, but at least three!

The blue moon was setting when a new moon rose, this time colored a dark green. It was considerably smaller than the other two, apparently about the size of our earth's moon.

For half an hour, the two moons hung simultaneously in the sky; then the green moon alone remained, glistening with a mysteriously dull light.

And now all nature was asleep. Everything was quiet as death, scarcely a whiff of air troubled the countless blossoms.

Hank's eyes became heavy-lidded and after three hours, of which only one had fallen within the green night, he was nothing loath to be relieved by Flitmore, during whose watch only the dark green satellite of Eden shone down upon the ground.

Three hours later came the turn of the Professor. For another three hours the third moon hung in the sky; as it disappeared under the horizon, the dawn came up.

Later on, our friends were to learn of still other attractions of Eden's nights, unfolded under the influence of the beautiful moonlight, depending upon whether two or even three moons were in the sky at the same time, at a greater or lesser distance from each other, in accordance with their differing periods of revolution. Completely moonless nights there were none, because of the short circling period of the green moon.

XLI

SUPERIOR BEINGS

WHEN day had broken, Schulze felt himself growing sleepy; and there was nothing surprising in that, for he had stayed awake for forty hours yesterday and then enjoyed a sleep of only six hours.

Before him appeared a wonderful vision.

It seemed to him as if he saw through the lashes of his softly closed eyelids a spirit floating towards him.

At first a charming countenance rose out of the glittering foliage, leaning forward half roguishly, half shyly.

Then the foliage parted with a scarcely audible restling and the whole figure slipped forward, moving over the ground without touching it.

Judged by its size, its features, and youthful appearance, the figure was that of a sixteen-year-old girl, but of a delicacy of shape and translucency of skin which would have made the most perfect creature on earth seem fat and coarse beside it.

The face was indescribably graceful and perfect, and the large eyes shone with a blue which did not have any counterpart on earth.

The hazy hue of the rosy moon seemed to stream through the white skin, and the transparent leaves of the heath-rose never attained such a delicacy of color.

Shining golden hair, finer than silk, fell in curly masses from its head and framed the clear oval of its little face.

A gay, clinging garment, which looked as if it had been spun of gossamer, flowed from its shoulders and enveloped the graceful form in a wonderful green shimmer.

Slowly this vision out of a dream came closer, sometimes retreating again like a bashful maiden; but at last it came quite close and bent down over the Professor.

Suddenly his eyes went wide open. The alluring vision took fright and fled back to the bush, with the speed of a meteor.

And the branches crackled and rustled and birds whirred aloft.

Schulze leaped to his feet and rubbed his eyes; the presence had disappeared like a wisp of haze carried off by the wind; yet he was awake! Had it really been an apparition?

"Here, old chap, what are you staring into the bushes for?" asked the Captain, who had already risen and dressed. "Do you see a serpent or a ghost?"

"I see nothing," replied the Professor, turning to his friend, "but I *did* see something; it did not look ghostly, more like a little serpent, but a most alluring one, I can tell you!"

"And which one of Eden's marvels is that supposed to be?" laughed Munchhausen. "You act as though we hadn't yet seen anything wonderful or alluring!"

Schulze was silent; for he was uncertain as to whether or not he had dreamed it all. That still remained to be seen.

Soon all were awake. They speedily consumed a breakfast of Eden's delicious fruits; all of them were burning with curiosity to continue the voyage of exploration and discover perhaps still greater marvels, even human traces, evidence of the existence of rational beings; for how could such a paradise fulfill its destiny if it were not populated?

They crossed through the shrubbery which surrounded their camping grounds and into which the lovely vision seen by the Professor had vanished. But not a word did he say about it.

When the shrubbery had been passed, the wanderers saw that they were on a plateau whose edge they were nearing.

But what halted them in their tracks and riveted their attention was the sight of two human beings, diligently engaged in activity.

One of them was a grown man with brown locks falling about his shoulders and a full brown beard. A white plaited garment clothed his body, like a toga, down to his ankles. His face had such a spiritual, serene, and radiant quality as would have aroused in any one a feeling of trust, even if the finely chiselled features had not been of such exceptional and perfect masculine beauty.

More slender, but no less handsome and winning, was the youngster at his side; compared with such magnificent beings, what did the figures of Antinous and Adonis, created by human art, amount to?

A blue garment covered the handsome limbs, clinging to their contours.

Both of them focussed all their attention on their work, which seemed to be a sort of forging. From the shelf of a rock rose a golden-yellow flame, the nature of which could not be determined. Neither wood, coal, nor any other fuel was anywhere to be seen; the flame seemed to break out from the rock itself.

In this sheet of flame, the youngster held metal rods and bars until they reached a white-heat, which did not take very long. Then he turned them over to the man, who must have been his father. He now shaped them as he pleased, with all sorts of remarkable instruments, tongs, and hammers.

"These people are careless, they take no precautions with the fire, which must surely be developing a tremendous heat," whispered the Professor; "we must tell them!"

"Suppose *you* tell them," retorted Munchhausen, ironically, "perhaps in your universal language, Latin, as you once did on Mars."

Schulze was silent. The Captain was right. How could he hold converse with these inhabitants of a strange world?

"Just look at that!" observed Mitzie. "Every moment the hem and folds of their streaming garments touch the flames yet they pay no attention to it, and the material doesn't catch fire, it isn't even singed."

"If I may permit myself an opinion," John now interjected, "then I would say that all this is, so to speak, hocuspocus, a deception, and not a burning fire at all; for, as you see, the old man grips the white-hot iron with his hands as if it were cold."

"But he is bending and shaping it," rejoined Hank; "so it must be heated close to the melting point."

"These Edenites," declared Flitmore, "seem to know of some preventive whereby the material is rendered uninflammable and the skin insensible to heat."

Turning for a moment from his work, the smith became aware of the strangers. Slowly he let the iron fall out of his hands.

He seemed astonished to see such unusual, unheard-of-looking beings, who nevertheless resembled him and his kindred in the structure of limbs and face, yet seemed to be made of far cruder material and lacking in that perfection which his and his son's beauty had attained.

But it was also possible that other Edenites were less handsome and delicate than these two; at any rate, the man revealed no boundless astonishment as might have been expected, and in particular he did not show any trace of fear. His surprise seemed rather to be a joyous one.

"Fliorot!" he called to his son, who now also looked up and appeared to be just as pleasantly surprised; indeed, the youngster clapped his hands for joy.

As these people had something celestial about them, so their voices in their harmony excelled the most melodious tone heard on earth. The sound of a bell or an organ seemed to be heard when the remarkable man cried out the one word "Fliorot"; and the clear shout of jubilation of the boy could best be compared to the tinkling organ-pipe which is called *vox humana*, the "human voice," but should be called "angel's voice."

"A thousand pities that we can't make ourselves understood by these remarkable humans, as we ought to call them!" Schulze regretted.

"How did Columbus manage with the Indians?" asked the Captain.

"That is true," said Flitmore. "The discoverers of the various coasts of America never found it a very serious difficulty when they had to enter into conversation with the natives and they learned their language very quickly; at least, there soon were gifted linguists who served as interpreters."

"Oughtn't we to be able to get as far as they did?" asked Mitzie.

"Come along, Prof," mocked Munchhausen, "how would it be if you did make another try with your old Latin?"

"Oh, no, you don't!" laughed Schulze, "but we have a young linguist in our midst; let Hank Frieding try his luck!"

"With pleasure!" said Hank seriously, without blinking an eyelash.

Schulze stared at him. "Come, now! I was only joking, of course! You don't seriously believe you can get along here with an earthly language? Even if you knew every tongue on earth and tried them one after the other, not one of them would be understood here, 25,000,000,000 miles from the earth—I can assure you of that!"

"To keep on trying would be to no purpose, it is true," replied Hank, "but there are natural laws, Mr. Professor, with which you are not familiar."

"But with which *you* are, my young friend?" laughed Schulze, somewhat mockingly. Did this otherwise so modest Hank imagine himself more learned than the much-travelled and highly educated Professor Henry Schulze of Berlin?

In the meantime, the two Edenites had approached them with light, elastic steps, barely touching the ground with their naked feet.

Hank Frieding spoke to them.

"We nom tu?" he asked boldly.

Schulze laughed gaily at this language, obviously invented by Hank himself on the spur of the moment. And this the inhabitants of the fixed-star world were supposed to be able to understand!

But the Edenite stared at Hank, surprised but visibly uncertain.

His son, however, uttered a cry of rejoicing; a sudden understanding seemed to dawn upon him, and as though to explain to his father what Hank had wanted to say, he called out to him: "Wai nuomi itu?"

"Nuoma Gabokol," the man now said.

"Ud itu?" Hank now turned to the youngster. But the father corrected him: "Onde itu?"

"Fliorot!" replied his son.

"Pa?" Hank asked the old man.

"Migu Pa," he said, indicating himself. "Seit failo mig."

Completely dumbfounded, the inhabitants of the earth listened to the young man, Hank, apparently holding a conversation with beings whose language nobody could understand.

Schulze exclaimed with awe: "But here is where all and

any science *does* come to an end! If you take a trip on earth of a few thousand miles, you can bet your boots you won't understand a syllable of what's being said by the natives of the strange lands you will come to, unless you have thoroughly studied their language. And you mean to tell me that you can make yourself understood here without further ado to people who live 25,000,000,000 miles from our planet?"

Munchhausen shook with laughter. "A magnificent joke!" he cried. "Don't you see, Prof, that this arch-wag of a Frieding is making fools of us all and only putting it on?"

"But then these people wouldn't be talking to him and giving him answers!" objected Mitzie.

"Everything is quite all right," said Hank. "Of course, I have never heard or studied the language of Eden, and that is why I cannot always strike the right word. Nevertheless I can talk it correctly enough to make myself understood. I said 'we' and it should be 'wai'; I said 'nom' and it should be 'nuomi,' 'nuoma' in the first person; I said 'tu' and it should be 'itu'; it should be 'onde,' instead of 'ud' as I said. But, as a rule, I hit on the right consonants, so that an intelligent Edenite would understand me and beside these corrected forms I have already learned a few new words; 'migu' means 'I,' 'seit' means 'this,' 'failo' is 'son,' and 'mig' is 'mine.' If I have got that far with three sentences, then I ought to be able within a few days to carry on a scientific conversation in the sonorous tongue of Eden."

"Well! But what have you learned from these gentlemen?" asked the Captain, still very much in doubt.

"Oh, not much, but I did learn what I asked about. We have before us father and son, 'Pa onde failo'; the father's name is 'Gabokol,' which means roughly 'open eye'; the son is called 'Fliorot,' which I might translate as 'fleet wheel.' That is all, for the time being!"

"How in blazes are you going to explain this?" cried Schulze. "I have seen many wonders, but this one seems to me the rarest of them all! 25,000,000,000 miles, I tell you, 25,000,000,000 miles separate the earth from Eden and you come fresh and green from the earth and without further ado start talking with the Edenites, and you both understand and make yourself understood! That passes my powers of comprehension!"

"Well, I am not quite so green as you imagine, Professor," laughed Hank. "You see, here is the whole thing: I have discovered the secret of the origin of human speech, and time and again I have succeeded in formulating the laws of sound on which the formation of words is based. Since it is a matter of natural law and not of arbitrary fancy, I can assert that wherever there are beings similar to ourselves, they must have formed their language in very much the same way and according to the same laws.

"So I addressed the Edenites, so to speak, in a primitive language; I formed the words out of the sounds characteristic of the concepts they were meant to signify. Now, if the language of Eden were not too far removed from the primitive form, they ought to be understood, and this proved to be the case.

"Just listen! When I say 'We nom tu?' perhaps you do not grasp immediately that 'nom' means 'name'; but think of the French word '*nommé*' or 'name,' and it becomes pretty clear that 'We nom tu?' stands for 'What is your name?' Now the Edenites say: 'Wai nuomi itu?'

"But, as I explained, the decisive sounds are familiar to them, so that they understood even my defective question. 'W' is the question sound: 'who,' 'where,' 'what,' 'when,' and so forth; in Latin and French it is 'Qu.' D or T, and sometimes G, is the indicative sound, the one used for 'thou,'

'thee,' 'thine,' and so forth, as well as for 'this,' 'that,' and
'those.' And in the same way I could tell you just what sound
comes naturally to the lips of man when he wants to express
himself concerning a given object or concept. This I learned
from the laws of the origin of speech as I discovered them,
and according to which I formed the words which must be
intelligible to the strangest beings, providing they speak a
language similar to that of man."

"In any case, it's a stroke of genius to think of trying out
this earthly knowledge in this way," Flitmore observed with
admiring praise.

The Edenites had listened attentively, but they must
surely have understood none of the words, or very few of
them; far simpler phrases would have to be used before they
would be able to get any idea of what was being said in this
utterly strange language.

At last Gabokol spoke up, turning to Hank.

"He is inviting us to follow him," explained the young
man.

"Accepted!" said Flitmore, and the company entrusted
itself to the guidance of its new friends.

The latter took a deep breath and rose into the air,
through which they now floated without touching the ground
again.

Our friends were indeed able to take tremendous leaps into
the air, but they could not keep floating in it for any length
of time.

When the Edenites noticed this, they descended and Gabokol said to Hank, in his tongue: "Why don't you want to
fly?"

"We are unable to!"

The man seemed highly astonished; but from then on he
and his son were courteous enough to accompany their guests
with leaps.

Fliorot was greatly interested in the two chimpanzees and asked if they were the sons of the Lady.

Mitzie uttered a cry of dismay when Hank translated the question to her. But the young man explained to Fliorot that the monkeys were animals and not men, and that they could not even speak.

The two Edenites thereupon examined the chimpanzees with the greatest interest.

"There!" declared Munchhausen. "These Eden people evidently are not descended from apes, for such animals aren't even known in these parts."

They had now reached the edge of the plateau.

Below, a river flowed into the distance, and on either side of it rose hundreds of blocks of stone in various shapes, sizes, and heights.

Our friends soon saw that they were ingeniously devised structures, the living-quarters of the Edenites. The stones revealed windows, galleries, and balconies; at the top they had flat roofs, which were, however, crowned or bordered with towers, pillars, and arches.

Broad avenues and narrow streets stretched out between the groups of houses.

All acknowledged that these crude, jagged buildings, with their galleries, arches, and towers, presented a most diversified and magnificent picture, a scene to arouse their enthusiasm.

The city resembled a bee-hive; over the roofs, through the streets, in and out of the windows, beings flew and floated in shining, colored garments, as fine as gossamer: men and women, boys and girls, and even little children.

They could not see enough of this richly colored picture, of these graceful movements.

When our friends later on had a closer glimpse of the

city's inhabitants, they discovered that Gabokol and Fliorot were by no means exceptionally handsome examples of their race, but that perfect beauty, comeliness and grace, as well as a noble-mindedness which was reflected in their eyes, were the general attributes of all Edenites.

Yet they were far from being alike. Rather the personal distinction of form and feature appeared to be more marked than it is on the earth; and, to look into the pleasant faces, or even the sunny eyes, of any of these people, was to be captivated by them at first sight.

XLII

IN A HOSPITABLE HOME

THAT day they did not descend, or rather float down, into the city; for Gabokol's dwelling was a residence on a level with the mountain rim which sloped down into the valley.

The house was in a garden of exceptional splendor and beauty. Only now did our friends see all that wealth of form and color with which the flowers, shrubbery, and creepers of Eden were endowed.

At first they thought that even the vegetables were ornamental plants, until later on the housewife explained everything to them.

The poultry-yard was especially fascinating; for our pheasants, peacocks, and guinea-hens come nowhere near the color and markings of the variegated kinds of laying fowl, ducks, and geese in which the place abounded. Even the eggs of Eden's poultry far excelled in flavor the earthly kind, and, moreover, they were colored like Easter eggs or speckled like the loveliest eggs of the earth's nesting birds.

Hank, who penetrated ever deeper and more swiftly into the mysteries of Eden's language, continued to serve as interpreter; but the others were already beginning to understand words here and there, after having had their attention called to them. Their knowledge of the natural relationship of sounds gave them the clue. Remarkably enough, John picked it up quicker than the others, perhaps because he relied more upon his inbred feeling for language.

Time and again, Gabokol assured them how happy he and

his would be to accommodate his esteemed visitors from another world. He would show each of them to his own chamber; they were so accustomed here to harboring guests, the oftener and more numerous the better—that in every house three quarters of the space was set aside for guest-rooms.

House-doors there were none; you entered through the roof, as was the case in all of Eden's homes. As the villa was a one-storied structure, they all managed the somewhat lofty jump. Gabokol and Fliorot floated in ahead of them.

"Ma!" called Gabokol, when they had entered the dwelling.

Instantly a radiant form appeared, an apparition of such grace, youthfulness, and beauty as none had ever before seen, with the exception of Schulze, who still recalled the even lovelier vision that had startled him on his morning watch.

But the lady of the house who floated towards our friends was enough to prove that on Eden too the female sex was the lovelier one, however handsome the men might be.

"Bleodila," Gabokol presented his wife, with the emphasis on the O of the melodious name, which Hank translated as "The Blossoming One," decidedly a fitting name for this flower-like woman.

Bleodila was overjoyed to have guests in her home, and she led them into the living-room, whose walls were built of rock-crystal and decorated with jewels in artistic flower patterns.

Here our friends were invited to seat themselves in comfortable chairs of multicolored, transparent basket-weave.

These delicately woven chairs had not been calculated for the weight of heavy earth-people, yet they proved to be tough enough to withstand even Munchhausen's weight without falling apart.

The Captain continued to use the same chair, the largest and strongest one, of course. The spherical shape which it immediately assumed, a rare departure from its original shape and that of all the others in Eden, gave the owners of this chair a lasting souvenir of the visit of the stout Captain.

When the guests had taken their places, the youthful mother of the household called in her oldest daughter; it was the custom in Eden to present members of the family to visitors one by one, rather than all at once.

The little twenty-year-old sprite who now appeared was clothed in a pale rose garment and her brown hair curled down her back in silken waves.

As they looked at her, our friends asked themselves if it would be possible to find still greater beauty and more delicate loveliness; for they had thought before, that the lady of the house represented the height of all possible allurements; while now they found these attractions far surpassed by those of the daughter.

Only Schulze knew that on this planet there was an even more fascinating loveliness than that which Glessiblora revealed.

The name of this enchanting maiden, Glessiblora, was translated by Hank as "Shining Flower."

Only a quarter of an hour later was the younger daughter, Heliastra, called into the room.

"She is but seventeen and a little rogue, a mischievous imp," explained her father before she entered, and Hank rendered her name as "Bright Star."

From afar they could already hear the silvery laughter of the approaching girl; for there was nothing with which the sound of this clear voice could be compared save the tinkling of silvery bells.

And now Heliastra appeared in the opening which took the place of a door; for real doors which could be closed at will were not to be found anywhere in Eden.

In the entrance, she halted her floating movements and as she stood there, her gleaming golden hair framed by the opening, truly she resembled a bright and glittering star.

Our friends looked up at the seventeen-year-old maiden: such a marvellously sweet face, such adorably merry blue eyes, such a translucent, petal-white skin tinged with a roseate gleam, in short, such a blending of beauty, gracefulness, and youth had not only never been seen by them, but they could not in their wildest dreams have painted such a fascinating picture.

Again, it was Schulze alone who had ever seen any one like her, and not merely like her; he instantly recognized in Heliastra the sprightly vision which had greeted him on his morning watch, while he was dozing off and did not rightly know whether he were asleep or awake.

The little one had recognized him too. After she had inspected the strange guests without embarrassment and responded particularly to Hank Frieding's admiring gaze with a bewitching smile and a friendly nod, she floated straight to the Professor and dropped him a deep curtsey; then she laughed musically into his face.

The others looked on enviously while Schulze was being thus favored, and he himself was proud of it. He beamed upon the charming creature through his spectacles.

To her mother, however, Heliastra's laughter seemed unbecoming. "Heliastra!" cried Bleodila to her youngest, in tones of soft reprimand.

"O Ma," replied the little one, "we already know each other. When I accompanied Pa and Fliorot to the smithy this morning, I flew around a little and found the camp of the strangers; this honorable gentleman was keeping watch; I thought he was sleeping and wanted to come closer. But he stared at me with such startled eyes that I took fright and fled. Only I think he was more frightened than I." And again she laughed her refreshing laughter.

When Heliastra saw that Hank understood her language, she began a lively conversation with him and asked him eagerly about the world from which the strangers had come. When the young man would jumble up a word now and then, she laughed until the others were irresistibly infected with her gaiety.

"I cannot help myself," she said to Hank apologetically, "I get so amused by the unusual words you use or the way you sometimes pronounce and alter them. It is really astonishing that you can talk our language, which you have heard today for the first time. We haven't anybody among us who is so clever. But I beg you not to learn to speak it perfectly or you will deprive me of a lot of fun."

Upon Gabokol's request, Hank now had to explain how he had succeeded in being able to make himself understood among the Edenites.

Even the girls followed his talk on the laws of the origin of human speech with eager interest and thorough understanding.

At the end, Gabokol expressed his greatest admiration and begged him to deliver a lecture on the subject in the principal city. "You will become a famous man among us; for while our scholars have discovered that all the tongues of our planet were originally related, they have racked their brains in vain over the beginnings of speech and have concluded it is a riddle human understanding cannot solve.

"Just think what light this new knowledge will cast, what a service you will render our science, the impetus you will give it. And we here shall gain a greater respect for the superior intelligence of the earth's inhabitants."

Hank laughed, but promised to deliver the lecture as soon as he had sufficiently mastered the language of the country.

The daughters of the house now served the midday meal, to the great satisfaction of the Captain.

During the repast, our friends made the acquaintance of new, undreamed-of foods, the wonderful vegetables of Eden, and the excellent pastries and confections which demonstrated that the Edenites had species of grain which supplied them with the most variegated flours.

Meats were unknown here. It would never have occurred to any one to kill an animal or to strip its body. Certainly, with the inexhaustible choice of foods, it would have been absurd to introduce meats, which would probably in any case have been repugnant to the Edenites.

None of our friends missed the meats, poultry, and roast, so much more delicious in their endless variety were the dishes of Eden.

Eggs, milk, butter, cheese, and honey were the only foods taken from the animal kingdom, and even these surpassed in quality the products of earth. Particularly was there a multiplicity of different sorts of eggs, of honey, and of milk, and from the various delicious milks were also prepared the greatest variety of butters and cheeses, each of which revealed its peculiar, inimitable merits.

The beverages were partly waters from the sub-soil, and partly concoctions of sweet and tart fruit-juices which contained no intoxicants but gladdened the heart and exhilarated the spirits to a far greater extent than the alcoholic beverages of earth.

Nor was the drinking of the exceedingly enjoyable wines of Eden ever harmful; on the contrary, they always buoyed up the strength and vigor of the body as well as the keenness of the mind.

XLIII

NEW KNOWLEDGE

HANK learned the language of the Edenites at a fabulous speed. He could now maintain a fluent conversation. Difficulties were encountered only with concepts foreign either to the earth or to the world of Eden. But by means of description and elucidation, he succeeded in making even these understandable in time.

Gabokol and his kin showed an unusual intelligence and very soon picked up and understood a whole series of "foreign terms" with which Hank enriched their language because it was lacking in the corresponding expressions. But here it was only a matter of finding terms for things which were familiar to earth-people but quite unknown to the Edenites.

Thus, it was difficult at the outset to make their hosts understand the meaning of poison, poisoning, wounds, illness, pain, hate, malice, and other woes and burdens.

And yet it was necessary to speak of such things if they were ever to learn about the conditions existing on Eden or to give information about those existing on earth. The foreign terms were therefore words, for the most part, of an evil significance, which the Edenites would have to learn and understand with painful astonishment, if they ever wanted to gain an insight into the strange world from which their visitors had come and, in turn, to make clear to the latter how much Eden differed from their own homeland.

The others also made speedy progress in Eden's language,

and Flitmore expressed the wish that the visit to the city be postponed until they had reached a point where they would understand the most essential words and be able to make themselves understood.

For the next few days, therefore, they confined themselves to short flights to nearby points on the plateau, and to vantage points from which they might gaze far out into the distances of this land.

One of the first questions which Schulze addressed to Gabokol was to inquire how it was that water here travelled upstream in some places and downstream in others.

"With us, the lighter always rises to the top," replied the man in surprise, "and the heavier goes to the bottom. Isn't that the case on earth?"

"In general, of course," answered the Professor. "Thus, for example, oil brought to the bottom of a stream would float to the surface of the water; but then it does not run upstream, but down. And oil, as well as water, whenever the bottom is inclined, flows downhill."

"Even when it is lighter than the bottom?" asked Fliorot in astonishment.

"Yes! In that case it is in another medium, in the air, and because it is heavier than air it sinks to the bottom."

Gabokol shook his head. "That is remarkable and contradicts natural laws as we know them. We have dense water which is heavier than earth or rock. But if it becomes lighter than the solid ground beneath it, through the dissolution of its firmer elements by heat, then it rises as high as possible and naturally flows uphill. The seas have heavy salt water which always remains at the bottom.

"Our planet also has a very heavy air and a very slight power of attraction. On our moons, it is quite different, for there you feel yourself held down to the ground. It is possible that water would not flow uphill there, provided there were water to be found."

"Can you fly as far as your moons?" inquired Mitzie.

"We can but we do not, unless it is necessary; for they are not suitable for living beings. They lack plant-life and water, they are like luminous flowers, but they are dead and fit only for the dead. Also, their strong power of attraction makes walking and flying there very difficult."

"How do you manage to fly, anyway?" asked Munchhausen, turning to Fliorot.

"We breathe air into our flying-lungs," he replied. "Just try it some time: as soon as you are filled with air, you float aloft by yourself and sink down again when the valves are opened. We practice this from our childhood. Why don't you do the same?"

"For the simple reason that we haven't such a remarkable second lung," retorted the Captain.

"I thought as much," asserted Bleodila, the housewife. "This internal organ is an advantage we have over the animals, which can only jump, or else must have wings in order to fly."

"And does the filling of your balloon lungs make you so light that you can fly to the moons?" Mitzie continued.

"No, not that!" she was answered by the master of the house instead of his wife. "Further up, the air becomes so thin and light that it no longer buoys us up; if we want to go higher we must make use of machines impelled by repulsive power until we shut off the power and, attracted by the moon, drop to its surface."

"Aha! My centrifugal power!" exclaimed Flitmore. "And don't you travel any farther with it than to your moons?"

"That we are unable to do. The air in between, up to the green moon, the one closest to us, is already scarcely enough for breathing; only very few bold and tenacious voyagers have ever reached the blue one; as for the rose moon, which is twice as far away, nobody has ever reached it. The air becomes so thinned that you must either turn back or die in the attempt."

"But if you were to rise in an enclosed conveyance filled with air?" asked Lord Flitmore.

Gabokol reflected. "That would be an idea! Nobody has ever attempted that," he said. "Is that how you came to us?"

"Yes!" confirmed Flitmore, briefly.

"A far distance!" declared Fliorot, and looked towards the sky.

"You can't see our earth!" laughed Schulze, who followed the line of his gaze and could not but reveal his admiration at the fact that the lad seemed to know exactly where the earth was to be looked for in the firmament, in the event that it were visible. But, of course, even with the strongest telescope nobody could ever have discerned that small dark planet.

But Fliorot replied: "Oh, yes, I can, I see it quite plainly. I am well acquainted with the position of your solar system. You have but one sun. At first there are two small planets——"

"Mercury and Venus," said Hank.

"Then comes your earth, as you call it," continued Fliorot, "I can even see its moon."

"Yes, Fliorot has keen eyes," Gabokol bore him out. "I myself cannot recognize the moon of your earth by daylight, only at night."

"But here is where all science *does* come to an end!" exclaimed Schulze, who observed with astonishment how the eyes of the lad were protruding slightly and staring into the far distance. "There's a range of vision which puts our best telescopes in the shade, and compared to which the visual faculties of the last inhabitant of Mars are as nothing! If this youngster is able to distinguish the earth and the moon as two separate bodies, then it is an optical parallaxis surpassing the fabulous. His eyes must be capable of distinguishing the incline of two lines to each other amounting to one third of an inch to the mile!"

Gabokol now led our friends to his smithy and explained to them how the flames arose, from the combination of two gases which he produced out of the earth by the admixture of metals and acids.

He was at work on an airship which was being built of extremely light metals and was to serve as the general means of transportation on the planet, as he explained, when it was a matter of moving more speedily than by individual flight, or of dispatching loads.

Magnetism served as the motive power, which he called parallel-power, because he drove the craft loaded with it in a horizontal direction over the surface of the planet.

Fliorot was greatly interested in Hank's revolver. When his friend warned him seriously to handle the dangerous weapon with care, he laughed; and before any one could stop him, he had fired a shot right through his arm.

The cries of horror of our friends left the Edenites puzzled. The arm was certainly bored through, and the bone shattered. Yet the wound closed instantaneously without any bleeding, so that not a trace of it was to be seen. The bones, too, were apparently so elastic that they could be pierced without injury. Feelings of pain were unknown to the Edenites and even completely severed limbs grew together instantly, as Gabokol assured them, when the severed bone sections were joined together.

"Are illnesses also unknown to you?" asked Mitzie, turning to Glessiblora. "There are no poisons here, you say, and the hottest fire doesn't affect you in any way—is there, then, such a thing as death amongst you?"

"Yes," replied the maiden, "die we must. One of our years lasts about 10 of your earth-years and from 300 to 500 years is the average limit of life."

"Three to five thousand years!" exclaimed Munchhausen.

"Rarely does any one die at a tenderer age," added Heliastra. "We are then old and tired, and yearn for the higher, more perfect life which God has promised us after death."

"When we feel our end approaching," Bleodila took up the thread, "we usually start our voyage to the green moon, the kingdom of the dead. There you fall asleep after a few days, never to wake again. If one falls into this slumber here, before he has started his last voyage, which happens very rarely, we bear his body aloft, where it soon dries up and crumbles into dust."

"So you believe, as we do, in a future life?" asked Flitmore.

Gabokol looked at him with astonishment. "Of course!" said he. "What would be the sense of it if life were to come to an end with death?"

"Well, you certainly have a task to perform in this life too," thought Schulze.

"Certainly! Many of them! Of work there is enough, for ourselves and for others; for we must always improve ourselves and improve our planet. Were we not, for example, to work seriously and diligently at the improvement of our globe, then our offspring would die of hunger: up to now only one strip around the planet is fertile and inhabited; everything else is wasteland, where both vegetation and soil are lacking.

"So our chief task is to pulverize the bleak stone, to mix it with vegetable material and chemical elements and thus provide a fertile soil with which we cover over the bleak areas. They are then sown and become forests and prairies which may at first be occupied by animal life until the population later expands.

"Besides this work, the production of the means of transportation and agriculture, everybody also takes part in the gigantic task of creating dwellings for the future generations."

"So that you might say," remarked the Professor, "that your aim in life is to prepare the ground for those who come after you and in whom you live all over again. Many people on the earth think as you do, without wishing to believe in a life after death."

"And those who come after us?" asked Bleodila. "They will also enjoy our achievements for a few hundred years and, in their turn, again prepare for those to come, to disappear finally into the eternal void. And is that how it is to continue until the planet, with every one that ever strove and worked upon it, perishes? And then? Then it wouldn't matter a bit whether or not rational beings had ever lived and worked here!"

"Yes," little Heliastra agreed with her mother. "If everything ended with death, then our lives would have been aimless and senseless, we should have been the puppets of an uncomprehending Creator. But the Power which has created and preserved us is Wisdom and Love; for that alone we may be joyful in this life and look towards the end with confidence and happiness."

"So you believe in a God from Whom all visible creation proceeds?" asked Mitzie.

A puzzled look came over Bleodila's face. "Yes, what else

should we believe?" she asked. "That this world, with its wonderful creatures and we ourselves, arose of itself?" She broke out into a hearty laughter in which both her daughters joined, so that it rang through the quavering air like the chimes of a little carillon.

"You may well laugh," said Mitzie; "nobody makes himself quite so ridiculous as he who doubts the existence of God."

XLIV

HELIASTRA

IT was remarkable how the air of Eden preserved,
strengthened, and invigorated both body and mind!

How many things they were able to accomplish in a day;
for to the twenty-seven-hour sun-day, after one hour of twilight, must be added the luminous night, which was far from
bringing with it fatigue or sleepiness!

They retired only when half the night had passed; they
rose, strengthened and refreshed, before the first sun rose;
eight to nine hours of sleep were sufficient, so that the day,
that is, the waking time, consisted of more than forty hours.

How much could be learned in a few days under such conditions was made especially clear to our friends by the fact
that they soon understood and spoke Eden's language as if
they had known it from childhood. Yet it is true that this
would have been impossible had it not been for the kinship
it had with the language of earth.

One evening, as the rose moon was shedding its fairy-like
glamour upon the landscape, the little company was assembled upon the roof of the house.

Gabokol was carrying on a serious discussion with Schulze
and Flitmore, to which John listened attentively, permitting
himself now and again one of his well-aimed questions.

Mitzie was conversing with Bleodila and the sedate Glessiblora about the life and activity of woman on Eden.

Fliorot listened raptly to the fabulous narratives of Captain Munchhausen, who had found a fervid audience in the
lad.

Somewhat apart sat Hank and Heliastra, regarding the

luminous starry sky, which revealed to the eyes of the young woman of a loftier world even richer wonders than to those of the young man of earthly origin.

"I love the stars!" said the young girl. "How countless must be the beings that take joy in their light! We have given names to the brighter stars as well as to the constellations apparently formed by them."

"That's just what we have done on the earth," said Hank, laughingly.

"Indeed! how remarkable!" cried Heliastra. "Just look, there on the horizon are four stars which form a square body from which a long throat stretches out; we call that constellation, which is the plainest in the sky, Ligela, after the long-necked animal you call the giraffe."

Heliastra had diligently picked up the words which Hank taught her, and she already knew the names of all the earthly creatures which bore any resemblance to those of Eden.

"We call this constellation Auriga, a part of Ursa Major," explained the young man. "With us, too, it belongs among the most familiar stars."

Heliastra shook her golden hair. "Ligela sounds nicer," she thought; "but look, there we have three stars in a row and two below them; this constellation we call the Throne, Sissal, and the bright star below to the right, Helor."

"We call the latter Rigel, but we add to the constellation the two upper stars, Betelgeuse at the left, Bellatrix at the right, and we name the whole Orion."

"Orion! Ah! what a lovely, tinkling name!" exclaimed the girl. "But just look: the two stars which you call Betelgeuse and Bellatrix, and we Fluir and Saila, we consider as a part of the lengthy constellation of the serpent, Slipilil; its head at the left there is the radiant star Glorhel."

"That is Sirius in Canis Major," explained Hank.

"And now look," continued Heliastra: "the rose-colored Fluir, which you call Betelgeuse, and above to the left the bright Blidal——"

"That is Prokyon in Canis Minor," explained Hank.

"Well, these two, together with Glorhel, the brightest of the distant stars, form a triangle in which only much feebler stars are situated."

"To our eyes there is hardly anything visible inside this triangle," Hank interrupted her again.

"Well, then, this triangle I hold to be the most magnificent group in the whole sky."

"That is just how I feel," agreed Frieding. And for a while a silence fell on them both.

Hank looked into the sunny eyes of the wonderful creature at his side. How proud he was that this celestial spirit should take pleasure at having met upon a different planet this poor son of the earth!

On the beautiful evenings that followed they continued to gather beneath the starry sky, and Hank and Heliastra preferred to sit side by side to talk about the stars.

Whole series of names of other stars and constellations they explained to each other, until it turned out that the astronomers of Eden had discovered, for the most part, quite different groupings than were known from the earth. Besides Ursa Major and even more so, Auriga, there was agreement only on the especially clearly defined constellation of Cassiopeia, which formed a large Latin "W," and Libra. Heliastra called them "Double-Triangle" and "Amber," or Dutri and Kolgor.

Over and over again was Hank obliged to tell about the earth and its people, and Heliastra listened to his accounts as to stories from a distant fairy world.

And when he narrated the sufferings, errors, and passions

of the earthly creatures, of the terrors and dangers, misfortunes and crimes, which disturbed the peace and welfare of the earth's inhabitants, he realized the deep feeling hidden behind this sun-child's roguish exterior.

"Oh," she exclaimed, "how much loftier and nobler are the tasks, the labors and the activities that are your lot, to alleviate pain, to battle against evil and to overcome hardships! We too strive towards ennoblement and perfection, but the difficulties with which you must reckon are unknown to us; your life must be truly heroic. If I could but once be amongst you, with all the misery you suffer, that I might battle together with you and with you overcome it!"

"Do not wish it!" said Hank, sorrowfully regarding the tender creature in her inspiring enthusiasm. "How much happier you are here!"

"Do you think so? I did indeed feel happy so long as I knew nothing of the suffering you describe. But now a burning desire has been aroused in me. Is it not the greatest fortune to be able to console, to minister, to help where misery cries to the high heavens?"

Hank regarded with wonderment this ethereal being who would joyfully sacrifice her enviable good fortune to shed light among those who loved their darkness more than light!

Indeed, with such a being at one's side, who would be unable to work so that the tormented and the misled might be made happier!

Hank had already felt the desire to dwell forever in this new world of peace, and nevermore to return to the misery of earth. But the high-minded response of this girl made him ashamed of his selfish thought of the moment. No! Return to the earth he would, a warrior for light and happiness!

XLV

IN THE KINGDOM OF PEACE

TODAY is the seventh day," said Gabokol one morning. "Wouldn't you like to visit the city with us for the first time? From time immemorial it is written that we shall gather on the seventh day to praise God, to worship Him and to hear the priest of the Eternal. On this day we leave all work and are happy together."

"Yes, it is the nicest day," added Bleodila.

"Amazing!" exclaimed Mitzie. "We too are accustomed to celebrate the seventh day as God's holy day."

"That's wonderful!" thought Bleodila. "It shows us again that you recognize our God as your own."

They then proceeded down into the valley as a group.

The meeting room was situated at the far end of the city, that is, it was the next building and it stood out among the others by reason of its height, extent, and splendor. Instead of the crude rock walls which most of the dwellings had, they found here shining, polished marble and pillars of transparent jewels, which had been taken for the most part from the moons of Eden, as Gabokol explained.

The whole population of the city was assembled here: sedate elders with noble features, without a wrinkle despite their hundreds of years; men, women, youngsters and young women, boys and girls, and even very tiny children floated in, and all of them shone with a radiant joy.

The appearance of the strangers from a distant planet,

created a sensation, particularly among the youth; yet even the smallest children showed no obtrusive curiosity.

Nevertheless, thousands of eyes were at first turned to the new arrivals; for while all of them had already heard of the unusual visitors, only a very few had seen them, in accidental encounters during their occasional promenades. Visits to Gabokol's had been deliberately foregone out of a feeling of delicacy and consideration; all waited until the earthly visitors had themselves decided to appear among them.

But as soon as the priest mounted the altar, he had the undivided attention of all and now there burst from a thousand throats a song of such purity and melodiousness that it seemed to our friends that they were listening to the celestial legions.

Then a common prayer was said, the priest speaking of the magnificence and beneficence of the Creator and of the thanks and obligations of His creatures. Again and again the tones and chimes of bell and organ swelled through the great hall.

When the inspiring service was at an end, the gray-haired priest came directly to our friends and said: "We have heard that you strangers from a distant world of God know the Eternal Creator and pray to Him even as we do. How happy we are to learn this! Now it would be a day of joy for this whole community if God's praises were to be sung to us for the first time by His creatures, in the tongue of another world. Therefore, if you would make us happy by singing one of your hymns, we should be thankful to you."

"The 'Rock of Ages!' " said Flitmore briefly to his companions.

And without hesitating for a moment they all joined in the chorus. It seemed to them as if their voices had become so vibrant that they carried the hymn to every nook of the hall, and the old chant preserved its sacred charm even in this loftier world, for the thousands listened to it quietly, respectfully, and visibly moved.

When the whole community departed from the House of God, our friends, in the company of their host, paid visits to numerous intimates of the latter and in the end accepted the invitation to lunch proffered by the Prince of the district.

They then proceeded to the outskirts of the city and admired the remarkable cultivation: the waving fields of grain with their transparent golden ears, the gardens of vegetables and nuts, and the pasture-lands.

The Edenites, clothed in festive garments, floated about in groups and it was a heavenly scene to watch them glide around so lightly, garbed in their gossamer-like cloaks, which shone in all the colors of the rainbow. It was an even greater delight to admire these perfect figures and the faces beaming with beauty, grace, and friendliness. And yet Hank could not but think that, however alluring were the maidens and young women he saw, there was not one among them who could equal in beauty the bewitching loveliness of Heliastra. She remained the pearl of Eden.

Here and there the youth played amid silvery laughter and gaiety; there was a whirling and leaping, a flying and scrambling on the ground and in the air, and the games were all so ingenious and full of so much exciting fun, that they might have looked on for hours at this colorful hubbub without losing interest.

When the rosy moon of evening gleamed, a feast in honor of the strangers was given in a huge park outside the city.

The entire populace, young and old, were there and took part.

During the course of the delightful repast, the Prince delivered a speech in which he emphasized the significance of the fact, that for the first time, so far as anybody knew, communication and friendly relations had been established between the inhabitants of distant planets. He praised the genius of these citizens of the earth who had made it possible, their courage which had dared the unknown, and the goodness of God which had preserved and guided them in their voyage through endless space.

Hank, as the only one who was already entirely at home in the language of Eden, replied in an excellent speech, and Gabokol and his family, especially Heliastra, admired the skill of his presentation, his noble flights of imagination, and the spirit of his thoughts.

They were exceptionally proud of their guests, and as jubilant applause rewarded the young speaker, Heliastra rose enthusiastically and, her eyes moist with tears, imprinted a kiss from her rosy lips upon the mouth of her friend, the highest sign of recognition that an Edenite can give.

The renewed applause and jubilation which followed this act, showed plainly that all the people shared this feeling of homage.

Hank felt himself in a dream, surrounded by rosy moonlight, honored and favored by the recognition of beings whom he rightly considered above him, but especially by the confusing mark of favor bestowed upon him by the most gracious of all creatures. He sat as if transfigured.

Heliastra read the thoughts in his eyes and took him by the hand.

"Come," said she, "let us seek out a quiet spot for a while, I see that your spirit requires peace."

Hank allowed himself to be led away.

They passed through some shrubbery to the banks of a quiet lake, which shone magically in the rosy gleam of the moon. Since the blue moon had meanwhile risen, the rosy light began to change into an uncommonly delicate violet.

Colorful swans, ducks and wild geese splashed about in the calm waters of the lake; herons, flamingos, ibis, peacocks, and pelicans strutted along the shore in their downy garb, birds that bore a resemblance to their corresponding earthly species, but were far more perfect and fascinating in form and color.

Giant lizards, like crocodiles, with scales of mother-of-pearl, lay on the strand or peeped out of the rosy mirror of the lake.

Hank followed the example of his companion who tenderly stroked these gorgeous lizards; here, even these huge amphibians had nothing hostile or horrible about them; by their soft eyes he could see how docile and friendly they were.

The rosy moon sank behind the horizon and its blue rival stood alone in the sky.

Heliastra laid her slender hand on the arm of her companion and said: "Come, let us turn back to our friends; the hour of homecoming is approaching and tomorrow we shall start the great journey to the capital of the country."

They turned back to the circle of the festive crowd.

XLVI

A JOURNEY ON THE PLANET

THE following day they undertook the contemplated journey on which our friends were to become acquainted with a part of the large planet and Hank was to deliver in the capital his lecture on the origin of language.

The monarch of the country and the teachers of the university had been informed by sound-waves of the impending visit.

For the journey, they had at their disposal the usual conveyance of the Edenites, a sort of large boat with covered sleeping-quarters and open decks which, driven by the so-called parallel power, flew through the air at a slight height above the ground.

The speed of flight, which could be increased to 300 miles an hour so that the whole planet might be encircled in 160 hours, was moderated to 60 miles an hour, so that the travellers might have a convenient view of everything.

Gabokol's whole family accompanied them, as did the Prince, who considered it both a duty and an honor to present them to the King in person.

"Our country is the largest and most important on the planet," explained the Prince during the journey. "The kings of the other countries have voluntarily submitted to the supremacy of our King, so that he is the supreme lord of the 400,000,000 inhabitants of our globe. To be sure, there is not much to rule over, since he leaves the other sovereigns full freedom and never has cause to intervene. In the other countries also, a citizen never thinks of neglecting his duties. The supreme power is consequently utilized only for a unified direction of our common labor, and in this it is certainly necessary to work consciously and according to some one plan, so that the inhabitable zone of our planet may be regularly extended and the growing population always find room in which to expand.

"Apart from numerous dialects, we have only four real languages, which are strikingly different from each other. The capital of our country lies in the northern hemisphere, beyond the equator, some twenty flights from here, that is about 3700 miles according to your measurements."

The Edenites measured by "flights," that is, by the distance they usually flew without stopping, and which amounted roughly to 180 miles by earthly measurement.

The air ship traversed country of wonderful beauty. Valleys and plains, rivers and streams, mountains, rocks and hills, large cities and idyllic villages were flown over, and when the rosy moon set, after a forty-hour flight, the travellers landed on the banks of a beautiful sea.

They flew over it the next day in twenty hours and on the far side rose the capital, right along the coastline, a large city of 1,500,000 inhabitants.

The rest of the day, as well as the two days that followed, were devoted to an inspection of the highly interesting settlement.

By his own wish, the King had our friends presented to him on the very day of their arrival.

He received them with the same heartiness and simplicity as would any other citizen of the land.

Especially overjoyed were the teachers at the university to make the acquaintance of the earth's inhabitants, and our friends had thousands of questions to answer, being constantly assured of the appreciation that was felt for the manner in which they so richly increased the knowledge of the Edenites.

When Hank delivered his lecture, the largest hall in the capital could not provide sufficient seats for the audience and he was obliged to repeat his performance three times in order to satisfy the thirst for knowledge of the masses that flocked to hear him.

The scholars assured them that they had gained a new insight into linguistic research, and Schulze kept thinking that up here, apparently, new truths did not have to endure the ridicule and passionate contradiction of professional scholars, whose vanity would not allow them to acknowledge that their previous investigations had yielded false results.

Of especial interest to our friends was their visit to the observatory. The Edenites also had telescopes, which were built along entirely different principles from those on the earth and made possible an incomparably better knowledge of the star world.

It is true that they owed the latter mainly to the remarkable eyes of Eden, for with the naked eye they could recognize worlds which remain forever concealed from our telescopes and even from photographic plates.

The astronomers were highly astonished to hear that the earth-people could barely see 2000 stars with the naked eye and that the catalogue of stars which Hipparchus had drawn up 2100 years ago contained only 1180 stars, though he marked down every visible star.

Schulze reported further that Argelander, by means of a telescope, had determined and noted down in his catalogue some 360,000 stars, a work to which he devoted virtually all his life, and that at the present time people were engaged in the task of undertaking to list the stars photographically, which would take another hundred earth-years and embrace more than 20,000,000 stars, of which 3,000,000 would have their position calculated according to the plates. About 1,000,000,000 stars could be taken by photographs.

The scholars showed Schulze a star catalogue with precise maps, containing more than 500,000,000 stars, among them also the earth's solar system with all the. planets and their moons.

Their long nights and long life enabled them, aided by the excellence of their instruments, to solve problems which man had found insoluble.

While the earthly astronomer must have a spectral analysis in order to establish with certainty whether a nebula, which also appears as such through the strongest telescope, is really a cluster of stars which are not distinguished as separate stars because their great distance from the earth makes them appear so close together, the astronomers of Eden could clearly distinguish nebula from star-clusters by means of their telescopes.

They were also of the opinion that most of the spiral-like nebula are the workshops of the Creator, in which new stars, and even whole new solar systems, are being created out of world-forming matter.

At the request of the astronomers, Schulze delivered a public lecture on the status and achievements of earthly astronomy. He set forth what David Gill had said in his famous speech on the movement and distribution of the stars in space: "We have learned to recognize the Milky Way as two majestic star-currents which wander in opposite directions; one of these currents carries the earth's solar system along with it into endless space, the other wanders towards the earth. The Milky Way dissolves in the telescope into masses of countless stars, which stand in part close to each other in dense swarms and are filled with conglobated nebula, and in part appear to be marked with dark, winding canals."

"Your main sun," continued the Professor, "wanders in the star current at a velocity of 114 miles per second. Our earth, with its whole solar system, moves towards the constellation of Hercules or Lyra at a speed perhaps as great as the orbital speed of our globe around the sun, namely, 95,000 feet per second, or about 18 miles, one tenth of a 'flight,' by your calculations.

"Spectral analysis, as David Gill says in his speech, has revealed the stars to us as enormous crucibles of the Creator, in which He shapes matter, under conditions of pressure, heat and environment, in a variety and on a scale which surpass all the conceptions of His creatures!"

For three weeks they remained in the capital, and then the return trip was started by another route, that gave our friends a glimpse of the immense rocky wastes of Eden, which had no soil and therefore no vegetation. The diligent labors of the Edenites, however, were slowly covering it with fertile earth.

XLVII

MUNCHHAUSEN'S FABLES

OUR friends became increasingly intimate with Gabokol's family; the inclination was mutual and extended to all; in addition, each felt drawn especially to some one else.

Thus, Lord Flitmore loved best his converse with Gabokol. Together they constructed photographic apparatuses and musical instruments, made flights for the purpose of photographing the country and more notable animals, and discussed the art of Eden and of the earth.

Mitzie's heart and soul beat as one with Bleodila's; they kept to each other in the kitchen, house, and garden and exchanged the experiences of housewives.

Professor Schulze found in Glessiblora his most fervent listener, who was more interested than any one else in the progress and peculiarity of earthly sciences.

Hank and Heliastra, in turn, felt themselves especially drawn to each other, as we already know; they shared their little secrets, and often went their own way together, enraptured by everything that was lofty and noble.

Captain Munchhausen, however, had selected Fliorot as his constant companion, for the youngster listened with devotion and curiosity to the fabulous accounts and stories which the old sea-dog knew how to tell about his earthly home.

John alone wavered between two choices, sometimes seeking education and instruction with Glessiblora and the Professor, and at other times drinking in the Captain's adventures by Fliorot's side.

When the wells of conversation dried up, they all gathered around the Captain who was inexhaustible and never silent, except during mealtime, of course, when he appeared, on the contrary, to be unfathomable, that is, insatiable.

It was Professor Schulze who made this observation by saying: "Munchhausen, when you eat you are a Cask of the Danaides, which was bottomless and could never be filled, no matter how much was poured into it; but in story-telling, you are a pure Charybdis, which Schiller said would never exhaust nor empty itself."

"Then what are you, Professor?" asked Munchhausen. "Scylla! For, whoever seeks to escape my profusion of words, is swallowed up in your wearisome and equally endless scientific whirlpool."

Thereupon the Captain continued with the story he had just started to relate to the inquisitive Fliorot.

"Well, as I was telling you, I made possible the voyage to you by having the comet Amina take our World-Ship in tow.

"That's just what comets are really made for, and they form, so to speak, the world postal-connections between the various solar systems; I was formerly a Captain at sea, but when I had had enough of travelling around on the limited earthly seas, I took the position of a World-Captain and frequently took trips with comets so that I know perfectly how to steer them. Every comet, you see, has a steering wheel in which its so-called force of gravity lies. All you have to do is to shift it and the comet takes another course.

"The astronomers on the earth have often wondered, when a comet suddenly takes a different direction from that which they had calculated for it. So they attribute it to the influence of Jupiter. I was really this Jupiter, for by turning the wheel, or the force of gravity, I gave the comet a new orbit in order to reach the point I was aiming at.

"A voyage with such a comet is extremely practical if you want to travel into the remote solar systems, for these cosmic vagabonds develop a terrific speed.

"Collisions and accidents, it is true, are not always to be avoided and it also happened to me that on such an occasion, a comet which I commanded went to pieces: there was nothing left for me to do but to continue my voyage on one of the pieces, for you can't get off them as you can off a ship. Storms and waves and torrents of water are not to be found in space, so that in the last analysis the dangers are not so great as on a sea-voyage, unless you plunge into the flaming sea of a sun, which is something easy to avoid, however, if you steer properly according to a good star-chart.

"Well, when Lord Flitmore entrusted me with the command of his World-Ship, the *Sannah,* I immediately decided to fasten her to the tail of some suitable comet, for I knew because of my knowledge of the conditions of world space that, with the relatively slow speed of our craft, it would require centuries to reach your planet, which we intended paying a visit.

"Then I succeeded in getting in touch with the comet Amina and grappling with it. I bound the *Sannah* fast to its tail with a long hawser, and then I mounted the comet itself so as to steer it here. Only when we had reached the realm of your solar system did I cut the towline and let the comet shoot along unguided, while we made a landing here."

Fliorot laughed; he knew the nature and orbits of the comets only too well not to understand that Munchhausen was joking; but he enjoyed these adventurous jests even if they weren't always particularly imaginative.

"But you promised to tell me about the wonderful animals on your earth," he now reminded him.

"Right enough! Well then, listen. Your animals up here are pretty smart creatures, but they don't come up to the animals of our earth.

"Look you, we have animals with long snouts like your mammoths; they have six legs and they can climb up a smooth, perpendicular wall without ever slipping, and even when they walk the ceiling, feet up and head down, they don't fall. They also have transparent wings like your birds and they fly around in the air in squads.

"We also have wingless animals, which make quite different leaps from those of your hopping colossi; for yours leap, at the most, three times their own height, while ours go from sixty to a hundred times as high."

Fliorot's eyes were wide open. Where it was a matter of animals with which he was unfamiliar, he was unable to judge whether the Captain was in earnest or joking, and he therefore believed that the Captain could be expected to tell the simple truth; for jokes which every one could see through, were considered harmless by the Edenites and were frequently invented for their amusement; but to exploit somebody's ignorance or credulity for the purpose of imposing on him, was unheard-of by this truth-loving folk.

Fliorot did not, therefore, entertain the slightest doubt about the Captain's reliability and exclaimed: "Ah! How I should like to see these amazing creatures!"

"Shame on you, Captain," said Schulze. "When you tell *us* your queer stories, it is very funny, for we are in a position to distinguish truth from bluff. But to swindle this young man, who is unfamiliar with earthly matters, isn't a very fine thing to do. You will be able to astonish him just as much if you depict our animal world as it actually is."

"Oho!" cried Munchhausen. "I myself should consider it stupid and malicious to have our young friend get false notions into his head when it's a question of things that are strange to him. With the comets it was different, for he already knew about them, but when I tell ! n about the earth I keep myself rigidly within the confines of the truth."

"That's a whopper of a statement to make! So you call it truth when you improve on the hopping mammoths of this planet by telling about earthly animals with wings and six legs, animals capable of walking a ceiling head downwards without falling? And about animals who leap into the air from sixty to a hundred times their own height?"

"You really astound me, Professor," replied Munchhausen, with mock wonderment. "I thought you were a Doctor of Natural Sciences and Professor of Zoology. Is it really possible that you don't know anything about the ordinary animals with which every child on the earth is familiar and which haven't their equal here on Eden? Is that conceivable? Professor Schulze knows nothing about flies and fleas!"

Now it was the Captain who had the laugh on his side and Schulze admitted dejectedly: "All right, you old jokester, there's no use quarrelling with you. You caught me napping that time."

XLVIII

DEPARTURE

IT was a lovely, a blissful time that our friends spent on Eden.

Every day they learned to know the serene people better, to esteem them more, and in going about with these thoroughly noble beings it seemed to them that they themselves were shedding all their earthly defects.

Even in a purely physical sense they had this feeling; for so healthy, sound and fresh, so spiritually elevated and vigorous, they had never felt as they did in the weeks and months they spent here.

They undertook several other journeys and viewed the most lovely landscapes and saw a large number of the native plants and animals.

But one day, Flitmore declared that it was now time for them to think of the return and since no comet could be used for the homeward journey, they would have to make up their minds that it would take several years.

In vain did Gabokol, Bleodila, Fliorot and Glessiblora seek to persuade them to remain for a longer period, or still better, to stay on Eden forever.

"God willing, this shall not be our last visit here," said Flitmore; "next time we shall bring you all sorts of earthly things, which will not enrich you but may yet be of interest. But now our duty calls us: our discoveries, particularly of the possibility of communication with distant worlds, are of the greatest import to our brothers on the earth. We must not allow them to be lost."

All of them, especially Hank, wondered why Heliastra

alone made no attempt to persuade them to stay. It affected young Frieding painfully. He had formed such a warm friendship with the girl that the thought of separation almost broke his heart.

When Gabokol saw that the departure of his guests was a settled matter, he said:

"As you have told us, it was a comet led you here. I have examined your World-Ship carefully, friend Flitmore, but it has one serious defect: By means of the centrifugal power, it is repelled from heavenly bodies, but you have no means of directing the voyage and must therefore leave it to chance whether you will return to your solar system or move away from it still farther.

"I should like to equip your craft with parallel power; the installation would take eight days at the most. Parallel power has some very important advantages for you: first, with its aid you can appreciably increase your speed through space; secondly, it conflicts neither with the centrifugal power nor with the power of attraction, so that it may be used while the current is turned on as well as when it is off. The third and most important advantage is of course that you can give your *Sannah* any desired direction, that is, you can steer straight for your solar system."

"You take a great load off my mind," replied Flitmore; "I could not conceal from myself what insurmountable difficulties might confront our craft on her return journey without such an arrangement. But I have learned from you the remarkable properties of parallel power and I know now how to manage it. If you care to take over the work of furnishing our craft with it, you will increase the gratitude we already feel towards you and yours.

"And then I have one more request: as you know, my *Sannah* has a great deal of extra room. On the voyage here, this served primarily for the storing of the large stocks of oxygen used to renew our air.

"We have now learned from experience that the World-Ship in space surrounds itself with an air-envelope of its own, which is constantly renewed. But what we do need is an abundance of provisions, for under certain circumstances the return voyage may take years . . ."

"Do not worry!" Bleodila interrupted him. "It will be a joy to all the women in the city to load your store-rooms with flour, vegetables and fruit preserves, as well as milk, butter, cheese and eggs, enough to last you ten years; you know that we have discovered a process whereby even eggs and milk can be kept fresh for years."

"You ought to have honey and wood, too, for our tree wood is as delicious and as nourishing as the fruits and keeps without any special treatment. And it offers you a delightful juice to drink that isn't soon forgotten," added Fliorot.

"Then we are well secured, if God's grace be with us, as I do not doubt it will," said Mitzie joyfully.

Now Heliastra came forward: "I also have a request to make," said she, her face lit by a lovely flush, "a request of you, dear friends: Take me along with you to your earth!"

Everybody was stunned! Even Gabokol and Bleodila, Fliorot and Glessiblora were taken by surprise!

But Hank was struck as by a bolt of good fortune out of the blue. Yet he thought immediately that it was far too good to be true. They could neither carry off this lovely maiden from her happy planet, nor would her parents consent to be parted from her.

Mitzie was the first to express this when she said: "My child, my dear child, how shall we dare to take you along into the unknown, to carry you off from your paradise into the misery of our earth?"

Heliastra smiled: "Do you not know that God is everywhere? Where is there an unknown? And you must know that it is my deepest desire to share your destinies and help you alleviate the sufferings of earth."

"It is a noble aim my daughter sets herself," said Gabokol thoughtfully.

"No, no!" cried Hank grievously: "God knows how my heart bleeds at the thought of parting from you; but here you are happy, and happy you shall remain and never visit our world of sorrow. I would rather spend my whole life longing for you than have you unhappy!"

"Do you love me so much?" asked Heliastra, and her wide eyes looked up at him.

"Yes; more than anything else: I shall never forget you!"

"And do you think I can be happy when you are no longer with me? From now on my lot is cast with yours. Or is it impossible for me to become your wife?"

"You! My wife? You are willing to come down from your starry heights to make a poor son of the earth like myself inexpressibly happy? But no! It must not be!"

"I see now how things are," repeated Gabokol, "and I see what is God's will. Heliastra, you shall make us feel the pain that has been unknown to us till now! Those who love should remain together, bound to each other, that is the highest command of God."

"Gabokol is right," said Bleodila with tears in her eyes. "Your arrival and your presence were a joy to us; your departure brings us greater pain than we dreamed of! Let Heliastra go, young though she is. If you take her as your wife, my young friend, we shall not try to keep her back. And if she can make you happy, we shall not be the ones to grudge you your happiness."

Hank knew not where he was when he opened his arms to receive the slender form.

"Will you remain with me like this forever?" he whispered, kissing her tenderly.

"Forever with you!" she said with a clear bell-like voice, and leaned towards him warmly.

In the course of the next few days, Gabokol installed the parallel power in the *Sannah* and repaired the hole which the meteorite had caused. Finally, he provided the whole casing of the ship with an uninflammable material known only to Eden, which was at the same time a far poorer heat-conductor than anything known on earth. The inhabitants of the city meanwhile came in squads to load the store-rooms with inexhaustible supplies of provisions, as well as with seeds of every kind, although Schulze strongly doubted whether Eden's marvellous plants would thrive on earth.

Then the solemn marriage of Hank Frieding and Heliastra was celebrated and the gray-haired priest of the city united the couple in the name of Almighty God and gave them his blessing.

The whole city took part in this extraordinary celebration, not just formally, but with a warm and loving heart. All of them approved Heliastra's decision and wished her God's richest blessings.

Then there was a festival of joy, such as was also customary on the departure of the dying. Finally, in the gleam of the blue moon, the roseate wife made her farewells to her friends and acquaintances.

The next morning she parted from her family.

Our friends also made their hearty, grateful, and touching farewells.

Heliastra, however, was filled with a radiant joy as she and her husband entered the craft that was to take her into the world of her desire, the world in which there was pain to assuage, in which there were tears to dry.

"God be with you and bring you back again!" was the cry that followed them as the *Sannah,* driven by her centrifugal power, shot into the air, and Hank and Heliastra waved a last farewell from the open window.

XLIX

THE QUEER PLANET

I T was evening when the *Sannah* ascended.

For the last time the rosy light of the most lovely of moons greeted our friends and the angelic creature who, from childhood, had been happy in its roseate beams.

Rapidly, with increasing speed, the World-Ship heaved forward, driven by the combined forces of repulsion and propulsion.

Soon the solar system of Toliman vanished from the sight of the voyagers, that is, its planets began to gleam as stars in the evening sky.

Only Heliastra, with her sun-eyes, was still able to see everything clearly and distinctly, and even to recognize the blue moon, which had by that time arisen.

And it was also she alone who, from the room at the other side, could report exactly which of the tiny stars was the earth's sun, so that right at the outset Flitmore was able to give the *Sannah* the correct direction.

Then they all retired to their rooms, except for John who had the first watch.

Three hours later, Munchhausen took over the middle watch and, finally, the Professor took the third and last.

Towards morning he saw how the *Sannah* was approaching a huge, dark body, if one can speak of approaching something that is still a few million miles away.

"Morning" and "Day" were mere time-conceptions now that the double-sun Alpha Centauri had once more become two fixed stars, which were already fusing into one before their eyes. Since, differing in this from their first voyage, there was now not even a feebly shining comet to give light from without, the World-Ship would have to go through her journey, lasting perhaps for years, in constant night: daylight or even sunshine were out of the question.

Not a very pleasant prospect!

It was time to waken the others, at least those who had not already aroused themselves.

The Professor pressed the various contact buttons which touched off electrical bells in the corresponding sleeping-quarters.

Flitmore was the first to appear.

"Milord," said Schulze, "there is a dark body in our path, a star, nearer to the earth than to Toliman. Shouldn't we come closer to it so as to see what it looks like there?"

"We don't want to be making long stop-overs on the way," said Flitmore smiling. "Our journey will take long enough without that! On the other hand, in a voyage which will probably last for years, another few days more or less won't matter much."

Hank had in the meantime appeared with Heliastra, and added: "Besides, since our journey, so far as we know, is to be through an endless solitude, without expectation of meeting anything until we reach the earth's planetary system, we ought not to miss what may be our last opportunity to make fresh discoveries."

"That's true!" said Lord Flitmore. "Turn off the centrifugal power, Mr. Professor."

The others had now come in and breakfast was eaten while the *Sannah*, attracted by the dark body, plunged downward towards it.

As they approached the surface of the mysterious star, Flitmore let a very weak centrifugal current stream through the metal casing, which just equalled the power of attraction of the sphere, so that the *Sannah* was kept floating at the same distance or height all the time.

The parallel power was now turned on and the World-Ship rode over the surface of the new planet at the low speed of thirty miles an hour.

Everybody went down into the Antipode room, so as to be able to observe the landscape below.

It looked sinister and dark: no sun, no moon illumined this celestial body; only a bloody gleam, not unlike the Northern Light, oozed down out of the atmosphere, apparently proceeding from phosphorescent matter or bacteria in the air.

For all this illumination, little could be seen; but what they did see left a revolting impression.

The land seemed to be fairly level, mostly swampy in character.

At certain spots, luminous fumes or vapor rose from the swamps, which shed a cadaverous, sulphuric light; in between, bluish and greenish tongues of flame shot up, so that the immediate surroundings were lit by a dull gleam which was more gruesome than the most infernal torches would have been, in a world of horrors.

Yes, a world of horrors! What kind of trees and plants were these! All of them seemed alive and at the same time repulsive: grasses which wound, twisted, and squirmed about on the ground in convulsive jerks like loathsome vermin, as if striving in vain to be free from the putrid soil in which they were rooted! Many-limbed trees, whose bleak, leafless branches curled like monster serpents or octopi, in constant motion, stretching out and drawing back, forming waves, arches, rings, and knots, as if the living branches of every tree were engaged in murderous combat.

And down below, the swamps teemed with ghastly creatures: whitish maggots, larger than elephants, bared their teeth in snarls; monster spiders, whose fat, spherical bodies were covered above, below, and at the sides with long, thin, hairy legs, so that they could revolve around themselves and always crawl with a number of feet while the others quivered in the air; greenish toads as large as buffaloes, with hideous eyes popping out of their wormlike heads; thin-legged mosquitoes as tall as giraffes, which sucked the life out of other animals with their long, transparent fangs or else were bitten and crushed to death by them.

Everything crawled and fought against everything else; not only animal against animal, but also plant and animal, were engaged in incessant, deadly warfare.

There a gigantic worm with crocodile's jaws bit off the branch of a tree and the branch twitched and jerked and squirmed convulsively on the ground, while a thick, greenish-black juice gushed from the stump, distorted as if in the ghastliest pain.

Here was one of the monster beasts with countless arms, seized by a tree and seeking in vain with desperate contortions to free itself from the fatal embrace: it was squeezed, strangled, and crushed into a shapeless mass.

And then slender vermin shot up out of the morass, sailed through the air, and bored through the body of a no less repulsive beast, finally to vanish completely into its bulk, there to commence on its entrails its ghastly work of destruction.

It was blood-curdling to watch such a monster-beast, itself gruesome in appearance, leaping about in terrific pain, to see it writhe madly and finally collapse in the throes of death, while its shapelessly swollen bulk suddenly burst open and revealed a mass of serpentine vermin which had devoured its still living body from within.

Then the livid flames shot up again through these teeming masses, singeing and devouring the bodies which vainly sought to escape: even these infernal fire-serpents seemed to be alive and to pursue their victims with bloodthirstiness.

Heliastra was deathly pale and filled with horror: "Is this what the earth looks like?" she asked uneasily.

"No," Hank consoled her. "This ghastly spectacle fills us also with a horror we have never known before!"

"Yes," the Professor reassured her. "Even scientific investigation revolts here and turns away in disgust. This is a realm of darkness in the fullest sense of the word, and I propose to give it the name 'Sheol,' as the Hebrews called their inferno."

"It is enough," said Flitmore. "Rather into the eternal night of solitary space than watch such a spectacle any longer!" And he switched the centrifugal power on at full force.

L

THE END OF A WORLD

"IF I may permit myself to make an observation on my own account," began John, as the *Sannah* started to move away from the appalling planet, "I see there another dark sphere coming our way, plunging down, so to speak."

"That might become dangerous to us," cried Schulze, looking out in the direction indicated by John. "A collision actually seems to impend between two enormous bodies. I judge Sheol to be ten times the size of the earth, and the body plunging down upon it at such a furious speed seems to be almost as large."

Lord Flitmore spoke not a word, but switched the parallel power on at full force and the *Sannah* moved away from the threatened spot with the velocity of light.

Suddenly everything became glaringly bright; a light, like that of ten suns, filled the room with blinding rays: the two spheres had crashed against each other and in less than a second they had fused into a glowing white mass from which flaming pieces were flung in all directions while tongues of flame, millions of miles high, shot out into space.

All life, with its dreadful struggles, must have been wiped out on Sheol in a flash; but the occupants of the *Sannah* were threatened with the same fate: the World-Ship was bathed in glowing gases, a tongue of flame had reached her; at the same time, however, she was flung ahead at a speed which surpassed anything she had hitherto been able to achieve.

The craft was shaken from one end to the other, and for a

time they all lay unconscious, suddenly thrown to the floor. Only Heliastra floated lightly above the floor and now helped the others to their feet.

A terrific crash and the rolling of thunder was heard. Once more the *Sannah* quivered in every part, shaken by exploded world-matter. A terrific heat developed in the Antipode room and all fled for dear life to the innermost chambers of the craft.

Here they could still stand it and the unimaginable fury with which the World-Ship was flung forward by the repulsion of collided planets soon brought her outside the range of the fiery tongues, so that she gradually cooled down again without having suffered serious damage. For this they had Gabokol to thank, who had covered the casing with his protective material.

"We have seen the end of a world," said Flitmore finally, "and it is far from a rare occurrence."

"To be sure," Schulze corroborated him. "Ever since the fixed stars have been studied closely and we have learned to look for such manifestations, we have observed the birth of new stars.

"Characteristic of this phenomenon is the Nova Persei, that is, the new star which flashed up in 1901 in the constellation of Perseus. At first, it appeared as a star of the twelfth magnitude, and in three days it became a star of the first magnitude, the brightest in the whole firmament except for Sirius: its light had increased two hundred and fifty thousandfold, but then diminished until it once more became so weak that it looked like a star of the twelfth or thirteenth magnitude. It must have been at least 100 light-years away from the earth and after its appearance it surrounded itself with a nebulous mass which measured at least 1400 times the diameter of the earth's orbit and revealed condensation lines and clots of light which travelled, moderately estimated, at a speed of more than 1800 miles per second."

"Then these new stars originate in the flashing up of two dark bodies when they are heated by a collision?" asked Hank.

"As a matter of fact, not much belief is put in that," replied Schulze, "for then the speedy cooling that takes place within a few weeks or months would be inexplicable."

"Then how are these occurrences explained?" Mitzie now intervened in the discussion.

"In different ways!" said Schulze. "Some think that they are extinguished suns which were invisible to us because covered with a congealed crust, but which suddenly flash up again when the internal glow temporarily breaks through the crust. The crash of a large meteor might also cause the sudden flash.

"Moreover we have just observed how one or, even better, how two bodies may flash up as the result of a collision. This phenomenon will probably have been observed from the earth also and we shall see what explanation the earthly astronomers have thought up for it."

"Will the Professor permit me to ask a question, with all consideration and modesty?" begged John.

"Go right ahead, my lad! What seems to be bothering you?"

"The Professor has said, as I have heard him on several occasions, that new fixed stars are being formed in the comic nebula?"

"Quite right, my good friend! Not in the 'comic,' but in the 'cosmic' nebula. You see, the Greek word for world is '*kosmos*.' Well, as you have so rightly remarked: from this world-nebula fixed stars are formed."

"And they shine for long periods of time, don't they?"

"Certainly! For thousands, hundreds of thousands, perhaps millions of years."

"Well then, you say that all new stars very quickly, so to speak, lose their strong light; but new stars, which were not noticed before and which will continue to shine as fixed stars, must be forming out of the nebula."

"Well, you see, this formation of new stars from nebulæ takes hundreds of thousands of years."

Here Flitmore spoke up: "And yet John is right; why shouldn't such a star formation be completed in our epoch? No fixed star known to us has yet been extinguished, never has a new one appeared. If a constant becoming and disappearing actually prevails in the universe, as is assumed, then this fact is inexplicable. At any rate, I believe that the days of the great sun-creations are gone."

"That's a very disputable view," objected the Professor, "for everything evolves so slowly that we should hardly be able to notice it."

LI

THROUGH THE SUN

THE terrific explosion resulting from the clash of the two dark bodies had, as we have seen, hurled the *Sannah* into world space with tremendous violence.

This proved to be an unexpected stroke of luck. For days, the World-Ship retained this speed, which diminished but slowly, and in a few days she traversed a distance which would otherwise have required as many years.

They could tell this from the terrific speed at which they were approaching the earth's solar system.

Four weeks had scarcely passed since their departure from Eden, when they crossed the orbit of Neptune.

But now a new danger was revealed.

"We are hurtling straight towards the sun," said Flitmore.

"And the centrifugal power?" asked Schulze.

"I am very much afraid that it is not helping us," replied the Englishman. "The violence with which the *Sannah* was hurled into its orbit is stronger than the strongest centrifugal power that we can develop."

"Then it ought to be stronger than the attractive power of the sun," thought the Professor.

"God grant it!" said Flitmore. "Otherwise we are lost."

The sun came closer and closer; the orbits of Uranus and Saturn had already been crossed without their being able to see these planets, as they were then at the remotest points in their orbits. Jupiter they saw only from afar. Of the planetoids, Mars and the earth, they could see nothing; but the

Sannah came very close to Venus, the bright morning and evening star which, when it stands away from the sun, shines more brightly on the earth than all the other stars and can even be seen by daylight if its position in the sky be well known; the only star whose light is so intense that when it strikes an object on the earth it casts a noticeable shadow, if the moon is not in the way.

Schulze was able to establish its hitherto unknown period of rotation. On this subject there prevailed such a lack of uniformity among the astronomers of the earth that it was sometimes supposed to be 24 hours and at other times as many days, even as much as 225 earth-days.

The Professor now found for Venus a period of rotation of some 700 hours or 30 earth-days.

Its annual revolution required 224 earth-days. Its atmosphere was very dense and strongly beclouded; its surface was a complete desert, a disconsolate solitude of regular, white sheen.

"In size and mass," said the Professor, "this planet is very similar to our earth, but receives twice as much sunlight. Its orbit is virtually circular; it has the strongest albedo, that is, more than all the other planets does it refract the light that it receives; perhaps it has some light of its own, in addition."

"It's too bad that we cannot reach the earth from here," sighed Hank. "We are so close to it: 25,000,000 miles! What good does that do us?"

"Yes, indeed!" said Schulze: "Regrets won't help us, we are being carried off mercilessly!"

The *Sannah* crossed the orbit of Mercury.

The sun looked like an enormous fire-ball.

Flitmore protected the windows of the *Sannah* with smoked glass so that they might be able to look up at the glow with the naked eye. Thus they succeeded in recognizing the sun-spots as enormous cindery islands which floated in a white-hot sea that sometimes dissolved them again.

A stormy sea of fire and flame, as if whipped up by a hurricane—that is what the sun looked like. Tremendous explosions and eruptions took place from time to time; then sheets of fire and beams of flame would be hurled, in a few moments, to a height of 46,000 miles at a speed of 100 miles a second.

And this raging sea of fire was what the *Sannah* was hurtling toward at a furious speed!

But even in this moment of terror, when all, with the exception of Heliastra, who watched this dreadful spectacle with childish curiosity, were filled with dread of the impending end—even in this anxious moment, Schulze proved to be the cool scholar for, in truth, he delivered a scientific lecture on the sun!

"This star," he began, "which dispenses light, life, and warmth upon our earth, is 300,000 times brighter than the full moon; yet the earth gets only 1 part in 2,735,000,000 of its light and warmth. Its diameter at the equator is 863,-376 miles, compared with the 7920 miles of the earth. You could put 1,300,000 earths into the sun, but it only weighs as much as 324,400 earths, for it is not much denser than water.

"We have virtually the same elements in the sun that we have on the earth; the spectroscope has shown us that.

"The extreme circumference of the sun-ball, or rather its atmosphere, forms the corona; it is composed, as we can plainly see, of broad clusters of rays, which extend in part more than a sun's diameter into space and often appear to be singularly distorted.

"This corona can best be observed from the earth during

a solar eclipse; it then forms a narrow light-ring of blinding brightness around the eclipsing lunar disc. This ring is surrounded by twelve times as broad a band of mother-of-pearlish brightness, from which there shoot out into world-space the beams which do not at all, or only barely, appear on photographs. This band is enclosed by a still broader light-zone which is lost in the sky in a rapidly diminishing brightness without visible boundaries.

"Beneath the corona, we see, near the so-called 'chromosphere,' a rose-colored ring which is formed out of the lightest gases known to us, hydrogen and helium.

"The innermost atmospheric envelope of the sun, finally, is the photosphere, which is composed of glowing metallic vapors and is the actual dispenser of light. We see it covered with a network of numberless pores and lines, which are constantly changing. They seem to be a collection of fleecy or cirrus clouds, the smallest of which, it is true, is as large as a continent; this phenomenon is called the 'granulation' of the sun's surface."

"Look here, Professor," said Munchhausen, peevishly, "what good is all this highly interesting information to us now? I mean, it is already becoming intolerably hot in here and we shall be burned to a crisp in no time. If you know of any way of preventing this, it would be better than all your other wisdom."

"The heat of the sun is not so great as is generally imagined," replied Schulze, coolly. "It must be about 7000 degrees Centigrade, that is, about twice as hot as the carbons of an electrical arc-lamp."

"Hot enough to turn us to ashes!" growled the Captain.

The Professor shrugged his shoulders. "All I can say to console you is that the great comet of 1843 sped through the glowing corona of the sun, 3,823,200 miles in 3 hours,

that is, 354 miles per second. It approached the sun to within
a distance of about the tenth part of its diameter."

"And it didn't plunge into it?" asked Hank.

"No! It was protected against that by the violence of its
impetus. The same thing happened with the comets of 1882
and 1883. They did develop an extraordinary brightness,
indeed they could be seen in the daytime right next to the
sun, and the comet of 1882 vanished when it came directly
in front of the sun; it was therefore just as bright as the
sun. At the same time, the comets developed ferrous vapors,
a proof that a part of their solid elements dissolved into
flaming gases under the influence of the heat of the corona.
Finally, the comet of 1882 burst into several pieces while
flying through the corona."

"A fine bit of consolation you've given us!" grumbled the
Captain.

"Is the Professor of the opinion that we are going to plop
right down into this frightful cauldron in spite of our
smoked window-panes?" John inquired anxiously.

"No!" replied Schulze, definitely, "I don't believe that at
all; for our speed surpasses that of the comet of 1843 by
more than a hundredfold."

"But that the *Sannah* will start to burn or dissolve into
glowing vapor, or that all of us will explode together with
it—do you believe that?" Munchhausen blustered.

"Since our World-Ship is not a solid, dense mass," rejoined the Professor, "it seems most probable that it will dissolve into a vaporous cloud. To tell the truth, I think our
last hour has come. But you may believe me, we shall not
feel a thing; in less than a second it will all be over."

Flitmore pressed a button and in an instant all the portholes of the *Sannah* were closed, that is, the thick protective
plates moved into place to cover the windows from the out-

side. At the same time, he turned off all the electric lights and said: "Let us go down into the innermost room, in the centre of the *Sannah*. In twenty minutes we shall reach the fiery atmosphere of the sun. Then may God have mercy on us!"

All of them hurried to the innermost store-room, which was lit by a single electric globe. All the hatches were closed, after they had passed through them.

Here the Englishman offered up a short, vigorous prayer, a plea for salvation, expressing at the same time a devout trust in the will of God, in the event that their end had been ordained. Then silence fell.

John sat down at the foot of his master, as if to express his desire to follow him as a loyal servitor even unto death. Mitzie leaned her head upon her husband's shoulder, Munchhausen held Schulze's right hand firmly in his grip. Heliastra snuggled into Hank's arm and felt its security, while her young husband was prepared to start the journey into a better life with his wife at his side.

The two chimpanzees, Dick and Bobs, cowered in a corner and understood nothing of what was happening; yet they behaved, quite against their custom, so quietly that it might have been thought that they did realize something of what was about to happen.

All at once it became terrifically hot; the air seemed to glow and weighed oppressively upon them.

Then Flitmore arose and uttered a hearty thanksgiving for salvation from the terrible danger of death.

LII

THE PLANET MERCURY

THE others did not know how to explain Lord Flitmore's expression of thanksgiving while they still fancied themselves to be in the midst of the sun's crucible; for only now did the heat begin to grow virtually insufferable.

Professor Schulze saw it all as clearly as Flitmore.

"We have come out of it alive!" he said, breathing freely again. "But the *Sannah*—what must she look like?"

"Are we out of the danger zone?" asked Mitzie, incredulously.

"Certainly, my dear," said Flitmore, "the mortal danger was that our craft, as a result of the terrific heat, would dissolve into vapor. But the warmth we now feel and which is certainly very irksome, and insufferable for any length of time, shows that we have already sailed past the corona of the sun and have it behind us. Had the catastrophe taken place, we should have felt nothing, so suddenly would it have happened. But this gradually rising heat indicates that the *Sannah* became very hot at her surface without, however, having suffered any serious damage. Thanks to the fire-resisting casing and the thick gutta-percha upholstering of the rooms, the temperature in this one rose but slowly and relatively little."

"I can believe that," said Munchhausen. "Why, on all sides of us there are no less than seven rooms, each ten feet wide, between us and the outside casing; seven rooms with rubber-covered ceilings and floors, so that fourteen layers protect us from the penetration of warmth, separated by seven air-spaces, not to speak of the strong outside casing and the excellent protective material with which Gabokol coated it."

"In any case, it is this protective casing from Eden that saved our lives," declared Flitmore. "No earthly material could have withstood the sun's glow."

"But isn't it possible that we may still be in the flames?" asked Heliastra. "In that case, the heat would rise gradually and would soon become too much for us."

"Entirely out of the question!" said Schulze. "With the terrific speed of our journey we must long ago have left the solar corona, even before the rise in temperature was noticeable down here."

"Then I should very respectfully like to express the modest remark," said John, "that we go above into the fresh air, for I am sweating, if I may be permitted to say so, like a ship's stoker."

"Patience, patience, my lad!" laughed Schulze. "I'm afraid we must endure this just a little longer. In the first place, we are still so close to the sun that a walk in the open is quite out of the question for the time being, unless you want to be roasted; in the second place, the heat in the upper chambers is undoubtedly much worse than it is down here. We must first wait until the *Sannah* has had a chance to cool off."

"Then we shall have to have a lot of patience," declared Hank, "for the sun is so close to us that it must be burning down upon the *Sannah* in a manner that doesn't bode well for a cooling off."

"In two hours," said the Englishman, "we can risk the ascent without worry. In the first place, a relative cooling must obviously take place, since the temperature is far greater in the corona itself than in its vicinity; in the second place, we are moving away from the sun at lightning speed; in the third place, our *Sannah* is revolving around herself and turns only one side towards the sun; the side turned away from the sun will cool off very rapidly."

As it turned out, the Englishman was right; the terrific heat diminished quickly enough and two hours later our friends were able to mount to the Zenith room, which was turned away from the sun.

Out of the hatchway of the Zenith room, Flitmore went to examine how much the casing of the *Sannah* had been damaged by the journey through the glowing atmosphere of the sun.

He found that the coating put on in Eden was entirely intact; but that the flint glass beneath was broken through everywhere. The outside metal casing was molten; in general it was still soft, but after leaving the solar corona it would quickly solidify again. In some places, holes showed where the casing had melted. But this was not disturbing, for they would not again have to go through a similar heat, and the protective covering supplied by Gabokol closed over the holes.

When Lord Flitmore had returned to the room, Mitzie said: "It is still a riddle to me how we were able to pass through the flaming atmosphere of the sun uninjured."

"It is surely a miracle of God's protection!" said her husband. "But the natural means by which He assisted us was the enormous speed with which our craft was moving. You yourself have found, my dear, how you can draw your finger through the flame of a light, without injury and without even feeling any warmth, if you do it swiftly enough. Of course, we did not stay in the flames of the sun for quite so short a time, but surely we were not there for more than half a minute, and our protective casing was enough to withstand the fire for a time. It required some time for it to break through the flint-glass layer. That the heat inside did not become entirely unendurable, although the metal on the outside was melting, ought not to surprise us when we remember that this is also the case with meteors."

The planet Mercury shone through the open window of the Zenith chamber with a blinding radiance. The *Sannah* was compelled to pass very close to it and it seemed to draw nearer at enormous speed.

This planet, which enjoys perpetual day on three eighths of its surface, and perpetual night on another three eighths, while only one fourth of it alternates between night and day, which lasts on an average forty-four earth-days, turned its almost fully illuminated side to the night-side of the *Sannah.*

In order to be able to observe it for a longer period, as well as to escape the heat of the sun, our friends proceeded, in accordance with the rotation of the *Sannah*, to that room in which midnight reigned. Every half hour this change of room had to be made.

Schulze felt himself called upon to express some remarks about Mercury. "The closeness of this planet to the sun," said he, "has placed the greatest difficulties in the way of observation of it from the earth. From the changes which Schroeter thought he perceived at the tips of Mercury's crescent, Bessel calculated its period of rotation at twenty-four hours. In 1883, Schiaparelli, on the other hand, deduced from spots and streaks which he perceived, a rotation of eighty-eight days; that is, Mercury would always turn the same side towards the sun, as the moon does to the earth, and would rotate around itself in the same period in which it revolves around the sun.

"Only it was proved that every sphere with a smooth, regularly colored surface shows dark streaks when it is incompletely illuminated, streaks which are based upon a natural illusion, so that Schiaparelli's calculations become questionable, since they were made upon the basis of observations of these very streaks.

"Mercury displays alternating light forms, or phases, like the moon, but, like Venus, it is fully illuminated when it is remotest from the earth, and appears therefore to be brightest when it is only half illuminated but nearer to the earth. Yet even then it is visible only to very good eyesight, because of its smallness and closeness to the sun; though it was noted in antiquity and in the Middle Ages by our clear-sighted ancestors.

"The light-boundaries of its surface are very vague, which indicates a fairly dense atmosphere. Its orbit is the most eccentric of all the planetary orbits, that is, it is the orbit most remote from the circular form and appears to be oval.

"Its density is one and a half times that of the earth, so that it may be regarded as a sphere of cast iron. Its surface is about three times that of the whole former Russian Empire. Its mass is only one twelfth that of the earth, its force of gravity is only three fifths that of ours. It receives seven times as much sunlight as we do and must suffer an intolerable heat on its sun-side and a dreadful cold on its nightside. The light it gets from Venus when closest, is 600 times feebler than the light we receive from our full moon."

This much Schulze was able to deliver in a short time. What was now seen of the surface of the planet from the *Sannah* was highly interesting: it looked like a smooth disc, not without hills and mountains, but even these were almost smooth; a few prominent hemispheres, which cast no shadow because the light, refracted a thousandfold by the mirror-like areas, illuminated everything.

Vegetation, and even forests, could be seen, but trunks, branches, and leaves glittered and cast off light to such an extent that at a great distance they vanished completely in a sea of white radiance.

"If animals and people live here," said Schulze, "they must certainly be the same kind of mirrorlike beings and this quality doubtless protects them from the harmful effects of either too high or too low a temperature."

They sped away swiftly from this planet, which moves in its orbit around the sun with a greater velocity than all the others. The *Sannah* once more approached the orbit of Venus, but the planet was far off: at the moment, the sun stood between it and the World-Ship.

LIII

BACK TO THE EARTH!

LORD FLITMORE switched off the centrifugal and parallel powers.

The momentum of the *Sannah* was still so tremendous that the power of attraction of the nearby sun did not suffice to hold her in her course, still less, naturally, the attractive power of Mercury.

It was therefore to be feared that the World-Ship might once again leave the earth's solar system; but the Englishman hoped, by switching off all motive power, to arrive at a point where the attraction of the sun and the whole planetary system would retard their speed to such an extent that in crossing the earth's orbit it would be diminished sufficiently to make it possible for the *Sannah* to sink to the earth.

Unfortunately, however, this was not the case; the earth was too far removed from the point in its orbit where our friends had cut through it, to be able to exercise any attraction upon the craft.

Only when Mars was being approached did the desirable influence manifest itself: the speed slackened perceptibly.

But then they passed beyond the orbit of Mars and drew close to Jupiter.

When Flitmore noticed that the momentum of the *Sannah* had so diminished that the mightiest of the planets was attracting her, he turned on the centrifugal power again, with the result that the World-Ship, now repelled from Jupiter, was hurled back.

Again it passed Mars and here too the centrifugal power

caused the *Sannah* to rush by the planet in an arc and approach the earth's orbit again. This time there was the favorable circumstance that the earth, travelling along its orbit, was moving closer to the point at which our friends would bisect that orbit.

"Now or never!" said Flitmore, and once more shut off the centrifugal current so that the earth might be able, if possible, to pull the World-Ship towards it.

With joyful curiosity, Heliastra peered at the sunlit sphere.

The *Sannah* plunged down obliquely toward its native earth, and they could already distinguish with the naked eye the seas and coasts, the mountains, and the larger rivers.

Hank, his beloved wife at his side, climbed out upon the surface of the craft and they looked down upon the globe which spread out beneath them. The better to see, now that the centrifugal power was switched off, they went below, holding on to the ramps, and sat down in a sort of observation basket which Flitmore had recently installed for such purposes near the entrance to the South Pole room.

"What high mountains you have!" said Heliastra. "And how is it that their peaks look so white and sparkle like diamonds?"

"Those are the Himalayan Mountains, the highest mountain-range of our earth; their peaks are covered with eternal snow; for at such heights it is very cold, so that the water and the precipitation turn hard and form those unfamiliar crystals which we call ice and snow."

"Oh, how lovely is the blue of your seas!" she exclaimed with rapture. "Just as with us! And how wonderfully green all these countries are. Haven't you the horrible deserts we have on our planet?"

"Yes, we have deserts; do you see those ruddy and gray

splashes to the right and left, at the foot of the mountains?
Those are the Mongolian deserts in the great Chinese Empire and the steppes of Sirdaria in southwestern Siberia.
And out there, in the far-off distance, you would be able to
see the glitter of the icy wastes of the North Pole, if we were
on the other side. But your planet, with the exception of the
blissful central belt, is one solitary, bleak desert of rock,
more extensive than the whole surface of our earth. At least
we have one advantage over you: our deserts extend over a
relatively small surface."

"I suppose you work just as industriously as we do to
make them fertile?"

"By drilling wells into the ground, something is being
done towards that end, but we are still far from having accomplished here as much as your brethren have on Eden."

Heliastra looked towards the southern sky.

"I see my native world!" she said: "A little star. I also
see its rosy moon! If you had my eyes, you would also be able
to see it. How far away we are from it, how far!"

"Do you feel homesick?" asked Hank, solicitously.

"Homesick, with you?" said Heliastra, and the blue eyes
danced with laughter. "No! My home will always be where
you are, and how happy I shall be on the earth, where I can
do so much more to be of help than was possible on our fortunate planet."

"You are an angel!" cried Hank, and kissed her ardently.

"What large island is that?" his wife asked again.

"That is Australia," explained her husband. "Do you see
the great desert? I nearly died of thirst and misery there
once."

"You poor boy," said Heliastra, and her eyes shone upon
him with a divine pity.

"And that great continent over there is Africa," Hank

continued. "Mitzie's brothers and her sister Sannah live
there. But look, the icebergs of the South Pole are rising beneath us! We are coming closer to the earth. I am afraid we
shall land on the ice!"

It certainly looked that way; for the diagonal plunge of
the *Sannah* led straight towards it.

"Come in!" Flitmore shouted out to them from the hatchway. "It is going to be dangerous to stay out there. From
now on, I must alternate my centrifugal current and also
work with the parallel power, so that we may locate a favorable landing-place, and you might be flung out of the basket while this is going on."

The young couple obediently re-entered the South Pole
room and the hatchway was shut down.

Night fell on the earth. The homeward-bound travellers
ate their last dinner in the *Sannah* and then Flitmore ordered them to retire.

He wanted to take the watch himself, this night, and manœuvre the landing at a favorable opportunity. For he had
a special plan, a surprise for them all; and, as he hoped, a
surprise also for others who were dear to him.

LIV

SANNAH

IN the quiet of night, the Englishman, thanks to the parallel power, directed his faithful World-Ship in swift passage over rivers, mountains, and lakes. The full moon lit up the landscape and Flitmore was able to find his way.

At last he found his landing-place and the *Sannah* sank down upon a green meadow.

The Englishman looked at his watch.

"Four more hours to sunrise," he murmured. "I'll turn in myself now, so as to be quite fresh when the morning comes."

He awakened John. "You keep watch this time, for the whole night. We are on solid ground and nothing will happen. As soon as the sun rises, wake me up first and then the others." This said, he lay down to rest.

John opened the window of the South Pole room and looked out. He was curious to see where they were situated.

What landscape was this he beheld? It was strangely familiar to Rieger. But it was not England, nor was it Germany; it could only be Africa!

Slender palms swayed in the moonlit night, thick banana trees gleamed in the distance, and not far away glittered the mirror of a lake along whose left bank loomed, in the east, the outlines of a massive mountain.

"This, so to speak, can be nothing else than Albert Edward Nyanza," said John to himself, "and that roof nearby among the treetops must be the farm of the old master, Peter

Rin! What a surprise this will be for my Lady Mitzie, as well as for the Professor, and for the family of Mr. Rin and Miss Helen—Ah, me! Mrs. Rin must be told about it now, Mrs. Hendrik Rin! And her husband, that fine Mr. Hendrik! If only that were done! And the heroic dwarf princess is surely with them. Ah! How happy I should be to see the lovely little Tipekitanga once more!"

He had to convince himself and went into the next chamber, which now lay northwards. Correct! There rose the enormous mountain-top of Ruwenzori, shining in the moonlight.

Beyond a doubt! They were right on the estate of the Boer, Peter Rin, on the banks of Albert Edward Lake! John smiled to himself; what a fine thought this was of his master, to look up his father-in-law.

In Peter Rin's farms, also, people were bestirring themselves. A blooming young woman had risen from her bed and looked out of the window.

She rubbed her eyes: what sort of an enormous globe was that, rising in the east above the treetops? How its curved surface glittered in the moonlight!

The young woman was Sannah, the daughter of farmer Peter Rin, who, with her husband, Doctor Otto Leusohn, a German physician who had settled in East Africa, was visiting at the time at the farm of her father.

She hastened to the bed of her husband and awakened him with a kiss.

"Otto," she said, "I had such a remarkable dream, as if a great big globe had flown here through the air—and just think who stepped out of it?"

"Well?"

"My sister Mitzie and our brother-in-law, Charles Flitmore!"

"A fine dream, that!" Leusohn said, laughing; he was now wide-awake, as was proper for a physician. "And do you believe that it will come to pass tonight?"

"I don't know! But when I looked out of the window, I saw the globe of my dream rearing above the treetops."

"Great Scott!" Leusohn exclaimed, and sprang out of bed. One look out of the window convinced him that something strange and amazing was encamped in the vicinity.

"Shall we go out and see what it is?" asked Sannah.

"I am with you!" replied her husband.

While his youthful wife dressed quickly, he knocked on the thin board walls which separated the sleeping-chamber from the neighboring room.

"What's up?" a drowsy voice inquired.

"I don't know," answered Leusohn, "but, in any case, something very curious has happened. Sannah and I want to examine the thing on the spot. Would you like to come along, Hendrik?"

"Certainly!" he called back. "I'll be ready in a moment."

"And I'm coming along, too," cried a woman's clear voice from the next room. It was Leusohn's sister, Helene, the wife of Hendrik Rin.

When Hendrik and Helene were fully dressed and had left their sleeping-quarters, a slender girlish figure met them in the hallway.

She was a strikingly lovely, well-formed little negress, with light-brown skin and magnificent, sparkling eyes. In truth, she was no longer a little girl, as might appear at first sight, but a grown-up woman, from the race of the pigmies. Despite her superior birth, for she was a royal princess, she served Helene as a faithful maid, and particularly as a companion on hunting-trips; for there was no more skilful huntress in all Africa than the lovely dwarf maiden.

"Are you going out into the night?" she asked. "Tipe-kitanga will go with you."

"Quite right, you faithful soul," Helene Rin said commendingly, and stroked the tender cheek.

Doctor Leusohn now appeared upon the scene with his wife, accompanied by her servant, Amina, an especially pretty Somali negress.

Sannah greeted her brother Hendrik and her sister Helene with a kiss; Otto Leusohn also kissed his dear sister and his brother-in-law heartily, then he narrated the dream of his wife and the remarkable spectacle that could be seen from the window.

In the meantime, they had already gone out into the open and hurried forward to where the enigmatic globe was situated.

When they came out of the palm-tree woods upon the grassy plain, they stopped in their tracks. Before them rose a dark colossus, an immense black globe. The moon had set and the enormous mass looked sinister and threatening, as if it might roll towards them at any moment and crush them to a pulp.

"The globe of my dream!" cried Sannah.

"But, according to your dream, Mitzie would have to be inside of it," Leusohn observed.

"A man is looking out there at the top!" Helene cried out.

The dark figure that leaned out of a window in the sphere now made his voice heard: "If I may permit myself to recognize the voices that are so endeared to me by a cherished memory, and if you will not take this recollection in bad part, then I believe you are Miss Helene and, moreover, as it seems to me from here, Mrs. Rin and Mr. Hendrik, as well as Miss Sannah, or, so to speak, now Mrs. Doctor Leusohn, with her honorable husband."

Helene uttered a cry of joy. "There! Such phrases are used by no man on this world," she said, "other than the one and only John Rieger, Lord Flitmore's noble servant."

"Oho!" cried Leusohn. "Then you did indeed have a prophetic dream, dear Sannah! If John is here, then Charles and Mitzie cannot be far off."

"Ah, how happy I am!" John rejoiced. "But excuse me, if I withdraw my humble person for a moment, for the sun is already commencing to rise and I am under an obligation to awaken my gracious master."

John disappeared, while the young people below babbled happily among themselves: what sort of a machine was this and how was Flitmore able to travel in it from England to Africa? But the main thing was: He had arrived, and Mitzie with him, an unexpected but wholly welcome visit!

Ten minutes later, the rising sun lit up the World-Ship as Flitmore and Mitzie appeared at the window.

"Hurrah!" shouted Leusohn. "There they are!"

"Hurrah!" answered Flitmore. "So you have discovered us. Welcome, Otto. Welcome, Hendrik! Welcome, my dear sisters-in-law, Helene and Sannah: the great *Sannah* has come to greet you."

"Oh, that you should both be here, Sannah and Otto!" Mitzie cried out in delight. "That's just too lovely! And there is our dwarf Princess and the faithful Amina!"

"Jambo, jambo!" the two negro girls cried out jubilantly.

Meanwhile, John had made the rope ladder fast and Lord Flitmore and his wife hastened to descend. Right behind them came Professor Schulze.

Mitzie and Sannah flew into each other's arms; Flitmore bestowed a hearty embrace upon his relatives and kissed the little dwarf Princess, who was worthy of such an honor. Just as warmly did Lady Flitmore kiss her brother Hen-

drik and his wife, as well as the Doctor, and then Tipekitanga and Amina.

In the meantime, the Professor also had approached the
group and was greeted by his dear friends with warm hand-
shakes, for they all remembered the many adventures
through which they had passed together on African soil.

Hank and Heliastra had now also left the *Sannah*.

They were still unknown here and remained somewhat
apart; but they were immediately noticed and great astonishment filled Hendrik and Leusohn and their wives when
they perceived the adorable figure and the divine countenance, radiant with beauty, of the strange maiden.

They fell silent and felt themselves overawed by the rare
charm of the being who stood before them, garbed in a
snow-white cloak. Their admiration was tinged with a certain shyness, too, for she seemed like a creature out of another, more perfect world. And they were right: Heliastra
did indeed come from a loftier sphere.

But besides this feeling of respectful admiration, a whole-
hearted love for the strange creature welled up in every
breast: they felt drawn to her immediately. The purity,
softness, and affecting friendliness that smiled from this
lovely, rose-shimmering face, and especially from the large
eyes, whose tender blue had no equal on earth, could not but
captivate every heart.

Heliastra, in turn, gazed with pleasure at the whole
group, her heart beating with joy, and she was especially
attracted by her new-found earthly sisters. How pretty and
kind they looked, if they were not so ethereal in appearance as Glessiblora and the other maidens of Eden! Even
her dark-skinned sisters, the graceful Tipekitanga and the
sinuous Amina, seemed lovely to her.

"Who is this divine creature?" Sannah finally stammered, her pulse racing.

"In truth, a divine creature!" said Mitzie. "For we brought her here from the celestial world of the fixed stars. And how dear and adorable she is, you will soon learn for yourselves."

"From the celestial world of the fixed stars?" exclaimed Helene perplexedly. What did these enigmatic words mean? And yet—she felt that only a heavenly mystery could explain it all; for the more she thought of it the more incredible it seemed that such comeliness could be bestowed upon an earthly being.

"It is so," Flitmore added. "Heliastra is a visitor out of the heavenly distances of the fixed-star world. How it all came about, we will explain to ycu later on. But now she pleases to regard our poor earth as her home; a noble desire brought her down among us and her love for our friend, Hank Frieding, who has drawn a prize such as no mortal before him has ever attained, with the exception of myself, for I won Mitzie Rin as my wife."

"Flatterer!" cried Lady Flitmore, and put her hand over his mouth. "How can you compare me with a Heliastra!"

"Is this the Hank Frieding who travelled through Australia with you?" Doctor Leusohn inquired of Schulze.

"Of course! A capital fellow and a hero! Never have I envied any one as I envy him his golden good fortune."

"Hearty welcome!" said Leusohn, and embraced the young man, who had long before been known and dear to him; just as warmly did Hendrik greet the new friend, whereupon Sannah and Helene also shook his hand.

Then the young women hastened to Heliastra; yet they continued to be restrained by a certain shyness from showing the charming creature all the affection they already had for her. They felt themselves unworthy and extended her a timid hand.

But Heliastra slipped her arm smilingly around Sannah's waist and then Helene's, and warmly pressed her rosy lips to theirs. "Are you not my darling sisters?" she asked blushingly.

"If we may be, then we are proud and happy!" replied Helene, and Sannah added: "I don't think I love anybody so much, with the exception, of course, of my dear husband."

"Yes, my darling Hank also takes first place with me," said Heliastra, with a tender glance at her husband. "But you come right after him. Oh, I have so much love, enough for you and the whole world."

Then she stepped light-footedly to Tipekitanga and Amina, who stood shyly to one side, embraced and kissed them, and said: "And aren't you also my dear sisters of the earth?"

Amina was struck dumb with joy and embarrassment, though her heart beat with blissful pride.

But Tipekitanga gazed at her celestial sister with radiant eyes and only whispered: "Oh, my darling, darling mistress!"

Heliastra gave her hand to Hendrik and Leusohn with warm heartiness; but the men did not dare to grip it firmly, so fragile did this hand appear when they pressed a respectful kiss upon it.

Suddenly a cry was heard from above and the bewitching spell cast by Heliastra's presence was broken for a while.

"Oh, vile earth! Oh, miserable, wretched humanity!" came the growl. "So we have landed again on the most miserable of all planets? And down there they are all greeting each other and nobody thinks of me, Captain Hugo von Munchhausen, the famous Abu Baten, Pasha of his Royal

Highness, the Khedive of Egypt! Me, me they leave to oversleep the celebration! Me, the most important personage of all, they treat as if I were a negligible factor! Come, Heliastra, thou angel-child from a better world! Let us leave this ungrateful soil together and turn back to the spheres of delight!"

"Hello! Munchhausen, our glorious Captain, the terrible Abu Baten!" they cried up from below.

This storm of greeting conciliated the wrathful colossus, and he skipped down the rope ladder with unusual nimbleness.

When he reached the ground, his friends encircled the wheezing seaman and hailed him with such hearty joy that he declared: "There, children! If you really like me as much as that, I'll have to decide, with heavy heart, to remain on this awful planet!"

Only now did the humble John come down, followed by the chimpanzees, Dick and Bobs, and he also was made welcome in the most friendly manner.

"Ah! And there is our lovely dwarf Princess!" cried Munchhausen. "Come to my heart, dear maiden, fly into my arms, alluring Tipekitanga! Your old uncle yearns to press you to his faithful heart!"

"Hold on there!" laughed Leusohn, as the Captain made to embrace the delicate form. "You would crush and strangle our little heroine. Such fragile creatures run too much of a risk from your caresses."

"You are right, as usual, wise Doctor," said Munchhausen, letting his arms sink to his sides. "Well, give me your little hands, most excellent of all princesses!" And he carefully pressed them in his own.

All at once, Peter Rin, the gray-haired Boer, appeared on the scene, followed by his other sons, Frank, Claus, and Danny.

Frank had seen the World-Ship from the farm, as she shone in the morning sun, and immediately noticed that Hendrik and Leusohn, with their wives and servants, had gone out. The sedate old man had immediately decided to run over and see what was up.

Overjoyed, he embraced his daughter Mitzie and his son-in-law, Lord Flitmore, heartily greeting the Professor, as well as Hank and Munchhausen, who were presented to him. Just as deeply moved, Mitzie's brothers greeted her, Lord Flitmore, and the other voyagers. Nor was John forgotten by them.

Amid the greatest wonderment, the pearl of the company, Heliastra, was made welcome; then they all marched off together to the dwelling of the Rin family.

On the way, Munchhausen fumed: "What a poverty-stricken earth this is, after all! How light of foot I was on the planet of Eden! Ah! When I think of that skipping and floating! And now? It's a shame to have to drag along such a majestic figure as mine!"

Heliastra had also noticed that it was not so easy to move along on the earth as it had been at home. She made an attempt to rise into the air, but here it could not be done! With a gentle, regretful disappointment in her voice she said to her husband: "Hank, I cannot fly here!"

But Heliastra's merry spirits quickly overcame her disappointment. Why should she fly if her Hank could not? And she skimmed so lightfootedly over the ground that no child of man could equal her.

"Like an elf!" thought Sannah.

Helene and Sannah hastened ahead to the farm, to prepare with the assistance of Amina and Tipekitanga, a substantial morning snack, in addition to which John brought out of the *Sannah* the fruits and preserves from Eden, which aroused great astonishment and afforded a pleasure such as had never been dreamed of on earth.

In the meantime, there was a lively discussion and a brief account of the wonderful voyage through the universe.

The account sounded like a fairy-tale and Leusohn declared: "If Captain Munchhausen were telling us all this, I should know just what is what; but as it is, I really am in a quandary! Is all this the real truth, actually experienced, or did it take place in some amazing dream?"

"Did you ever see or taste such fruits and preserves?" Helene asked her skeptical brother. "Can you find on this broad earth of ours milk and honey, butter and fruit-juice resembling those just now brought and served up to us from a distant world?"

"And above all," added Sannah, when her husband could find no reply to make, "is this angelic creature, Heliastra, not a visible evidence of the truth of everything we have just heard?"

"You are right, my dear," the Doctor now admitted, "and when I have convinced myself that I am not dreaming either, then I shall have to believe it all. As a matter of fact, I seriously doubt whether even our Captain's amazing imagination is powerful enough to think up such marvels."

"Oho!" boomed Munchhausen. "Just wait till I begin telling you some things about the six-legged people of Mars, and the like!"

"And did you name your fabulous craft *Sannah* in my honor?" Leusohn's wife asked of her brother-in-law.

"Certainly! And she was worthy of you; she proved faithful and trustworthy," was the reply.

Tipekitanga beamed with pride and joy when she learned that she also had been deemed worthy of an exceptional honor, and that a heavenly body had been named after her, a small one, to be sure, but rich in wonders and beauty. Just as proud was Amina that a comet had been given her name.

Our friends spent several weeks at Peter Rin's farm, happy amongst their dear ones, before they made their departure, though not forever.

Once more they climbed into the *Sannah*; Munchhausen was let off in Adelaide; Professor Schulze, Hank and Heliastra left the World-Ship when she reached Berlin.

Shortly thereafter, Lord Flitmore, together with Mitzie and John, as well as the faithful chimpanzees, landed before his castle in England, to remain there for a while, but later on to equip the *Sannah* more thoroughly for a new voyage into the unknown, utilizing all the experience gained on her first trip, which he now regarded as merely a test flight.

A second visit to the planet Eden was already a settled matter with Lord Flitmore and Mitzie; this they owed to Hank and Heliastra, whom they had promised to take there in a few years, so that the daughter of Eden might be able to report to her parents and relations concerning her life and experiences upon the distant earth-world.

In addition, Lord Flitmore was determined to build several world-ships, on the model of the *Sannah*, so as to establish regular communications between the earth and the planets and the world of fixed stars.

On the next voyage, a well-manned fleet will probably rise at one time from the earth into world space, and the loveliest and most perfectly equipped of these world-ships will bear the loveliest and worthiest of all names, the name of Heliastra.

THE END